Praise for *Brown Dog*

A Heartland Indie List bestseller

A *Publishers Weekly* Best Book of 2013, one of the *New Yorker*'s Books to Watch Out For (December 2013), and an Amazon Top Pick for December 2013

"There's no mistaking Harrison's signature style. . . . *Brown Dog* is rich in character and incident, rude humor and melancholy. It is both heartfelt and ruefully real."
—*San Francisco Chronicle*

"Harrison's writing is funny, generous, and bittersweet, with an unexpected, plain-speaking poetry." —*New Yorker* (Online—Books to Watch Out For)

"Brown Dog himself is a born wanderer and romantic whose common sense and good luck see him through comic adventures and some heartbreak as well."
—*Wall Street Journal* (online)

"One of Harrison's most recognizable characters. . . . [Harrison's] process, like his protagonist's, is unintellectual, wild, and elemental." —*Atlantic*

"Lovable . . . Brown Dog . . . is a big-hearted rascal who is always getting into deep trouble with the ladies, and often with the law. . . . strong and spirited, and there is some great storytelling here." —*Minneapolis Star Tribune*

"An indelible character . . . *Brown Dog* is a robust, ribald, and irreverent tribute to the idea and ideal of maximum life." —Daily Beast

"Jim Harrison's amazing late-career run continues with *Brown Dog*."
—*Oregonian*

"Is there another novelist in the last hundred years who has developed a character as vivid as Brown Dog? . . . If Jim Harrison or Brown Dog are new to you, *Brown Dog: Novellas* is a marvelous way to meet them both."
—*New York Journal of Books*

"B.D.'s adventures are quirky, sometimes humorous, sometimes illegal. . . . But his simplicity is all on the surface. As Harrison artfully shows, inside B.D. roils the complexities of his past, a past that dances in ancient choreography with his present—and his future." —*Cleveland Plain Dealer*

"One of literature's great characters. . . . An essential collection from an American legend." —*Publishers Weekly* (Best of 2013)

"Few American writers—Mark Twain comes to mind, the early Hemingway of the Nick Adams Stories or, in short bursts, Henry Miller—leave so much of their own blood and sinew on the written page as does Jim Harrison, that fearless and open-hearted storyteller. Nowhere in his fifty-year career does so much of Harrison the man saturate the page as in his cultish and gregarious tales of Brown Dog." —*Kansas City Star*

"Brown Dog is, as his best buddy and sometime sex partner Gretchen says, 'absurdly endearing,' a backwoods mensch with the wisdom and compassion of a bodhisattva. . . . [B.D.] keeps readers coming back for more."
—*Associated Press*

"*Brown Dog* follows that great tradition of short novellas that pack a punch and a punch line, offering the reader a world that's both emotionally moving and bawdy, high-spirited fun. . . . B.D. is a breath of fresh air, albeit one that would fail a Breathalyzer test. . . . In the tradition of Pete Dexter and Tom McGuane, Harrison is an American original, with his tongue in cheek and his heart in the right place." —*Dallas Morning News*

"A modern-day Huck Finn . . . B.D.'s honesty and lack of pretense are refreshing—and often hilarious." —*Detroit Free Press*

"Pity poor Brown Dog, the Everyman of the North Woods, whose luck would be nonexistent were it not bad. Still, Brown Dog's countenance is as cheerful as Don Quixote's was woeful. Harrison's comic hero—and in some ways alter ego—is as quixotic as they come, depending on kind winds to blow him a little money, some booze, and a bit of righteous loving. . . . [*Brown Dog*] is just right. . . . Rollicking, expertly observed, beautifully written. Any new book by Harrison is cause for joy, and having all the Brown Dog stories in one place is no exception." —*Kirkus Reviews* (starred review)

"Rollicking comic novellas . . . Brown Dog is very much an American hero—not the macho blowhard kind but the picaresque variety, a la Huck Finn."
—*Tampa Bay Times*

"[An] essential collection . . . Brown Dog [is] a pure Harrison creation and a glorious character who will make readers howl with delight. . . . One of literature's great characters." —*Publishers Weekly* (starred review)

"Jim Harrison is . . . the literary equivalent of Keith Richards. . . . The wise but profligate Brown Dog is a signature Harrison character in much the same way that Richards's open-tuned chords define the Stones. . . . He is one of the great characters in American literature—as American as Twain's Huck Finn or Hemingway's Nick Adams." —Shelf Awareness

"Despite his numerous dead-end imperfections, B.D. is as deeply magnetic a character to readers as he is to the women who enter his orbit. In Harrison's hands, he leaps off the page with the same comedy and verve that Ignatius J. Reilly does in John Kennedy Toole's New Orleans classic, *A Confederacy of Dunces*—B.D. is an exceptionally funny character." —*Toronto Star* (Canada)

"If you have read Jim Harrison, more than likely you were blinded by his poetry and prose. . . . Brown Dog . . . is a hellacious character of wit and lewdness. . . . You can't help but love him." —Three Guys One Book (online)

"Brown Dog can't seem to stay out of trouble. . . . The character's observations highlight the foibles and hypocrisy of modern life. Readers new to Harrison's sagas will be happy for this full introduction. Those already familiar will find here a satisfying conclusion that leaves open the possibility for further adventures." —*Library Journal*

"The comedy, despite its bawdiness, recalls Mark Twain. . . . Brown Dog is certainly an endearing character." —*Santa Fe New Mexican*

"There's much to be said for Harrison's prose, which in many ways mirrors the northern landscape: hard-edged and not too showy, yet gorgeously attentive in its detailing of place (and of home-cooked meals) and exuberant in recounting the travails of the titular character." —Bookreporter

"Harrison gives his character such an incisive and deadpan outlook . . . Like Huck [Finn], B.D. holds his tarnished mirror up to America and lets the reflection speak for itself. . . . Whether or not you're a fan of Harrison's other work, the character of Brown Dog is probably somebody you'll want to meet."
—*Missoula Independent*

"In these novellas Harrison masterfully satirizes the absurdities of modern life through B.D.'s grounded gaze. . . . One of the most memorable characters in American fiction over the past quarter-century. . . . Reading any of these novellas puts you in the presence of a character whose humanity contains the unadorned wit and innocence of Shakespeare's Touchstone as well as the peccadilloes and calculation of a modern-day Falstaff." —Arts Fuse

"In all six stories here, Harrison demonstrates the ability to elevate memory, whether win or loss, without stooping to sentiment. More than that, however, he tells laugh-out-loud stories." —*Petoskey News* (5 out of 5)

Brown Dog

Also by Jim Harrison

FICTION

Wolf: A False Memoir
A Good Day to Die
Farmer
Legends of the Fall
Warlock
Sundog
Dalva
The Woman Lit by Fireflies
Julip
The Road Home
The Beast God Forgot to Invent
True North
The Summer He Didn't Die
Returning to Earth
The English Major
The Farmer's Daughter
The Great Leader
The River Swimmer

CHILDREN'S LITERATURE

The Boy Who Ran to the Woods

POETRY

Plain Song
Locations
Outlyer and Ghazals
Letters to Yesenin
Returning to Earth
Selected & New Poems: 1961–1981
The Theory and Practice of Rivers & New Poems
After Ikkyū & Other Poems
The Shape of the Journey: New and Collected Poems
Braided Creek: A Conversation in Poetry, with Ted Kooser
Saving Daylight
In Search of Small Gods
Songs of Unreason

ESSAYS

Just Before Dark: Collected Nonfiction
The Raw and the Cooked: Adventures of a Roving Gourmand

MEMOIR

Off to the Side

JIM HARRISON

Brown Dog

Novellas

Grove Press
New York

Copyright © 2013 by Jim Harrison

"Brown Dog" originally appeared in *The Woman Lit by Fireflies*,
copyright © 1990 by Jim Harrison
"The Seven-Ounce Man" originally appeared in *Julip*, copyright © 1994 by Jim Harrison
"Westward Ho" originally appeared in *The Beast God Forgot to Invent*,
copyright © 2000 by Jim Harrison
"The Summer He Didn't Die" originally appeared in *The Summer He Didn't Die*,
copyright © 2005 by Jim Harrison
"Brown Dog Redux" originally appeared in *The Farmer's Daughter*,
copyright © 2010 by Jim Harrison

For permission to publish "Brown Dog Redux" in Canada, Grove Press gratefully acknowledges House of Anansi Press Inc, who originally published it there in 2010

All rights reserved. No part of this book may be reproduced in any form or by any electronic or mechanical means, including information storage and retrieval systems, without permission in writing from the publisher, except by a reviewer, who may quote brief passages in a review. Scanning, uploading, and electronic distribution of this book or the facilitation of such without the permission of the publisher is prohibited. Please purchase only authorized electronic editions, and do not participate in or encourage electronic piracy of copyrighted materials. Your support of the author's rights is appreciated. Any member of educational institutions wishing to photocopy part or all of the work for classroom use, or anthology, should send inquiries to Grove/Atlantic, Inc., 154 West 14th Street, New York, NY 10011 or permissions@groveatlantic.com.

Printed in the United States of America
Published simultaneously in Canada

ISBN: 978-0-8021-2286-5
eISBN: 978-0-8021-9300-1

Grove Press
an imprint of Grove/Atlantic, Inc.
154 West 14th Street
New York, NY 10011

Distributed by Publishers Group West

www.groveatlantic.com

14 15 16 17 10 9 8 7 6 5 4 3 2 1

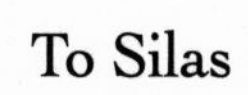

To Silas

Contents

Brown Dog

Just before dark at the bottom of the sea I found the Indian. It was the inland sea called Lake Superior. The Indian, and he was a big one, was sitting there on a ledge of rock in about seventy feet of water. There was a frayed rope attached to his leg and I had to think the current had carried him in from far deeper water. What few people know is that Lake Superior stays so cold near the bottom that drowned bodies never make it to the surface. Bodies don't rot and bloat like in other fresh water, which means they don't make the gas to carry them up to the top. This fact upsets working sailors on all sorts of ships. If the craft goes down in a storm their loved ones will never see them again. To me this is a stupid worry. If you're dead, who cares? The point here is the Indian, not death. I wish to God I had never found him. He could have drowned the day before if it hadn't been for his eyes, which were missing.

These aren't my exact words. A fine young woman named Shelley, who is also acting as my legal guardian and semi–probation officer, is helping me get this all down on paper. I wouldn't say I'm stupid. I don't amount to much, and you can't get more ordinary, but no one ever called me stupid. Shelley and me go back about two years and our love is based on a fib, a lie. The main reason she is helping me write this is so I can stop lying to myself and others, which from my way of thinking will cut the interesting heart right out of my life. Terms are terms. We'll see. Shelley believes in "oneness" and if we're going to try to be "one" I'll try to play by her rules.

I'm a diver, or was a diver, for Grand Marais Salvage Corporation, which is a fancy name for a scavenging operation. You'd be surprised what people will pay for a porthole, even though they got no use for it. An old binnacle is worth a fortune. We sold one last July for a thousand dollars, though Bob takes three quarters because he owns the equipment. Bob is a young fellow who was a Navy SEAL, the same outfit that lost the hero, Stethem, who was beat to death by the towel-heads. Bob is still damned angry and hopes to get revenge someday.

"Vengeance is mine; I will repay, saith the Lord," I quoted.

"Do you believe that, B.D.?" he asked.

"Nope. Can't say I'm sure. But if you believed it, it would save you from going way over there and having the Arabs shoot your ass off."

Bob is a hothead. A salvage bunch up in Duluth owed him a compressor so we drove over. The three of them were sleeping off a drunk so we took two compressors, and three portholes for interest. Two of the guys woke up punching but Bob put them away again. I'm not saying Bob is a bully, just a bit quick to take offense.

I've been reminded to get the basis of my salvation out of the way, to start at the beginning, as she says. Shelley is twenty-four and I'm forty-seven. That means when I'm one hundred she'll be seventy-seven. Age is quite the leveler. She is a fair-size girl by modern standards, but not in the Upper Peninsula where you would call her normal-size, perhaps a tad shy of normal. In a cold climate a larger woman is favored by all except transplants from down below (the southern peninsula of Michigan where all the people are) who bring girlfriends up here who look like they jumped right off the pages of a magazine. Nobody pays them much attention unless the situation is desperate. Why take a little girl if you can get a big one? It's as simple as that.

Anyway, on a rainy June evening two years ago Shelley came into the Dunes Saloon with two fellows who wore beards and hundred-dollar tennis shoes. They were all graduate students in anthropology at the University of Michigan and were looking for an old Chippewa herbalist I was talking to at the bar. They came over and introduced themselves and Claude announced it was his birthday.

"How wonderful," said Shelley. "How old are you? We've driven three hundred and fifty miles to talk to you."

Claude gazed at the three of them for a full minute, then sped out of the bar.

When the screen door slammed Shelley looked at me. "What did we do wrong?" she asked.

"Goddammit, we blew it," said the redheaded fellow with a big Adam's apple.

"You missed your cue. When Claude says it's his birthday you're supposed to ask if you can buy him a drink. If someone else is buying he drinks a double martini," I said.

"Is there a chance we can make up for this?" said the third, a blond-haired little fellow in a Sierra Club T-shirt. "We were counting on talking to him."

Shelley pushed herself closer, unconsciously using her breasts to lead. "Are you related? I mean are you an Indian?"

"I don't talk about my people to strangers." Now I'm no more Indian than a keg of nails. At least I don't think there's any back there. I grew up near the reservation over in Escanaba and a lot of Indians aren't even Indian so far as I can tell. What I was doing was being a little difficult. If you want a girl to take notice it's better to start out being a little difficult.

"We're really getting off on the wrong foot here. I didn't mean to intrude." She was nervous and upset.

"How the hell could we know he wanted a double martini," whined the redhead. "You don't push drinks on an old Indian. I've been around a lot of them."

"What do you know about my people, you shit-sucking dick-head?" I yelled. The three of them jumped back as if hit by a cattle prod.

I moved down to the end of the bar and pretended to watch the Tigers-Milwaukee ball game. Since we are much farther from Detroit than Milwaukee there are a lot of Brewers fans up here. Frank, the bartender, came over shaking his head.

"B.D., why'd you yell at those folks when the lady's got beautiful tits?"

"Strategy," I said. "She'll be down here with a peace offering pretty soon."

The three of them were huddled by the window table, no doubt figuring their next move. I began to question my yell. In fact, I'm not known to raise my voice unless you set off a firecracker right behind me. Finally she got up and walked down the bar toward me with a certain determination.

"I'm Shelley Newkirk. Let's start all over again. The three of us have a great deal of admiration for Native Americans. We love and respect them. That's why we study them. We want to offer you an apology."

I stared deeply into my glass of Stroh's while Frank darted into the kitchen. When she spoke I thought he was going to laugh, but he's too good of a friend to blow my cover.

"The name's B.D.," I said. "It stands for Brown Dog, my Anishinabe name." At this point I wasn't bullshitting. Brown Dog, or B.D., has been my nickname since I was in the seventh grade and had a crush on a Chippewa girl down the road. I played ball with her brothers but she didn't seem to care for me. Their mother called me Brown Dog because I was hanging around their yard all the time. Once when she was slopping their pigs this girl, Rose by name, threw a whole pail of garbage on me. I actually broke into tears on the spot though I was fourteen. Love will do that. Her brothers helped clean me off and said they guessed their sister didn't like me. I didn't give up and that's why the name stuck with me. I was sort of following her around before a school assembly to see where she was going to sit when she hit me on the head with a schoolbook and knocked me to the floor. "Brown Dog, you asshole, stop following me," she screamed. I got to my feet with everyone in the gymnasium laughing at me. The principal tapped the microphone. "Rose, watch your language. Mr. Brown Dog, I think it's evident to all assembled here that Rose wishes you would stop following her."

So that's how I got my name and how, much later, I met Shelley. Right now it's October outside and already snowing though we're sure to have a bit of Indian summer. I don't care because I like cold weather. The farthest south I've ever been is Chicago and it was too goddamned hot down there for me. It was okay when I got there in March but by June I was uncomfortable as hell with the bad air and heat. That was when I was nineteen and was sent off on scholarship to the Moody Bible Institute, but then I got involved with the student radicals who were rioting and my religion went out the window. It was actually a fire-breathing Jewish girl from New York City who led me astray. She wore a beaded headband and flowers in her hair and kept telling me I was "one of the people," and I had to agree with her. At her urging, when we were camped in the city park, I led a charge against the cops and got the shit kicked out of me and got stuck in jail. She bailed me out and we went off to a commune near Buffalo, New York, where they didn't eat chicken or any other kind of meat. They supposedly ate fish though I didn't see much of it around, but that's another story. At honest Shelley's insistence I will add here that I was kicked out of the commune because I snuck off to a bar, got drunk and ate about five hamburgers. They didn't drink either.

Just four months ago in late June was when I found the Indian. You'll have to understand how the cold at the bottom of Lake Superior preserves things. It was hard on my partner Bob. On one of our first dives together off Grand Island near Munising he came across a Holstein cow as big as day and looking damn near alive. He said the cow scared him as much as any shark he'd seen in the tropics. Then, as if to cap it off, a week later we found a new wreck off Baraga and the cook was still in the galley of the freighter. The cook didn't look all that unhappy in death except for his eyes, which like the Holstein's plain weren't there. The cook seemed to be smiling but it was the effect of the icy water tightening his lips. After the Holstein and the cook Bob was ready for anything, which didn't prove true when he saw the Indian.

Shelley just came in from the cold and sat down next to me. Before I get on to our drowned Native American friend, she wants me to lay down a few more background effects, partly so I won't appear to be worse than I am when we get to what I did. I keep wanting to get to the Chief, he was dressed in the old-time clothes of a tribal leader, but she says my actions will not be understood without an honest "confrontation" with the past.

To me the past is not as interesting as finding a three-hundred-pound ancient Indian chief sitting bolt upright on the bottom of Lake Superior. Your average man on the street doesn't know that the hair continues to grow after death and the Chief's long black hair wavered in the current. Besides, you can't walk right up to your past, tap it on the chest and tell it to "fess up." It has reason to be evasive and not want to talk about the whole thing, which for most of us has been a shitstorm.

Luckily there are methods for digging up the past and confronting it, and Shelley knows these methods like the back of her hand. This knowledge didn't come from her university training but from her troubled youth. Her dad was and is a big deal gynecologist in the Detroit area and his overfamiliarity with women on the job made him act remote and impersonal to Shelley. Or so she tells it. "Too much of a good thing?" I offered, which she didn't think was funny. The upshot was that Shelley went to psychiatrists, therapists and psychologists, and learned their methods. How you tell the difference is the first can give medicine (not cheap), the second goes deep into your past, and the third offers cut-rate tips on how to get through the day. That's my rundown on it anyway.

So we set aside an hour or two each day and she asks me questions in a professional manner. She calls this "probing," just as she was probed because of her haywire times with her dad. They're in fine shape now. He even gave her a new 4WD made in England when she got her master's degree. I'd call that a top-drawer relationship for a father and daughter on a certain level. Anyway, Shelley was probed from eight to eighteen at who knows what cost because she says there's no way to add it up. It seems the real problem was that her mother's younger brother, Uncle Nick by name, used to make Shelley play with his weenie on camping trips. Between this and her father's occupation father and daughter kept their distance until it all came out in the wash. I suggested we go find Uncle Nick and kick his ass but she said that was missing the point. What's the point then, I wondered. She's pals with her dad and fearless about weenies? That was part of it but mostly it's that she's not upset for mysterious reasons. That made a lot of sense to me because you can't even shoot a grouse or a deer properly if you're upset about something vague.

And now that she's at one with herself and the world she can work my brain over with high horsepower energy. For instance, she nailed me to the wall on the story of how the student radicals in Chicago had ruined my future in Christian work. She got me all soothed on the sofa by talking about things I love like all the different kinds of trees and fish in the U.P. Sometimes her voice gives me a boner but I'm out of luck because this business does not allow a quick time-out, sad to say, for fucking.

We went back to the ordinary sadness of those hot days in Chicago and what really happened, not all of it my fault. The church treasurer in Escanaba had made a mistake and sent the scholarship check directly to me instead of to the Bible Institute. I didn't even open the envelope right away because I thought it was just another letter saying that everyone in the congregation back home was praying for me. I just sat on my bed in the Christian rooming house (no smoking or drinking) and had a sip of after-school peppermint schnapps. I remember I was thinking about Beatrice who was a bubble-butted waitress at a diner near the school. She was a dusky beauty but when I asked her what nationality she was she said, "What do you care, you snot-nosed little Bible thumper?" We had to carry our Bibles (King James Version) at all times. I guess I looked so downcast that she came over when I finished my oatmeal and said she was part black and part Italian. I told her that to me she was the most beautiful woman in the world. I'd have my oatmeal and breakfast coffee and spring a hard-on just watching Beatrice wipe off a table.

So I was sitting there in my room thinking of Beatrice, and not wanting to exhaust myself on unclean thoughts I opened the letter from the church. It was a check made out for three hundred and ninety dollars. The possibilities hit like lightning so I dropped to my knees and prayed for strength which did not arrive.

I hit the bank as if shot from a rocket, then trembled my way over to the diner for an early supper. Mind you, I didn't order thirty-cent oatmeal for breakfast out of choice but because it was all the budget would allow. It was irksome to sit at the counter and watch a neighbor eat ham, eggs and potatoes. I have always had a weakness for catsup, but it didn't go too well with oatmeal. I tried it once and it wasn't a popular move at the diner. For days afterward other customers would look at me and shake their heads. So when I got to the diner I took a full-size table in Beatrice's section and ordered a T-bone steak with all the trimmings. She doubted I had the money, so I flashed my roll and she smiled. I had become handsome between breakfast and dinner. The owner even nodded to me when he saw me eating a steak. I admit I was feeling like an instant big shot when I asked Beatrice to go out.

"You looking for a chance to talk about yourself or are you after free pussy? In either case, the answer is no."

"I'd be a fool to think anything was free in Chicago except hot weather and bad air," I said, catching the drift. I'd always flunked the courtship routine so I might as well try to sin boldly and quick.

Well, she wrote down her address and told me to come over at nine, but not unless I had a fifty-dollar bill in my pocket. I said I'd be there, though fifty bucks about equaled the largest amount I'd ever made in a week. This fact and a lot more caused the next three hours to be pretty uncomfortable. There was a sense in my small room that I was wrestling with Satan and I somehow knew I was going to lose to His power. I felt the overwhelming heat of His presence in the room though I realized it was mostly the weather. I prayed and almost wept and even gnashed my teeth. The guy in the next room, Fred, a poor kid from Indiana who was also a Moody Bible Institute student, heard the noise and came over to pray with me. Of course I didn't tell him the nature of the problem. The trouble with Fred's prayers was that he sounded like the popular comedian from Indiana, Herb Shriner. At one point the devil made me laugh out loud. I gave Fred ten bucks and he ran out with plans to eat a whole fried chicken. My food budget was two dollars a day and his was only one. The week before his mom had sent him cookies and he ate them all at once and puked.

I worked on my term paper on Nicodemus but the bubble-butt of Beatrice seemed to arise from the page and smack my nose. How could I think of spending fifty bucks straight off the collection plate of the poor folks back home? Few unbelievers and upper-class-type Protestants understand this kind of test and the fact that deep faith is a surefire goad to lust. Forbidden bubble-butt fruit is what I was dealing with. Years later when President Carter spoke of the lust in his heart I sure as hell knew what he was talking about.

To be frank, as some of you might have guessed already, I failed the test. I still feel a trace of shame over my five days in Beatrice's school of love. That's what we jokingly called it. We started slow but soon enough we were on the fast track, me to perdition, and for her, business as usual.

When I got to her small apartment the first evening she was still in her waitress uniform making late dinner for a little boy about four years old. While she took a shower I read the kid a book called *Yertle the Turtle* about ten times, which was not much of a warm-up for sex. She came out of the bathroom in a blue satin robe and white furry slippers and took the kid down the hall to a babysitter. While she was gone a mean-looking black guy peeked in the door and tried to give me a bad look which didn't work. I was known around my hometown as a first-rate fistfighter and I had dug enough eight-foot-deep well pits by hand not to take any bullying.

So she came back, we went into the bedroom and it was over in less than three minutes. What I bought was what she called a "half-and-half" which is half "French" and full entry. She took off her robe and had nothing on but a teeny pair of red undies. I was dizzy from holding my breath without knowing it. She undid my trousers and let them drop to my ankles, went down on me for a few seconds, and when I groaned she jumped up, pulled down the undies and bent over. I had barely plugged her when I shot and fell over backwards to the floor, where I thought for a moment of my young love for Rose. I looked up in despair at Beatrice's fanny, then she turned and started laughing. She put her robe back on and went out to the other room still laughing. Was it for this that I had betrayed all my principles?

We sat on the couch and had a beer and I became cagey. I pointed out that at her current rate for work done she was making a thousand bucks an hour which was more than the President of the United States. "Fuck the President," she said, still laughing. I tried to slide a hand in on her breast and she slapped it away. I developed a lump in my throat and got up to leave with shame sweating out of my pores. She stopped me and said for another twenty bucks we could transfer the deal to an hourly rate. She let a breast slip out of her robe and I agreed. I also had to do the dishes because she was sicker than shit of dishes and food.

It was while washing the dishes that I realized I was in the hands of forces far larger than myself. There was a temptation to cut and run, reduce my losses to the T-bone dinner and seventy bucks (I had immediately turned over the twenty for the hourly rate). I could tell the Institute that the money had been stolen from my room while I was at prayer service. Tears formed at the image of me on my knees while some craven thief stole the church's money, stealing money from God Himself. Only that isn't what happened, I corrected myself.

I turned then to see Beatrice on the sofa, now with her robe off and only the red panties to cover herself. She was reading *Life* magazine which seemed to me a coincidence.

"What I was wondering is this. Is the dishwashing time using up my hourly rate?"

"It depends. It all depends. I'll take another beer."

I brought her a bottle of beer and she set the cold bottom of it first on one nipple, then on the other. The nipples perked up and she shivered.

"It concerns me that you don't know fuck-all about what you're doing. You're an amateur at this, aren't you?" She slid off her undies and took another drink.

"You're crazy if you think it's my first time. I'd say you were about number eleven. Maybe twelve."

She was actually number three. The first, by the name of Florence, was thin as a chicken carcass and we did it standing up against a pine tree in a cloud of mosquitoes. The second, Lily, was enormously fat and drunk, and I can't even guarantee I was on target, though I suppose it's fair to count it.

"Let me tell you, B.D., I don't like men who don't know what they're doing. It's simple as that. You're one of them. I have feelings. We all need pleasure, you understand."

She tugged my arm and I knelt down by the couch. She rubbed a hand through my hair and laughed. "You got the ugliest head of hair in the world." True, my hair is bristly and will stand straight up without a good soaking of Vitalis. She tugged my ears, then pressed a hand on the back of my neck, pushing it downward. And thus I faced the beautiful mouth of hell.

Five days of this and I had run out of money. I went over on the sixth evening and she was friendly enough but it was no dice. Her "professional standards" made what she called "freebies" out of the question. Her heart of gold was actual gold and not very warm at that. She was cooking spaghetti for her boyfriend and served me a single meatball before showing me the door. I tried to get a little sentimental and she just shook her head like she did the day I tried catsup on my oatmeal. It is hard for me to admit that I didn't turn her head one little bit. But still, a wise man would do well to go looking for a woman who's half black and half Italian. There's no point in searching the U.P. because the population is too scant for such a combination.

Within a week I was locked out of my room for nonpayment of rent and was bumming around the park. When I think of that room now I wonder what they did with the new robin's-egg blue suit Grandpa gave me, my schoolbooks and Scholfield Reference Bible (KJV), the single dirty picture of Beatrice, a present, stuck under the mattress. The last must have been an eye-opener for the kindly old landlady, at least she was kindly until I ran out of money. I was lower than a snake dick until I cast my lot with the student radicals in the park who assured me I was one of the people. I couldn't wait to disrupt a political convention, though we never got inside to see the big deals. At least there was plenty to eat. I didn't realize at the time that college students were expert thieves.

I'm running on at the mouth a bit here at Shelley's insistence. What happened to me was in her terms a "key experience." This doesn't mean what I thought it would. According to Shelley, what I did with the church money and Beatrice wasn't necessarily wrong, only that it established a pattern of failure as a self-fulfilling prophecy that I never got over. I was involved in failure as a habit, according to her. This is curious as I never felt I did all that badly at life, at least for up here. I'd say half the men I know are worse off one way or another, either from drink or jail or because a tree fell on them while cutting pulp. I never owned a house but my van is free and clear, though it's a '78 Dodge and could use some work. I rent deer cabins real cheap to keep a roof over my head. You just have to be out during the season from November 15 to December 1. Sometimes I live rent free if I do some improvements.

Also I relish parts of what Shelley calls my professional guilt trip. The battle between good and evil is entertaining and is supposed to be instructive. Just about everything seems to be in the gray area these days, at least according to the newspapers. I only read the newspaper on Sunday like Grandpa did. I was just remembering that right after the brief trial Shelley's father called me a scoundrel. Ten minutes later he asked me not to tell his daughter that he called me a scoundrel, to keep it between us. I agreed which lightened up his mood. After all, he paid my legal expenses, otherwise I'd be in jail like my partner Bob, or any other poor guy without a first-rate lawyer.

To be frank, my life in crime started right after Rose hit me over the head with the schoolbook. About a week later when I still wasn't feeling all that well a sheriff's deputy shot my dog Sam for killing chickens, domestic ducks and geese, ripping the mailman's trousers, chasing a stray cow into a fence and tearing the tire off a kid's bike, that sort of thing. I'll have to admit he wasn't much of a companion, but I loved him, and he stood for something to me, something like Old Glory to a veteran. He even bit me once when I tried to take a fresh deer bone from him to destroy the evidence that he had been running deer.

Grandpa had found Sam two years before while he was skidding logs in Dickinson County. The dog had no doubt been lost by bear hunters as he was part terrier with some Plott hound on the other side which made him large. Sam's muzzle was full of porcupine quills, also his sides, as if he had bowled it over after biting it. Sam wanted help in a real unfriendly way and Grandpa said the only reason he tried is another logger bet him a quart of beer he wasn't man enough for the job. It wasn't that hard, he said. He took a tarp from the truck, threw it over the dog, wrestled him down and rolled him up in the canvas with the dog's head poking out. Then he wedged a stick sideways in Sam's mouth, tying it behind the head, and pulled the quills out with a pliers. When he unrolled the canvas the dog stood still for the side quills and Grandpa had the notion this had happened before. Certain dogs are so ornery they can't learn from their first porcupine experience. He washed Sam's mouth out with whiskey and water, then the dog jumped in the truck and went to sleep, so we had a dog.

Unfortunately, as we were to see, a dog that is bred, raised and trained to chase bear was not the best choice for our small farms, one near Bark River and the other outside Escanaba, where we lived depending on where Grandpa was working. To call them farms is a bit of a joke as both of them were Depression brick shacks sitting on forty untilled acres of swamp, woods and meadow. I liked the one in Bark River better as there was a small creek and a beaver pond where you could catch brook trout. Living in two places allowed two school systems to share the load of my behavior without totally outwearing my welcome.

In her search for problem spots and "glitches," as she calls them, Shelley sometimes gets a bit loony in my book. For instance, she made a big deal about the fact that though Escanaba and Bark River are only twenty miles apart they are in different time zones which must have confused me. I said no, though I generally preferred the central time zone in Bark River, but I couldn't say why. Grandpa said all the world cares is that you get to work on time. I never owned a timepiece but I could see the need for one if you had to catch airplanes, or were having business-type dealings. Of course Bob had an underwater watch for me when I was diving. When you're down deep you have to come up slow, otherwise you'll get the bends and die. If you don't time your air and leave enough for a slow climb you may as well cut your throat and stay down there. The late afternoon I found the Chief I had to spend a full half hour moving slowly up the line, looking down at his black hair wavering below. It made me want to draw up my feet closer to my body.

But what I said about time isn't what Shelley means. If you don't have a sense of time you tend to drift along without any plans. You'll just be another working stiff waiting for his next day off. That's what she means by calling it a glitch in my brain, not thinking ahead pure and simple. For instance, if I had kept closer track of Sam the deputy wouldn't have had to shoot him, she said. Just try keeping up with a bear hound, I replied. Then keep him tied up, she said. He would just be a piece of meat tied to a dog house if he didn't get a daily run. Mind you, the dog has been dead nearly thirty years.

What happened was that I was walking home looking for Sam when he appeared with a white chicken in his mouth. I tried to get it away with no luck. I heard a car and turned to see the deputy coming at me at top speed, then I tried to get Sam to run but he stood his ground. In the winter he'd stand in the road and the county snow plow would stop and lay on the horn. The dog would piss on the snow blade and walk off. The deputy jumped out with this woman from down the road screaming "My chicken!" The deputy drew his gun and when I tried to get in the way he pushed me in the ditch. Maybe he tried to shoot Sam in the head, I don't know, but I do know he caught him in the gut which was sad indeed. Sam started howling, still with the chicken in his mouth, and ran into our yard with me right after him. When I reached him the chicken was turning red from the blood coming out of Sam's mouth. He was hanging his head but unwilling in death to let go of the chicken. The deputy came up to finish the dog off but Sam tried to attack him and the deputy ran backwards while I hauled on Sam's collar. Then Grandpa drove into the yard, home from work and beered up. He read the situation right and grabbed the pistol from the deputy, then walked up to Sam, gave him a goodbye pat and a bullet in the head. He threw the deputy's pistol across the road into the weeds and told him if he came on our property again he'd stomp him until he had to be hauled off in a gunny sack. We buried Sam with the chicken still in his mouth. Even now, across all these years in between, my eyes get wet thinking of my beloved dog.

Shelley and I had a terrible shitstorm of an argument. She hates animal cruelty and the story about Sam. I said that I was only writing what had happened. The argument went on to my other shortcomings and my lack of sympathy for her work. She wants to dig up this old burial mound I found way back in the forest exactly thirteen miles from the nearest people. She said it dates from the time of Columbus. I showed the burial site to Shelley the day after we met so she'd make love to me which she did on the spot, so she fulfilled her side of the bargain. The trouble is that when I had showed the spot to Claude he asked me never to disturb it and I promised. My word is not too reliable in most matters but this one was important. I took the precaution of using a roundabout way and Shelley could never find her way back. Now she nags at me like a sore tooth over this matter. The Chippewa are tough folks and won't stand still for the digging up of their relatives like they do out west.

After the big argument I ran off to the bar, which violates my probation. I came home just before dawn smelling of perfume. Who wore the perfume I can't say except she was not local. I finally made peace with Shelley when I got up in the afternoon. She is to continue probing me an hour a day but will not interfere in or read this story until I'm done. In turn I had to promise to drive her down to Escanaba and Bark River to see where I grew up, something I don't want to do. When Grandpa died about ten years ago I sold both places for a total of thirteen thousand dollars, bought my vehicle and took off for Alaska to seek my fortune. I never made it past Townsend, Montana, where I got beat up by some fellows in a misunderstanding about a girl. The money went for repairs at the hospital in Bozeman, but that is another story.

I was just thinking that my mind became a tad criminal after my dog was shot. Shelley told me that suffering, as opposed to what they say in the newspapers, does not necessarily make you a better person. I'd have to agree with that notion. I waited for two months before I burned down the deputy's chicken coop, though at the last moment I took mercy and opened the coop door so the chickens could escape. My friend David Four Feet, who was Rose's brother, stood watch. He got his name Four Feet because when he was a little kid his spine was haywire so he scampered around on his hands and toes like an ape. Then the government took him away for a year and when they delivered him back he could walk, only the name stuck.

The deputy had a pretty good idea who burned his chicken coop but he couldn't prove it. I hoped it would make me feel better but it didn't. You can't compare a chicken coop to a dog.

For Christmas that year Grandpa bought me a big heavy punching bag. He knew I had set the fire though he didn't say anything, and I think he wanted to get me interested in something, which was the sport of boxing. But boxing turned matters worse. I worked so hard on it for two years I became a bit of a bully, winning all my bare-knuckle fights in the area. I wasn't any good at anger so I had to rely on technique, most of it taught to me by an Italian railroad worker from the east side of Escanaba. My fighting career ended when I was seventeen one night over in a field near Iron Mountain. My Italian railroad worker organized the thing to win some betting money. I only weighed about 170 at the time and my opponent was a big pulp cutter in his thirties, real strong but too slow. There were two rows of cars lined up to cast light. It was supposed to be a boxing match but right away the guy chokeholded me in a clinch and I got the feeling he was trying to kill me. I got free by stomping on his instep and then, since he smelled real beery, I worked on his lower stomach and then his throat. The feeling of nausea and choking will weaken a man faster than anything else. Finally the guy was down on his knees puking and holding his throat. What ended it all for me was when a little kid about five ran to the guy and hugged him, then came at me and hit me in the legs with a stick over and over. I never knew my own father but if I had I sure wouldn't want to see him get beat up. The whole thing was awful. I never fought again except on the rare occasion when I was attacked by surprise in a bar.

It just now occurred to me that Bob was right when he yelled at me during a recess in the trial. He said that if I had acted like a real partner we wouldn't be in this mess. The afternoon I found the Chief I was off by myself in the rubber tender dinghy near the Harbor of Refuge at Little Lake. Bob was farther down west in the main skiff with a metal detector where the *Phineas Marsh* went down in 1896. Mind you, everything we do is against the law as all sunken ship artifacts are the sole ownership of the state of Michigan. When I made it up to the surface and to the dinghy I rigged the smallest buoy I had so it wouldn't be noticed, then thought better of it. Any diver will check out a stray buoy and I didn't want the straight arrows over at the Shipwreck Museum at Whitefish Point to find my prize redskin. I sat in the dinghy for a long time making triangulation points on the shore about a mile distant.

When I joined up with Bob an hour later at the Little Lake dock I had good reasons, or so I thought, for not telling him about my find. I was still sore over my arrest in the Soo (Sault Sainte Marie) a few weeks before. Bob had sent me over to sell a brass ship's whistle to a nautical antiques dealer. Most of the time we work through a dealer in Chicago to escape detection, but we needed some quick cash as the lower unit of our Evinrude was in bad shape. I dropped off the ship's whistle and got the cash in a sealed envelope which was an insult in itself. I said, How's a man to count the money? The dealer said he was just told to give a sealed envelope to a messenger.

The downfall in this situation was that I only had gas money to get back to Grand Marais and I was hungry and thirsty. I went into the bathroom of a bar down the street, opened the envelope and took out a well-deserved twenty. I had a few shots and beers and went over to a cathouse for a quick poke with a black girl I knew there. This girl has three years of college yet works in a whorehouse, which shows that blacks don't get a fair shake. Maybe I just liked her because she reminded me of long-lost Beatrice, though like Beatrice she wasn't especially fond of me. Anyway, it was slow time in the afternoon and I worked up an appetite doing "around the world" instead of the usual half-and-half. It cost me an extra twenty bucks but I was still within my share of the take on the brass ship's whistle. Then I figured Bob wouldn't want me to drive home hungry so I went out to the Antlers and had the Deluxe Surf 'n' Turf for the Heavy Eater, which was a porterhouse and a lobster tail, and a few more beers to fight the heat of the evening. I had every intention of leaving town, but was struck by the notion I could get some money back by going to the Chippewa casino and playing a little blackjack. Wrong again. I was out another hundred bucks when I walked over to the bar at the Ojibway Hotel for a nightcap to help on the lonely ride home. This turned out to be the key mistake of the many I made that cursed day.

The seafood had given me a tingle of horniness which it is famous for and I asked a real fancy woman to dance. She and her girlfriends were all dressed up from their bowling league banquet, and her pink dress was open-necked like a peck basket. She said, "Get out of here, you nasty man." I went back to the bar feeling my face was hot and red. I admit I wasn't looking too good in my jeans and Deep Diver T-shirt. I hardly ever get turned down when I'm in fresh, clean clothes. Sad to say, the weight of failure of the day was pissing me off so I went back over to the table and asked her to dance again. She said the same thing and all the women at the table laughed, so I poured a full mug of cold beer down that big open neck of her pink dress, then I said something impolite and stupid like "That should cool off your tits, you stupid bitch." I was not prepared for what happened next. All five of these women jumped me as if they were one giant lady. They held me down with the help of the bartender until the cops came and hauled me off.

The upshot was that the next morning in jail when I called my partner Bob to come bail me out he wouldn't do it. He said, "Use the money from the ship's whistle and bail yourself out." I had to explain over half of it was gone which left me fifteen bucks short of bail. He yelled "Then fuck you, sit there" into the phone and let me cool my heels for three full days. A lesser man might have sat there and moped, and I could have called Shelley down in Ann Arbor, but I decided to guts it out. Grandpa used to say "Don't Doggett," meaning don't act like his second cousin with the truly awful name of Lester Doggett from Peshtigo, Wisconsin. Lester used to stop by for a visit and piss and moan about the likelihood of a forest fire. That's about all he talked about, and true, his grandparents had died in the great Peshtigo fire which killed thousands, but that was over seventy years before. "Don't Doggett" was what Grandpa said to me when I whined, complained or expressed any self-pity. It still means to stand up and take your medicine, though it doesn't mean you can't get even, and that's what I was doing two weeks later when I didn't tell Bob about finding the Chief.

One afternoon it was wet and windy and we were almost done with our probing when Shelley's cousin Tarah and her boyfriend Brad showed up at Shelley's cabin. I had heard about this Tarah and was curious to meet her. Tarah is not her real name but was given to her during a ceremony of "empowerment" in a place called Taos in New Mexico. That's what Shelley told me anyway. I could believe it as this Tarah had green eyes that could almost hypnotize you. She was a bit thin for my taste but her satin gym shorts pulled up her butt in a pretty way. She was brown as tobacco and had a clear musical voice. The minute they arrived this fellow Brad unloaded a thick-tired bicycle from his van and dressed up a bit goofy in black, shiny stretch shorts, a helmet, goggles and special shoes. He was a real ox and I asked him what the bike set him back and he said a thousand dollars. I was not inclined to believe the figure and I said for that amount they should throw in a motor. He said "Ha-ha," asked directions and rode off at top speed on the dirt road, farting like a bucking horse.

Back inside Tarah made us some tea out of secret Indian herbs and we sat before the fire. I can't say I felt anything different from the tea but I had high hopes, sobriety being a tough row to hoe. Then Tarah spread out a velvet cloth and put this rock which she said was crystal in the middle of the cloth. She stared at Shelley and me and said in a soft, whispery voice, "You are more than you think you are." I didn't exactly take this as good news because what

I already was had gotten my ass in enough of a sling. Then Tarah said a whole bunch of what sounded like nonsense symbols as if she were trying to make a rabbit jump out of a top hat, though maybe it was another language. I wasn't concentrating too well as Tarah was sitting cross-legged like an Oriental and you could see up her crotch past her shorts to where we all come from. I already said she was a bit thin but she was also smooth and healthy. She had Shelley and me put our hands on the crystal. "We all go back many, many eons. We started when time started and we end when time ends. We have been many things. We have been stones, moons, flowers, creatures and many other people. The source of all beingness is available to us every day."

I admit I was a bit swept away, at least for the time being, by this mystical stuff. We had to sit there in complete silence for a half hour just like you do for long periods when you deer hunt. It sounded good because since I was a kid I wanted to be a bear or a sharp-shinned hawk or even a skunk. If someone gives you a hard time you just piss in their direction and they run for it. At one point Shelley frowned at me, thinking I was looking up under Tarah's shorts when I was supposed to keep my eyes squinted almost shut. "Seeing but not seeing," Tarah called it. I was wishing my old buddy David Four Feet were here. We used to spend money we earned hoeing at a raspberry farm to send away for books we saw advertised in *Argosy* or *Stag* or *True* magazine that would give us what they called secret powers. If you're hoeing raspberries for thirty cents an hour in the hot sun what you want is secret powers. We never got back anything we could understand but neither of us was good at school. The toughest book was about the Rosy Cross put out by the Rosicrucians. It mostly reminded me of David's sister Rose, the one who knocked me down and also threw pig slop on me.

Tarah rang a little chime to end the period of silence. I remembered when the bell rang that what I was supposed to be doing was getting in touch with a past life. Shelley went off to start supper because Tarah wanted a private time with me. Tarah moved closer to me and held my wrists. She was sitting in what she called a "full locust" and you couldn't help but wonder what was possible with a woman with that much stretch in her limbs. She fixed her green eyes on me.

"What did you become? I could see your trance state was very deep."

"I became a big condor from olden times. I was feeding on a dead buffalo I scared off a cliff." I fibbed, remembering a trip to the Field Museum when I was on the bum in Chicago. If you're in Chicago you should go see these ancient stuffed animals.

"That's truly wonderful, B.D. It means your spirit wishes to soar far above your current problems. Your spirit wishes to use your condor being and blood to help you. In order to do this you must not deny the proud heritage of your people. You must let us help you rediscover your heritage."

I dropped my head as if lost in thought. Despite how many times I've told Shelley I don't have a drop of Chippewa blood in me she refuses to believe it. She feels I am ashamed of my roots and how do I know anyway since I'm not all that sure who my parents were? I've said I'm just as likely to be an Arab or a Polack, but she won't hear of it. All of her anthropology friends think I'm at least half Chippewa but she's told them I won't talk about it. I've been tempted a few times but then was worried about being caught out. After all, these people know more about Indians than any Indian I ever met, except what it is like to be one. I never saw David Four Feet's family having all that much fun.

"It would be nice if you'd give me a hand during these troubled times," I said. "Sometimes this probing I do with Shelley just wears me out."

"There are many ways rather than a single Way. Shelley is dealing with your past and I'm trying to reach into the past before your past. Do you understand?"

I nodded as she stood up stretching a few inches from my nose. I breathed deeply so as to catch a general whiff. It was somewhere between watercress and a rock you pick out of a river, way up near the top along with wild violets and muskmelon.

"I sense that you are responding to my womanness," she said, twisting at the waist to loosen up. "But you are not responding to me, Tarah, but to the female porpoise that has been my other mode for the last month or so. Porpoises are deeply sexual."

Then Brad came in from his bike ride. It turned out he had ridden all the way to the Hurricane River and back on a dirt road in less than two hours. That happens to be about thirty miles which I found amazing. I got out my topo maps and he was thrilled to see that there were hundreds and hundreds of miles of small dirt roads in Alger County. I was brought up short when I asked him if he had seen the moose that had been hanging around the Hurricane. "I see nothing but the road," he said. Then he grabbed a towel to go swim in the bay even though the temperature was only in the midforties and the foghorn was going full blast. I watched him through binoculars and he swam all the way out to Lonesome Point and back which was three miles. I didn't bother asking him if he had seen any fish.

It was during my after-dinner nap that I got a real eye-opener. Tarah and Shelley had fixed the food of far-off India which didn't sit real well in my stomach, mostly because there was no meat, chicken or fish, just rice and vegetables. Old Brad really tied on the feedbag. It was the most quantity I had seen anyone eat since I watched a friend of mine eat twenty-three whitefish fillets. It was all-you-can-eat for a fixed price and he wanted to get a deal. Tarah said Brad needed ten thousand calories a day while he was in training. Brad didn't talk while he ate or after he ate. Anyway, while I was napping and trying to digest the food I heard my name mentioned through the thin wall by Shelley and Tarah who were in the kitchen cleaning up. I pretended I was snoring to urge them on. I just heard bits and snatches but it was a plot for me to take Tarah out to my secret burial mound and for her to try to remember the route. Shelley knew I'd never take her back there and here she was trying to rig it for her cousin to do the job. My feelings were so hurt I eased out the window and walked down to the Dunes Saloon.

Morning dawned bright and clear for me, if a little late. Shelley couldn't very well say anything about my getting drunk when she was busy hatching a plot. She sat at her desk surrounded by a pile of books, writing a semester paper on how Indians preserved their medicine herbs for use in winter (they hung them out to dry after they picked them). Tarah was in the kitchen packing a knapsack of food for Brad's all-day ride. While I poured my coffee I saw her stick in twelve apples, a sack of carrots, a head of cabbage and a jar of honey. She wondered if I could catch some fresh fish for dinner and I said yes. She was all dressed up in the Patagonia clothes that Shelley wears, including green shorts that did a good job on her rump. She had on great big hiking boots that looked funny at the end of her brown legs. Meanwhile, out the window I could see Brad stretching with a leg so far up a tree you'd think he'd split himself. Two old Finns I knew were standing out on the road on their way for the morning opening of the bar. They were watching Brad with polite interest.

Finnish people don't judge other folks too harshly. My partner Bob says no one knows where their language comes from and that they migrated to the U.P. because they liked pine trees and cold weather just like me. Grandpa said I liked cold weather because of the sunstroke I had once when hoeing. Also, when I was a baby I had been left in this closed-up cabin for two days and when he found me I was about dying of thirst. Ever since those two experiences I can't handle hot weather. I like to dive to the bottom of Lake Superior and be cold, and in the winter I keep my cabin about fifty degrees which also means you don't have to cut so much wood. Sometimes in winter I'll stand outside in shirtsleeves just for the fun of getting cold.

I turned from the window where Tarah was giving Brad his ten-pound bag of lunch. I was wondering what he was going to do with that whole cabbage when Shelley came into the kitchen. She asked me to take Tarah out to the burial mound, not to try to fuck her if you please, and perhaps she could go along though she already knew the answer was a "negativo" as Bob says. He had picked up a lot of Spanish in the tropics and owns a bunch of treasure coins from diving on the *Atocha* wreck off Key West. I tried to act stunned at the idea that I'd make a pass at Tarah, but Shelley just crossed her eyes which is what she does when she knows I'm bullshitting.

"Take my car. It's more comfortable," she said.

"Nope. You got a compass on the dashboard. I'm wise to your tricks."

"Do you think Tarah is sexier than me?"

"Of course not. She needs some more meat on the bones. You might catch a splinter with that girl."

That seemed to satisfy Shelley. Then Tarah came in and when they were standing next to each other the idea came to me how nice they'd look naked in bed with me in the middle. I mean for the contrast, like autumn leaves, brown grass and white melting snow. Something like that. I did it with two big ole girls over in Munising once but I didn't write home about it. One of them fell down in the motel shower and we had a deuce of a time getting her out until I turned on the cold water to sober her up. I had met them at the Corktown Bar with Frank my bartender friend, but he backed out. "B.D., you better go it alone," he said. I went ahead so they wouldn't feel bad, also I was curious. On the way out of the house with Tarah I saw her slip one of those flat compasses out of her knapsack and into her pocket, so driving out of town I asked her for it. I slowed down and tossed it out by a hemlock where I could find it on the way back.

"I'm getting the vibes you don't trust me," she said.

"I don't want anyone digging up my grandparents," I said, remembering that's what Claude said when he saw the mounds.

"How can they be your grandparents when Shelley said the burial site was from the Hopewell Period? That's why it's so important to her. It would be the northernmost Hopewell site. She'd be famous."

"Fuck famous. Everyone who came before is my grandparents." I was getting on thin ice here and wanted to change the subject. Once when she went for groceries I tried to read one of Shelley's books on the Chippewa but it was slow going. I either needed some pointers or had to keep my mouth shut.

"I don't want to dig up graves. I just want to communicate with the Ancient Ones." She twisted in the van seat and put a hand on my leg. I was already noticing how sharply she looked at the landscape. I was sure I could confuse her, though, because she was used to out west and in the U.P. you don't have the elevation for landmarks. It's just woods beat up by logging, or bare gullied areas where the soil is too weak to grow a tree, or just plain bogs and swamps. She put her feet up on the dashboard and squinted her eyes. I could see pretty far down the underside of her shorts but wasn't going to let myself lose caution. I was willing to bet that within her "seeing but not seeing," Tarah was trying to remember all my turns.

I could tell this girl was playing hardball when I parked near the river and said from then on we had to go by foot. I could have damn near reached the site by two-track in the van but thought I'd make her pay some dues. It had become a fair day for mid-October, what we call Indian summer, but I knew the river water would be cold from the frosty nights. I waded right in, then turned to watch her take off her boots and socks, shorts and panties, so she was only wearing her shirt. She plunged right in and crossed the river's waist-deep water and scrambled up the far bank ahead of me, a pretty sight for the eyes. I just stood there waiting for a few minutes while she air dried and got dressed. My plan was not to be a pushover for any tricks but my heart was like a deer's that's been chased by dogs, so I just stared off in the distance, taking only the shortest peeks at the lady.

I hauled ass off on a zigzag route for the burial ground, but I sure was wrong thinking I was going to tire her out. When I paused after two miles to catch my wind she wasn't even breathing deeply, and this raised a certain resentment in me that came from a lot of directions. For instance, how could Shelley really care for me, then try to trick me out of my secret place using her cousin? There's no way I'm going to try to jump this girl, I decided, just to spite Shelley who thinks I'm going to try. Maybe they even talked about it.

"I just can't do this," I said, and sat down on a stump, facing away from her.

She walked around the stump and faced me with tears coming into her eyes. "I can tell what you're thinking by the way we walked here. You don't trust me. I want to commune with these people, not dig them up."

I reached out and caught a tear that had made it to her chin and was about to fall off. Tears have a powerful effect on me because I doubt if I ever cried myself since I was a baby.

"I'll tell you what. We'll go there but if you try to bring Shelley back I'll put a Chippewa curse on you that will short-circuit your entire life. You'll damn well wish you really was a porpoise. In fact, within a year you'll be praying to die, *wagutz*." *Wagutz* is a real dirty Chippewa name for a woman but it was the only thing I could think of.

She nodded and put her arms around me. This had to be the best-smelling woman in the world, despite the hike. I thought she was going to kiss me but I slid off the stump, not wanting to lose control of the situation. I never have been in control which means someone else is, and at this moment I didn't want it to be her.

So we came to a natural clearing in the woods and I pointed out to her the seven large mounds and four smaller ones about thirty yards away, then I sat down under this small tree that had been blasted and burned by lightning. I don't have an ounce of superstition in me but you have to draw the line and I wasn't going near the mounds this time.

When I thought about it later it seemed that the light was too clear, the clearest I had ever seen, and the area was full of ravens whirling and croaking. She walked right out there and sat in the middle of those graves and began chanting in another language. After a while she lay facedown on one of the larger graves which I wouldn't have done at gunpoint.

As luck would have it, from way off there came a howling and bawling sound. Now I knew very well it was just a baby bear trying to locate its mother but there was a split second of doubt and I jumped up before relaxing again. Tarah out there on the mounds heard it and started flopping around and crying out. I thought, Jesus Christ, she's gone goofy on me, and I shouted out it was just a bear at least a mile away. Now she was rolling around shrieking and I had half a mind to leave her there. Of course I didn't. I ran out and grabbed her, dragging her away. She was flat-out hysterical for the first ten minutes I led her back toward the van. She didn't hear anything I said about the noises bear cubs make when they've lost track of their mothers.

It didn't take us long to get back to the river because I could see I was safe not retracing the crooked route. In fact, I was worried because she was acting like some of the crazy folks in the County Home I saw when I visited Grandpa before he died. She just lay down on the bank of the river and cried, then started to take her boots off but I had to help her. She lay back in the sand and I pulled off her shorts and undies. It was at this point I got an idea, and not the one you might think, as my notion of fun isn't fucking a crazy woman. First I bit her on the leg to get her attention, then picked her up and threw her headfirst into the river. By the time she came up sputtering I was right beside her, shaking the living shit out of her. "In the name of the sacred coyote, get the fuck out of here, demons," I shouted. I used coyote because I couldn't think of anything else at the moment but raccoons and woodchucks and they didn't seem right. Then she calmed way down though she was still crying. I went back to the bank, picked up her stuff and helped her across the river and up to the van.

Everything was going fine up to this point, all considered, until I looked at her tiny white panties in my hand. Without question I deserved something for my efforts. I got an old blanket out of the van and used it to towel her off. Then she grabbed hold of me so legally speaking it was more her fault than mine, not that I was exactly a victim though this girl was as strong as any. It was quite a chore getting me out of my wet trousers and shoes and my body was real cold so that it made her seem hot as fire. To be frank we wore off some skin right there on the ground which at least served to make her stop crying.

We returned home to a tragedy of sorts though Shelley had the situation well in hand. It seemed that Brad had been riding full tilt on a deer path off the Adams Trail and rounded a bend and ran smack-dab into the Golden Age Dirt Trackers, which is a fine club of senior citizens who ride three- and four-wheel ATVs. I hate the racket these machines make which is worse than a chainsaw or snowmobile but it's the only way real old folks can get around in the woods. The collision was of such force that Brad got a spiral leg fracture when he flew through the air and about crushed an old man. The local rescue squad took Brad to the Munising Hospital, then on to Marquette because a spiral fracture was too much for Munising to handle.

The upshot was that Shelley and Tarah took off right away for Marquette and I got a few days of solitude. I was about peopled out anyway though my solitude didn't start too well. It was a fine afternoon and Frank stopped by and we went out bird hunting with his springer spaniel. We shot three grouse and five woodcock, and picked up two T-bones down in McMillan at Rashid's, also making the mistake of buying a half gallon of wine and a bottle of whiskey because it was Frank's day off. We grilled the birds and steaks over a wood fire and finished off the beverages to the last drop.

I woke up early not feeling too well and drove out to the deer cabin. I brought along some groceries, my tablet and three pencils (Dixon Ticonderoga number 3's) so as to get on with my "memoirs" as Shelley calls them which is another word for your memories. I partly wanted to get out of Shelley's place because of the phone. Not just Shelley calling, because if I wasn't there she could check with Frank, but all the phone calls she gets from her friends in the anthropological business, and her parents who she talks to nearly every day, and whoever else. When the phone rings it's not for me is the rule of thumb. I've lived pretty well at times on what she pays out in phone bills. When the people I know have to talk long distance they keep it under three minutes. With Shelley it's like talking across a kitchen table.

By midmorning a northwester had come up and the temperature dropped thirty degrees so I let the deer cabin get real cold before I stoked a fire. I don't take aspirin for a hangover because Grandpa said if you do you'll never learn anything. I drank about a gallon of water from the spring and just sat there hurting and collecting my thoughts. About midafternoon I had a glass of peppermint schnapps to settle my stomach.

Now hangover thoughts are real long thoughts and I was feeling damned near like an orphan because I was standing outside listening to the wind and waves come up on Lake Superior some two miles distant through the woods. The stormy season was beginning.

About ninety percent of all the shipwrecks that Bob and me dove on took place in late October and November. You'd think someone would learn from this fact. I was out near Whitefish Point when the *Fitzgerald* went down with all hands that November afternoon. The wind came up to ninety knots and the waves were cresting near forty feet. That day a friend of mine was on the ore freighter *Arthur Anderson* which was trying to stand by for help. When he reached the Soo he got off the boat and never got on another. The Coast Guard didn't agree but my buddy said he knew the *Fitzgerald* sprung her hull on Caribou Shoals and despite having four seven-thousand-gallon-a-minute bilge pumps she went down in six hundred feet. Not a single body was found, for reasons I already said. Those thirty-four men will still be down there when the world ends as it surely must. Our preacher used to say nothing manmade lasts except real big stuff like the pyramids and even they show signs of wearing out.

Anyway, I was standing outside the cabin in the cold wind thinking these thoughts when I saw a big snowshoe rabbit. At the same time it occurred to me that Shelley might have been helping me out this long in hopes of finding my ancient burial mounds and becoming a famous anthropologist. A friend of hers had become famous for finding a prehistoric stone prayer wheel on Beaver Island even though a Chippewa lady had found it in a dream three years before. Maybe I was just glum from the liquor burning off and I knew Shelley really cared for me but I couldn't figure in her long-range plans. It had to be the mounds that made her hang in there and pay the legal expenses and all that. The thought was too obvious for me to be struck dumb. I stared into the evening woods behind the snowshoe rabbit which was taking bites of grass in between keeping an eye on me. I was feeling right at home all by myself. The woods can be a bit strange. It takes a long time to feel you belong there and then you never again really belong in town. It's a choice made for you by your brain at a moment you don't notice.

When I had this notion of Shelley helping me out for mixed motives I can't say I was real upset. Grandpa used to say to me, Don't just listen to what people say to you but why they say it. Shelley and me have a fine time together but my future is more of the same which I don't mind, and she's bent on making her mark. Be thankful when a woman's not kicking you in the ass one way or another, I said to myself. Also, there's the point that I'm forty-seven and Shelley is the best I've ever been under the sheets with. She's like Beatrice, with four more gears plus overdrive. If I start acting betrayed I'll screw the whole thing up.

There was no point in standing there in the wind getting a hard-on thinking about my girlfriend so I went in the cabin, opened the window quietly, took my .22 rifle (Remington) and shot the rabbit for dinner. I skinned and gutted it, cut it in pieces and browned the pieces with a little bacon. The rabbit was a big male and I knew it would be tough so I stewed it with a few turnips, potatoes, onions and a head of garlic. Shelley started me on garlic for my high blood pressure and I got to liking it even better than her. Sometimes I boil up a head and spread it on toast because I don't like butter. I put my Dutch oven on the stove and sat down to think recent events over step by step.

Your thoughts jump around when you are real hungover and hungry. For instance, I laughed out loud at the idea that Tarah mistook the bawling bear cub for the voice of an Indian dead for seven hundred years. An owl hitting a rabbit makes the rabbit scream like a woman which will startle you when you're in the woods at night. The yelping a bunch of coyotes make chasing a deer or rabbit will tend to make you lighthearted while a wolf's howl makes your mind lose its balance. The worst, the most horrifying noise I ever heard, was when the Chief asked me to bury him. How could this be, you might wonder, if he was found in seventy feet of water and his eyes were missing? When I walked to the stove to check the stew my feet dragged and the hairs rose on the back of my neck.

It's like I murdered someone and I'm pretending it was in a dream and I can't admit it to myself let alone confess it in public. The judge said I was "delusional" and that's why I got off so light while poor Bob was thought to have a "sound mind" and a bad lawyer so he's doing two years.

What happened after I found the Chief was that I made a plan. Probably lots of folks make the same mistake. Your number one step on your plan might be wrong, therefore all the other steps will be even more wrong. The morning after finding the Chief I had full intentions of getting the advice of Frank who is the only man I can trust, but when I got there Frank was babysitting his kids and they were all on the couch watching the exercise girls on television while his wife was at work. Frank likes these exercise programs on television as you don't get to see all that many girls in bathing suits in the U.P., what with summer being known locally as three months of bad sledding. Well, Frank didn't have time for any advice but sat there with a kid on his lap eating eggs with its hands, and he was yelling stuff like, "I want the one in blue on my nose."

The first thing I did after Frank was to call Shelley in Ann Arbor and ask her for two eyes. She had friends over at the medical school and I was sure they'd have some spare glass eyes lying around. I'm proud to say I've treated my girlfriends good enough so that they trust me and will help out when I'm in a pinch. I've lived with a half-dozen ladies over the years and none of them left me over any unkindness but because there was no future in staying. Grandpa always said I'd be a late bloomer so something might happen yet. I have my own theories about what people think of as the future. Imagine yourself lying in bed sleeping and dreaming of things people dream of, say fish, death, being attacked, diving to the bottom of the ocean, the world exploding, the undersides of trees, screwing women or men without faces, that sort of thing. It makes the world seem blurred and huge. Then you wake up and you're just B.D. in a ten-dollar war surplus sleeping bag in a cold cabin.

The first step is to pee and make coffee, which I can deal with, and after that what happens is not in firm hands.

Part of the problem of handling the future of the Chief was the article I had read in the *Reader's Digest* in a barbershop in Munising, where like Beatrice of yore the lead scalper thinks I have the worst head of hair in the Christian world. According to him, every single hair goes a different direction. This article said it is given to every man to have a few main chances in life, opportunities that will turn the whole thing around. While getting clipped it came to me my first chance had been when I sold Grandpa's land cut-rate because I was in a rush to get to Alaska. This opportunity ended in the hospital in Bozeman. It was clear as day to me when I found the Chief that he was my second chance.

My first problem was to get ahold of one of those small trucks that deliver bags and blocks of ice to gas stations and grocery stores. I would also need a piece of gill net for towing the Chief into Little Lake. The man looked pretty big but I was sure I could boost him up onto the dock and then into the back of the ice truck, the one I didn't have.

My ace in the hole was Avakian, the nautical artifacts dealer in Chicago. I always felt that he paid us fair prices though Bob wasn't so sure and he was dealing from our side. When Avakian came to the U.P. on buying trips it was a top secret operation because, as I've said, everything we do is a tad illegal. We'd meet way out in the boonies, or in an odd place, and every time Avakian would be driving a different fancy car. Well, once this man got me aside alone and said if I came up with anything weird he'd be interested. When I asked him what he meant by weird he just said, "Think it over, think it over," twice in a row in the slick way Chicago men talk which I could remember from so many years back. Being an honest fellow I later asked Bob what Avakian meant. Bob said Avakian had pretended he wanted an old-time body for science to study the qualities of preservation in cold water, but Bob had said to him,

That's bullshit. Then Avakian had said he'd pay twenty thousand for a shipwrecked body because a private customer wanted one to freeze in a big block of ice. When Bob had asked why, Avakian had just said, Who knows?

The problem for Bob was that before he signed up for the SEALs he was in a different part of the Navy working for some dentists and doctors identifying dead men by their dental records and body parts. Bob signed up for this duty because he was tired of San Diego and wanted to travel. What happened was the Navy would have an accident somewhere in the world like a plane would crash or a part of a ship would blow up. Bob and another assistant would fly to the place with a doctor and dentist and figure out which victim was which. After a half year of this Bob got sick and tired of sorting body parts and loose teeth and signed up with the SEALs. I say this because when I cut Bob in on the action with the Chief he wasn't much help because he had developed a phobia about dead bodies and he only looked at the Chief straight in his empty eyes once.

The upshot was that the first of July I stole an ice truck in Newberry by hot-wiring the ignition. I drove the truck full of sacked ice cubes directly to the deer cabin where I repainted it with seven aerosol cans of camo green spray at five bucks apiece. The next day Frank drove me to Newberry to pick up my van. I told him it had broken down, not wanting him to be involved in my criminal activity. He was my only character witness at the trial and the judge wasn't too impressed because Frank made it clear he wasn't one bit impressed by the judge.

Anyway, I switched license plates with my van and drove the ice truck to Little Lake at about three AM with the deflated rubber dinghy and the gill net squeezed inside with the cubes. I had told Bob I had an earache and couldn't dive so he busied himself trying to fix the Evinrude. You shouldn't dive on wrecks alone as there is too much that can go wrong. You develop an excess of nitrogen in your blood and you get what they call rapture of the deep which is about the same as smoking too much dope. I have nothing against smoking hemp except it puts me dead asleep and it's not what you'd do right before diving.

I found the Chief just after daylight as soon as I could pick out my triangulation points. I dove with a single tank and the gill net and a light to help me find the body. The Chief had tipped over on his side as if he were sleeping. There was a school of lake trout that looked like they were standing guard. I was all business and wrapped the big body in the gill net and towed it upward with a rope. I can't tell you why things weigh less under water. I tied off the body at about fifteen feet to ensure clearance when I towed it through the channel to Little Lake.

So far so good, you might say. I thought I was making smart moves while I was doing it, all cool as a cucumber. I pulled the body up to the dock where the ice truck was parked. How was I to know there was this old Audubon-type woman down the beach trying to find a kind of plover that is nearly extinct? She was watching me all the time through binoculars and she said in court that when she saw me load the Chief into the ice truck it struck her as "peculiar." And there was another thing I was missing out on that would have given me cold feet. I always listen to country music on the Ishpeming station and never the Top Forty out of Newberry. Little did I know that the town of Newberry was treating the missing ice truck as the crime of the century. Not much has happened there since the state closed down the nut house. I bought a whole roomful of their furniture once for twenty bucks to fill an empty deer shack. I don't know why but it was comforting to have furniture that was all worn out by crazy people. So there I was driving down a two-track in a dark green ice truck not knowing that an old woman was on her way to the Rainbow Lodge at the mouth of the Two-Hearted River to call the cops.

When I reached the cabin I hid the truck in the woods and drove my van into town to the hardware store to see if the eyes had arrived by UPS. This wasn't suspicious as Bob sends out artifacts through UPS all the time. The eyes had come and I opened them in the van and rolled them in my hand. They were sort of disappointing as they were blue and not too realistic. There was a note from Shelley that read: "Dearest B.D., Here are your eyes. My tits and pussy ache for you. Behave yourself. Your Love Pumpkin. P.S. See you this weekend."

Shelley is quite the potty mouth for such a high-class girl. I never ran into this before in a woman and it threw me off balance. After I met her in the bar that night two years ago we agreed to meet the next day. That was a downfall of sorts as I took her out to the burial mounds to impress her in order to screw her. In a way I was like Adam in the Garden I guess. We started necking out there in the clearing in the woods and she shrieked, "Stick your dick in me, you asshole," and it stopped me cold for fifteen minutes or so. I never even heard the lowest-class lady talk like this when making love. This talk took some getting used to during a sacred act (or so I am told) but I've learned to like it a bit over the past two years.

Anyway, I put the two eyes in my pocket and went in the Dunes Saloon to calm my nerves. The weather had turned hot which put me on edge and meant I'd have to keep the truck's refrigeration unit running nearly full time. My nerves forced me into a double whiskey when I realized I hadn't yet looked the Chief full in the face from close up, then I had to order a beer chaser because the whiskey was catching in my throat. Bob came in with grease to his elbows from working on the Evinrude. He asked about my earache and I said both of them were ringing. He was pretty upset because the diving season was just beginning and he didn't have the money to replace the lower unit.

"How about I offer you five thousand dollars for a day's work?" I found myself saying. I sketched out the story in a whisper leaving out the fact that the truck was stolen. At first he was angry over my breaking the bonds of our partnership so I edged up his share to seventy-five hundred. All we had to do was drive the Chief to Chicago. He said he'd call Avakian and meet me at the cabin. Meanwhile, I should install the eyes as he didn't want to fool with the body.

I drove out to the cabin all warm with the feeling I was no longer in the scheme alone. It was easy enough to burn down a chicken coop years ago but now I was in the big time and I had to act strong like Robert Mitchum does in the movies. Just by the way Mitchum talks or lights a cigarette you know he's not fooling around. When I got to the cabin I stood there in the gathering heat and watched the last of the south wind stop in the trees. I could hear the soft *putt-putt* of the ice truck's refrigeration unit in its hiding place out in the woods. I strode right toward it rattling the eyes in my palm as if they were dice. I paused at the back of the truck in full sweat because of the heat, then opened the door.

The Chief was still wrapped in the gill net and the sunlight struck across his chest, his head still in the shadows. It occurred to me I shouldn't have painted the truck camo green from its original white because it was absorbing too much sun and heat. I got halfway in and unwrapped part of the gill net around the Chief's head and slid him down so I could see better what I was doing. He owned the biggest head I've ever seen on a man so there would be plenty of room for the eyes. I looked down and saw there was some water on the floor which told me I was dealing with meltage. This didn't bother me too much as we would be driving mostly at night which would cool it off. I figured after I got the eyes in I would throw some boughs and bed sheets on the truck top for the time being. Just then, as I was looking up the Chief let out a moan and some air which flubbered his lips. Suffice it to say I threw myself backwards out the door, knocking my wind out when I hit the ground. I felt like I was full of hot jelly I was so scared. I hadn't even moved a minute later when Bob drove up and came down the trail into the woods.

He looked down at me, then in the truck door at the Chief, quickly slamming the door. "Jesus," he said, "that's fucking Frankenstein." He helped me up and I told him what happened. "Just gas," he said, having seen it before in dead bodies. Bob suggested we start right away instead of waiting for dark so the wind could help cool off my paint job. Avakian wanted us there before dawn and the trip was over five hundred miles. I'd wait and see if Avakian would pay extra for the eyes. Little did Bob and I know that bodies aren't a case of finders-keepers.

Right now I am back in present time with my rabbit stew bubbling on the stove. Old Claude just walked in without a knock. He said he smelled something to eat a half mile away, then asked for a drink. There is something in the air up here that makes us lie a lot. For instance, if you catch three brook trout you say you caught fifteen, and if you caught fifteen you say you caught three. If things are terrible you pretend you're okay, but if things are going too smoothly you tend to piss in the whiskey and create a problem. I'm not sure why this is true. I told Claude I didn't have any booze in the cabin and he started sniffling loudly and said he smelled schnapps, McGillicuddy's Peppermint Schnapps, in fact. I got the bottle out of the cupboard and took a big swig first in case he had it in mind to hog the rest. When I handed him the bottle he sat by the stove and just looked at it for a long while before drinking. He always acts like this when he has something important to say.

Claude is in his midseventies and he just walked seven miles out here to tell me something but he was in no rush. He carries a big garbage bag folded up in his pocket to crawl into in case it rains or the snow is wet, or he just wants to take a nap. Claude's the one who told me that every tree is different from every other tree. I thought about this for a week, then told Bob who didn't think it was such a big deal. Claude has a weak spot for Shelley even though he thinks she's up to no good. He tells her a lot about the old ways of the Chippewa though I know he makes most of it up on the spot.

It wasn't until I set out two bowls for supper that Claude told me the news. First of all Shelley wanted me to come over to Marquette tomorrow because she and Tarah were feeling blue. Claude said they were at the Ramona Inn but I was pretty sure it was the Ramada. Then came the shocker. Just this afternoon while Claude was wandering around in the boondocks for reasons of his own, he came upon two fellows setting up camp despite the bad weather. It just so happened that the two guys were Shelley's friends and classmates, the asshole with the red hair I'd met several times and the small blond fellow who walks around being sincere about everything. The blond guy had given me a book of poetry by a fruitcake Arab by the name of Gibran that I couldn't understand, so I gave it to a tourist girl and it made her horny as a toad.

When I heard about the camp certain things were clear. Claude said when they drove off he came out of hiding and snooped in their tent, finding a whole tube of marked-up topographical maps. It dawned on me Shelley wanted me over in Marquette so I wouldn't run into the two guys looking for my burial mounds out in the woods. I got so angry that I couldn't eat my rabbit stew, then I calmed down in a few minutes and it was so good we finished the whole pot. Sad to say we didn't have a single beer to go with it, and the schnapps was gone.

I drove Claude back to town and we decided on the spur of the moment to have a nightcap at the Dunes. Sure enough Shelley's friends were there. To protect their identities I'll call them Jerk and Jerkoff. They were all smiles and pretended surprise that Shelley was in Marquette. After buying us a drink they said they were headed back to the Superior Hotel for a night's rest. When they left Frank came over and warned me that the two of them were talking about me to Shelley on the pay phone. I felt my muscles tighten as if they were steel. "I'm going to deal hard with those shitsuckers,"

I said. Frank offered to loan me an axe but I thought that was going a little far. You never know when Frank is kidding.

The next day dawned bright and clear. I wasn't feeling great but a lot better than the day before. I made a thick bacon and raw onion sandwich which always gives me energy. It was about seven and I knew I should wait until ten before I checked out their camp as they would likely be out on their burial search at that time. If Shelley was blue I was a whole lot bluer. I'm not talking about feeling betrayed, because I saw that coming, but the idea that far too much had been happening in the past four months for me to get my balance.

When Shelley probes me she can't get over what she calls my "preferences" and "life choices." For instance, my favorite thing is just plain walking in the woods. I can do it days on end without getting tired of it. I mix this up a bit with fishing and hunting. Of course I like to make love and drink. That goes without saying. Before I started diving for Bob I sometimes had to cut pulp which is hard work. When I cut pulp my favorite moments were drinking cold water, making my dinner, then falling asleep because I was bone tired. I think I've seen every bird up here but I don't know their official names which irritates Shelley. Perhaps no one is who they seem to be. Shelley also thinks that what with my being pretty much an orphan, and with an old man as a parent, I was raised as if I myself were an old man with no expectations, no drive and ambition. When I agreed she didn't want me to, so I said I've been around a bit and there's a lot worse things than that. To be sure, it is strange to be an orphan and have to invent yourself because you don't know the facts. Having parents would give you an anchor on earth, but when you're an orphan you're always dreaming about how you came to be, and you could well pass your life dreaming. Or walking around in the woods.

This reminds me of the finest thing I ever saw, and which upset Shelley so much we skipped the next day's probing. I was about ten at the time and we were living over west of Escanaba. It was the day before school let out before Christmas vacation and a storm had begun in the morning so we were let out of school early. The problem was that the wind had been coming from the south up across Lake Michigan bringing in rain because the lake hadn't completely cooled down. But then the wind, as it always does, came around to the west, then the northwest, increasing to about fifty knots and we had a full-blown gale and blizzard sweeping down all the way from Manitoba. First it was the rain turning to ice, then a foot or so of wet snow freezing up as it turned cold, then another foot or two of dry snow casting in drifts so it came halfway up the kitchen window. It was a hellish storm and by late afternoon the electricity went off. That didn't matter to us as our heat was wood anyhow and we had twenty cords stacked against the back of the house, with another two cords of dry maple in the pump shed. We just lit the oil lamps and continued to play cribbage which we always did during storms.

Somewhere in the middle of the night the wind stopped and moonlight came in my frosted-up window. I blew my breath on the window to make a peephole in the frost. I remember staring at the field outside and the woods beyond and feeling quite satisfied that I wasn't an animal freezing my ass off. Then I saw a movement way out in the field near the edge of the woods, a black shape wobbling around and coming slowly toward the house. My skin pricked up with fright before I realized it had to be our neighbors. I also remember Grandpa was worried about David Four Feet's mother because she was due to have a baby and her husband was in jail for getting drunk and slugging the deputy. The upshot was that I woke up Grandpa and he got dressed in a hurry and went plunging through the deep snow to help out. It was David, his two brothers and sister Rose dragging a toboggan with their mother aboard. She was in labor and the kids, none of them over ten, were upset and their legs were bleeding from the crusted snow.

Grandpa put the mother in his bed and the kids in the parlor where he attended to their wounds with me helping out and fetching hot water, bandages and iodine.

He made the kids stay in the parlor, then put another pot of water on the stove, and we went in to help the mother. I mostly stood there and let her squeeze my arms and hands and within a half hour out came a baby girl with the help of Grandpa giving a tug or two. When he held the baby up and cleaned the gunk off and it started crying he said to me that this would be the finest thing I'd ever seen and this was how every person came into the world. I believed it though my arm hurt and was all bruised up from her squeezing. They all stayed with us for four days and we had a grand time playing games and cards and tobogganing though it didn't make Rose and her mother like me later on. I must have been an unlikable kid.

That afternoon in July before Bob and I took off for Chicago with the Chief we had more than a few cold beers to fight the heat, and me with a plumb empty stomach. The beer filled me with courage and I took an easy chair out to the truck and tied the Chief down on it so he wouldn't be sliding around in an undignified way. A thing worth doing is worth doing well, they say. I also stuck in the blue eyes. It was then I made an important discovery I have divulged to no one. It was possible the Chief had been murdered because of the piece of frayed rope around his ankle. On a whim I ran my hand through his ice-cold hair until my fingers touched a hole that could have been made by a bullet. It was then I checked his trousers and came up with a thin wallet which never occurred to me before. Everything in the wallet had turned to mush except a plastic-coated driver's license that read Ted Sleeping Bear and a Marinette, Wisconsin, address. The license had an expiration date of November in 1965 so the body wasn't nearly so old as I thought, right around twenty-five years in Lake Superior. I pitched the wallet in the brush and hid the license in the outhouse where it still is today.

I drove first and only made it halfway between Grand Marais and Seney before the hot air and the truck's bad exhaust system made me sick. I rinsed my face in some ditch water but it was warm and green. I was dizzy and my clothes stuck to me and Bob was anxious to get going. I said I'd ride in the back with the Chief and cool off and he said, "B.D., you got a real set of balls." By this time, though, I wasn't afraid of the Chief, and to be truthful, while riding back there in the cold dark I got to thinking he might be my dad. Of course I was half drunk and sick, also afraid of being caught, so my mind was a bit crazy. This is what the court called "delusional." There was nothing to say the Chief wasn't my dad. Marinette is across the river from Menominee which is less than fifty miles from Bark River. Of course Shelley has pointed out just about any man near sixty years old or older could be my dad. Be that as it may, the idea set itself in concrete in my mind, which shows again I had no talent for crime. All Grandpa would ever say was that his wife was a bad woman and so was their daughter, so he finally kicked them both out when I was a baby and raised me himself. Just before he died in the old folks' home I tried to badger him out of more information but he just said, "B.D., cut that shit out," and told the story he had told so many times about how he started to cut a big hemlock to get it out of the way for the skidder and it tipped over uprooting itself. Out popped a big bear that had been hibernating under the tree roots but the bear was still too sleepy to be pissed off. The bear just looked at him and walked away. Then when Grandpa was near death he was mumbling about Beaver Island. Sometimes in the summers we'd catch a ride with a fish tug out to Beaver Island and that was where I first learned how to dive. There's nothing to equal being down there on the bottom looking around except walking in the woods on a cold morning. Shelley couldn't quite believe how I'd take a stroll on a cold blustery night in just a T-shirt. Anyone who's not a fool should try walking in the woods on a cold night when the moon is full. That's when I learned most of life's secrets that I know.

Sitting back there with the Chief I could tell when we hit Seney because Bob stopped and turned right, heading west on 28 on a part of the road called the Seney stretch. This country strikes some as a thirty-mile swamp but it is beautiful when you get inside it. We were about five minutes or so down the stretch and I was having a chat with my presumed dad when I heard the siren and knew the jig was up. As the truck slowed I scrambled around behind the Chief's easy chair to hide which was pointless but I did it anyway. The truck stopped and in a minute or so I heard two voices besides Bob's, then the door opened and flashlights shone in because it was evening. Partway as a dumb joke I let out a howl and the police yelled. I peeked out quickly and saw one cop throw his hands back, dropping the flashlight, and accidentally hit Bob square in the face. I'll tell you that to hit Bob is to light a stick of dynamite because you better run for it. I jumped out and watched the three of them fight and it was quite a struggle. Just then I had the bright idea of jumping in the truck and taking off which is exactly what I did.

It is now nine-thirty AM and time to take my vengeance on Jerk and Jerkoff. I made sure I had what I needed in the van and took off for the woods. After I settled their hash I would take a powder and head over to Marquette to see Shelley and Tarah to try to lighten their hearts. I stopped short of the campsite, put on my camouflage suit, loaded my Colt .22 pistol and grabbed a gallon of gasoline I keep for the dinghy's old three-horse Scott-Atwater. The can was red so I sprayed it green with the last of the aerosol paint I used on the ice truck four months before. Waste not, want not, they say. I moved silent as a shadow through the woods, then came down a dry, brushy creekbed that only carries water during spring runoff. Just as I thought, there was no one at the campsite. Their Toyota was parked far enough from the tent and for a moment I thought of burning that too, but settled for letting the air out of all the tires. I doused the tent full of expensive camping gear with the gasoline, threw on a match and leapt back, and she burned with a fine roar. With a forefinger I traced a skull on the dusty side of their Toyota though it looked a bit more like a shmoo. For no reason at all I fired three shots in the air and hightailed it for my van. From my reckoning they'd have a thirteen-mile walk on their hands, by which time I'd be in Marquette.

Somewhat to my surprise I didn't get much pleasure out of the tent and equipment burning. On my way down toward Seney and over to Marquette I thought long and hard about protecting those ancient burial mounds. You better not hold your hand over your ass until you come up with thinking that makes a difference, that's all I can say. Mine was the original sin of taking Shelley out there in the first place in my pussy trance. I knew Tarah had been confused enough afterward, but maybe on the way in she'd been smarter than I thought. Country people are always underestimating just how smart outsiders can be. I've seen men come way up here from Flint, Grand Rapids and Detroit with a bunch of high-price bird dogs and shoot more partridge than any fifty locals. Sometimes these same folks catch more trout on flies that you can hardly see than anyone who fishes with worms. Maybe Tarah had one of those brains like a camera you read about. The fire might slow down the effort for a while but in the long run you couldn't stop these people if they kept up their gumption. Sad to say, in my thinking there was no way to get myself off the hook.

I had to laugh when I crossed the Driggs River Bridge because this was where Bob had had his duke-out with the cops that got him two years along with illegally transporting a body. I wish I could have stayed to watch the fight. The one cop who was supposed to be the toughest around ended up in the Munising Hospital but so did Bob for a few days. While they were fighting I had turned off 28 and headed down the first of many log roads at top speed. I went so far into the brush I doubted the sunlight would ever reach me, deep into bug hell where you could grab a handful of mosquitoes out the truck window if you had a mind to. What's more, I knew that at daylight the blackflies, horseflies and deerflies would join the cops and mosquitoes in the search for the truck. I had no insect repellent and nothing to drink but two beers that were getting warmer by the minute. There was nothing to eat and though I knew I was close to creeks, the Stoner and the Creighton, I had no fishing tackle. The fifty-one dollars in my wallet couldn't buy a thing out in that black hell. If I needed to lose weight it would have been a fine time to diet.

Rather than tire myself out with fear I curled up and slept for a few hours until so many mosquitoes managed to get in the truck cab I awoke to a swollen face and hands. I got out and checked on the Chief and found it was warming up in there. Above the whine of the mosquitoes I could hear the ice melt. I started the truck and the refrigeration unit to cool it off which wasn't taking much of a chance as the search for me probably wouldn't start until daylight. I was disappointed to see that I had less than a half tank of gas which would limit the time I could hide out. I was pretty sure Bob wouldn't say anything as in the Navy SEALs he had been taught how to resist confessing under torture. And what could he say besides that he was driving a dead Indian to Chicago in a stolen truck? Of course he could name my name but everyone in Alger County knew we were partners and it wouldn't take Dick Tracy to figure out I was involved.

I turned off the ignition and the refrigeration unit and got in back with the Chief to avoid the warm night and the mosquitoes. I thought of moving him off the easy chair and taking a snooze but it didn't seem right, so I sat on the arm and leaned back just touching his left side. It remains to be seen if I was asleep or awake, and maybe I'll never know, but the Chief spoke to me there in the ice-cold dark. It didn't seem to be in English, though that's the only language I know by heart. Some of it was in a jumble but I remember it pretty well. *"B.D., my son, you haven't exactly panned out but then you didn't start with much. To whom the Lord gives much, much is expected so you are not on the hot seat in regard to gifts. Someday branches and leaves will grow out of you and you'll understand how fish, birds and animals talk and I don't mean in chirps and growls. You'll be a green man is what I mean, with leaves coming out of your ears. Don't cross the Mackinac Bridge and don't go south of Green Bay toward tropical places. Your greed got you into this. Beware of women with forked tongues. Buy yourself a hat because your hair is thinning on top. Don't rely on alcohol so much for good times. Sneak up on animals and just say hello. Don't try to take vengeance on those who killed me or they'll kill you too. It wouldn't hurt you to read a book about nature cover to cover. Remember when you were so good at square dancing in the seventh grade?"* How did he know this? *"Well, don't come tromping into the Halls of Death, but live your life with light feet. Before I forget, bury me in the forest where I belong, not with the fish."*

That's pretty much what he said. I started to relax when he stopped talking and he sang me a few songs like nursery rhymes which were beautiful. I imagine this is what fathers do for sons who are hurt and grieving.

I awoke bone-chilled on the Chief's lap to the sound of water trickling on the inside and bird songs on the outside. I opened the door to let the light in and heard the first of the spotter planes above the bird sounds. The treetops above formed a pretty good canopy and I added to it with brush. It was about six AM and already warm and the breeze was from the south so I knew it would be a hot one. This made my heart ache for both myself and the Chief. I cranked up the truck and sat on a stump trying to make a plan, mindful that the original one had been short on good sense. I quickly drank the two warm beers out of thirst and for courage. Why hadn't I put the beers inside with the Chief to cool off? It showed that in desperate straits you can't think clearly. By and large, though, I felt pretty strong from my talk with the Chief. There was no way I was going to get away scot-free, and the best plan had to take this into account. We should have been leaving Chicago now with a paper sack full of twenty thousand dollars. I was going to buy a newish used van and check out some locations in Canada as the U.S. seemed to be filling up. Shelley was due in the evening and would get her ears full of my fuck-up. In short, the whole damn situation didn't look good.

I opened the door and it was cooling down nicely. About all I could manage by way of a plan was to bury the Chief properly and turn myself in. I decided to remove the blue eyes but they were stuck so it meant the Chief was swelling up. I took off on foot out of the woods and across the marsh and the Stoner Spreads toward Worchester Lake where I hoped to break into a cabin and find something to eat. It was a tough walk as the marsh was spongy and two of the creeks were neck deep. I watched an otter family fooling around so long I about forgot what I was doing, but was brought awake by the DNR (Department of Natural Resources) spotter plane. I wriggled under a clump of elder until the plane got tired of crisscrossing the area. At the Stoner Spreads I drank my fill at a cold spring I knew about from brook trout fishing and smeared some silt mud on my face and arms to try to slow down the blackflies.

The cabin I had in mind hadn't been used yet this year so the pickings were slim. I ate at a can of baked beans and a can of green beans until I was all beaned out. I took a bottle of water and half ran back the Creighton truck trail because the Chief would need cooling off. Twice I had to jump off into the brush, the first time for a State Police cruiser with a big German shepherd tracking dog in the back, and the second time for a County Sheriff's car. It made me feel important for about ten minutes, then I saw the back end of the deal. I'd hate to miss the big storms of winter in a jail cell.

There's not a lot more to this part of the story. As soon as it got dark I drove over to the Bear Trap Inn near Melstrand. I knew the bartender and he sold me a six-pack and fifteen bags of ice through the side door, and let me use the phone in the back room. He said I was getting real popular with the police as they had stopped by three times that day to check on my whereabouts. I called Frank and asked him to drop off a shovel and a bottle of whiskey at a certain part of the woods. Frank said, "B.D., you got your ass in a sling." I asked if there was a reward for my capture because I wanted him to have it, but he hadn't heard of any reward. Shelley was in the Dunes Saloon waiting for me to show up and Frank put her on. "B.D., I beg you to give yourself up, my darling." I told her where she could meet me at dawn with the cops and hung up. I instantly regretted this as I had a hard night of work ahead of me and would need a nap before I turned myself in. Then I tried to call David Four Feet to see how you went about burying an Indian chief. There was only one number under their American name and I got an older woman. I said this is B.D. and she said "I know it." This was the same woman who I had helped have a baby over thirty years ago. Sad to say, she told me my buddy David had got himself killed in Jackson Prison ten years before. She said Rose was living in the house with her two kids and I asked to talk to her. There was a pause and voices, then she said Rose was watching *L.A. Law* and wouldn't come to the phone. Maybe if I stopped by someday with a present she'd be likable. I hung up the phone with a bad feeling in my stomach from Rose just like in the old days. The power of love to make you feel awful is something to see.

I took log trails all the way to Grand Marais and past it, picking up the shovel on the way. There was a note from Frank taped to the shovel handle: "Do not shoot it out as if you get your ass shot off we will not get to hunt and fish anymore. There is no cold beer in hell. Yr. friend, Frank." This note scared me a bit as it had not occurred to me that the cops would shoot me.

I reached the location a half mile past the burial mounds and spent the next four hours digging a hole the size of a well pit for the Chief. I hauled him out and set him down, then sat next to him and had a cigarette and a cold beer. I put my arm around him and looked up at the moon, listening to some whip-poor-wills from along the river, and way in the distance a gang of coyotes yipping after a rabbit. I said "Goodbye, Dad" and almost cried, and gave him a shove so he toppled into the hole. By the time I filled in the hole there were the first traces of daylight in the eastern sky and I knew I had to give myself up to the law.

Now it's October and I am a free man driving to Marquette to see the woman who saved me, Shelley, and her dingbat cousin, Tarah. I imagined Brad might be having problems getting his ten pounds of vegetables per day at the hospital. I stopped at the Corktown in Munising for a pick-me-up and felt lust in my heart for the barmaid who had a large, solid fanny. I was nervous as the thought came to me that burning up the tent and expensive equipment might be a violation of my probation. No doubt it was, but someone has to stand up for what's right. For some reason I couldn't remember why Jesus came into Jerusalem on a donkey and why they threw palm branches in front of him. There was the idea that back then they maybe didn't have riding horses. Grandpa bought me a horse once for twenty bucks and you could hardly ever catch him, but you could see him at dawn and in the evening from the kitchen window, way out at the end of the field hanging out with the deer.

I checked at the desk at the Ramada Inn but the clerk didn't want me to go up to Shelley's room until he called ahead. I should have dressed better, I suppose, and when I felt my head my hair was sticking up. I went on up and found they had two rooms, what is called a "suite" with a living room and a bedroom. If you ask me, neither of them looked too good. They were both edgy and pale around the gills and I figured they must be sitting up day and night with Brad, but I discovered later it was something else. Tarah gave me a bleak hug and went off into the bedroom to take a nap.

Shelley closed the door on her and immediately became crosser with me than ever before. She accused me of playing a trick on Tarah so that she heard a voice when she lay facedown on the burial mound. This had given her a nervous breakdown as she had never got an out-loud response from the spirit world before. Shelley said she thought of herself as a scientist type and didn't believe in this bullshit but I had to have done something to freak out her cousin who was also her best girlfriend. I said I couldn't throw my voice like Edgar Bergen did to Charlie McCarthy and Mortimer Snerd, but she had never heard of these people, which shows the difference in generations. I explained like I did to Tarah that the noise was just a bear cub crying for its mother. Then Shelley accused me of fucking Tarah when she was practically passed out from fright. Shelley was standing right in front of me so I had to stonewall it by saying that Tarah was "delusional" just like they'd said about me at the trial. It seemed to work as Shelley gave me a beer from a tiny refrigerator like a boat refrigerator over in the corner. She took a vial from her purse and snorted white powder that I knew was coke with a miniature spoon. This was out of character, I thought, as she is usually down on drugs. She said she and Tarah had been tired and sad from their problems so they bought a bunch. She offered it to me and I said no. A few years before, Bob and me met some tourist girls in the bar and went to their motel room and did some coke and whiskey. I got real excitable but my weenie wouldn't stand up so I got drunk. The idea of paying a hundred bucks for a half-master is beyond me. My head hurt so bad the next morning I rolled around in the weeds next to the cabin and yelled.

Shelley perked up fast and took a sport coat she bought me out of the closet. I hadn't worn a coat like that, except a borrowed one to a wedding or a funeral, since I lost my graduation suit back in the Moody Bible Institute days. Things were looking up again, I thought, staring at myself in the bathroom mirror and wetting down my hair. Shelley came in and took off her clothes and we tore off a quick one watching ourselves in the mirror, and me with my new sport coat on. Shelley made a loud hooting noise and Tarah woke up and came out of the bedroom to see if Shelley was okay. We could see her behind us in the mirror and we all started laughing. It looked like it was going to be quite an evening.

I had the rare treat of watching cable television while the girls spent an hour getting dressed. The cabins I live in never have electricity and Frank doesn't turn TV on in the bar unless someone wants to see a sporting contest. Strange to say, there were twenty-seven channels and nothing interesting to watch. Shelley only let me have one more beer because we were going out to dinner at someone's home and she wanted to guarantee my good behavior. I busied myself catching glimpses of them dressing through the bedroom door while I pretended to read the catalogue that lists every single Ramada Inn in the entire world. I caught Tarah bending over in a rear shot that made me wish I could work a camera so I could save the view for future generations, or at least for my cabin wall. She finished dressing first and came out and sat on the couch next to me with a dab of white powder under her nose and glittery eyes.

"Shelley said that noise I heard was a baby bear."

"I told you that about five times." I was nervous when she put her hand on my thigh because I was still a bit swollen from seeing her butt in underpants.

"No you didn't. It doesn't matter anyhow. The voice spoke right into my stomach with a weeping sound."

"That was a bear cub," I repeated. She traced a finger along the shape of my pecker and I glanced at the bedroom to make sure Shelley wasn't coming out.

"I think it's the way the dolphins used to tell me to get involved with Native Americans," she said, giving my weenie a pinch.

"Might be," I said. Then Shelley came out dressed for church and we went off to dinner.

After I thought it over later I can't say I didn't enjoy myself though I never got my balance back after Tarah's pinch. The house was big and old but inside it was brand new which was peculiar. It was owned by a doctor younger than me who was taking care of Brad. He had a beeper on his belt and didn't get to drink or do any drugs. Everybody else kept glugging drinks and disappearing into the bathroom for reasons I guessed President Bush wouldn't approve of. I'd like to take him fishing as according to the newspapers, he never catches much in the ocean. According to Bob, the Japs are raping the oceans of fish for their yellow hordes.

Meanwhile, at dinner there was also an attorney who kept saying "Super" and a newspaper guy who had been at my trial for a short period and who ignored me. The women were more pleasant than the men, also they were pretty and smelled better at close range than any bunch of women I had ever met. One of them could see I was uncomfortable at such a high-class deal and talked to me about her kids. Her husband had left for a while and came back with a fresh sack of coke. He was a nice fellow and we talked about fishing, exchanging our least-best locations as fishermen do. His wife said she was glad to see we were "bonding," and went into the kitchen to help out. I said to the guy that I always thought bonding was when you repaired your waders or an inner tube and he agreed, though he was staring across the room at Tarah as if he wanted to jump her like a flying squirrel. All the men were paying the most attention to Shelley and Tarah because they were new in town, which pissed off the other women, who pretended they weren't pissed off as they helped set out dinner.

The main part of dinner looked like a huge cornish pasty but it was baked dough covering rare meat with a liver-tasting sauce. To be frank, it was the best thing I ever ate. The doctor's wife was real happy because no one else was eating much, so she kept serving me more, and with it I drank two whole bottles of delicious foreign red wine. There was also a dish of the tiniest carrots and onions and I said the onion was one of the most perfect things God made, and everyone was eager to agree. This made me feel more comfortable though the wine might have had something to do with it. In fact, the wine was creeping up on me like a dread assassin, and when everyone got up to go to the bar where they were playing music, I went to the bathroom and washed my face with cold water. When I got out they were all gone except the doctor's wife who was cleaning up. I felt sort of forgotten but she said she'd told them she would give me a ride. I think she was fibbing but I let it go and pitched in with the dishes. There was some gravy left and I asked if she minded that I drink it to settle my stomach and that pleased her. She was the plumpest of the ladies and I couldn't help but flirt a little. Her face got red and her eyes all teary.

"I know Fred is chasing that slut friend of yours, Tarah." She threw a glass against the refrigerator and it broke all over. By Fred she meant Dr. Fred, her husband.

"Don't worry, she won't be caught. She's engaged to this fellow in the hospital." I swept up the broken glass so I wouldn't have to face her. I knew if Tarah was primed up she'd probably fuck a rock pile if she thought there was a snake in it. I could see Mrs. Fred didn't believe me either, so I gave her a simple enough hug, and when we kissed she stuck her tongue in my mouth which sets me off, but then she pushed me away though not too far.

"I'm not going to screw you. I'm pregnant and it wouldn't be right." She put her hand on my pecker under my trousers and I put one down her blouse and gave a nipple a tweak. She unzipped me, then poured some dish soap in her hand, saying she'd be glad to "release my tension" which is what she did. It might not seem like it to the naysayers but it was sort of romantic.

Mrs. Fred dropped me off at the bar with a big French kiss and squealed off in her foreign-made car named a Volvo, my first ride in one. The music was so loud it was deafening me but I still felt sleepy after love when you ordinarily take a short snooze. I went to the bar and had a couple of 7 Crown doubles to wake myself up, then looked around just in time to see Shelley going out the back door with the lawyer. I felt low for a minute but I can't say I blamed her as he was cut from the same cloth as her, and I wasn't. Tarah was dancing and smooching with Dr. Fred and the others hadn't seen me yet so I left. It was the noise of the music that drove me out. I'm not used to loud noise in my life and it's the same reason I quit cutting pulp. A chainsaw is just too loud.

It was a long walk back to the motel and I was feeling low so I stopped at a few workingmen's bars along the way, also an all-night grocery store where I bought the new *Outdoor Life*. When I got back to the rooms Tarah and the doctor were fooling around on the couch. He jumped up grabbing at his clothes so I said "Peace, brother" like the radicals did way back in Chicago. I went into the bedroom, got my clothes off and started to read an article called "How to Nail a Big Swamp Buck" when I remembered the burning tent in the wilderness. It hardly seemed this could be the same day but it was, as I was to find out the next morning.

When I got up to pee at very first light Shelley and Tarah were also in the king-size bed, one on each side. You would think this would be the most exciting thing possible but I wasn't feeling too good about the ladies or myself. The world was moving too fast and I had to get my balance back. I picked up my sport coat from where I had thrown it on a chair when I came in and interrupted Tarah and the sawbones. There was a gravy splotch on the sport coat which sent me lower and I thought, B.D., you ought to wear a bib. It did warm my heart, though, to look out the window and see my van down in the parking lot in the dim morning light. There was also a guy who was asleep in his car who might wake up feeling worse than me, though that's like saying you feel great because you're not a roadkill. It's time to take stock, I thought, which is hard to do when you are bare naked and far from home. For some reason, I could remember a cold October morning when Grandpa and me got up at dawn and cut firewood all day. When we took a break at midmorning for breakfast, he fried two partridges and cornmeal mush and made gravy. Late in the afternoon the day got warm and he let me have a big glass of cold hard cider to ease the aches of a day spent on the end of a crosscut saw.

I went back in the bedroom, picked up my *Outdoor Life* and sat down on a chair at the end of the bed. The room was too warm and the girls had moved around so the top sheet was half off. Shelley was snoring ever so little and her arm was on Tarah's back. I looked at this page in *Outdoor Life* that is in there every month about a sportsman's perilous adventure in a cartoon-style drawing. Usually a guy gets attacked by a bear or rattlesnake, or charged by a wild pig or moose, or maybe falls through the hole when ice fishing. This month a fellow was going down a river in a rowboat, just fishing and not knowing there was a waterfall ahead. The artist did a good job on the guy's face as he shot over the waterfall, probably screaming "Holy shit" and having his close call with doom, but the person always survives the adventure or it wouldn't make much of a cartoon.

There was a rustling from the bed and I was all slouched down so I lifted the magazine for a look. They were on their stomachs and both of their bare bottoms were showing plain as day. The room was getting lighter and if their butts were cameras it seemed like they were taking my picture. In a way I was having a stare-down with the source of life, then I thought of a weird ancient story Shelley had told me. It was an Indian story from out west about when we were first on earth. Every time a man would screw he'd bleed to death because women had sharp teeth in their articles. It wasn't until a coyote came along and pulled the teeth out that men could screw without dying and get the human race started. This is why the coyote is thought to be sacred.

Men like to say that a hard dick has no conscience, but I've never believed that as I like to think I have free will even when I'm drunk. I moved closer to them for a better look and, though I was still upset, I began to think it was time to forgive and forget. Let bygones be bygones. A bad night had passed and now it was a new day, also it was hard to think of anything more purely beautiful than those two bottoms. I got a lump in my throat and couldn't quite catch my breath. Given their behavior they could hardly turn me down. Man is not exactly built for two at once and I was going to have to keep real busy so they wouldn't lose interest. I stood there at the ready, like the Olympic diver on the Dunes TV dedicating his dive to the Lord. The first ray of sun came in the window, a sign I thought, and I went for it. I almost yelled "Geronimo" but I didn't want to startle them.

It couldn't have been better and I still felt warm all over when I returned from getting some containers of coffee for myself, also sweet rolls and Diet Pepsi for the ladies. All I can say is I did my best and we all agreed we had sweated out the worst of our hangovers. Afterward, in the bathroom mirror, it looked like I had been saddle-soaped.

Unfortunately I may as well have gone back to a room in hell itself. Tarah was taking a shower and Shelley was on the phone and talking excitedly. When she put down the phone she started screaming at me so I couldn't even understand what she was saying. She kept saying, "I carried you, I saved you, I've been carrying you so long, you hideous dumb bastard. I even loved you, you worthless fucker, and now you did it, you're going to prison now, you asshole." The upshot was that Jerk had called about the burned tent and equipment and all of Jerkoff's "field notes." It was a shock to hear the State Police had come out to the boonies and taken my fingerprints off the vehicle where I had drawn the skull and crossbones that looked like a shmoo. It was easy as they had fingerprinted me a few months before, and my name came up right away in the burned tent accident.

I denied everything, saying that I had made the drawing in the road dust the night before outside the bar, but she wasn't having any of it. She started sobbing there on the couch and wouldn't let me comfort her, then she calmed down and became cold and mean. I had never seen her like this before and it chilled my poor heart. She told me to go out in the hall while she made a few calls and I stood out there like I was waiting for a dentist to jerk my teeth. It was all I could do to not cut and run, but there was a problem of the State Police and my slow van.

It was an hour before she came out, and by then I wasn't sad and I wasn't mad. She stood there with her hands on her hips as I studied the big girl vacuuming the hall.

"Look me straight in the eye, B.D.," she said, so I came up to her until my nose was about an inch from her forehead, then I tilted down.

"You don't love me and you never did," I said. "You just want my graveyard."

I was using a woman's wiles and it slowed her down for a few seconds, then she wanted to take a ride so off we went. She had a small bag and told me to take my toothbrush. When I hesitated she promised me she wasn't turning me in to the police, though they were looking for me. I smelled a small rat and wondered what she wanted.

I won't say it was a bad ride, because it started what I hoped was a new part of my life, but a lot of it made me sweat blood. The cool sunny air of October had cleared my head to the point I realized I could sure as hell do some time for torching their camp. Probation was supposed to make me walk the straight and narrow for three years and I had only made it four months, no matter that my heart was in the right place. I thought of my buddy David Four

Feet getting killed in Jackson Prison and shivered. I did not want to die for the good cause of protecting my burial mounds, which would be like dying for the dead.

Shelley wanted to go down to Escanaba and Bark River which was only about seventy miles or so to the south. She said the ride was our "swan song" and I had promised to show her where I was brought up which would "complete the circle." I didn't know what the hell she meant by this and didn't care because a squad car had passed us on the outskirts of Marquette and this had churned up my stomach. I agreed to show her around if we could eat something first, but she said she wasn't hungry, so we stopped at a store and I ran in for a six-pack and a chunk of pickled bologna. At the counter I couldn't help but check out the place for the back door as an escape route but I was breaking my last twenty-dollar bill and the notion was hopeless.

We took back roads to get down to the old place near Bark River. This was to avoid any Saturday traffic caused by what the tourist people call the "fall color tour" in their brochures, where Jack Frost uses his icy paintbrush to color the woods red and gold. A storm will come along and take off all the leaves overnight and the tourists who drove a long way are pissed off like it was the local people's fault. I showed Shelley a two-track where once the game warden had cornered me and David Four Feet and his brothers. We had my 1947 Dodge I'd paid fifty bucks for, and a case of beer, and we had been out shining deer. We shot a spikehorn buck for the larder, threw it in the trunk and got ourselves chased by the game warden to this two-track where the game warden stopped and waited us out. He knew the road went into a big area where there was only about forty acres of high ground surrounded by thousands of acres of swamp, and then the road dead-ended. We felt real smart so I built a fire while David and his brothers skinned and pieced out the deer. Our plan was to bury the hide and bones in the swamp, roast and eat all the meat, thus destroying the evidence.

We must have eaten about ten pounds apiece and drunk all the beer. David's younger brothers got sick and wanted to go home so he had to pound them a bit. David said if the warden wanted to locate the dead deer all he'd find were turds. The trouble was we got convicted on the basis of the blood and deer hair in the trunk.

Shelley didn't think this was too funny as it betrayed an early start in the life of "petty" crime, crime that authorities kept records on and doomed the criminal to failure. I wanted to tell her to go fuck herself but then I got upset over the fact that they wrote down every little thing you did wrong. For instance, at my short trial the thing about pouring beer down the woman's neck came up, also my so-called resisting arrest when I pretended to fall on the stairs dragging the cops down with me, even the scuffle in Montana, shining deer, everything. What chance did a fellow have to improve when they had files to pull the rug out from under him? Especially when I never intentionally hurt anyone. Don't Doggett, I thought as we entered Doggett country with a potential forest fire starting in every swale. Take your medicine and reform yourself, however that is done.

Then Shelley started laughing for no reason which lifted my spirits, even though she was beautiful and obviously bent on ridding herself of me. She described again what it was like to be down near the marina in Grand Marais at dawn with the sheriff, two deputies, and two state cops. They had all thought this meeting place meant I was coming by water, then they heard the roar from the hill at the far end of town. That was me in the ice truck, cranking it up to top speed for no reason but to make my giving up a big deal. I didn't want to putter into Grand Marais in third gear. Shelley said the bunch of them got off in the corner so they couldn't be run into and watched me heading down the hill into town at sixty miles an hour, swerving around the corner and down over the embankment. My idea was to drive the ice truck into Lake Superior and half drown myself but I got bogged down in the sand about fifty feet from the water. Even though it was barely daylight a lot of people came out to see the show because squad cars are rare in Grand Marais. I got to wave to Frank and his kids in pajamas before the cops subdued me. I put up a little tussle so the people wouldn't feel disappointed they got up so early.

I was pretty upset at my so-called trial because I didn't even get a jury I could explain myself to. The sharpie lawyer from Detroit Shelley's dad got for me said we'd be better off throwing ourselves at the mercy of a judge, a notion I didn't care for. I had plenty of friends in Munising who knew my heart was in the right place and I thought a couple of them might squeeze onto the jury. The lawyer told me just to "act like a geek which shouldn't be too hard" which upset me. I told the silly little fucker I was going to jerk his ears off which was held up as an example of my "unsoundness" to the judge, who had already thrown the book at Bob, which put him in a good mood. I could also see that the judge liked Shelley's father, probably because they were both big-deal Republicans. When Bob started yelling "Retard" at me at a hearing they just took him away. Shelley cried a lot and grasped my arm. I liked that even though at the time I suspected she had other motives, such as being a famous anthropologist. Frank wasn't too helpful as a character witness because he didn't dress too good and lipped off to the judge. Frank is his own man and doesn't like the authorities. What gave me the most trouble was convincing them I had dumped the Indian back in Lake Superior. The State Police divers even had a look but of course couldn't find anything. This is where my asshole lawyer came in handy because the police couldn't prove there was a real body before their fight with Bob. When I went into the judge's office, just the two of us, he asked me why I thought the body was my dad's and I said there was nothing to prove that it wasn't. He was plainly glad to give me probation and see me drive off with Shelley.

Now we were getting near the old homestead and I was pretty nervous. I don't know why for sure, and I began to fiddle with the buttons on the electric seats that could put you in any comfortable position. Shelley had said the seats were calfskin but when I smelled them I couldn't catch the scent of calf. I had her stop by a culvert so I could check out my old-time fishing creek. I walked downstream and felt bad that when they widened the road they had silted up the rocky creek with sand which meant trout could no longer spawn. Rather than keeping track of the likes of me the authorities might better be tending the health of their creeks, I thought.

Around a curve was another shocker. David Four Feet's house had burned down and all there was around the foundation were dry burdocks and chokecherries, and one sugar plum the bears had broken down to get at the fruit. Another quarter mile and there was our old place with David's mom bent over putting bales of straw around the foundation to insulate against the coming winter. She hadn't told me about this move when I called but she probably thought I knew. I had Shelley pull in the drive which she was glad to do as she knew this was the mother of my first love, Rose. The old woman admired Shelley's vehicle for its great big tires. In the U.P. it's the car that doesn't get stuck that gets the admiration. She pointed over about a hundred yards to the old orchard where she said Rose was picking apples with her two kids so we headed off across the bumpy field in the car. I asked Shelley if she had something I could give Rose and she said there was a nice scarf in her bag. I took the scarf out and it smelled nice with a foreign name on the corner.

"Your hair still looks like shit," is the first thing Rose said to me after all these years. She was wearing overalls and had picked four bushels to make a batch of applesauce. To me Rose looked real good though she was quite round, to be frank. I had read in the newspaper that the circle was Nature's most perfect form so that put Rose up there on the top. She introduced us to her boy Red who was called that after redskin. That's what the kids called him at school and he didn't seem to mind. Red was twelve and the little girl she called Berry was seven, though it was plain to see something was wrong with her. Berry was called that because all she knew how to do or liked to do was pick berries. Berry wrapped herself around my leg like a monkey and I had half the notion she might take a bite but she didn't. Rose told Shelley not to get drunk when she was pregnant because that's how Berry came out haywire. Red wondered if it would be okay to take a look in Shelley's Rover so she took him for a ride around the field, partly to be nice and leave me alone with Rose.

"That's the whitest woman I ever saw," Rose said when Shelley left.

"Why not? Always thought I was white myself," I said.

"You never were that white. How did you ever get such a high-class lady, B.D.?"

"A lot of women see things in me you were blind to." It was then I handed her the scarf which she shook out and tied around her neck without a word. She reached down and selected an apple, polished it against the sweater covering her big breasts and handed it to me. We looked off to where Shelley was coming back at us across the field. I was nervous but I didn't know if she was, so I bit into the apple.

"If you don't mind I'd like to stop by and visit," I said with a bit of quaver in my voice and almost choking on the apple.

"Suit yourself," she said, which wasn't much to go on, but when Shelley pulled up and Rose pried Berry off my leg Rose gave my ass a good pinch. Later at the hotel I checked out the red spot and it made me feel good.

It was at dinner that Shelley described to me what was going to happen, depending on my cooperation. We were sitting in the fancy dining room of the House of Ludington Hotel in Escanaba, and I was glad I had on my new sport coat despite the dried gravy spot. I was agitated because Shelley didn't want me to have a drink until she discussed the deal she had cooked up on the phone. The upshot was that either I told her where my burial mounds were or I was facing three to five years in the prison down in Jackson for the crime of arson, added on to the other stuff.

"I'll sleep on it," I said, mostly because that was what people seemed to say when they were discussing a big deal. A man at the next table who was eating alone finished his whiskey and water, then poured himself a full glass of wine with a burbling sound. Three to five years was a long time. I couldn't remember exactly what I was doing that long ago.

"No you won't sleep on it. You'll sleep on shit. You're always sleeping on it." She was angry and sounded like her dad when he was pissed at me. "You think each day is a fresh new start, which it isn't."

"I don't get why you and your friends are always doing rundowns on people. You're always taking people apart in pieces, especially me." I felt my ears getting red. I had never been real mad at Shelley before but now she was squeezing my balls too hard. I was close to the point I had been when I poured the drink down the lady's neck in the Soo.

"I need to know your answer. People are waiting to hear. My dad and my lawyer are waiting. A State Police detective is waiting. My friends whose tent and field notes you burned up are waiting. You're going to tell me or you're going to prison. If you tell me, I'm going to help you out with some money and we'll say goodbye. Also, you can't go back to Grand Marais for one year."

"Why's that?" The man next door had finished one glass of red wine and was starting another.

"Because I can't trust you to not sabotage our field work. That's the whole deal. Take it or leave it, but tell me now. I've got to make some phone calls."

"I'll tell you what. If I don't get a drink I'm going to kick over this fucking table on your lap." I stood up as if to judge my leverage. Shelley signaled the waitress and I ordered two doubles and sat back down. There was something in her face of the school principal who used to tell me I was headed for the reform school down in Lansing, the same one who made fun of me when Rose hit me over the head with her books. One night David Four Feet and me snuck up on the principal's house and poured a couple pounds of sugar into his gas tank to generally get even.

"What do you say now?" Shelley asked as I was eating my shrimps for appetizers and sipping whiskey. She wasn't touching her soup and slid it over when I looked at it. There was nothing in the soup but beef-tasting water but it was so good I could have drunk a quart.

"I'm lost in thought over your proposition. Who is to say which of us is right? I know I could use a bottle of red wine to go with dinner."

"You are fucking driving me crazy." Now she was hissing and called the waitress over and ordered a bottle of red. The waitress knew something was wrong and brought the wine in a hurry.

"You know you got me cornered. I've been taken prisoner in the war of life. That's how I look at it. Maybe they keep the prison too warm in winter and I couldn't stand that. I'd have to hang myself with a sheet."

"You wouldn't do that," she said. Shelley can't stand the talk of suicide because she had an aunt who did herself in.

"Yes I would. You know I can't stand the hot air, and there wouldn't be any walking or fishing or trees. In fact, if you called the police right now I wouldn't be taken alive. When I got my toothbrush out of the van I also got my pistol which is in my back pocket."

"I don't believe you, but you're putting off the answer."

I reached toward my back pocket where there wasn't a pistol and she waved at me with alarm. The waitress brought my huge porterhouse and Shelley a little piece of fish.

"What's to happen to me if I can't live in Grand Marais? The son of man has no place to lay his head."

"I'd give you a thousand dollars and you could make a fresh start, maybe over this way."

"I wouldn't accept more than seven hundred," I said, which sounded like a solider figure to me than a thousand.

"Then we have a deal?"

"Of course," I said, and she got up to make her phone calls. "You're not going to eat your dinner?" I asked.

"Go ahead," she said and rushed off.

I took her plate and dumped the piece of fish alongside the steak. A portion of bird meat would have completed the circle. It wasn't exactly a happy meal but I cleaned my plate. If you live on the railroad tracks the train's going to hit you, Grandpa used to say. I had a notion to call up Frank and ask him the name of that tribal lawyer he knew over in Brimley. Maybe they could organize a welcoming party for the grave diggers, but suddenly I was tired of the whole damn thing. The steak had heated me up as beef will do, so I went outside and stood under the awning, letting the cold wind blow on me. I stood there like a statue until I got real cold, then I stood there longer. Grandpa and I used to drive past the hotel but neither of us had ever been inside. He said it was a place for the men who owned the trees, not for the ones who cut them down. Come to think of it, I was not likely to return myself.

After a while Shelley came running out as if I had made an escape. "There you are," she yelled. We took a long walk without saying much. I had an urge to haul her into Orphan Annie's striptease club but it didn't seem to go with the evening. There would be other times for that, I thought, if I came back this way for a year. We took a turn down a side street so I could show her the church that sent me off to Chicago so many years ago. I had been sentenced to attend church by a juvenile judge after a couple of unfortunate accidents. David Four Feet and me found a source for black-market fireworks, serious stuff like cherry bombs and M-80s, and there was a lot of noise around town for a month. Before we got caught for that we had cabled a county snowplow to a fire hydrant outside this diner, with a lot of slack so the truck would have a head of steam before the cable came tight. Little did we know the truck would uproot the fire hydrant and cause a flooding problem in the middle of winter. I had to shovel city sidewalks all winter for free, and attend church where everyone was nice and thought of me as the prodigal son.

We went back to the hotel because Shelley was cold and tired, probably because she didn't eat her dinner. She got us two connected rooms again with the living room having a big flat-top piano in it. I said it was wasting money but she said that this is where we were to have our meeting in the morning. Nice to have something to look forward to, I said, wandering around the room hunched up like I was a lot older, which always irritates her. I admit I was a bit blue so I sat down at the piano. Back in my church days I could play "The Old Rugged Cross" with one finger, also "Chopsticks," but now I didn't feel up to it despite the rare opportunity of a piano.

Shelley tuned me in a hockey game on TV while I sat there on the piano bench. Hockey's the only sport I was ever good at except boxing. I suddenly got this idea I was a great piano player whose hand had been crippled when his girlfriend had slammed it in a door, so near to greatness but yet so far. I told this to Shelley and she gave me a big hug to cheer me up and she said she had brought along my favorite nightie for our last night. This nightie is purple and smooth as satin because that's what it's made of. It clings to her and you sort of peel it off until bingo, you're there.

She went to take a shower and I sat down by the phone with an urge to call Frank and give him the sad tidings. There was a card attached to the phone that said to dial 33 for room service so that's what I did. They asked me what I'd like and since I had already eaten I wondered if they could bring me a couple of drinks. Presto, a guy was there in minutes. They let me sign my name as I only had fifteen bucks after the six-pack and pickled bologna and wasn't counting on the big payment mentioned. I took my drinks over to the piano and tried to noodle along singing my favorite country songs, but I couldn't get the piano to go with the words and, what's more, the drinks weren't making their way through the load of shrimp, fish and steak in my gut. I had just about decided to ask Shelley if she had ever loved me or was she just hanging in there for the burial mounds when she came out in the purple nightie and I didn't have the heart to. She came right over and I lifted the nightie and a lot of shower heat escaped. "It's like a blast furnace in there," I said, dropping the hem. She laughed and had a slug of my second drink. I asked if she'd mind getting up on the piano and laying out so I could sing to her. She scrambled up with no problem and lay there leaning her head on a hand. I tinkled along singing a mishmash of my favorite lines from country music, including one I made up: *"Our love was not meant to be, at least not in the long run."* She was getting tears in her eyes so I swiveled her legs around so the backs of her knees were over my shoulders and I sang, *"Yes, we have no bananas,"* and she started laughing. I stood partway up and she slid down, her butt hitting the keys in a nice way like the lost chord. We did it right there which wasn't easy.

I woke up from a bad dream where I was suffocating in a hot cabin and I couldn't walk, then I saw where I was and lightened up. The first of the morning sun was red in the east and there were black rolling clouds and snow flurries, sure sign of a coming gale. The red sun made the room pinkish and I turned to look at how Shelley's nightie was pulled up all the way under her arms. I opened the window which squeaked to cool it off.

"B.D., is something wrong?" she asked.

"Not so you would notice. Red sky in morning, sailors take warning. That's all I know."

She said "Oh" and went back to sleep. It was then I had the notion that I'd better memorize her body as another one this fine was not likely to pass my way again. I started with her face but I knew it well enough so I went down to the feet and stared at them, then the ankles and knees. I thought of the old grade school song which we used to sing to the tune of *"I'm looking over a four-leaf clover."* The dirty version went, *"I'm looking under a two-legged wonder"* but I couldn't remember the rest. Also, in the pink light her body was too lovely to be thinking of nonsense. She didn't wake up until I turned her over to memorize the other side.

"B.D., what are you doing? It's too early." She checked her watch on the nightstand and put her face in the pillow.

"I'm memorizing your body because we're going to part," I said, and she went back to sleep with another "Oh." I said I never cried but I think I was getting pretty close by the time I got the memorizing job done, also I remembered how the Chief told me to keep my feet light. Luckily other emotions took over and by the time she fully awoke she was making yodeling sounds like Judy Canova on the *Louisiana Hayride* program.

The meeting wasn't all that it was pumped up to be. I was the sailor who took the red sky as a warning and played it hard and cold as Robert Mitchum. I had had breakfast in bed for the first time since I was sick as a kid so I was in a good mood except I couldn't get a beer. I had eaten Shelley's ham and mine too, so I was a bit dry, but when I called room service they said it was state law—no beer on Sunday until noon. I asked them what kind of low-rent hellhole they were running and they apologized. It was a comfort somehow that rich folks had to wait until noon just like everyone else.

First to arrive was Shelley's lawyer fresh off a stormy ride on the morning plane from Detroit. He kissed Shelley on both cheeks, like I've seen on television, and told her her dad couldn't come because he had to do a "C-section" on an important lady. He just looked at me and sighed, deciding not to offer his hand for a shake, partly because I was staring him down like he was so much dog shit. Then came the State Police detective and the two of them whispered in the far corner while I watched snow swirling up the street which was putting a jinx on the color tour. Along came Jerk and Jerkoff with a tube of topographical maps which they spread out on the lid of the sacred piano. They glanced at me out of the corner of their eyes. I told Shelley that they had to stand over against the wall or the deal was off and I wouldn't trace a route on the map. The lawyer and the detective came over and gave me some papers to sign that said the arson charge would be resumed if I showed up in Grand Marais within a year. I was given two days to move my stuff out. I signed the papers and the detective said he'd be keeping an eye on me.

"No doubt you will because you can't find honest work," I said with a sneer. Then I went over and worked on the map with Shelley, using the lawyer's gold pen I intended to swipe. She gave me a pleading look that said "Please no tricks," but it was too late in the game for that. When I finished with the topo map she said she was surprised how close she had been several times. She waved over Jerk and Jerkoff but I yelled, "Stay in the corner, shitsuckers," so they did. For some reason I picked up the cover of the piano bench and looked at some sheet music. There was a piece by Mozart, whose name I'd heard on the NPR station out of Marquette. I took it out and sat down to play.

"A little Mozart for Sunday morning," I said, then beat the hell out of the keys. Everyone left right away except Shelley. On the way out the lawyer picked his gold pen out of my pocket and gave me the envelope of money which I didn't stop to count.

That was that. We checked out of the hotel without saying much of anything. While she warmed up her car I cleaned all the wet snow off her windows, looking at her as she sat there shivering. She wasn't built for winter. She almost ruined it by saying maybe we'd see each other again someday, but I said "I doubt it," and off she drove.

So there I stood in the Sunday snow with my toothbrush in my pocket wrapped up by Shelley in Kleenex. I felt the toothbrush and envelope of money and it was then I remembered my van was parked at the Ramada Inn up in Marquette. Worse things have happened, I thought. I'd just have to hitchhike up there. Just then a taxicab dropped off a lady at the hotel and I walked over. I asked the driver who was an old man how much was the eighty miles to Marquette, and he said things were slow so he'd make the drive for fifty bucks. I got in but before he'd start he wanted to see the color of my money just like Beatrice when I ordered a steak back in Chicago. I drew a hundred-dollar bill from the envelope and off we went. It was quite the shock when he asked me if I wasn't B.D. who he saw fight a pulp cutter over in Iron Mountain twenty-five years ago. It wasn't the biggest thing on earth but it made me feel life was holding together somehow.

We were out on the edge of town when I had the idea to stop at the supermarket and pick up a bunch of chickens, also a six-pack for my trip, to drop off at Rose's. Maybe she and her mom would cook Sunday dinner. I'd see if her boy Red might want to ride up to Marquette since he probably had never been in a taxi before. And that's what I did. A pinch and a "suit yourself" wasn't much to go on but it didn't hurt to try.

The Seven-Ounce Man

I

BACK HOME

It was the darkest and coldest summer of the century in the Upper Peninsula, or so everyone said. When in groups people spoke in muffled dirge noises; alone, their soul speech was a runt-of-the-litter whimper. If you were awake the night of the summer solstice, perhaps driving home from a tavern, you saw snowflakes. You wanted them to be a hatch of summer bugs but they were definitely snowflakes. Then the night of the Glorious Fourth, when multicolored pyrotechnic bombs burst in the air over Escanaba's harbor, folks huddled in their heated cars or sat on blankets in their snowmobile suits. By dawn every tomato plant in town lay supine under a crust of hoarfrost. The sturdier peas survived but the pods were already atrophied by the frigid dankness of June.

It was to be a summer without the pleasures of sweet corn, tans, beach parties, and most disastrously, tourism. Bridge crossings over the "mighty Mackinac" dropped to an all-time low along with beer sales. A trickle of diehard, dour downstaters with shiny vehicles arrived—RVs towing compact cars that in turn towed boats—but few of them other than the campers, known locally as bologna eaters, unlike the most welcome kind of tourists who stayed in motels and ate in restaurants. Even the bears suffered and became scrawny from the failure of the wild berry crop, invading the outskirts of town for garbage cans and tooth-some household pets.

Since Brown Dog was not given to lolling on beaches he did not mind the weather which stayed right around a daytime high of forty-nine degrees, actually his favorite temperature among all the possibilities. He liked the symmetry involved in the idea that his favorite driving speed and temperature were the same. His grandpa had always said that nobody ever got killed driving below fifty so Brown Dog kept it at forty-nine, kissing the inside limit of fatality. The real problem was that he no longer had his own vehicle, what with Rose totaling the old Dodge van against a birch tree on her way home from her job cleaning the Indian casino. He visited the junkyard as if it were a grave site, fondly patting the undamaged parts, caressing the metallic wounds, a lump forming in his throat as he said goodbye to his beloved vehicle.

Where Brown Dog hurt the most, though, was in the double of love and money. The truth was that he was out of both, the pockets utterly empty, and there didn't seem to be a philosophical or theological palliative for the condition. The presence of one somewhat consoles the absence of the other, and when one possesses neither, the soul is left sucking a very bad egg indeed—say, one that got nudged into a corner of straw in the hen house and was discovered far too many months later. What's more, he was dealing with a bum knee from a logging accident, and the five percent of the net from the Wild Wild Midwest Show had not "eventuated," as they say these days.

* * *

The October before, he had rediscovered his childhood sweetheart, Rose, though it must be said that Rose had never offered a single gesture of affection in their youth, and she wasn't overly forthcoming in the present. To think of her as a sweetheart at all would be called a far reach, in sailing terms. She was born mean, captious, sullen, with occasional small dirty windows of charm. The pail of pig slop she had dumped on Brown Dog's head when he was the neighbor boy might have been a harbinger for a sensible man, but as a sentimentalist he was always trying to get at the heart of something that frequently didn't have a heart. For instance, the afternoon Brown Dog had showed up after twenty-five years and taken off with Rose's thirteen-year-old son, Red, and eight-year-old retarded (fetal alcohol syndrome) daughter, Berry, for the first taxi ride for any of them, all the way up to Marquette to retrieve Brown Dog's van, he had returned to discover that Rose had drunk ten of the twelve beers he had dropped off, plus eaten most of the two chickens. There was a leg apiece for Berry and Red, and two wings for Brown Dog. Rose grandly split the remaining two beers with him, which made the score eleven to one. Her mother, Doris, only said, affably enough, that Rose was a pig.

Still, it was a homecoming, and when he stepped outside to quell his anger (and hunger) in the cold air he was amazed that Fate had brought him back, with her peculiar circuitry, to the small farm where his grandfather had raised him. It was a pretty good feeling that after the real threat of prison he had arrived back here even though the home was no longer his. But well behind his boyhood love for Rose and its resurgence at the not very tender age of forty-eight, back in some primitive dovecote, there was the worry that he might not be invited to stay. The Son of Man might not have a place to lay his head, he remembered from the Bible, and this was not allayed by the nine hundred bucks in his pocket. He was one of the few poor people in creation who actually knew that money didn't buy happiness, this knowledge due to the fact that he always squandered money at touch, which left the dullish feeling of a head cold.

The front door opened behind him and he braced himself against the rotting porch railing without turning around. He hoped it was Rose asking him to stay, prayed though he had no verbs in his possession that might get a prayer going. He felt the retarded Berry clutching his leg, whispering insistently something that sounded like "whooper." He turned to see Rose standing somewhat groggily at the door.

"Ma says I should ask you to stay. There's no room out of the way except under the kitchen table. I need the couch for TV."

"Thank you. May as well." He looked down at Berry who continued her whispered incantation. "What does she want? What's 'whooper'?"

"Her and Red want Whoppers. Make yourself useful."

At the Burger King they ate Whoppers, largish burgers loaded with condiments, and Brown Dog tried to make some plans. There was a specific peaceful feeling of being here with the kids like a real father, and the mood lent itself to thinking about his future. The authorities had allowed him a single day to return to Grand Marais and pick up his belongings, but he doubted it was worth the three-hour drive to gather a winter coat, boots, and an old single-shot .22 rifle. He'd call Frank at the Dunes Saloon and have him hold the stuff.

It surely was time to take stock, as Grandpa would say. Brown Dog shuddered at his two brushes with prison, the first as a salvage diver when he found the dead Indian down in fifty feet of water for fifty years, perfectly preserved in the icy waters of Lake Superior, then stealing the ice truck in an attempt to transport the body to Chicago, followed by the arson of the anthropologist's tent and camping equipment—all to protect the secret Indian graveyard from certain excavation, the only Hopewell site in the northern Midwest. His so-called girlfriend, Shelley, was right on the money as Eve in the original Garden tempting him, or so he thought, barely noting the commotion that had begun to gather around him at the Burger King. His beloved Shelley, whose pinkish body he had tried to memorize that morning at first light before the meeting with the detective, lawyer, graduate student, and Shelley herself, where he diffidently marked the graveyard site on the map, was given a thousand dollars, and once again was forgiven for his mayhem.

His mouth was full of now tepid Whopper when he realized that the yelling was directed at him. A short man in a uniform was shouting, "Get her out of here," his prominent Adam's apple bobbing. Brown Dog then noted that Berry was jumping from table to table. Red had given up in embarrassment and was standing outside, looking in the window with the strange grin young boys affect when the nervous shit hits the fan.

"She's not right in the head," Brown Dog said, standing and making a shattering whistle at Berry, then closing in and missing the grab. Many diners were standing as she leapt the tables, making the cries and voices of birds and animals. When Brown Dog caught her she clutched his body like a frightened cat. He barely heard the shrieked insults of the restaurant employee: "You Indians catch all our fish, shoot all our deer, get drunk, and can't mind your own children, you welfare bastards." That sort of thing. But then the voice trailed off into a gurgle. Brown Dog turned to see a gawky, rawboned younger woman in a black turtleneck sweater shaking the man by the throat.

"Shut up, you racist pig, you piece of filth," she hissed.

Back at Rose's, he brought in his second-best war-surplus sleeping bag (the best was back in the cabin near Grand Marais) and arranged it under the table where Rose's mother, Doris, had pointed out a place. Both mother and daughter were watching a tiny TV with a cloudy picture. During a commercial Rose turned to him with a winning smile that fluttered his heart.

"Could I trouble you to get me a six-pack?" she asked with an imitation pout.

He crawled out from under the table wearing what he assumed was a sexy smile, though by then Rose's attention was fixed again on the television. He stood near the couch squinting at the wretched set. It required a lot of imagination to detect the outlines of floating images.

"Looks like you could use a new TV. Want me to pick one up with the beer?"

It was a real big-shot line, but not one he would regret since he had always proved himself an anti-magnet for money. Their reaction was slow but the brown chins of Rose and old Doris turned upward to him as he rocked confidently on his heels, the kind of physical gesture brought to success by the late actor Steve McQueen.

"How come you're talking new TV? You don't got a pot to piss in," Rose said, turning back to the visual mire of the screen. Doris, however, continued to look at him, her face as crinkled as a shucked pecan, her eyes shining out from the dim cave of her age. He wondered for a millisecond how such a lovely old woman could breed a screaming bitch like Rose, but this observation was mitigated by the worm turning in his trousers at the sight of Rose's big breasts rising within the confines of her blue sweater. There was still the fine warm smell of fried chicken in the room, one of his favorite odors along with a freshly caught trout, lilacs, the fermenting berries in a grouse's crop, the dense sourness of a bear's den, not to speak of a vagina within a few days of a shower.

And so it was that he flashed his remaining nine C-notes from the payoff from Shelley and they were off to Wally's Discount Palace at nine in the evening of his very first day with Rose. The purchases included a color TV with remote, a sewing machine for

Doris, Taiwanese-made bikes for Red and Berry, a down payment on a satellite dish (fifty dollars a month for three years), a wall clock in the shape of an angry leopard, an army cot and a big roll of duct tape for Brown Dog himself. It had occurred to him the house was going to be too warm for a solid sleep and the barely heated pump shed would be a better idea. On the way home he swerved into a liquor store for a case of beer and a half gallon of the butterscotch-flavored schnapps Rose had requested. This shopping frenzy left him with only thirty-seven dollars but since the sum was in dollar bills it still felt like a lot of money.

It was well past midnight before he closed the romantic deal. The television set and sewing machine were unpacked from their commodious boxes and both worked perfectly. Rose began to watch and drink, and Doris to sew, laughing at the sweet and luxurious hum of the machine. Red took off into the darkness on his new bike but the toy was plainly impossible for Berry. Brown Dog wheeled her around until he was breathless, trotting down the gravel road until he reached the county blacktop, a big moon lighting their way but the night growing palpably colder. Berry just couldn't get the hang of the bike. He meant to work with her until she was a champion at the sport, no matter how unlikely the notion seemed. On the way back to the house they nearly hit a curious deer with Berry shrieking, clutching to his back, her teeth locked on his jacket collar.

Back at the house Doris patched up Red's scraped knee. Red was soon dozing from exhaustion and Doris whisked both grandchildren toward the bedroom, with Berry bidding Brown Dog good night in a jumble of Chippewa.

"She's too simple for school so she may as well know the old language," Doris said, glancing at her daughter on the sofa, sprawled before Jay Leno with a jam jar full of butterscotch schnapps. Doris winked at Brown Dog and he recalled that day she gave him his name while he stood in her yard in the cold rain waiting for a peek at his beloved Rose. He was only nine years old at the time, truly a young romantic. "Get on out of here, you brown dog," Doris said, and the name stuck though he wasn't, so far as he knew, one bit Native.

With Doris and the kids gone he plopped himself down on the couch beside Rose, wishing he liked butterscotch schnapps so he could calm down his trembling.

"You're a good boy, B.D. What happened to your fancy girlfriend?"

"Shelley and me called it quits just this morning."

"Bullshit," Rose whispered drowsily. "She gave you some money and told you to hit the road. Nobody can bullshit me." She gestured to the bookcase overladen with mystery novels and crime magazines to explain her prescience, then lifted her blue sweater, revealing two very large brown tits, the captured heat rising to his face. He suckled one as her eyes closed to a commercial, his member setting up a wild twitching in his pants, then she drew it out while clicking the remote with her other hand. Arsenio Hall was talking to an actress who only ate fruit and cheese, so Rose went back to Leno. She flopped back and he had a difficult time pushing her tight skirt up to her waist, making the additional mistake as he mounted of not taking his trousers all the way off, allowing limited movement as the trousers constricted his ankles. He pumped away in unison to her burgeoning snores, his orgasm seemingly timed to when Leno changed to Letterman and her eyes popped open.

"You should know I love only Fred," she said, and then slept.

It rarely is, but it can be a blessed event when a dream dies. The bigger the dream, the bigger the vacuum when the dream slips off into the void. First love is always a somber though colorful thicket of images, and when Brown Dog pulled on his trousers and went outside the images tumbled and wavered through his mind: tracking Rose at twelve when she picked berries with her mother, looking so lithe and petulant in the patch of wild raspberries, wiping the August sweat from her eyes as she filled her bucket with the red fruit. He was sitting well up in a white pine to spy on them, and they stayed so long his need to pee became ungovernable and he hugged the pitchy trunk for courage, looking down at Rose and Doris as a bird might. At last his friend and Rose's brother, David Four Feet, came to help them home with the berries and he was able to pee out of the tree with shuddering relief.

This happened thirty years back but could have been only a moment ago, thought B.D. as he peed off the pump shed steps. The moon looked too big and in the wrong place and the wind had increased since the bike ride with Berry. One vast round cloud with a black bottom looked very much like an angry Mother Westwind in an illustration from a children's book barely on the edge of his memory. The big mother's face contorted into a howl and through her cloud mouth blasted the cold damp air that meant snow.

Now he felt his love sweat drying as if into a film of ice and the cold wind became so delicious he wanted to drink it. Far off across the fallow pasture dotted with ghostly clumps of dogwood he could hear a small group of coyotes yapping in chase. Three or four or five at most, he thought, taking the army cot from the van and setting it up in the pump shed, deftly patching the holes in the wood and the slat cracks with duct tape. As a mongrel anchorite he could not bear the heat of the house, or the way the TV seemed to attack you like a barking dog, or to sleep within the dank scent of heating oil. He had finally achieved his dream of making love to Rose and the feeling was much emptier than the pocket that had held all the money that morning. But then, just on the verge of opening the door, he had a sodden wave of homesickness for the deer-hunting cabin in Grand Marais, for Shelley's dainty undies, for his lost move up in the world and his plummet back to his original home. He could almost hear himself as a child pumping the morning water in this very shed as his grandfather cooked breakfast in the winter dark.

He dismissed his melancholy into the sound of the wind. He might be B.D. dragging along the earth but he actually was a lot lighter in the mind than nearly everyone else, save a few sages and master adepts sprung from the Far East. There was also the hot memory of the time he and David Four Feet had snuck up on the swimming hole up the creek and watched Rose and Ethyl, a plump pinkish girl with a cleft palate and David's main crush, swimming in the nude. Then the girls knelt on the bank drawing pictures in the sand with forefingers, their bottoms aimed at the boys, with Rose's bottom so trim and beautiful compared to Ethyl's big pink one. Now, just over thirty years later, he had fondled that bottom, albeit in a much larger state, and felt a sure and certain accomplishment though it was joined to the perennial problem all artists feel on finishing a work—what's next? Not to speak of the fact that he had nothing to show for his efforts except the lineaments of gratified desire.

Thinking Rose asleep he tiptoed into the living room, but there she was, big as life, cooing on the phone and watching David Letterman drop watermelons off a tall building, an activity B.D. instinctively recognized as worthwhile. Rose looked up, lifting her spare hand from her pubis, and made a shushing motion. "My pen is running out of ink, Fred, just know that I'm real hot to see you," she said to the phone and hung it up. She watched B.D. gather up his sleeping bag from under the table. "We could do it once more but it would have to be the last time." She held out her glass and he poured a few fingers of the schnapps. She smiled fetchingly and his legs hollowed. "I also got to send thirty bucks to Fred up in Amasa so he can get his carburetor fixed. Or else he can't come to see me. Can you spare it? If not, no pussy."

That left him with seven bucks after he counted out the stack of ones. And the thumping set-to that ensued gave him a back spasm, so he slept in the painful cold of the pump shed quite happy that love had died.

B.D. awoke temporarily famous but he was not to know it for an hour or so. Doris fixed him a breakfast of fried cornmeal mush with maple syrup which he shared with Berry wriggling on his lap. Though it was only late October the world was bright and beautiful with a full foot of fresh snow, and he had wakened to the grinding of the county snowplow on the section road, soon followed by the school bus to pick up Red. Rose was still on the couch, a green mound that snored, totally covered by an old army blanket. Doris showed him the empty refrigerator, a wordless cue that meant to get cracking, while he drew pictures of bears for Berry so she could fill in the outlines with her crayons.

"She saw her first bear in August when we were picking blackberries," Doris explained. "She run right toward it and the bear waited a second before it took off. She must have bear medicine. Rose told me she didn't eat no bear meat while she was pregnant but she might have done so when she was drunk." Doris looked off at the lump of her daughter noncommittally.

It was at the employment office that B.D. discovered the unpleasantness of fame. He stood there in his cold wet tennis shoes wishing his boots weren't back in Grand Marais but facing up to the fact that they were. There was nothing fresh up on the bulletin board except a crying need for snow shovelers—and him without even gloves, let alone his icy tennis shoes.

"I don't believe I recognize you. You'll have to register with us," a voice boomed out from behind the counter. It was a middle-aged man sucking on a dry pipe while he kibitzed with the secretaries. He beckoned B.D. back to his office with the amiable boredom of a midrange civil servant. There was a plaque on the desk that said his name was Terrance Stuhl and framed diplomas on the wall from Michigan State University, four hundred miles distant, down in East Lansing.

"First things first." Terrance chuckled, pushing a long form across the desk for B.D. to fill out. B.D. had an aversion to such forms, in fact had never completed one, in part because he didn't know his father's name and had never seen his mother, so her name didn't mean much to him beyond giving him mental quavers. Besides this, he didn't have a Social Security number, which invariably closed the business of the day and he was sent packing off to the Social Security office to get one, which he never did. All through his youth his lumberjack grandfather had railed against Social Security as being communist inspired, and what's more, the government had no right to keep track of its citizens, a caveat that included the census and voting for any of the "mind controllers."

"I guess there's no point in this. I don't have a Social Security number," B.D. said, flushing at his hair roots. He ached to be in a swamp cutting cedar for fence posts. You didn't need a number for that.

Stuhl looked up from his morning *Detroit Free Press*. "You what? You don't have a Social Security number?"

"Nope. Never had a use for one."

"Then how do you pay your taxes?"

B.D. stonewalled, and then Stuhl threw back his head, laughing with his mouth wide open so that B.D. could see down his pink throat past the twittering gizmo known as the uvula. It was curiously the flip side of a porn magazine where you could see way up inside women. Stuhl wheezed as he picked up his fallen pipe and turned the *Free Press* and shoved it at B.D.

"So we have a felon with no Social Security number. You're out of my department, bub!" Stuhl continued to chortle as B.D. hastily read a large article in the Outstate News section featuring a big photo of Shelley with the rubric U.M. STUDENT DISCOVERS

ANCIENT INDIAN BURIAL GROUND. The article went on to say that it was the northernmost Hopewell site and plans were being made, of course, to begin excavation the following summer. Off to the side there was a small photo of B.D. himself and a paragraph describing him as a "grave robber" who had attempted to sell the body of a dead Indian chief found at the bottom of Lake Superior, and that his further activities would be under surveillance by the State Police.

"Gretchen, Gretchen," Stuhl brayed into the intercom. "I've got a live one." He turned back to B.D. with a not unkindly look. "We're not involved in law enforcement here. I suspect you've never even filed for income tax, which could make you liable for twenty years in federal prison. Rest assured, your secret is safe with us. Our aim is to make you self-supporting, not to punish you."

B.D. sat there feeling, in a general sense, like he was leaking, his life's fluid draining away. When he stood he could not feel his feet. Twenty years in federal prison would just about take care of the whole thing, yet how could he make a run for daylight with only seven bucks in his pocket?

"I've got you an unemployable," Stuhl said, and B.D. turned to see the same young woman who had defended him and Berry at the Burger King, still dressed in a black turtleneck, all angles but with a fine set of breasts. Stuhl handed her the newspaper. "A little background." He chuckled.

Gretchen looked at Stuhl as if he were a dog turd and led B.D. out into the hall. "I'm tied up until after lunch," she said. "Could you come back at two?"

"Count on me." B.D. was wary but at least he was talking to a woman.

"That asshole put you in a state of panic. You're not coming back, are you?"

"Nope." B.D. began to edge backward down the hall.

"How's your little girl doing?" She took his arm, restraining him.

"I bought her this bike but she can't get the hang of it," B.D. said lamely, desperate for escape.

"You just come back and I'll find you something. Do you understand?"

He mopped the frightened sweat off his brow with his coat sleeve, returning her direct glance just to get some courage back. She had the aura of a man but a lot nicer. He nodded then and rushed off, grabbing the pull tabs for snow-shoveling jobs as he left the lobby. You'll never starve if you're a good shovel man, he thought, out in the cold sunlight that glistened off the snow, the working folks leaning into the cold wind as they would for the ensuing six months or so until spring came in May. The wind rejuvenated him, made him a man to be reckoned with, somewhat the desperado what with his mug shining from the *Detroit Free Press*, a desperado falsely accused, but then he never put any stock in the offense of being misunderstood. As Grandpa used to say, it is not in the nature of people to understand each other. Just get to work on time, that was the main thing.

In the next four hours B.D. earned thirty dollars by shoveling five walks and two driveways. Rather than striking a deal before he started, he had depended on people's generosity, a specific mistake during the recent hard times. One old woman had given him only a buck for shoveling her walk, telling him he was probably going to spend it on liquor anyway. He didn't mind, assuming she was covering up for being broke herself. He ran out of work at about one o'clock when the wind clocked around to the south and Lake Michigan's waters raised the temperature to over freezing, and it occurred to everyone at once that the first big snowstorm of the year wasn't going to stick around. It was a disappointment to B.D. to see his employment begin to melt away. Before having lunch he went to a grocery store and bought pork chops, a pot roast, salt pork, potatoes, rutabaga, and pinto beans, plus a six-pack of orange soda for the kids. There was always the danger of stopping at a bar and getting carried away and he didn't want to face Doris without a sack of groceries.

He stopped at Shorty's, a crummy old diner he remembered from his youth as being famous for large portions, and ordered the hot pork sandwich at the counter. On Saturday afternoons his lumberjack grandpa and his cronies used to sit at a big table in the corner, drink coffee, and argue, allowing B.D. to walk down to the harbor if it was summer and watch rich folks fooling with their boats. It was unlikely that any of the local boaters were actually well heeled but to B.D. anyone who owned a boat must be rich. Boats, unfortunately, reminded him of diving for the dead Indian chief and he deftly cut a miniature trench in his mashed potatoes so that the gravy could sweep out over the fatty pork. He paused after his first taste, though ravenous, determining that it wasn't, in fact, pork gravy.

"Something wrong, dear?"asked the waitress, who was saucy and well built, if slender, though one of her legs was shorter than the other and there was a light hobble to her walk. She also spoke with a peculiar accent he couldn't trace, but then he had only been out of the Upper Peninsula twice.

"The gravy on the hot pork sandwich is not pork gravy," he said. An observation, not a complaint.

"Like it or lump it, dear. It's generic gravy and we use it on everything. It comes in thirty-gallon barrels straight out of Chicago. You're new here, so don't complain." She tapped her pencil and tried to stare him down. There was a grease stain about where her belly button would be and he lifted his eyes from the grease to her neck and lovely pale skin.

"Didn't say I didn't like it. Only said it wasn't pork. Besides, I was eating Saturday lunch in here when you still had pot rings on your ass." Quite suddenly the idea of any mark on her ass seemed desperately attractive.

"Should I call the manager?"She was smiling now in the curious way of women with not very straight teeth.

"What you should do is have a beer with me after you get out of work. Where'd you get that way of talking?"

"Louisiana. Near Bayou Teche. I come up here with my husband who's up at Sawyer Air Force Base."

She went off to service other customers and B.D. noted how trim her waist was in contrast to her firm but ample bottom, then he remembered his hunger and cold wet feet and shoveled the pork home, daubing up the gravy. Fuck, he thought, fondling the pepper shaker, I forgot to put pepper on it. He felt a hand on his shoulder and swiveled on the counter stool to face the breasts of the waitress. With a goofy edge he decided not to look up but to keep his eyes on the prize.

"What can I do for you? I hope it's something," he quipped.

"Nothing, you dickhead. Chief wants to see you." She gestured over at a very old man drinking coffee at a table in the corner, the same table at which his grandpa sat when he was hanging out with his cronies.

B.D. approached cautiously with a weather eye on the exit, but then this ancient creature couldn't very well be from the IRS. The man gestured at him to sit down and pulled a silver flask from his well-tailored, if rumpled, three-piece suit. B.D. swigged deeply and the whiskey hit the pork with a pleasant thump.

"This is not a good time to be wearing tennis shoes, you fucking numbskull. Doris called and said you were back in town. And I don't believe this for a moment." The old man pushed the morning *Free Press* toward B.D. "For Christ's sake, don't you recognize me?"

"Now I do. You're Delmore Short Bear, my grandpa's friend." Delmore was famous for being the only rich Native anyone had heard of when B.D. was young. Delmore had worked in the auto factories of Detroit for years and bought a farm just north of the city because he couldn't stand cities. His farm was now part of the swank suburb of Bloomfield Hills and it was well known that Delmore had sold it off for a pretty penny.

"Delmore Burns to the world at large. You can't have people knowing your medicine. Now Doris told me you spent all your money on them. I assume the anthropologist paid you off. You're a goddamn nitwit like your friend David."

B.D. stood abruptly and turned to go. He was used to taking criticism but the mention of Rose's brother and his boyhood friend caused a lump in his throat. David Four Feet had died in a fight in Jackson Prison, a fact that had been easier to accept before B.D. came back to home territory and saw reminders of David in every thicket, on every street.

"Guess I don't care to hear another rundown of me," B.D. said. "I help out a family, then wake up to see I'm known far and wide as a grave robber. If all you got is criticism, why don't you go fuck yourself. I don't need some mouthy old geezer with a fat wallet giving me a hard time." B.D.'s umbrage grew with his speech but had no apparent effect on Delmore.

"Twiddle-twaddle. None of us believe you're a grave robber. I owe it to your grandpa to keep an eye on you. How come you think the judge let you off so easy and gave your partner time when you stole the ice truck to sell the body in Chicago? It wasn't just that Republican cunt friend of yours and her rich father. You've always been up to nothing over at Grand Marais and I'm here to help you get good at it."

"Good at what?" B.D. slumped back to his chair.

"Good at nothing. It takes talent to be good at nothing. You were a master at it out in the boondocks but now you have to deal with Escanaba, a big city to you."

"I handled Marquette okay," B.D. said without conviction.

The waitress brought him a cup of coffee and a giant wedge of apple pie "to make up for the pork," she said. He watched her wobble to the end of the counter where she sat down with the *Free*

Press, then glanced back at him. Word was getting around and he didn't give a shit. Beneath the odor of fried food, he detected the faint scent of lilac on her skin. His balls gave a pleasant twitch.

"You're pussy-struck is your main problem, among hundreds," said Delmore. "I want to warn you about Rose's boyfriend, Fred. He's a phony pulp cutter over in Amasa. He's mean and he's a lot bigger than you."

"How can you be a phony pulp cutter? There can't be a worse job other than pumping septic tanks." The pie wasn't much good but B.D. ate it so as not to offend her.

"He went to college and played football, I hear. Then he read a few books and is trying to go Native. He likes to get in fights and thrown in jail in order to have genuine experiences. It's our times that cause people to act this way."

This notion transcended that of imminent danger to B.D. He liked the surprises offered by odd behavior himself, and he remembered waking early one morning a couple of summers before when he was supposed to help Frank, the owner of the Dunes Saloon, roof his house. Instead, he ate a can of beans and walked in a straight line for eighteen miles, over hill and dale, through gullies and creeks, skirting tamarack swamps, to a hummock he liked near the roots of the Two Hearted River. He carried a giant Hefty bag folded in his pocket for instant shelter, on the advice of old Claude, a Chippewa herbalist. At dark he drank a lot of cold spring water, climbed into the bag, and watched the first full moon in August out the hole near the drawstring, smoking an occasional cigarette to keep out mosquitoes. Before dawn he poked a hole and peed right out of the garbage bag.

"I like the way you think things over before you talk," said Delmore, watching B.D. think. "You're wondering why this guy Fred is after Rose if he went to college? Imagine Rose as an evil mudhole and men are pigs and can't help but wallow there. That's your basic answer. Women are a machine with a big panel of buttons like a drop forge. You can't ever hit the right combination of buttons without getting one of your limbs cut off. Meanwhile, stop by my place and get some boots and warm clothes."

Delmore got up and took both of their checks from the waitress, adding, "I'm not loaning you a penny so don't get any ideas. I just don't want you to get left sucking the mop." On the way out Delmore gave the waitress a five-spot as tip and pinched her butt. B.D. quickly followed to pick up on the good will.

"So your alias is Brown Dog?" she said, waving the paper at him.

"You might say that. What's yours?"

"Maybe it's Pink Pussy. Maybe it's Happily Married."

"Which is it today?" They were nearly nose to nose and the lilac scent now was working up through the sheen of cooking oil.

"I'm not sure. My husband, Travis, is way over in Somalia helping to feed black folks. It wouldn't be real patriotic to fuck you, would it?"

"Depends on how you look at it. I could just lay next to you. I wouldn't do nothing. In fact, we could leave our underpants on." B.D. was feeling like a smooth talker but it didn't seem to be registering with her. She looked off out the window, then made her way around the corner and poured herself a cup of coffee, paused with her back to him, then turned.

"If I go to bed with you, kiddo, I'm going to be in your face. Now get out of here. Check me tomorrow if you like. No promises." She limped into the kitchen without turning again.

He fairly pranced the first block toward his van. This was the promise of American life. You wake up wishing you were back in the cabin near Grand Marais. You have your ups and downs. You're down in the cold dumps of the employment office. You shovel snow after being slandered in the newspaper. You have a hot pork sandwich and love strikes you deep in the gizzard, besides which blessing your disappeared nine hundred dollars is just another burnt-out bulb. He nearly swooned with the thought of balancing the waitress on his nose when he was brought back to earth with a shrill cry.

"There you are! Where the fuck have you been? Hurry, goddammit." Gretchen grabbed him by the arm and dragged him up the street to the employment office. "You've been the victim of a media rip-off and you've got to stand up for yourself and your people." She batted at him with a rolled up *Free Press* for emphasis.

Parked before the office was a van from the local television station. Gretchen rapped at the window and out came the cameraman and the newsman, the latter chortling like Stuhl but with the dank, mellifluous baritone of his trade. B.D. got prickly heat when it occurred to him he was going to be on TV, but then summoned up the training he got from church, plus his aborted stay at the Moody Bible Institute in Chicago where he had enrolled in Preaching 101. The newsman did a flimflam intro including the notion that a local citizen had been accused of a "grave, possibly heinous crime," though in fact he had been convicted of nothing, due to an agreement between the "aggrieved parties."

B.D. closed his eyes and leaned against the van in the attitude of one lost in thought. He strained to come up with a Chippewa word to use other than *"wagutz,"* a real nasty thing to call a female; all his other words in Anishinabe were names Claude taught him for birds, animals, and plants which would be hard to drag into this situation. The point would be to present oneself as the wronged party, coupling this with quiet moral superiority. He opened his eyes to the baffled mike approaching his face, and to the question, in a game-show timbre, "And what do you have to say for yourself?"

"Sure, I brought the body of one of our grandfathers up from about a hundred feet. I was a salvage diver making a living before all this happened. I wanted this chief to have a correct burial. We're land animals and don't want a watery grave. As far as the ancient burial mounds are concerned, I'm the only living person who knew their location and I was sworn to secrecy by a medicine man. I was tricked by these Ann Arbor anthropologists, including the famous *wagutz* Shelley Thurman, and then framed for burning one of their tents. I was facing thirty years in the slammer. Now the sacred ground is frozen, but by next late April and May these college folks will start digging up the graves of our relatives. I call upon all Ojibway peoples in the U.P., even Wisconsin and Minnesota, to defend this burial mound—"

"Do you advocate violence?"the newsman interrupted, a little embarrassed by B.D.'s quaking voice and the tears streaming down his cheeks.

"What would you do if you went to the cemetery on Memorial Day and discovered a bunch of folks with shovels digging up your grandpa who died in the war to keep this country free?" B.D. waved the newsman and camera away, realizing he was about to lapse into nonsense, though he couldn't resist finishing with a quote a woods hippie had taught him which he brayed into the mike: "Don't forget, stagnant water cannot contain the coils of the dragon."

An hour later, after dropping off the groceries with Doris, B.D. was making himself busy cleaning up a partially flooded church basement. The church janitor hadn't drained the outside faucet used to water the lawn, and the pipe had broken with the early storm and hard freeze. Gretchen had got him the job, demanding for him in advance fifty bucks cash on the barrelhead.

After the adrenaline of the media event their little interview hadn't gone well. He resented the notion of being unemployable and being chucked into the bin with others she termed "learning and physically disadvantaged"—what they used to call dummies and cripples. B.D. was in a third category of malcontents: crazies, outcasts, felons, the plain pissed-off residue of society. He felt typecast when all he had done was spend his life at odd jobs and at what Delmore Short Bear had described as "nothing." Gretchen wanted to pin him down about his background and "ethnicity," so he had acted remote and distraught over the TV experience in order to get out of there. When you got pinned down by questions from anyone, especially those in any branch of government, they were going to take advantage of you or try to keep track of you. Of course that was what they were in business for and it was all well and good for them, but there was no way he was going to be involved. Gretchen kept saying she needed to "share" his work experiences in order to help him, so he settled for one example, avoiding diving with scuba tanks to illegally pillage sunken ships in Lake Superior, a summer occupation that had gotten him into a lot of trouble.

"I get up at daylight and take a little stroll in the woods to see what's been happening there overnight. I make coffee and breakfast. I cut and split a cord of wood and sell it to a cottager for twenty-five bucks. I got plenty of orders from hanging out at the bar. Then I have a little lunch followed by a snooze to change my thought patterns."

"How's that? I mean, what you're saying about thought patterns." She was taking notes.

"The woods business can make you nervous. If you take a snooze, you can forget the stress of the guy acting like he's doing you a favor for paying for the wood he doesn't know how to cut himself. You lay back and think pleasant thoughts, say about birds and animals, like the time I saw a great horned owl blast a red-tailed hawk out of a tree just at daylight, or two deer fucking in late September, or a big raven funeral I watched."

"Birds have funerals? You're bullshitting." She was irked.

"Ravens do. I can't tell you about it for religious reasons. Anyway, after the snooze, I go do a little fishing or hunting depending on the season. Catch a few trout or pot a grouse and woodcock for dinner . . ."

"I personally feel hunting is shameful," she couldn't help but chime in.

"Tell it to someone who gives a shit. I'm answering a question you gave. After dinner I have another snooze, then read for an hour, then go to the bar for an hour or two. Maybe longer. That's it."

"What do you read?"

"*Popular Mechanics. Outdoor Life.* Girlie magazines. I also been reading this south-of-the-border novel called *One Hundred Years of Solitude.*" He hadn't actually gotten beyond the first fifty pages of this book given him by a tourist lady but he liked the title and the parts about the discovery of ice and magnetism.

"How extraordinary," she said, and it was then she got the call-in about the church basement. He noted the poster on the wall proclaiming "The Year of the Woman" and readily agreed. Despite his experience with Shelley, Rose, and dozens of others, women still beat the hell out of men to be around. You weren't always cutting and bruising yourself on their edges.

In fact, the church basement proved the point, a mudbath for the mind and body. Neither the pastor nor the janitor wanted to get wet, and watched standing on chairs as B.D. found the drain and reamed it out with a coat hanger, then worked laboriously with squeegee, mop, and pail. It was a good two hours' sweat, but then he had the two twenties and a ten already in his pocket, and kept his mind busy with thoughts of the waitress and Doris's promise that she would make pork chops, also pinto beans with salt pork and hot peppers, a condiment he had taken to when he had worked welding on a gas pipeline and met two Mexican laborers from Texas. The pastor was annoying with his spit-shined shoes, asking B.D. if he had "come to the Lord," to which B.D. responded that he was meek, and "the meek shall inherit the earth." This piqued the minister's interest but B.D. clammed up, preferring as he worked an involved sex fantasy about the waitress, all the more tasty because it was fabricated in a church. They were picking blackberries on a hot afternoon and she pulled down her jeans, leaning over a stump for a quickie. That sort of thing.

B.D. was wet and tired when he pulled into the dark yard, puzzled at the fairly new three-quarter-ton step-side pickup parked there. He scrambled back in the old van to sort through a pile of clothes, looking for something clean and praying that he would be allowed a hot shower or bath. His favorite flannel shirt had a crunchy BBQ stain on it which he sniffed for clues to the occasion. Doris tapped at the van window and he slipped open the side door. In popped Berry with a screech, another screech, and a *hoo hoo* in the manner of an owl in the half-collapsed barn out back. Doris held out a plate of chops and beans steaming in the cold air, the steam rising across the moon, and a warm can of beer.

"Fred's in there with Rose. They just finished the butterscotch schnapps. It wouldn't be safe for you. I'm real sorry."

B.D. gave Doris a pat. It was hard to think clearly what with Berry starting her bluejay renditions, so he ate his plate of food in a trice. Doris could fetch his sleeping bag from the shed but that might not be a good idea since it wasn't more than twenty degrees, a little cold for sleeping in the van. B.D. said, "The sucker's real big, I hear."

"Real big and mean. He ate a pork chop raw, covered with black pepper. He just don't care about man or beast." Doris shivered. B.D. sent her and Berry back to the house, starting the van and lighting their way with his deer-shining spotlight. Fred appeared at the front door, filling the frame, his eyes reflecting yellow like an animal caught in the headlights, raising his arm to shield his eyes. He brushed past Doris and Berry, knocking Berry over, and came down the steps.

"Hey, you motherfucker, shut off that light!" Fred bellowed.

B.D. backed the van in a half circle to prepare an escape route, keeping the spotlight in Fred's eyes. Fred roared and began trotting, then broke into a run, with B.D. keeping just barely ahead of him as he drove out the driveway onto the wrong side of the road. He was a man with a plan, sucking Fred toward disaster. Fred slowed and B.D. pretended to have problems shifting, spotting the mailbox just ahead. Sensing victory, Fred moved into a sprint, his hand on the locked door, when B.D. wiped him off against the mailbox perched on the cedar fence post. Not smart. But fun, he thought, shining the spot back at the huge man writhing in the snow-filled ditch.

The cheapest motel he could find was out on Route 2, next to the filled parking lot of a bowling alley. He stowed his van in back just in case Fred came out on the prowl. The room was only fourteen bucks but luxurious by his standards. He bought a pint at a party store next door and took a long hot bath, sipping the whiskey and trying to sing along with MTV. Out of the tub, he dried while watching go-go dancers jumping around in undies in a big cage while the singer kept snapping at the cage with a bullwhip. B.D. favored letting them out of the cage and being nice. He peeked out the window to make sure the bowling alley had a bar. Some did, some didn't.

Fortune struck true, a boon, a blessing, a gift probably not from heaven. It was ladies' night at the bowling alley, and when he stood in the bar looking out at the lanes he picked out her trim figure on lane 7 in a gaggle of plumpies. He shuddered, easing out of the bar toward her like a crawling king snake. He reached her lane as she held a ball, stooped with her taut butt protruding, then skipped to the line and threw a strike which seemed to mean more than it actually did. She turned, shrieked with joy while her friends jumped and clapped and then she spotted him, rolled her eyes and danced in a circle, waving her hands in the air as if at a minstrel show. She came toward him, trying her best to minimize her limp.

"You possum dickhead! How did you-all find me?" she hissed, giggling.

"I just followed your lilac scent through the cold, dark night, Frieda." Her name was on the bowling shirt, which made it easy.

"I borrowed this shirt. The name's Marcelle. Maybe I'm ready. Maybe I'm not. What you got in mind?"

"I got a pint and a motel room next door. I want to root like a hog and turn you to butter. That's just for starters."

"That so? Sounds pretty good to me. What's your room number? I don't want these ladies knowing I'm fucking over Travis."

He paced the room, his breath and throat constricted as if on death row—or better, Saint Augustine in his monastic cell in a frenzy of religious doubt. He turned on the Weather Channel and watched the digital seconds tick away at the bottom of the screen. On his way back he had picked up another pint and he tried to sip sparingly on the first he had begun in the tub, knowing that whiskey was good for the noodle only in small doses. Then, just over the edge of despair, the knock came and she whisked in, immediately turning out the lights except for the bathroom. He almost said he liked to see what he was doing but remembered she might be shy. She took a slug from the proffered pint and went into the bathroom, closing the door all but an inch of yellow light. He decided not to peek, and flicked through the TV stations until he arrived at country music videos, somehow more appropriate than MTV, or so he thought. Back on the bed he slipped off his shoes to avoid the potential ankle trap, then leaned far out of bed, supporting himself awkwardly with his hands on the floor, feeling he deserved a peek. Times change. She was washing at the sink but the opening was too slim for more than a thin slice of the picture. Suddenly the door opened and out she came with her bottom half wrapped securely in a towel. Surprised, B.D.'s hands collapsed and he scrambled awkwardly back on the bed.

"Window peeker!" She turned, glancing at the TV, the light flickering off her breasts. "Garth Brooks sucks. Give me George Jones any day."

"I was just a door peeker." His voice had become very small. With her clothes off there seemed to be a lot more to her. She moved to the side of the bed, right above his face. He glanced up and then away at the TV, then back, with Marcelle smiling down at him over her breasts.

"You might say I'm ready to get turned to butter." She laughed. "Cat got your tongue?"

"Nope.

She did a free fall over his head and he went down on her like the no-hands pie-eating contest at the county fair, an event he had won at age thirteen.

II

THE MIND OF THE MAKER

Gaagaagfhirmh! I found this on my notepad I kept for Shelley. It is the word the Chips use for raven. Claude told me so. Sounds like one if you say it right, not too loud from the throat's back end. The days they come and go as always. Delmore is hard on my case and loaned me this cabin which is only fourteen by fourteen he and his son built the summer of 1950, the year I was born. Delmore hasn't seen or heard of his son since 1952. He's got me logging my days and thinking to pay my rent. It's not like Shelley, who was always looking for the secret poison in my mind. I also have to cut Delmore's firewood which comes to two cords a week for that big drafty farmhouse. You don't have to be a scientist to know I am not getting a deal because I also shovel his drive and do repairs, like I had to dig up the main pipe to his drain field with a pickax because the ground was frozen and the pipe broke by a tree root. If you count up the worth of everything, I am paying about four hundred dollars a month for this midget cabin with an outhouse. I also have to haul my water about a quarter of a mile from Delmore's on a toboggan, and there's no electricity so I use oil lamps.

Read this and weep, Delmore, you old fuck. You're taking me to the cleaners but I've been there before.

Delmore said this morning at Shorty's when we ate breakfast that he can't help but get the best of any deal he ever gets involved with. It's part of his training in the Saramouni Brotherhood he went through when he was in the auto factories in Detroit. Their main saying was there is no God but reality, and if you look for him elsewhere you're out of luck. Something like that. It was up on the wall of this cabin but I took it down and threw it in the stove because I don't have to live every day with someone else's bullshit. Just remember, Delmore, you don't own me, you just got me rented for a short time. Here is the so-called clear thought for the day you asked me to come up with. A horse that shits fast don't shit long. I take this to mean you have to conserve your energies. I also advise you I'm moving over to Duluth when I get three hundred bucks saved. You could say this town is getting too small for me after one whole week. I can't get my breath if Fred is breathing down my neck, also Travis is bound to get home from Africa. I said to Marcelle, how come Travis will know about me? She says they exchange stories of their sex wrongs to energize their marriage. They like to go into rages, then feel peaceful afterward. She also told me Travis is a black belt which didn't have too much effect. These weenies were always getting out of the service saying they were black belts, and the same pulp cutters as before would kick their ass. I hate to get hit myself as it digs a hole you don't quite get out of for a couple of weeks.

Tragedy struck Sunday morning. I've been bowled over for a couple of days so I couldn't work at the odd jobs Gretchen digs up for me. First of all, I loaned my van to Rose. Actually she took it out of Delmore's driveway but she left a note. Fred hasn't been around since he ran into the mailbox because he went down to Flint where his dad is sick. The van's not there when Delmore and me go off to Sunday morning breakfast. We stop at Doris's and the van isn't there and neither is Rose. We take Berry to breakfast with us because she likes both Delmore and me. She and Delmore say Chippewa words to each other.

It wasn't but about seven A.M. with few customers that got out of Mass, too early for the Protestants, and Shelley's photo was on the cover of the Detroit Sunday magazine which is part of the newspaper. She was dressed up to climb Mount Everest and was called "The New Woman" for her famous discovery of the anthropological site. I was only mentioned once as the grave robber that she sent packing. This in itself didn't ruin my biscuits with sausage gravy partly because Marcelle sat down and put her hand under the table and gave my pecker a little squeeze. Berry also poured some imitation maple syrup on Shelley's picture which was justice indeed.

Then in comes the State Police detective who warns me that my TV interview could be thought to be "inciting to riot" which is a laugh. He called Delmore "sir" and that shows just how much pull Delmore's got. Delmore then tells the detective that I am under his care and direction. This seems to please the detective who leaves but then is followed by the local sheriff's deputy in about ten short minutes. This cop wants to arrest me for leaving the scene of an accident. Delmore invites the cop to sit down and have breakfast and explains that Rose borrowed the "vehicle in question" to drive to her new job cleaning up over at the Indian casino in Hannahville so that I am innocent of all possible charges. The deputy calls Delmore "Mr. Burns" and "sir." I already got a lump in my throat about my van because the deputy said it was totaled. It all made sense to him because he had arrested Rose later on over in a bar in Bark River for drunk and disorderly.

I guess I broke down when I saw the van out behind the garage that had the towing service. Delmore stayed inside because it was real cold. It tore me apart because it seemed to be the last of Grandpa because I bought the vehicle over ten years ago when he died and I sold the house to a realtor who sold it to Doris after her house burned down. I got fifteen grand and went west in my first and only new van and ended up spending the leftover money in the Bozeman hospital after a fight with three cowboys this girl got started. Now the roof was stove in and the frame buckled. Berry was upset when I started to cry so I quit and she helped me gather up the spare stuff like the shovel and chain, kindling, candles, a couple cans of beans and a pint of whiskey, all in case I got caught in a storm. On the way home Delmore said it was a cruel lesson but I was going to learn it by doing a lot of walking. I didn't answer. I just walked down the trail to the cabin saying to myself fuck the world that takes my last possession from me.

It's only early November but it snowed three days, strange indeed as Escanaba is thought to be the Banana Belt of the U.P. Just seventy miles up the road, Marquette on Lake Superior gets twice as much snow, and over in Houghton they often get more than three hundred inches. That's thirty feet but it settles a lot or there wouldn't be any Houghton.

I spent three days and three nights down in a mind hole. I am forty-eight with no vehicle and about fifteen bucks in my pocket. If Fred showed up I'd just plain shoot him but my .22 and my single-shot 16-gauge are both over in Grand Marais along with my boots. I remember some of my Bible training from Chicago about Jonah in the belly of the whale this long but I don't get how he breathed. It's supposed to stand for something else but I don't know what. I can't say I feel sorry for myself, I just don't believe in the world for the time being. I didn't even eat the first day, if you don't count breakfast when I got the bad news.

The second morning, right at daylight, I was watching it snow and a grouse ran into the window jamb. I hurried outside and there was a great horned owl in a tree and that is what scared the grouse who broke her neck. I studied this wonderful bird for a while and found aspen leaves and a few dried wintergreen berries in the crop. The bird felt real warm but dead. I peeled, cooked, and mashed a few potatoes. The bird's bad luck was my good. I plucked, gutted, split, then roasted her over the potatoes in an iron skillet in the oven, basting her with butter and pepper. It takes a while to get the hang of a wood-burning stove and oven but I'd used one for a whole winter before. I must say it was a meal fit for a king.

Come to think of it, the main good thing out here snowbound in this cabin is that nothing is happening. Think of smoking that one in your pipe, Delmore. I've got this personal feeling things are not supposed to be happening to people all of the time. At least I'm not designed for it. There should be more open spaces between events. That's my clear thought for today.

The third day of keeping away from the world, the snow stopped and the wind eased up which is the pattern of a three-day blow out of the NW. I read in this old-timey bird book stored here along with Zane Grey and Horatio Alger (what a name) exactly how to build a raven feeder so that's what I did. You build a four-by-four platform about twelve feet up a tree and try to keep it supplied with roadkills. Didn't have a ladder so I built it in a white pine with good climbing limbs, made a large space, then cut off the limbs on the way down. The question is how am I to pick up roadkills without a vehicle? Now that I've calmed down I got the notion this problem will be solved by fate. Meanwhile, I'll hoof it, maybe get an old sled for roadkills. Not a bad idea.

This is the fourth dawn and I didn't even have a drink yesterday, an act which was made easier because I didn't have any booze left. I'd say it's time to stop the grief about my stone-dead vehicle. Goodbye, old pard. November tenth and it's already twenty degrees instead of the ten below me and the creatures have been dealing with these past few days. My homesickness for Grand Marais is gone because I'm in the same kind of cabin. Woke up in the middle of the night with this idea I should dig a huge hole and bury the van like a dead friend. Now this morning it is a dumb idea, besides being a lot of unpaid work. Got to get out for groceries as I'm down to the last of my pot of pinto beans. Sad to say I dumped a whole can of chopped jalapeños in them so they're damn near too hot to eat, also uncomfortable the next day in the outhouse though a handful of snow cools the butt, something they can't do south of the border. Bet Gretchen wonders what happened to me, also Marcelle though Delmore will tell her I'm out sulking in the woods. She was almost too hot to handle but this morning now that my tears have dried I'm about ready for another run at it. It was the least sleep I can remember. The Bible says a woman's womb is a horse leech that cries out *I want.* I'll buy that fact. In her defense it's a fact that Travis has been gone two months. The short leg is just like the other one only shorter. She says she was born with it just like I was born not to cooperate with the world. All I can say is my tongue was raw so my morning coffee stung like hell and my pecker was plain out of commission for a few days. Take that, Delmore. I saw you pinch her ass, you cheese-brained old fuck. Just wanted you to know I delivered the goods you can't anymore. I won't always be around to cut free wood. I just looked at your 1952 Sears Roebuck catalogue and those girdle ad pictures are looking pretty good though they don't show the women's chests and legs.

Doris and Berry showed up at noon with a loaded toboggan. This threw me off when I saw them out the window because they're a section away, a full mile of woods, not even thinking of the swamp and creek. Then I saw their trail and figured they came down from Delmore's. Right away Berry shinnied up the tree to my raven feeder and when I came out of the cabin Doris was trying to get her down. I had gave away my pound of popcorn kernels to a flock of yellow pine grosbeaks, so couldn't make popcorn to my regret. The grosbeaks were making their odd calls in the trees and Berry was talking back at them. Then she jumped off the platform a full twelve feet into a big snowbank, and we ran over sure that she was hurt but she was burrowing around under the snow.

We unloaded the toboggan which was good and bad. Doris had brought along her late husband's rifle because she wanted me to shoot her a deer. I tried to say the season didn't open for almost another week and I was a little close to town for violating but she just said again, "Shoot me a deer." Something smelled good and it turned out to be a small kettle of stew she'd made out of a bear neck someone had given her. She put this on the stove while I looked at the other stuff which turned out to be warm clothes from Delmore which were not exactly modern. I had seen stuff like it in army-navy surplus stores when I was a kid and wanted it then so I wanted it now. There was one of those coverall-type flight suits lined with sheep's wool, a lined pilot's cap, and a pair of good boots. Right away I knew you could sleep in a snowbank and stay hot as a sauna rock. I put the suit on and it was a bit short and the boots a little tight but I ran out and burrowed like a vole or gopher with Berry. You could wriggle along the ground blind as a bat, then pop up in a new place.

Back in the cabin I was in for a surprise. I was eating the bear neck stew (with onions and rutabaga) and Doris hands me this letter from Delmore and then three other letters to me that he already opened. I sat there trying to think of when I got some mail. There was one letter from Shelley the year before, then once a year from the state of Michigan with my license plate sticker. I fill out the top form. That's it. And this mail comes to the Dunes Saloon. So if you only get the one piece of mail a year and you know what it is, it's hard to handle the four pieces. So I didn't. I put them aside.

Just before dark I shot Doris a little spikehorn buck, gutting it and saving heart and liver. I shot it on her side of the creek so I wouldn't have to drag it through the water. Delmore, you're a sure-thing old asshole but I can't tell you how toasty that outfit is. I put a rope around the spikehorn's neck and got it through the snows to Doris's which was a bit hard as the snow was melting during the day, then a crust froze as the sun was going down. I can't tell you how thrilled Doris was. She fried up the heart and liver pronto, also a pan of potatoes and onions. Rose sat there like a dog turd on the couch with nary a word of apology for my van. She was watching TV as usual so Doris brought her a plate of food. Red and Berry ate so fast I could tell they didn't have meat for a while. When I got ready to go Doris told me to make sure I took some meat and I said no, I'm going back to work tomorrow. During a commercial then Rose told me Fred would likely kill me when he came back from Flint. I said, "Sounds fair to me," showing no fear. Then she said that the crippled waitress stopped by. She had already been to Delmore's looking for me. I left feeling good about being in demand. First a deer for Doris and her family and now Marcelle for whatever. Sad to say I could not track Marcelle down on foot so I headed home.

Flushed a group of roosting wild turkeys on the way home in the dark which scared the living shit out of me. These birds weren't here when I was young but the state game folks brought them back. I'm going to eat one to get even for my fright which was closer to home than the idea of big Fred trying to kill me, not to speak of Travis in a far-off land who will have the same idea no doubt. It was a fine walk making my way back by the moon and stars if you don't count the turkeys.

Back at the cabin I stoked the fire and laid out the letters in a row, saying eenie-meenie-miney-mo to choose the first one, which came to Delmore's, so I changed the rules and went from left to right. The first one was from this reporter from the *Marquette Mining Journal* who needed to talk to me about the violation of the burial ground, and whether me and "my people" intended to use force to defend it. Yes and no, I thought, getting into the mood. The next one came from another reporter. This one for the *Detroit News,* the other Detroit newspaper you didn't see so much in the U.P. This asshole was on the muscle a bit, suggesting that during all the years he had covered Native politics in Michigan he had not been aware of me as a spokesman, and on viewing the TV tape he had wondered if I might represent a group "advocating a more radical approach." The reporter added that none of the local Anishinabe leaders seemed aware that I was politically active or had any idea if I was Native or not since I wasn't on the tribal rolls, though Tom Deerleg Koonz said that my uncle Delmore Short Bear was on the rolls.

"These fucks got everything wrong!" I yelled out to the cabin's silence. Koonz had hit me over the head with a two-by-four in the seventh grade when there had been the promise of a fair fight, a battle over the honor of Rose because Koonz had been spreading it around the school that he had screwed Rose. Rose was an early starter in the fucking sweepstakes. Koonz is an asshole spreading confusion. I might look him up with my own two-by-four.

The third letter pulled at my heartstrings. It was from Marten Smith who was really Lone Marten (named after a real tough weasel), David Four Feet and Rose's little brother. Doris told me he was out in California and that's where the letter came from, in a place called Westwood. Had a nice ring to it. Marten thanked me for standing up for the People, and a Red Brother had sent him the TV tape. Help was on the way. I wasn't sure what help he was talking about. Then he said he was coming home before spring and had an investor for a business that would help the cause. I'm confused but it would be good to see Marten who was always a crazy bastard. He stole a little sailboat from the marina once and got way out in Lake Michigan but couldn't get back because he didn't know how to turn it around. Some commercial fisherman from Naubinway picked him up way down by Hog Island.

Delmore's letter was short and not too sweet:

> Maybe by now you have learned not to loan your vehicle. There's an old Studebaker pickup in the barn. If you can start it, you can borrow it. Meanwhile, I am not your enemy. I'll be needing some wood in a few days and I need you to take down a maple that is endangering my aerials. I opened your mail by mistake so went ahead and read it. See what trouble your big mouth is getting you into? I hope so. The media is a cruel mistress. Be here by seven AM if you want a ride to town. Doris called to say you got her a deer. I could have used a piece if you had thought of your benefactor. To show you I am not a bad old guy, go to the southwest corner of the cabin. The last board is loose. There is a bottle of whiskey. You can have two short drinks. There is also a shotgun and shells. I would like some grouse to eat. Marcelle showed up looking for you. She ran around naked in my living room. Ha ha.
>
> Yours, Delmore

The whiskey and the promise of the Studebaker made up for something. I had my two drinks then went to sleep. Woke up in the middle of the night with a boner thinking about Marcelle which got lost in a whirl feeling I was getting in over my head what with Marten and the reporters. I tried to think of the advice the frozen chief in the ice truck gave me but what I could remember is about reading a book about nature. I lit the oil lamp and chose between *Riders of the Purple Sage* and one by Ernest T. Seton called *Two Little Savages* about two little white kids trying to be old-timey Indians. It was real interesting but put me to sleep. Here's my clear thought for cabin rent, Delmore, you driving limp-dicked old nut case. You never regret the ones you do, you always regret the ones you don't. I got that from a nature book.

* * *

My strength is about gone after a day of ups and downs. It seems I am unfit for the life of the city, however small. First of all Delmore gives me a ride to town and some more free advice so I turn up the radio. Things are not going well overseas. Then we have breakfast and Marcelle is all over me like a decal. She whispers you can't get a woman way up there in the air and drop her. I said that somehow I'd take care of the problem that day, and I was back in the woods in mourning for my vehicle.

"You chose that old piece of shit over me,"she said real loud. I couldn't help but remember after our night of love she wasn't too impressed with the van. Still, it was like someone making fun of a recently dead friend so I walked out of the diner without finishing the last few bites.

Gretchen was glad to see me at the employment office. She and her roommate decided they wanted their bedroom and living room painted. She asked if I could paint and I said yes because I've painted a lot of cabins though nothing on the inside. She took me over to her house which wasn't much on the outside but real nice indoors. She showed me where she had got started but was too busy to finish. Afterward I remembered that she said something about her roommate Karen being upstairs doing painting but artist-type painting and we wouldn't disturb each other.

But I got carried away and forgot this little item. What happened was that Gretchen left and I did some looking around which was natural. It is important to know where you are at any given moment. Since I was to start in the living room I looked in the kitchen first, seeing that there were a lot more cookbooks than most people have regular books. I noticed a half-full bottle of jug wine and took a sip, then a couple of gulps what with not having a drink in four days, almost breaking the record from when I had Asian flu twenty years ago. I didn't open the refrigerator because I just ate breakfast an hour ago.

The real problem started when I went into the bedroom which I shouldn't have done because the door was closed, though not locked. The room for sure was dolled up like a love nest with art-type posters of naked women hugging each other so my red head started thumping a bit. I was about to leave when I began to wonder what kind of undies Gretchen wore. I guessed probably plain white cotton ones but when I opened a dresser drawer they were pretty fancy. I couldn't help but take a few sniffs and there was the telltale smell of lilac that sets me off. Also under the undies there was a Polaroid photo of Gretchen and another girl buck naked on a tropical beach. I couldn't help but wonder who the lucky guy was who took the picture. By now I was breathing pretty hard and had to wedge my pecker under my belt. I called information then got Marcelle at the diner and asked if she could take a fifteen-minute break and get on over here. She could, and she was at the door in a few minutes. It was like setting off five sticks of dynamite under a stump. We just exploded, doing it like dogs with her waitress skirt up to her waist and her breasts hanging out. We made about three revolutions of the living room floor just getting traction with Marcelle real noisy, yodeling and yelling.

I don't know how I forgot that Gretchen's roommate was upstairs doing her art, but after about ten minutes—you lose track of time—Gretchen came running up the steps and in the door without knocking. Of course it was her house but we didn't get any warning. We were just finishing and Marcelle didn't notice anything like she was unconscious and Gretchen started screaming, "How dare you! How dare you how dare you you pig you pig I'm calling the police!" The roommate Karen was looking in from the kitchen and also was yelling and screaming. Marcelle was up and out of there in a split second leaving me to face the music. Once again I made the old trousers-around-the-ankle mistake. When will I learn, I thought, falling the first time I tried to get up. I covered my face in shame, also because I didn't want to look Gretchen in the eyes.

It stayed quiet though I could hear her breathing. "I guess I was lonely," I said, and that set her off again. "Get out of here before I call the police," she said. "You're fired and don't come to the office again." I walked to the door trying to think of something right on the money to say. "I don't think love is against the law," I said.

My heart was heavy as I began the long walk back to Delmore's. It lightened up a bit when I noticed the wind had clocked around to the southeast and the snow was slushy, also I stopped into a bar setting a limit of two shooters with beer chasers because it wasn't noon yet. I can't say I was proud of myself but I sure as hell didn't shoot the President. Sure I made a mistake, but a mistake is not exactly a crime.

So I hoofed it back to Delmore's and the sun was out and glistening off the snow. When I got there a tow truck was just leaving and the old Studebaker pickup was out of the barn and running. There was another car behind Delmore's and a big man in a sport coat. Delmore was giving the man a drink out of his flask so I knew he could not be from the IRS. His name was Mr. Beaver or something like that, and he was from the *Detroit News*.

Delmore took me to the side. "This guy is fine but don't get sucked in by the media," he said with a chicken cackle.

"As I said on the phone, the tribal leaders up here, including those in Sault Ste. Marie, seem to know who you are but don't know what organization you represent, if any." Mr. Beaver eyed me like that State Police detective but I wore my poker face.

"Our operation is top secret," I said, thinking there could be a group so secret that no one even knew if they belonged to it.

"Can you give me any indication what you intend to do come spring about the anthropological site?"

"Just write down that it's a lot more likely to be hot lead than bows and arrows. I'm sorry but I can't say any more. The brotherhood might kill me."

"Can you clarify 'brotherhood' for me?"

"Nope." I made a sign like my throat was being cut and then went over and took a good look at the Studebaker. The side windows were broke out but the windshield was fine except for a crust of swallow and pigeon shit from sitting in the barn for forty years. It was real thick on the roof and frozen hard. I had the clear choice of hammer and chisel or letting Mother Nature clean it off with wind and rain. I got in and took her for a spin, waving goodbye at Delmore and the reporter.

Shot two grouse out of a tree for Delmore. There were four but I left two for seed. If you start at the bottom you can get them all. I'm only a fair wing shot which is the better way to hunt but it was almost dark and I had to work in a hurry. Delmore invited me to dinner and I must say the old coot knows his business at the stove. He boiled diced-up salt pork to get some of the salt out because he's got blood pressure, then he browned up onions and carrots, browned the grouse I plucked, then put it all in the Dutch oven for forty-five minutes. All the stuff on the bottom ensures a good gravy, and the short cooking time keeps the bird juicy. He fried pieces of cornmeal mush and served the birds on top. He poured some red wine which, like Gretchen's, wasn't sweet enough to have much punch. Once me and David Four Feet stole a case of Mogen David from behind the supermarket when the workers took a coffee break from unloading a semi. We got about three bottles apiece down our gullets that day before it backed up on us. Since that day so long ago I haven't been partial to red wine though I will drink it if there's nothing else at hand.

I told Delmore the terrible story of Gretchen catching me with Marcelle and the geezer laughed so hard he slid off the couch. I said it probably was funny if you weren't there and maybe it would be funny later on but I lost my job. He said I got a forty or two you can cut the pulp off. I said what makes you think I can cut pulp and he named three outfits I worked out of in Munising, Newberry, and Grand Marais. I said will wonders never cease, you're a fucking spy on top of a slave driver. He said I just kept track of you, we're second cousins but I knew he was lying there because Grandpa never said Delmore was his cousin, an old-time friend. I said if you're Grandpa's cousin then tell me about my mom and dad I didn't get to know. He looked at me a full minute and took me off to see his radio room.

In his radio room which had RADIO ROOM on the door I understood why he had all the aerials and wanted me to cut the maple tree with dead branches down. The room had a whole wall of equipment and Delmore is what you call a ham operator. It's hard not to think of hams smoked off a pig when you hear "ham operator." That's just the human mind at work and there's no connection. Delmore said name a country and I said Canada but he said that's too easy name another. How about the lost country of Atlantis, and he said fuck you B.D., we'll contact old Mexico. Sure enough in a few minutes he was talking to a guy named Ricky about this and that including politics and the guy's family. He sent me to get the whiskey bottle and he contacted a lot of countries. Delmore's got this theory, not ready for the man on the street, that the world hasn't fit together since the Korean War. With these ham radios he can tell you where the shit has hit the fan anywhere at anytime within minutes, that way he is never caught off guard about anything. I didn't say so but I like surprises though I am not exactly up to date on the fate of the world.

Then I got a bit of surprise when Delmore took me into his Indian room though it didn't say that on the door. It was full of snakeskins and shells of different kinds of turtles, some of them real big snapper and mud turtle shells. Over in the corner there was a full hooded bearskin, a war club, and a bunch of rattles hanging from a hook. Then Delmore says that the bear medicine he got as a boy up by Ontonagon was too hard to maintain unless you could give it full time. It was too much medicine for him when he went south to work in Detroit but on his farm north of town he had lots of dreams about serpents and turtles so he turned to them and they had stood by him. Then he asks about what animal I dream about and I said I dream about animals every night of my life because I've lived full time around them. I also dream a lot about dogs which seems reasonable given my nickname. He said he'd have to think that over and gives my face a little scratch with a snapping turtle claw for good luck. You're a true mongrel, B.D., which isn't all that bad.

There's not a lot you can say about cutting pulp all winter long except that it's easier than in the summer when the woods can be chock full of blackflies, mosquitoes, ticks, deerflies, and horseflies. I'm partial to the cold and live in the right place for it, and would rather freeze to death than boil any day. Grandpa told me I had been left in a hot cabin in August when I was a baby and that accounted for my love of cold weather and cold water. He said in another day I would have looked like a miniature mummy, the way Egyptians buried their dead like they were making venison or beef jerky, not that the dead minded that much.

Anyway I didn't write my memoirs for three months because pulp cutting didn't give me any memories. Everything was used up, simple as that. You cut the tree, trim the branches, cut the logs to the proper length, then every few days when you have a load a custom skidder comes in to haul the logs out to the nearest two-track where a log truck with its own hydraulic lifter can load up. There's a saying that there aren't any old pulp cutters. You wear out before that, or a falling tree bucks back and catches you, or a "widow maker," which is a loose branch or a tree that gets caught up on another, falls on you and you are so much crushed meat. What saves the job is that you're outdoors, and if you're troubled in mind you are too wore out at the end of the day to give a shit, period.

Delmore is only giving me fifty bucks a week plus room and board, which means the cabin plus the groceries he picks up, a free breezy use of the Studebaker without any windows but the shitty windshield. He says all that's worth about eight hundred a month in value so the fifty bucks cash per week makes me overpaid. You're not likely to argue if you don't have a choice, let alone a Social Security number. We should all be grateful for work if we don't push it too far.

Also, a few days after he showed up Mr. Beaver's article was in the paper speculating that I represented some secret "Red Power" group from Wisconsin or farther west. He also said I was a well-known U.P. drifter with several scrapes with the law, and come from our "outcast subculture," the "forgotten outsiders" from the lowest ten percent of our wage earners. It was no wonder that I was outraged when my religion was going to be violated by anthropologists and archaeologists and that I and my organization might consider violence. He also added that the university people were within the law, and the State Police said I was being closely watched.

Delmore said the article should teach me to keep my mouth shut and it was easy for them to find a reason to put me in jail, far from whiskey, pussy, and a decent meal. I admit I got scared though I was interested in seeing myself described in print in better terms than in the court papers in Munising. There is supposed to be free speech in this country but you say a few things and they come down on you like a ton of shit. To be frank I was afraid to go to town and Delmore encouraged my fear because he liked my company for dinner. He said my spirit and body would die in prison and I would come out a shrunken man.

Every night after dinner and Delmore's lecture about life I'd head down to my cabin with whatever was left of my whiskey ration (a pint of Guckenheimer every three days) and stoke up the banked fire. One thing about a well-built cabin is that once you get the walls warm it's not too hard to maintain fifty degrees in winter. I can't say your body will cook in that temperature but it will maintain life.

Sad to say Marcelle only came out twice, the second time after a deep snow, and she had trouble walking with her one short leg so I pulled her on the toboggan and being from Louisiana she couldn't stand the coolness of the cabin. Also, Travis was being sent home from Africa with a case of amoebas in his intestines, all of which left me out of luck except for an occasional poke with Vera from the country bar, the Buckhorn Tavern, two miles down the road from Delmore's. I only go there on Saturday nights out of my police fear but it's hard to imagine them hanging out there. Sometimes Delmore comes along and he'll point out some old backwoods, scab-faced stewbum and say he might be working undercover for the police so I better behave.

Vera has been married three times and is not exactly a dieter but is full of affection which makes up for a lot. She said that before her family moved over to Felch she was in the third grade when I was in the sixth. I admit that I didn't remember her but she said that was a hundred fifty pounds ago and starts laughing. We sneak off to the storage room at the back of the bar for a quick one and it's comforting to see beer stacked in cases and rows of liquor stored on shelves, neat as a pin. The first time we did it she got to kicking and broke a few bottles. There was no way to save a single drop.

Late in January and I had a big nature day that filled my thoughts. First off there was just a bare hint of day when I got to the logging site. There were almost too many stars above and west and a trace of light in the east. There had been a small thaw the day before, then it went down to zero, so I could walk right on top of the snow. I carried my saw and a can of gas way back to the corner of the forty near the

edge of a tamarack marsh. I stood still for a while thinking of where to start a fire to warm up my hands during the day when I heard a whooshing sound. I didn't have time to think before a snowy owl hit a rabbit on the edge of the swamp. There was a squeal from the rabbit then that's all folks. I had to stand there stock still for a half hour to make sure the big bird got his meal without me roaring him off. These owls come all the way down from the Arctic certain years when they run out of food up there, but it can be a long time between seeing one. Then around midmorning I looked over about a hundred yards to where I had been clearing out smaller trees to fell a big one the day before and there were three deer feeding on the slender popple tops. When I shut off the chain saw they'd get edgy, but when I cranked up again they'd go right back to feeding. Some people know a chain saw is a dinner bell. Hunger must be a lot stronger than fear.

Delmore had filled a wide thermos of chili and I shook a bunch of hot sauce in it. I have to keep the hot sauce in my pocket or it will freeze up. I was feeling good so I took a stroll across the county road from the forty. I wanted a snooze but it was no fun waking up cold and stiff on the pickup seat so I headed into this real thick stand of cedar that even got thicker. It was grand being able to walk on top of the snow so I made a pretty big circle with an eye on the sun so I wouldn't get turned around. I came upon a small pond with a steep bank and a pile of deadfalls on the far side. I was about to pass it by when I noticed a small black hole in the snowbank by the tree roots and I smelled a musty smell in the cold air. I could have jumped for joy but I didn't want to make a racket. What happened is that I found my first bear den blowhole in my life. Grandpa showed me one when I was a kid and I did the same thing I had done years ago. I lay down and smelled the strong scent coming out of the hole which was an inch wide, then I put an ear to it and listened to the slow stretched-out snores. I couldn't remember when I felt luckier. I would have to bring Delmore back here to help the bear medicine he gave up.

* * *

It was Thursday and when I told Delmore about the bear den he shook his head no and said it would be too much for his heart. He had killed a bear as a young man and that was its skin in the other room. His point was since he had abandoned his bear medicine this one might come out and get him. Then he wore another long face and said Marcelle told him that morning that Travis was looking for me and I shouldn't go to Vera's Buckhorn Tavern on Saturday. She was baiting me, for sure. Just when I get over the worry about the State Police spying on me even out in the woods I got this black-belt nut case on my tail. I told Delmore to tell Marcelle that this country was too small for both me and her husband. Delmore asked what movie I got that from and I said I thought it was one I saw with Randolph Scott when I was a kid.

Friday was a mean and blustery day in the woods and I damn near quit but there was no point in stewing in the cabin. I built an extra-big bonfire because it was darkish with low clouds whistling past out of the northwest. I tried singing while I worked but I don't know whole songs, only parts. "Yes, we have no bananas, we have no bananas today."And there was one my pardner in the diving salvage business, Bob, used to play on his pickup stereo called "Brown-Eyed Women and Red Grenadine" that was beautiful though I could only sing the title. I didn't know what grenadine was until I met Shelley and she bought it to pour in rum drinks. It is a kind of sweet syrup that wouldn't be good on pancakes. While I was singing "Row, row, row your boat, life is but a dream," it occurred to me why Travis, or Fred for that matter, wouldn't attack me in the woods. If you jumped a man running a chain saw you could get cut up pretty bad. I thought of this because once in the Soo, when Bob sold some ship's lanterns we got off an old wreck, we saw this movie called *The Texas Chainsaw Massacre.* I walked out halfway through and went to a bar. My idea of fun is not seeing people get sawed up. I also swore I'd never go to Texas. Delmore has been there and said they got a lot of cowboys but drove all the Indians out.

On Saturday morning I didn't work because I was fretting about my face-off with Travis that was coming up. I tried to read a book about nature with plenty of photos that Delmore gave me back at Christmas at my request. When I asked for it I was remembering that the dead chief in the ice truck told me to read a book about nature. Under a picture of a cottonwood tree it said the tree drinks two to three hundred gallons of water a day. This didn't seem possible but then I'd never seen one. Come spring I might just have the urge to head out west again like I did when my dead van was brand new. I'd check out cottonwood trees. Then there was a bang on the cabin door and I jumped for the rafters. It was Berry on her Bushwacker skis I got her for Christmas. They cost me more than a week's pay but I was thinking she might never get the hang of a bicycle, and these cross-country skis are short and wide, more like snowshoes so she can get around in the winter. What surprised me is that Berry only visits on Sundays. She comes in sounding like a flock of pissed-off bluejays and gives me a note from Doris. The upshot was that Fred was back in town from burying his dad in Flint and was on my trail. Doris heard Rose tell him she'd heard I was in the Buckhorn every Saturday night. Rose isn't allowed in the bar because she had a pretty mean duke-out with Vera last summer I was told.

Fine. Two on one, if that's fair. I made Berry hot chocolate in a soup bowl because she always wants seven marshmallows in it. We played one game of Chinese checkers though she doesn't know how and I sent her on her way so she could ski home before dark. Then I went up to dinner at Delmore's before the big showdown. Delmore knew about Travis but when I added Fred he was troubled indeed. He took me back in his pantry where he's got a big flour bin full of every lightbulb he's ever used up. When I asked him why he said "Waste not, want not." From another drawer he took out a pair of old-time brass knuckles and gave them to me for extra help. They had a nice heft to them, especially on a haymaker. He also put a German Luger in his suit-coat pocket but he didn't have any shells for the pistol. He said he was willing to scare someone for me but wasn't going to jail on my account. He had made a good little venison roast plus the heart for dinner to give me strength. He made me eat the heart and I said deer aren't all that strong. "But they can run," he yelled, laughing his guts out, which picked up my spirits. It had been a long time since I'd had a fistfight but it wasn't likely to be the end of the world, just a real expensive way to pay for getting laid a few times.

Delmore and me got to the Buckhorn fairly early so we could get set up. We decided to sit at the bar and we played a few games of cribbage while we waited. There was extra size to the crowd which was usually twenty or thirty, the kind of drinkers who wore out their welcome in town. I guessed that some of them heard there was going to be excitement and showed up for it. I was glad to see Teddy, a great big mixed-blood I'd been to school with. His dad put him to work in the woods so he had to drop out in the eighth grade like a lot of my friends. Grandpa made me finish school so I'd have a diploma. I misplaced this diploma somewhere. Teddy waved to me and pointed at the ball bat he had leaned up against the fireplace on the far side of the bar. I had Vera take him a pitcher of beer as Teddy always drank straight from the pitcher. The ball bat made me feel a trace warmer in my very cold guts.

About eight o'clock in comes this tall, wiry guy dressed up like he was God's own commando. He was sort of dancing on the balls of his feet as his eyes swept the bar. He had to be Travis as Fred was a lot thicker when I saw him on Doris's porch and in the rearview mirror of my van. It was then it came to me that these guys wouldn't exactly know what I looked like. Marcelle must have given him a general description because he sidles up and asks if my name happens to be B.D. I naturally say no, but B.D. is a friend of mine and is due any moment because we got a pool game coming up. I estimated Travis to be only about one-eighty but his arms were made up of cables. He orders a drink next to me and Delmore, looks around, and heads to the toilet.

Just at the moment Travis goes into the toilet (Bucks and Does at the Buckhorn) in comes Fred, half drunk with his eyes boiling red, his neck real thick like the football players on TV. To be frank I'd rather fight a bulldozer. The bar is silent except the jukebox which is playing George Jones's "He Stopped Loving Her Today." Again, he comes up to me and asks if I'm B.D. and Delmore interrupts and says what I was about to say, that B.D. is in the pisser. Fred starts jumping up and down to juice himself up, then heads toward the corner just as Travis comes out. Fred looks back at Delmore for a split second and Delmore nods yes, then they were engaged in mortal combat.

It was a real bar sweeper and enjoyed by all. Fred was more powerful but Travis had the moves. Travis whacked and kicked him about thirty times and would have been the clear winner if he hadn't tripped on a chair. Fred came down with a knee on Travis's guts, then got him in a choke hold but Travis reached up and gouged Fred's eye and Fred whirled him around by the neck and threw him against the pinball machine which broke. That was enough for Vera who called the sheriff. I was surprised when Travis bounced up but he did. Teddy made his way up to the bar and said he thought I was the one supposed to fight and I said shut up. Then this old guy and other folks started screeching because Travis drew a knife, and Fred took out one of his own. I was sure glad I wasn't involved. They started circling through the tipped-over furniture and it was then that Delmore jumped off his barstool with a war whoop. Delmore always wears his old three-piece suit so he could be someone official. That and the fact he had drawn his German Luger got their attention.

"Fun is fun, boys, but now you are destroying public property. Throw down your knives or I'll blow you both to hell." They threw down their weapons so Delmore took it a little further. "Now lay facedown. The law is on its way. Teddy, if they move you bash the skinny one while I shoot the other through the skull." Teddy bonked his ball bat on the floor near Travis's head.

So that was that for the meantime. The deputies came and took them away without protest. Everyone knows that the cops in the U.P. like to mix it up so there was no further trouble. Delmore who had only let me have two drinks to start bought a few rounds for the house. Vera said the pinball was on lease and nobody played it much, though I will miss the painting behind the glass, part nude woman and part robot. Next morning on Sunday we had pork chops and potatoes and coffee royals, a popular special-occasion morning drink in the U.P. (coffee, whiskey, sugar). Delmore liked to add a lesson to everything and said that spuds and pork had made America. He was still high with the last night's excitement and almost turned on the TV. He had pulled the plug during a thunderstorm years ago, then didn't watch again because Ronald Reagan said a lot of Indians were oil rich on their "preservations."

March came as it does every year and not a moment too soon. Except the weather didn't know spring was coming, and after that summer—March was as bad as December and January, and a lot worse than February. Delmore and me went over to the winter powwow at the junior college gym and next morning he took off on a bus for the Milwaukee airport with about thirty members of the senior citizens group to go on a jet plane for a week in sunny Las Vegas. He had a bunch of brochures about what they were going to do and see including the Hoover Dam, Wayne Newton, and a show with Siegfried & Roy who had trained albino tigers. To me, Siegfried & Roy looked as weird as a Christmas tree in June.

I enjoyed the powwow because I'd never been to one before, also I was tagging along with Delmore who was a pretty big deal among the local Chips. He got introduced to the whole crowd of about a thousand Indians, including some from over in Wisconsin and Minnesota. Then to my shock I also got introduced because I was a "wild"one who had been in the newspapers and on TV. A bunch of people clapped, mostly young men who then raised their fists so I did too thinking it must be some sort of sign. Until that moment I tended to brood about the newspaper saying I was an outcast and an outsider. When I had said something to Delmore about it he said not to worry because there were too many people inside which didn't exactly cover the situation. The best part of the evening was Berry in the crow and raven dance that all the little and younger girls took part in. There must have been fifty of them dancing around and around in a circle with the five drummers, beating faster and faster, and all the girls acting like crows and ravens, bobbing their heads, strutting, waddling, beating their wings. Berry was by far the best and Doris said it was probably because Berry didn't know she wasn't a crow or a raven which didn't take anything from it. There were also a bunch of white people of the better sort at the powwow, and in a room where they sold food I ran into Gretchen and Karen eating frybread. They just turned red as beets and walked away so I judged I wasn't forgiven.

We had to leave early on account of Delmore. What happened was that an old man of about a hundred years did his last bear dance of this life. He was completely caped in a bear head and hide and even his hands were hid by paws. He danced all alone real slow and every few steps he'd shake his war club at the gym ceiling. Delmore couldn't handle it so we left. He was shedding a lot of tears and it was lucky he was going to Vegas next day so he could get over it. I got a little edgy out in the parking lot because someone was following us. I slipped on the brass knuckles I had taken to carrying just in case Travis or Fred wanted another go-around. Under the parking lot light I could see it was a dark man in a dark suit wearing a ponytail. It turned out to be Marten, Rose's little brother, who I had seen earlier but didn't recognize with a bunch of huge braves from Wisconsin who showed up on Harleys. Marten whispered we can't be seen together because of State Police spies and he'd meet me tomorrow night at the Buckhorn and off he went. Delmore was already in the car and asked who it was. When I said Marten he said Marten was an agitator and whenever he came back to town he started trouble among decent law-abiding Natives. Californians always did that. On the way home I argued how did he know about California if he'd never been there and Delmore used the old biblical saying "By their fruits ye shall know them."

While Delmore was in Vegas I was supposed to stay in the house but such was not to be. I was even going to plug in the TV but then tragedy struck. The wind had clocked around to the south and by midmorning the deep snow was mushy and hard to move around in. I was trying to cut a big birch low to the ground so as to not leave too much stump. I wasn't paying too much attention because I was horny as a toad and was having sex thoughts about this Indian girl I met at the powwow who was so smart she went to the university up in Marquette. She was a third cousin of Delmore so she might have thought I was a bigger deal than I was. Delmore said she was "crane clan," whatever that meant, probably sandhill cranes. Anyway, in my mind we were out in the woods laying on sweet moss with her dress up when all of a sudden the birch fell, hit another tree, and bucked back. In a split second I came out of my pussy trance and threw myself backwards or the tree would have caught my head or chest and I'd be dead as a cleaned fish. Instead, the butt end of the tree caught my knee and blasted my kneecap up a few inches. It was a full minute before I felt anything. I just sat there looking at blood coming out of my torn pants, and then the pain hit and soon I was flopping around and yelling. Somehow

I knew I had to crawl a quarter of a mile out to the road where Teddy had been trying to get the skidder started. I must have left quite a blood trail.

III

POINTS EAST AND WEST

To most, a hospital is a bright, shrill, utterly lonesome place—inhospitable, in fact. Visitors fail to make the slightest inroads on the notion that one wishes to be elsewhere, the nights full of slight but unaccountable noises, a factor of illness that penetrates even the vases of flowers, the professional smiles that you never quite forget are concealing skulls.

Brown Dog, however, was enjoying his stay after the initial postoperative discomfort natural to having a smashed kneecap put back in place and a few tendons reconnected. His only other time in the hospital, in Bozeman, Montana, had been far less pleasant for the simple reason of the subdural hematomas covering face and head. He was confident he could have handled two cowboys, but three were out of the question. Walking out of the bar for the fight, he had wrongly assumed there was a code of the West that guaranteed against gang rape. The good thing this time was that, unlike the head, you could distance yourself from your knee. It was simply there, the sharp edges of the pain dulled to a smooth roundness by drugs.

Before being wheeled into surgery he had made Teddy, who had accompanied him in the ambulance, promise to get the other half of a frozen roadkilled deer up onto the raven-feeding platform at the cabin. Teddy was strong enough to pitch the carcass up there and wouldn't need to use a ladder. B.D. was mindful despite his inchoate pain that once you get the ravens coming in, you didn't want to disappoint them. He liked calling to them out the cabin window and often one or two would respond, though when he tried to slip quietly outside to get closer they'd fly away. On Berry's Sunday visits, however, there was the thrill of watching her gargle out her *gaagaafbirmbs*, her chortles from deep in her throat, caws, chucks, clucks, and whistles. The ravens would wheel around the yard in a state of frantic interest, resettle on the platform, and peer down at the small brown girl who spoke their language.

On the second day, when he was out of intensive care and ensconced in a ward with two very old, terminal men and a motorcyclist who had hit an ice patch without his helmet, B.D. enjoyed a train of visitors. Vera brought him a pint, which he slid under the mattress, and a real nice hamburger with plenty of onions wrapped in tinfoil, allowing him at his request the briefest glance of tit. Doris came with Berry but didn't stay long because Berry immediately took to imitating the groans of the motorcyclist. Doris brought him a cold venison steak between homemade bread and a packet of salt and pepper. She said Rose still couldn't figure out how he beat the shit out of Fred. Delmore had told Doris the real story which she thought wonderful. On the way out B.D. had Berry do her raven renditions and this brought a nurse on the run.

Being full from the snacks, B.D. was somewhat critical of the single pork chop, applesauce, and salad brought for dinner by a nurse's aide named Elise. He complained that the pork was dead and affected tears which confused Elise, who stared at the chop in a new light. She was pretty cute though hefty, with just a trace of a downy mustache. He kept a hand at the edge of the bed in hopes she'd rub against it, which she did. "Look at my little tentpole," he said, pointing at the risen sheet around his pecker. She blushed and fled but he was confident of her return because he couldn't very well sleep with a tray above his chest.

During evening visiting hours Marcelle showed up but was slack-jawed and sullen. She wanted to know if she should alert Delmore out in Vegas to the accident, and B.D. said no, Delmore was getting old and should have a trouble-free vacation seeing Siegfried & Roy. Then Marcelle got all teary over the fact that B.D. had beat the tar out of Travis. It had never happened before and now Travis was pissed about their wayward life.

"You must have really got the drop on him," Marcelle said petulantly.

"You might say that," B.D. agreed, deciding not to correct her wrong impression. He tried to force her hand under the sheet but she was intent on whining about her marriage, so he grimaced in fake pain so she'd shut up. She made a halfhearted attempt but her hand was cold and her fingernails sharp. Finally Marcelle was put off and left when the old man in the next bed started vomiting. So much for love that can't overcome circumstances, B.D. thought. Even Elise made a rush job out of retrieving the dinner tray.

His last visitor of the evening took him by very real surprise. The nurse had just given him his bedtime Demerol and he was feeling the delicious tingling consequence when in walked Gretchen, a vision of loveliness in her habitual black turtleneck. He speculated on which of the dainty undies he had sorted through in her dresser she was wearing. The drug helped him see their pale, silly renditions of the rainbow. Unfortunately, Gretchen was in a business suit.

"Let's just forget your bad behavior, although I'd like an apology. Karen thought you'd like these fruit and bran muffins. I doubt you get enough fiber." She dropped a brown bag on the nightstand and took a pen and forms out of her shoulder bag.

"I apologize from the depths of my painful heart." His eyes became misty but when he reached for her hand she moved farther back from the bedside.

"Your employer, Delmore Burns, hadn't paid any workers' compensation insurance so we'll file through the state to make him liable. Let's start with your full name and Social Security number."

"Delmore's my relative. He'll take care of me. I can't be getting him in hot water." In his dope haze B.D. hadn't the strength to reenter the Social Security nightmare, with visions of the government carting him off to lifelong rest in prison.

"I need at least to know how much he's paying you so we can prorate a claim," she said. "We can do the rest tomorrow."

His look was so full of grief that a remnant trace of the mother arose in her. She leaned over and impulsively cuddled him, a breast brushing his face. When he told her he got fifty bucks a week, room and board, she flushed with anger and hugged him tightly. The situation was worse than the Chicanos she had worked with in Leelanau County.

B.D., with his face between Gretchen's breasts, drew in a new scent that reminded him of the Chicago student riots after he'd been booted from the Moody Bible Institute, having blown his tuition on a hooker. He would never know the scent was called patchouli. "It would be nice to know you when you're not working," he squeaked, nose to nipple, and she turned loose as if he were a hot potato.

"I have to be honest with you. Karen and me are twilight lovers if you know what I mean."

"I'm not sure I get you." There was the image of these two nifty women walking at twilight, his favorite time of day.

"Lesbians. We love each other all the way." Gretchen was almost embarrassed but made yet another of dozens of leaps out of the closet with gusto. She rather liked B.D.'s naïveté and lack of presumption, the absence of bristling showmanship that repelled her in men.

"You don't say. Well, there's more than one way to skin a cat, that's for sure. Can't say I've ever met one that I knew of. If there's any way I can help out with you two, just let me know." His mind had quickly become a whirl of intrigue and pleasure, also he was flattered that this fine young woman had confided in him. She was a bit of an outsider just like himself.

"Thank you, but we can manage." She gave him a peck on the cheek, letting the alternative of being insulted pass by. He was such a goof, sort of like discovering a long-lost retarded brother.

When she left, B.D. struggled to remember the movie he and Bob, his partner in the salvage business, had seen in the booth at the porn shop over at the Soo. These two women who ran a flower shop were working each other over in the back while they filled the vases. One had the tattoo of a lizard on her ass. One of their customers was this jerk-off guy whom they tied up and beat senseless with dildos to get back at their mistreatment at the hands of men, or so they said. Gretchen and Karen were clearly a higher sort of people than these flower-shop women and he hoped to become their friend.

Meanwhile, B.D.'s errant comments to the media had set in motion a troublesome set of decisions for the State Police detective, Harold "Bud" Schultz. He rather liked his temporary duty in the U.P., as his marriage back in East Lansing was in a state of travail—his wife had gone back to college and his two teenage sons scorned his profession. Schultz had quickly determined that B.D. was up to essentially nothing despite the media blarney, and that tailing the man resembled following around a stray dog. The prospective felon was being sponsored by a prominent Native citizen, perhaps a blood relative, of impeccable reputation other than being a registered Democrat. B.D.'s rap sheet was dreary indeed, including a scrape in Montana, a number of drunk and disorderlies, suspected illegal selling of maritime salvage, the business of trying to sell a long-dead body from Lake Superior, the theft of an ice truck from Newberry, the arson of the anthropologist's tent near Grand Marais, all of which did not add up as a threat to public order. Still, Schultz liked the idea of spending his spring in the Upper Peninsula, far from domestic discord and the very real crime in southern Michigan.

The true impetus for the surveillance was that his superiors in the State Police and the governor's office did not want a replication of the civil discord in Wisconsin over Native fishing rights which had a measurable impact on tourism. The upshot was that though it was relatively easy to determine that B.D. was a loose screw representing only himself, it was difficult to file such a simpleminded report in a political climate where conspiracy was the only satisfactory free lunch. B.D. appeared to be a happy-go-lucky pussy chaser, and the fact that he consorted with Gretchen Stewart, a feminist activist out of Ohio State, Marcelle Robicheaux who was from a family of Louisiana malcontents and small-time dope smugglers, and Vera Hall whose second husband was an auto thief from Duluth, added up to nothing whatsoever. Schultz's job therefore boiled down to the simplest imperatives: merely stop the nitwit from breaking the injunction to keep out of Alger County until the University of Michigan could do their gravedigging. In order to maintain the state's interest in the project and his own soft duty, Schultz would continue to plant intriguing items in the press. The sole, small mystery in B.D.'s file was that neither Social Security nor the IRS could come up with a trace of a record, nor the Selective Service for that matter. The only string on the man was his driver's license.

Schultz proceeded on his somnolent way, even reading Densmore and Vizenor on the Chippewa and their arcane customs, until the night of the powwow when a lightbulb blew up and he spotted a true dissident, Lone Marten, a.k.a. Marten Smith, thought to be residing in Westwood, California, but from the local area. Schultz felt juiced indeed while he watched Marten talking to B.D. in the gymnasium parking lot, but the energy was somewhat dissipated when he got back to his quarters at the Best Western and did a sleepy phone check on Marten. As he reread his notes in the morning, it occurred to him that though he was an ex–American Indian Movement member, Marten was small-time indeed, having shown expertise mostly in getting government grants from Interior, Health and Human Services, and the National Endowment for his dissident films on contemporary Native life. Marten had also raised funds as the chairman of the Windigos, a supposed Native radical organization, but the best intelligence had not turned up any other members. There was a dropped charge for manufacturing crystal methamphetamine, three motorcycle accidents, and the most miserable credit record Schultz had ever seen. In short, Marten was a chiseler, no doubt looking for a little excitement while he was home visiting his mother.

Or so Schultz thought out on the county road as he watched the ambulance carry B.D. away. He drove over to a pine grove down the road from Doris's house and glassed Marten as he pissed against a maple tree, then tailed him as he drove his rent-a-car, gotten with a suspicious credit card at the Marquette airport, to a realtor's office. There Marten made a three-thousand-dollar cash down payment on an abandoned fake fort out on Route 2 that had once been the entrance to a shabby zoo for tourists, then a failed RV court, then a local flea market that expired when everyone was rid, finally, of their recirculated junk. Schultz found all this out when he opted to talk to the realtor instead of doing further surveillance of Marten. He picked up Marten's trail again that evening, when Marten appeared to be waiting for his co-conspirator B.D. at the Buckhorn, not knowing that B.D. was in the hospital. Just about everything led to nothing, Schultz thought, as he hit his Best Western sack with a two-week-old copy of *People*.

B.D. was more than a little annoyed the next morning when Elise was giving him a sponge bath and a new doctor interrupted. B.D. had almost got her to touch ole Mister Friendly when in walked this asshole sawbones and sent Elise away. Since B.D. was decidedly proletarian he lacked the bourgeoisie's reverence for members of the medical profession, thinking of them as body mechanics who were no more reliable than the grease monkeys at the local garage. The doctor merely stared at him from behind the austerity of white suit and surgical mask and B.D. looked away with growing anger. He thought of Elise as

Fuzzy Wuzzy for her downy skin, and they had been talking about religion which he knew instinctively was the best sexual approach. When he was sprung from the hospital she'd go out with him if he'd go to church with her. Why not? he thought, as he guided the hand that held the sponge toward his pecker, truly a beautiful moment that had been destroyed by the doctor, who was flipping through his chart at the bed's end.

"Up to your old tricks again, Brown Dog," said the doctor. "You'd fuck a rock pile if you thought there was a snake in it."

"Kiss my ass, you dickhead butcher," B.D. barked, but then it dawned on him the doctor was none other than Marten. "Jesus, Marten, I didn't know you were a doctor."

"I'm not. I swiped this disguise down the hall. There's a detective following me and I need a little time to sort things out, man. How many people do you have behind you? If we're going to protect that burial site from the *wasichus,* we have to get organized."

When B.D. told him the grim news that he was working alone and at random, Marten admitted that he suspected as much, adding that his own group, the Windigos, was presently shorn of membership. "It's just the two of us to man the battle lines. In fact, today I bought an old fort as a cover for our operations. Actually I represent a group of investors—a fancy word for dope dealers, I suppose. My first love is film, but my integrity as an artist depends on my becoming *engagé* at times."

B.D. tried to buy time by offering Marten one of Karen's fruit and fiber muffins. He had taken a bite of one earlier and it reminded him of fruitcake pumped full of air. He didn't like fruitcake. Even gravy couldn't help fruitcake. Marten's comment about manning the battle lines brought to mind Delmore's Korean War theories. "The bottom dropped out and the top came off," Delmore liked to say. You could start as B.D. once had, with so simple an act of justice as pouring a cold beer down the neck of a truly mean-spirited woman, and end up in jail. The idea of standing with Marten and defending the ancient burial site against the college people, not to speak of the police, did not appeal to him.

"I'm going to have to think this over. They got an injunction until next October against my showing up in Alger County. Prison would make me a shrunken man."

"Go ahead and think this over," Marten said. "Just don't cop out on me. You got this thing started and I came from California to help out. I already invested in a fort."

At that moment B.D.'s actual doctor came in and Marten slipped out after advising a polio shot.

Five days later, against all advice, B.D. checked out of the hospital wearing an elaborate knee brace. He had been through a dark time what with the administration of fewer and fewer drugs and the brutal fact that Elise had been transferred to another wing of the hospital after having been caught toying with his weenie by her superior. He had written Elise an affectionate note and her reply had been discouraging: "You got me in dutch. My career is at stake and you're doing the devil's work. Don't be bothering me anymore." Somehow far worse was that all animals had fled his dreams and he realized the extent he had counted on them for good feeling to start the day. Now there were mostly people with big pink faces squeaking a strange language. With the bum knee and crutches he doubted he could even make it down the trail to the cabin. How was he supposed to live without ravens and other birds? That was the question. Also it was April Fool's Day, which meant trout season would start in three weeks—not that he was a great observer of seasons—and how was he supposed to wade creeks and beaver ponds in his current condition? This was not an occasion for self-pity, an emotion alien to him, but a question.

Delmore, fresh out of Vegas, was waiting in the car. An orderly helped B.D. in and Delmore, without a greeting, waved a letter from Gretchen in his face. This cunt Gretchen Stewart was threatening Delmore with all sorts of financial mayhem over B.D.'s logging accident.

"I took you in as an orphan and now this," Delmore said, pulling up in front of the fanciest hotel in town, the House of Ludington, the same place Brown Dog had stayed with Shelley last October. In the dining room they were met by Delmore's lawyer, who patted B.D. on the back and said, "Just call me Fritz," so he did. B.D. was completely ignorant of Michigan's generous workers' compensation laws. He was plied with a half-dozen drinks and a T-bone steak which mixed wonderfully with the Percodan he had taken for knee pain. Before dessert he was asked to sign a paper releasing Delmore from all financial liability for his accident and injury for the consideration of fifty dollars a week for one year, plus the use of the cabin for that same period. To the consternation of Fritz and Delmore B.D. became cagey, almost captious, leaning back and staring at the paper as if it were a tout sheet. Finally he handed the paper to Delmore, ignoring Fritz.

"You forgot to put in the grub and two pints of V.O. It's time I move up to top-shelf whiskey. I also want one dancing girl a week and your bearskin for keeps. I need it and you don't. You agree to my terms or I'll sue for five thousand." He drew that laughable figure out of the hat because it seemed enormous at the moment. He had thrown in the dancing girl as a negotiating ploy to ensure the bearskin. Old Claude over in Grand Marais had told him that when your dreaming goes sour you should sleep outside naked, wrapped up in a bearskin.

"You drive a hard bargain, B.D.," Fritz said, holding up a hand to shush Delmore. He knew his client was getting the deal of a lifetime and wanted to close it forthwith. Such injuries most frequently result in a lifelong sinecure for the wounded.

B.D. slept off lunch on Delmore's sofa during which time Delmore burned Gretchen's letter with satisfaction, put the signed release in his strongbox, and checked B.D.'s coat for incidental information.

There was a short note from Marten saying that "the plot had thickened" and to "burn" the note, which in fact contained no useful information other than that B.D. was needed back on board the revolutionary express.

The afternoon's *Mining Gazette* had printed an article and interview with Marten that would immediately have gotten him locked up in any other country in the world. Delmore suspected it was a case of reefer madness, as before Marten left for the outside world he and his cronies had filled the local forests with patches of low-grade marijuana, so that every time the sheriff and deputies uprooted a small patch they'd proclaim a million-dollar drug bust (street value). Delmore would have to speak to the detective to find out if there wasn't some way to ship this crazed urchin out of town without attracting the attention of the sharpsters from the ACLU. At least with Marten hogging the microphone, his idiot grandnephew might be saved from prison.

Vegas had done a real job on Delmore and he trusted the oncoming spring to eventuate a recovery. He had been semi-hot on a local rich widow until she insisted they sit through the Wayne Newton show three nights in a row. That nasalate dipshit had driven him hysterical with boredom. And the chintzy banality of Siegfried & Roy brought desperate tears, so he climbed over tables and chairs to get out of the room. What saved him from heading home was a dark lounge where a luscious black woman sang the old Mabel Mercer–type tunes he had loved in jazz clubs in Detroit in the late forties and fifties.

And now he had to give up his bearskin because Fritz had told him if B.D.'s case ever got into the hands of a good compensation lawyer, it would cost Delmore a minimum of a hundred grand. He went into the storage room and held the skin but not too close. The last time he wore it he had been dancing after a Mediwiwin ceremony up in Wisconsin when he was about B.D.'s age, thirty-five years before. For security he put on his turtle claw necklace and took the skin out before the fireplace where he examined it to the tune of B.D.'s slobbering snores. Goodbye my youth, thought Delmore, a somewhat pretentious emotion in that he was seventy-seven. His own son should have been wearing it, or his sister's son, who had been murdered in a scuffle on a fishing boat off Munising back in 1950, after he had knocked up B.D.'s grandpa Jake's worthless daughter, who had then run off with Delmore's own son to disappear forever. How much Native blood anyone had never meant anything to Delmore—true Indians were those who observed the religion and the attitudes. Where it did matter significantly was in the area of fishing rights where Delmore figured a man ought to be one half by blood, and also when it came down to the pathetic benefits offered by the government. In the old days in the U.P. the bottom quarter of whatever background married whoever was available. He had even read how the Finns up in the northern areas of their country were actually a different kind of Indian. Delmore had never needed a free dime from anyone so a lot of the prolonged Native nightmare meant nothing to him. He had also read enough to know that notions of genetic virtue had caused the world a lot of problems in its sorry human history.

Delmore laid the bearskin over B.D. on the couch so that the great toothed mouth was open near his face. He had shot the bear, a male of about three hundred and fifty pounds, up near the Fence River between Crystal Falls and Witch's Lake. It took him two full days to drag it out, and when he brought it home his mother and young wife and all the neighbors had quite a celebration, though without alcohol, as they were traditional.

B.D.'s eyes opened to the fierce countenance and he kissed the bear's nose—a good sign, thought Delmore, who had been hoping for a frantic wake-up call. He made B.D. take a hot bath, then put on some fresh clothes, including the old plaid hunting shirt Delmore had shot the bear in and saved. Any more ceremony would have been wasted, though he relented a bit and opened his medicine bundle. He took out a small leather bag containing the bear's gallstones. B.D. treated them as if they were diamonds before he pocketed the pouch.

B.D. was wondering again if he could make it to the cabin on crutches, so they went out on the porch to check the weather. It was the beginning of twilight, the air warm enough for the crutches to penetrate the snow, with the sky's cumulus billowing a promise of the first rain. Delmore wanted company for dinner and his post-Vegas depression but B.D. was eager for the cabin with its deep, non-hospital scent of pitch pine, the sound of a running creek rather than groans, pukes, moans, and nurse whispers.

There was no way for B.D. to carry the heavy skin, so Delmore wrapped it around him, tying the arm and leg thongs and fitting the hollowed head over B.D.'s own. He had become a standing bear on the porch, then a walking bear on crutches as he headed off down the trail toward the cabin. Delmore had wanted to give him a hug for the first time but then thought it would increase his own internal quakiness. After the rifle shot so long ago the bear had stood up, its forepaws on a deadfall log, and howled and roared at Delmore for taking its life. That was certainly too much medicine to deal with at his age.

At the cabin B.D. lit a lantern, then burned a green cedar bough over the kindling to remove the musty odor. He had fallen three times on the trail for lack of a flashlight, but by God he made it, throbbing knee and all. He pumped a quart of cold water, then frightened himself when he looked in the small mirror on the kitchen cupboard. He quickly shed the bearskin, listening to the hiss and crackle of the fire. It would take hours for the cabin to warm, so he got in his sleeping bag, drawing the bearskin over him so the head was on the pillow beside his own and the lantern light shone off the teeth.

Deep in the night he got up to stoke the fire and take a pain pill. The rain was deafening on the roof, and over that he could hear the roar of the rising creek down the bank. There was only one pleasure on earth to equal that of a hard rain on a cabin's tin roof, or so he thought as he peed out the door into the night. He suspected the tiny creek in the gully between the cabin and Delmore's place would be filling with water, so he was doubtless trapped on this island in the forest, far from his only problems on earth which included Marten and his own big mouth. He had known it was wrong to show Shelley the ancient graveyard in the first place, but then she was that rare college woman who could have taken first place in any skin show. It was definitely her wiles that led him astray, and though he could not specifically name the principle he had wronged by showing an anthropologist the burial mounds, he knew there was one.

At daybreak he noted that he was ill provisioned for his isolation. There were three cans of pork and beans and one of Spam. He didn't care for Spam unless it was fried hard in lard, and the closest lard, he thought, was around a pig's ass on the farm down the road from Doris's place. He heated a can of beans, reflecting that Mr. Van Camp was cheap with pork. At least there was flour and a single egg left. He could make a loaf of bread which would be a bit chewy as there was no yeast. Better to use the egg for cornbread. He glanced over at the bearskin and remembered the idea old Claude spoke of: going without food to purify your mind and body. It was called fasting and he thought he might give it a go-around after the beans. The minute in which you got thrilled with an idea passed into the next minute when you weren't. For instance, at the hospital Marcelle was a pea-brain dipshit and he didn't want to see her again, but with the first spoonful of beans halfway to his mouth he remembered the charming way she cocked her bare butt at him like a house cat.

By noon he had reached page one hundred of *One Hundred Years of Solitude* and marveled at how people bore up under the burden of all the things that happened to them. He liked a genuinely empty future, and his own smoke-blowing ideas for disrupting the excavation, plus Marten's solider plans, stood off on the horizon like an immense nugget of doom, definitely spoiling the view. He was staring into the cracks of the floor when last night's dream came to him. He was holding his childhood teddy bear to his chest. It was missing one leg and the fur was crinkly and singed from the time he put it in the oven to dry it out. The teddy bear started out cold and damp, then got warmer and warmer against his chest, then began to squirm and move of its own accord, wiggling and stretching, coming to life, then stood on its hind legs and looked around, whuffed as bears do, then curled up and went to sleep. What a relief, B.D. thought, to have my dreaming back, then he heard three rifle shots in succession and scrambled for his crutches.

It turned out to be Teddy and Delmore standing on the other side of where the gully was filled by the feeder creek, Delmore in a yellow Great Lakes Steel slicker and Teddy with a bag of groceries, his rifle leaning up against a tree. It was a good thing Teddy was there, because Delmore never could have pitched the cans of food across the water, especially a fair-sized tinned ham. When it came to the pint of whiskey B.D. leaned his crutches against a tree and caught the bottle, falling in the process, but then it would have been quite the kick in the balls if the whiskey had broken.

"Delmore, you cheap sonofabitch," B.D. yelled, noting it was Four Roses, not the agreed-upon top-shelf V.O.

"I forgot. I'm real old." Delmore laughed, flipping him the bird and turning back to the trail.

"You got any pussy over there?" Teddy yelled, his voice booming through the rain.

"Not so as you would notice," B.D. called, trying to figure out how he'd carry the stuff back to the cabin on crutches. It wasn't as if someone would steal it if he left it there until needed. He settled on taking the whiskey, a fatty piece of chuck steak, a loaf of bread, and a can of peas. Halfway back he dropped the peas and let them lay for the next trip. At that moment he remembered that the Chippewa name for bear was "*mkwa*" and kept repeating it over and over until he was yelling it out to the downpour by the time he reached the cabin. On the platform three ravens fed on the remains of the deer Teddy had tossed up there for them. They let B.D. pass unremarked.

A full week later he was out at the fort, unable to further avoid Marten, who had appeared the night before at the cabin, stoned almost senseless and making chicken sounds through the window. There was a temptation to shoot him but he ran off in the dark, hooting and clucking. When they were young if someone called you a chicken as Marten had, you either took the dare or fought on the spot.

Rather than barge right in, B.D. pulled his breezy Studebaker off the road a few hundred yards away and peered at the scene through an old spyglass he borrowed from Delmore. At the fort they were as busy as bees. The rickety structure was made of upright half logs that had become quite warped. A half-dozen motorcycles were parked outside and it occurred to B.D. that they must be owned by those tough Red Power types from Wisconsin he had seen Marten talking to at the powwow. There was a pretty good-looking woman in a tight Levi's outfit and B.D. zeroed in when she leaned over to pick something up. Now that he was out in public again he might as well track down Marcelle. He swerved the spyglass, seeing a low-flying hawk cross far down the road. He didn't pick up the hawk but back in the evergreens there was a man with binoculars watching the fort, then swiveling to look at B.D. himself, who lowered his spyglass. It was the detective who had come into the diner when Delmore had defended him the same morning after Rose totaled the van.

At the fort B.D. told Marten about the spy in the underbrush. Marten looked through the spyglass, then went into what he called

his official office, coming out with a couple of cherry bombs and an M-80, which he lit one by one and launched with a slingshot toward the vicinity of the detective, who had disappeared. B.D. was introduced as the original hero to the Red Power guys, who were generally immense, with long black hair in braids and favoring tattoos. He was wondering what happened to the woman in Levi's he had spotted when Rose came around the back corner of the fort with her dreaded boyfriend, Fred. B.D. made for his Studebaker as fast as his crutches would carry him but Marten stopped him.

"It's time to put aside our petty bourgeois miseries for the sake of the cause," Marten said, drawing them altogether.

B.D. couldn't get over what Rose looked like. He recalled that three months ago at Christmas Delmore mentioned she was taking the cure but he hadn't paid attention. She must have lost thirty pounds of her bloat after she quit drinking. He was stunned.

"B.D., you started this fucking thing and it's time for you to stop hiding out,"she said, giving him a hug.

"You don't look like you're supposed to. You're the other guy at the bar with that old man," Fred said, puzzled but amiable.

"A case of mistaken identity in the great north," B.D. said, glancing over to where two Red Power guys were hauling out the big sign Rose had been painting. The sign read WILD WILD MIDWEST SHOW and everyone but B.D. stared at it with solemn admiration. You had to be light on your feet to keep up with Marten.

"Give me a ride to town," Marten said, drawing him aside. "The shit-sucking Nazis came and got their rent-a-car."

They went to a used-car lot down Route 2 owned by the brother of the realtor who sold Marten the fort. B.D. stood nervous and well aside as Marten made a thousand-dollar down payment on a three-year-old black Lincoln Town Car with a phone that had been repossessed from one of the thousands of developers who tour the Midwest every summer looking for fresh land meat. The dealer was enthused as the car had been on the lot all fall and winter eating up interest. He decided to sell it to Marten, who his brother told him was a "live one," for only twice what he had paid at the wholesale auto auction. When they were drawing up the papers a local signature was also needed, or so the dealer told B.D., handing him a pen. B.D. noted that Marten had signed "Luke Olsen, Pres., Windigo Corp.," so he signed B.D. Robicheaux because he was thinking of Marcelle's fanny.

B.D. followed Marten downtown in the Studebaker to the army-navy store and when Marten got out of the Lincoln he gave the finger to the detective passing in his car. While Marten was in the store, B.D. wondered how much, if anything, his phony signature meant. "B. D. Robicheaux" had a certain substance to it. Marten came out with a hard-billed cap and put it on B.D.'s head while explaining the whole deal. Because his injury prevented him from doing hard work, B.D. would busy himself driving Marten around so Marten could keep his mind clear for the goal ahead. The proceeds of the fort would go into a kitty, but since B.D. had started the whole movement and couldn't live on air he would receive five percent of the net profits of the Wild Wild Midwest Show, the cover for the revolutionary activities which would start with a demonstration at the burial site when the anthropologists showed up. Marten had a spy at work down at the University of Michigan who would tip them off.

"I told you I got an injunction on me," B.D. said angrily.

"Injunctions are made to be broken. It is clearly unconstitutional to keep you out of Alger County for a purported unconvicted crime. Also it's time for lunch."

Lunch at the diner wasn't all that pleasant because Travis had punched Marcelle around and she had a few bruises on her face, neck, and arms. B.D. couldn't remember when he had been too angry to eat. He seethed as he stared down at the congealing fat of his liver and onions, finally demanding from Marcelle Travis's number at the supply depot up at Sawyer Air Base. They didn't want to put B.D. through, so he said he was Travis's brother and there was a tragedy in the family. B.D. smiled out at his diner audience as if on stage.

"Travis, B.D. here. In case you don't remember, I kicked your ass out at the Buckhorn. If you lay another hand on Marcelle I'm going to squeeze your fucking head clean off and cram it up your ass. You understand?"

Many of Marcelle's customers cheered and clapped. Marcelle reheated the liver and onions in the microwave and B.D. was able to sit up and take nourishment, his anger subsiding, though Marten was pushing to get to a camera shop.

"You got a prize coming and it's not a tamale," Marcelle said after French-kissing him at the door, the taste of her snapping Dentyne merging with the liver and onions. Love was grand again.

A few days later the mystery of Marten's camera was received rather brutishly by Detective Schultz when he was suddenly called back far south to headquarters in East Lansing. The chief of all chiefs and an ACLU lawyer from Ann Arbor met Schultz with a large envelope of photos that Marten had taken of him in the act of spying on the Windigos, including a photo of Schultz asleep in bed with Rose at the Best Western. Schultz felt as if his bowels would empty while viewing the adverse evidence. His curiosity about the Chippewa had gotten the best of him and when he had met this handsome, albeit husky, Indian maiden at the casino she had been all over him like a washcloth. After fucking him into a rag pile she had obviously opened the door to the photographer. The real point the lawyer was making was that the State Police had been instructed years before by the legislature and governor to stop spying on political groups. The lawyer said he was keeping the photos for insurance against further noisome forays against the Windigos and walked out of the office after demanding and receiving Schultz's files on the case. The chief had a real aversion to the threatened rush of newspaper reporters and handed over the pathetic sheaf of notes. Schultz was sent off to do the prep work on a case of pill-popping osteopaths in Kalamazoo who purportedly were black-marketing the French abortion pill, or so tipped a pro-life group.

B.D.'s trout season opener was without the usual solitary grace. Marcelle had slept over at the cabin, which he couldn't very well blame her for because he insisted, partly to avoid the walk up the trail on crutches in the dark to take her home, and partly because she had been telling him her sexual history starting with when she "came out of the chute, kicking and bucking" at age thirteen. Southern girls weave a better tale than those in the North and B.D. lay there with a sore weenie listening to her dulcet-voiced confessional, quite sure that he had missed out on a lot of life but that couldn't be helped.

The upshot was that he didn't get up at dawn to fish, though he had taken the precaution of catching a half-dozen illegal brook trout for dinner the night before. Marcelle did a beautiful job frying the fish, evidently another Louisiana art, while describing a set-to with a couple of good old boys from the New Orleans Saints at a Breaux Bridge motel. Several times he put his hand on his head to see if his hair was standing straight up. He was rigging his fly tackle at the time, looking at the Wheatley box of terrestrials given to him by one of his cordwood clients, an old cottager from Birmingham, near Detroit, who was the best fisherman that B.D. had ever known. The man would look at the bugs in the air and the ones crawling around on the banks of the stream or beaver pond and then select the closest imitation from his fly box. B.D., who had always fished with worms or spinners, had been astounded at the man's skill and success, guiding him back to a number of top-secret beaver ponds. Once, at B.D.'s holy of holies, his more remote pond, the man had caught a four-pound brook trout on an ant imitation, an incalculable trophy, then broke down in tears and gave B.D. his six-foot Bill Summers midge rod as a present, an expensive item indeed.

So B.D. blew the opening morning by taking Marcelle to work in the Lincoln. On the way she called on the car phone to advise that she'd be a few minutes late—her feelings toward B.D. had warmed considerably since the advent of the fancy car. She pushed the electric seat back and put the heel of her good leg on the dashboard and scratched her lovely thigh with no more modesty than if she were serving a slice of banana-peach pie.

He was supposed to pick up Marten at Doris's house but figured he'd fish for a couple of hours first. Marten had been distressed by success of late. Not only had the gumshoe been withdrawn but the university had announced to the press that no excavation would begin until their right to do so had been established in court. Marten was pissed that his infighting skills had sent the excitement flying out a dirty legal window. He was reassured, though, when his Ann Arbor spy reported that Shelley and some other graduate students were still coming up to Grand Marais in May to survey the site, a technical exercise to establish the boundaries of the dig. To Marten that was blasphemy enough to plan some sort of assault, especially since he was running low on money, his troops from Wisconsin were getting surly and restless, and his latest arts fellowship required that he be back at UCLA in mid-June to head a colloquium: "Will Whitey Ever See Red?"

While B.D. was struggling to make it along the creek into the swamp to where a burbling spring emptied its contents into a stream, causing a deeper hole, Delmore was taping a note to the Lincoln's windshield: "B.D., take this auto back to the dealer. I know him and also know you didn't sign your right name. I won't tell if you return the auto. You should know that falsifying a credit application can get you three to five years. Your guardian angel, Delmore."

Delmore was splenetic over Marten, who reminded him of the low types who stuffed the confines of Vegas, full of glassy-eyed greed and rabid behavior. Delmore had tried to talk to Doris about the problem but she was mostly pleased that Marten wasn't violent like David Four Feet and had limited his criminal activities to credit cards, dope, and an infatuation with fireworks that had started early. Delmore even stopped by to see Gretchen, hoping she could figure out how to extricate B.D. from Marten's clutches. She began the encounter in a hyper-abusive state over Delmore and Fritz's con job in regard to B.D.'s accident, relenting enough to hear the old man out.

"He's just a big baby," Delmore said. "He acts so ordinary he can't see anything coming. If you don't help, he'll end up in the Big House." Delmore had a flash where he envisioned B.D. as James Cagney up on a tower, taunting the police, firing on them until he was riddled with bullets and his world burst into eternal flames. "In the old times he could have gotten along acting that way but nowadays the world is full of sharp edges."

Gretchen promised she'd look into the matter and Delmore left the employment office casting about mentally for reinforcements. Back home it occurred to him to call his third cousin Carol, since B.D.'s eyes had lighted up when he met her at the powwow. Her family were fire-breathing traditionalists and had always made Delmore feel uncomfortable, as they thought he had the makings of a spiritual leader and shouldn't have run off to Detroit to make money. While at college Carol also worked as a stringer for the Native newspaper in Minnesota, and her mother had proudly sent Delmore some of Carol's articles, which were dry and analytical. The thinking of the sanest of the Anishinabe seemed to be you could only fight the white man for land and fishing and hunting rights with superior lawyers, since the entire white modus operandi was conducted in legalistic rather than moral terms.

He called Carol and she wasn't encouraging, saying she was aware of what Marten, B.D., and the other worthless nitwits were up to—all you had to do was read the newspapers—but she'd give it a try to honor Delmore. The only other thing Delmore could think of was to withhold the fifty-bucks-a-week payment but Fritz had warned against any loss of punctuality that might invalidate the agreement. Delmore held his turtle claw necklace to his chest, trying to remember the details of an old movie about an alcoholic woman called *Leave Her to Heaven.*

Moment by moment, B.D.'s days altered in mood from manic confidence to feeling like a dead fish, the contents of his life dissolving in the push-comes-to-shove slag heap that is the substance of nearly everyone's life, but a conflict with which he had little experience. He dreamt twice of the Munising judge's stern warning to stay out of Alger County, and in the dream the judge's face was scaly green and his tongue forked like a snake's.

After the night in the cabin he had tried to see Marcelle but the proprietor of the diner told him she had flown the coop back to her husband up at the air base. B.D. couldn't help but see a very pink, featherless chicken flying above the forest from Escanaba to Gwinn, soaring low over one of his fishing spots at the confluence of the West Branch and the Big Escanaba, a pink chicken with women's parts dipping her wings goodbye. Marcelle had been the best he ever had, saving perhaps Shelley, who wouldn't have been afraid of the dark at the cabin like Marcelle had been. According to Marcelle, way down where she lived cabins out in the swamps were threatened day and night by alligators longer than a car and moccasins bigger around than a man's arm. The fishing was supposedly good but given the other horrors it reaffirmed B.D.'s notion that he lived in the right place.

That afternoon Marten tracked him down at the cabin where B.D. had been rigging a rope and small pulley to hang his bearskin. While he was out fishing some mice had worked over a paw and he felt that in itself this was a dire omen. Marten was utterly pissed and lectured B.D. on his failure as a limo driver and revolutionary, saying that he was nothing but a pussy-crazed backwoods rooster. B.D. was inattentive to the dressing-down, lost in the thought that his beloved skin had been raped by rodents while he was fucking off elsewhere.

It was definitely time to pay attention to the things that mattered, though he couldn't pin them down with Marten prancing around and shouting. He took the cane that had replaced the crutches and jerked Marten's ankle, upending him, putting the foot of his good leg on Marten's neck, and explained Delmore's note about the car purchase. He released the foot pressure and Marten scrambled up, white-faced with rage.

"I'm fucking sick of your middle-class worries. Let's go. Everyone's waiting for rehearsals. But if you want to betray the people over a car, maybe you should stay here and trade your balls for another can of beans." Marten hurled a can of beans through a window which delayed their departure until B.D. made repairs with cardboard and duct tape.

Rehearsals turned out to be sort of fun because there was a case of cold beer and the day was warm and sunny. Marten played the director as the six Wisconsin braves rushed out of a pine thicket and mimicked a rifle attack on the fort, shooting B.D. and Fred, who stood in open windows, at which point B.D. and Fred would fall backward on cushions. When B.D.'s leg got better they would fall from a platform up on the top edge along with some other white boys they'd hire. Rose, in the part of a vicious squaw, would run into the fort and cut off everyone's ears and balls and reemerge with a full bloody platter, what Marten called "a real showstopper." B.D.

wondered if this wasn't going too far for tourists and Marten said his integrity required "absolute historical verisimilitude," to which they all nodded in sage though uncomprehending assent.

The Wild Wild Midwest Show would be repeated every half hour between ten AM and six PM, and the charge to the inevitable hordes of tourists would be five bucks a head. B.D. quickly toted up that that would be sixteen plummets a day in addition to driving Marten around to keep his hands free for the phone. It would be a real busy summer, but then Marten assured him five percent of the net proceeds might well be an astronomical amount, certainly enough for a new custom van to replace the Studebaker.

They were all feeling effusive and glittery, a true showbiz high aided by the beer and joints Marten rolled, when up drove Carol to throw a wet blanket on the afternoon. She was calm and deliberate which made her points more effective, accusing them of political adventurism, histrionics, meddling, interfering in a process of grave legal consequences that tribal leaders and their white legal allies were already dealing with in negotiations with the university's archaeologists and anthropologists. Marten was too stoned to deal with her, and she insulted him in Anishinabe, then turned to the six Wisconsin warriors and began shrieking at them in the same language. Marten had forgotten most of the words he did know, and helplessly watched three of the men pack up their Harleys and the other three scatter to hide in the woods. Marten, in his dope haze, flapped his arms like a wounded crow, thinking that if all the Native women in America joined the feminists, they could blow the country sky high. It would be a real party, he thought, relieved as Carol drove off.

B.D. generally avoided dope, as it made him cry at the beauty of nature or women, depending on where he was, then fall dead asleep, waking up an hour or so later with a passionate need for a cheeseburger. He was busy weeping over the afternoon light shining off Lake Michigan when Gretchen drove up, looked around with an angry maddened glare, especially at Marten, and drew B.D. aside.

"You're coming with me. I can't bear to see that dipshit lead you into prison."

"It's too late for that," B.D. said, carried away by waves of sentimentality, his throat filling with sobs. He couldn't seem to get off the upended pail he was sitting on. He wanted to stand and embrace Gretchen goodbye.

"It's not too late for anything, goddammit!"She stooped beside him and took a hand. "You can finish painting the rooms minus that slut."

"Nope. We move out at midnight tomorrow. I have nothing to look forward to. Our love was never meant to be." The tears were still streaming but he felt the approach of sleep. He buried his face in his hands, thinking that he'd likely fall off the bucket, but then, worse things had happened. She scratched his head as she had her girlhood dog so many years ago. He heard her walk away across the gravel and her car start. With tremendous effort he lifted his head but she was gone.

When they were fully conscious B.D. and Marten drove off to get topographical maps, then on a whim they picked up Berry and Red at Doris's and took them to the Burger King for cheeseburgers, though as a precaution B.D. settled on the outside carry-out window. Marten let Berry make bird and animal noises to the operator on the car phone, and at Red's request Marten dropped a lit string of Zebra firecrackers out the window as they left the Burger King. B.D. had snooped in Marten's tote bag and it was full of wonders, including a couple of swiped license plates, all sorts of fireworks, dozens of credit cards, and various prescription bottles full of ominous-looking pills, a couple of slingshots, a makeup kit to disguise Marten in criminal situations.

That evening for their farewell dinner Delmore had made a batch of snapping turtle soup. B.D.'s spirits were diffused into melancholy by scratched Bach organ music on the old Zenith phonograph that Delmore said he had bought back in 1956. Delmore paid him a week ahead on the allowance, which was somewhat startling but Delmore said he had had a dream that B.D. was going away and would miss most of the summer of beautiful clouds, Delmore's favorite natural objects.

"You mean jail?" B.D. was nervous.

"Worse than jail but not death. I sent you a plane ticket and you came home in a new haircut afflicted with insanity. You lost the last part of your ticket and I had to drive clear over to Minneapolis to pick you up. Then the dream ended."

B.D. pushed his luck on the solemn occasion and tried to get some information on his parents, but Delmore just held up his hands and said "Nope." They played a game of cribbage and B.D. had the specific feeling Delmore had cheated while he went to the bathroom. It was only a matter of thirty cents, and he supposed that to stay ahead in this life you had to work at it all the time. When they said goodbye Delmore gave him his first hug since he was a boy and had brought Delmore a mess of trout.

It was a warm night for May, with bright roundish clouds scudding across the moon, and the ravens croaked above him as he passed under their roosting tree. There was also the call of the whip-poor-will from down by the creek, the mournful notes doom-ridden and settling beneath his breastbone. How could he leave this lovely place for a series of acts that might land him in prison? He stopped to think things over in the cabin clearing amid the friendly whine of mosquitoes. All of the ifs of his life descended on him: he could have been a preacher, a licensed welder, a captain or even a mate on an ore freighter, an important guy in a high skyscraper, a world-famous lover. Instead, he felt like the small print of a painting in Grandpa's living room called *Orphan in a Storm* where a tyke in a thin coat faced the wintry blasts alone, perhaps to die a frozen death. Grandpa would never tell him whether the kid died or not, though he did warn him against trying to fight the battles of others. He certainly wasn't an Indian, or not enough so that it mattered. It wasn't as if a noble and ghostly voice had told him to further defend the burial site he had betrayed. He had already gotten his ass in a sling trying to balance that score. But maybe not enough of a sling, and as he drew closer to the cabin he felt, at least for a moment, that he should die for this cause. It was a real difficult concept for him but there was no question that he had fallen in love and betrayed his honor. Shelley was a beautiful woman and she had dangled him on strings as if he were Howdy Doody, finagled his secret, paid him off, and sent him packing. "That bitch!" he screamed at the night.

In the cabin it occurred to him that he had done so much worrying he had been neglecting his drinking. He poured the last two ounces of a pint, then remembered that Delmore, the tightwad peckerhead, hadn't given him his new ration. A dim lightbulb lit up when he recalled that the burial site couldn't be more than a mile from the Luce County line. If he parked on the main logging road south of Potter Creek, then walked up the trail across the makeshift bridge, he would only be a half mile from the site and maybe be able to get back to Luce County before being caught. Perhaps he could wear a disguise. He had always fantasized about having a giant ruffed grouse costume to scare snowmobilers. Maybe a giant beaver or woodchuck costume, but they were all out of the question. In the pale yellow light cast by the oil lamps he stared up at his hanging bearskin. Of course it was sacred, but then so was the burial site. He couldn't very well leave his most prized possession behind. He hadn't slept outside in it yet, as Claude had instructed, because the nights had been pretty cold. Also he had forgotten to. He lowered the skin with the clothesline and pulley and embraced it, his father bear. He filled a plastic milk bottle with cold water, grabbed his mosquito dope, and headed out near the raven platform, wrapping himself in the skin and staring at the moon as if she might tell him something. He had thrown a nice, fat roadkill raccoon up on the platform a few days before and he hoped he might wake up to ravens. There was the mildly troubling thought that bears can help you if you stay out in their world, but not in your own. Time will tell, as Grandpa used to say.

B.D. awoke at dawn from bear dreams to a very real bear, a full adult weighing over two hundred pounds, its neck craning toward the carrion on the raven platform while the ravens whirled and pitched, trying to drive the bear away. The air was thickish and dew-laden, and when B.D. growled at the bear it scooted off through the grass in a shower of mist, turning for an instant at the edge of the clearing to see the source of the noise rising upward from the grass.

The Muskol had worked fine on the mosquitoes save for a protruding ankle covered with welts. B.D. scratched, yawned, shivered, peed, figuring it had been the best night of sleep ever, peering out now and then at the drifting moon from beneath the bear's jaw. His mind was empty, clear as a ringing bell or spring water, and he did not say what ancient warriors had said on the eve of battle: Today is a good day to die. Such an awesome utterance would have distracted him from the course that was set, locked into, predestined by everything that had happened to him in the past two years.

Out in Doris's yard he played a version of ring-around-the-rosie with Berry while Marten ate his breakfast and packed. He and Berry twirled until they were dizzy, then Berry would shriek like an osprey and they would throw themselves on the ground. It made his knee hurt so they stopped and he showed her the incision scar which she traced gravely with a forefinger. The school bus arrived and Red came running out with his lunch bucket, yelling to B.D. to "kick ass."

Out at the fort they had their war council on a picnic table pilfered from a roadside park, moving the table inside after a few minutes because Marten's paranoia was growing by the moment.

B.D.'s attention was distracted by a pail of fresh smelt the Wisconsin warriors had seined the night before, also by the two cases of beer and loaves of bread he had noted in Fred's truck. That morning he had been full of bears and ravens, and after his last cup of coffee at the cabin he decided to fast to prepare for battle. Now a couple of hours later he had changed his mind about fasting. Of all possible meals God had concocted, fresh fried smelt with salt, bread and butter, and a couple of cold beers were one of the best. It was like Jesus with the loaves and fishes for the multitude.

Marten stirred him by barking, "B.D., are you in a pussy trance? Pay attention. You know the fucking area and we don't."

Luckily one of the braves and big Fred could properly read a topographical map, so B.D. was able to trace their intended route from Escanaba east to Grand Marais, then south into the outback, on only thinly defined log roads. B.D. was startled to discover that one of the warriors had been a schoolteacher and another a master sergeant in the army. They never said much but even B.D. sensed that they had a purity of intent lacking in both him and Marten. Perhaps even Rose had it. Meanwhile, he and Marten would be coming up from the south, walking about a mile in the dark before they started their cherry bomb and M-80 barrage at first light. Rose would be in Fred's 4WD pickup and the braves would haze the camp on their motorcycles. Rose was going to leap out of the truck and throw red paint on the anthropologist campers, for whatever reason. Fred's noble mission was to subdue any aggression with his bare hands, for which he was eminently qualified. Fred told B.D. that ever since he was a baby he had liked to knock heads, and that was what made him a successful football scholar in the Big Ten until he had pummeled an assistant coach into a rag doll.

When the wind turned and fog came in off Lake Michigan, B.D. started a bonfire as a tip-off to start thinking about a smelt fry. The fucking hogs must have hit the Burger King before he showed up, he thought peevishly. When the coals were ready he raked a flat bed of them aside, set the Dutch oven in place, and filled it half full with oil. Since the smelt were small there was no need to go through the onerous duty of cleaning them, to which no one but Fred objected. "Then clean your own, asshole white boy," Rose said. There was no flour to dust them in, but there was a lot worse things to be without, B.D. said, whipping the bottle of hot sauce out of his coat to applause.

They ate the whole pailful and drank most of the beer, sleeping it off until near sundown. There was a quarrel about omens when the sunset made the foggy lake look like it was on fire. Marten said sententiously, "We push off at midnight."

B.D. went back in the woods to gather firewood and the notion occurred to him that he could keep on going. But no, the cards were on the table, the dice and gauntlet had been thrown, the genie had been unleashed, the circus animals were ready to make war. Fred wanted to sing "We Shall Overcome" but no one could remember the words beyond "someday"and their voices trailed off to the crackling fire. Marten applied some war paint to the Wisconsin braves' faces, then went out front with Fred to change license plates on the Lincoln Town Car and Fred's pickup. Rose beat on the upended pail and sang what she knew of a war song in an eerie, quavery shriek. The braves danced around and around the fire with contorted and violent motions, a mime of war, but always keeping an intricate step to Rose's thumping. B.D. thought the braves sure beat hell out of anyone dancing on *American Bandstand,* a program he had watched with Frank back at the Dunes Saloon for the obvious reason of all the beautiful pussy, especially the black girls. The immense difference was that the dance of the three warriors scared the shit out of him, as did Rose's chanting. Fred and Marten came back and one of the braves grabbed B.D., forcing him to dance with his cane in hand, then all were dancing right up until departure. Marten made everyone take a black beauty, a type of magnum speed, to ensure alertness. Fred, Rose, and the braves were sent up and over by

Route 28 while Marten and B.D. would take Route 2 over to 77. In case either group got stopped by the police the others could carry out the mission.

B.D. had been bright enough to let the black beauty spansule slip under his tongue, then to spit it in the weeds before getting into the car. The world was going fast enough all by itself without cranking up your brain. One night his salvage partner, Bob, had chopped up some white crosses and hoovered them, leaving a line for B.D. to snort before going out to a bar. B.D. had drunk ten drinks instead of the usual three, danced alone for an hour in front of the jukebox to Janis Joplin, slept with his feet in the river to slow down the world, and caught a bad cold.

In the car Marten was rattling on as if he had way too many batteries, so B.D. listened closely to the undercurrent of the radio on a golden oldies station and it was like hearing all of your used-up emotions. Before Manistique he had a brainstorm, to which Marten agreed, and called Frank at the Dunes Saloon from the car phone. Marten's Ann Arbor spy had been right on the money. Frank had snuck up for a look-see in case B.D. called, but all Shelley and her friends were doing was pounding in stakes and measuring. Frank hadn't seen a single shovel but had noticed a couple of deputies from Munising on the closest log road, no doubt waiting for a possible appearance by B.D. Also, when Shelley and the other graduate students came in the bar they had a real big guy with them who wore a sport coat and didn't act at all smart like a college graduate does. In addition, the man drank boilermakers, and Frank supposed the guy was someone Shelley's father had sent along to look after her.

Marten was thrilled by the news but B.D.'s sole operable thought was how he was going to outrun the deputies if they showed up, what with a bum leg and a cane. The main thing going for the Windigos was the earliness of the assault and the weather, which was getting bad with the wind coming around from the northwest and rain turning to sleet, not an uncommon thing for May in an area that has seen sparse snowflakes on the Fourth of July. B.D. was not one to deny his emotions, and as they drew near Old Seney Road off Lavender Corners he remembered Grandpa's remarks about Italian soldiers turning to froth and jelly. If you added incipient diarrhea and strange needle pains shooting through the neck, B.D. thought, you'd be right on the money.

When he turned off onto the final log road he made a prayer to a god unknown. The rain and sleet were picking up and the wind was bending the treetops. Marten had flicked on the dome light and was sorting through his munitions, stuffing them in a parka pocket. B.D. mused that if Marten caught on fire there would be shreds of him all over the landscape. One blockbuster was too big for the slingshot and Marten announced that it could only be used in the manner of a grenade if the enemy drew too close or chose to pursue them, or in any way hindered their escape.

"Where we escaping to?" B.D. asked, peering into the dark for the narrow trail that ran to the north. The trail had once been used by off-road vehicles until he had laced it with carpet nails which had settled the noise problem. He had also weakened a small wood bridge over a culvert they used.

"Westwood. I got a colloquium." Marten now had his ordnance sorted, jacket zipped, and was beating out a dashboard tattoo to the fading song "Young Girl (Get Out of My Mind)."

B.D. decided to pretend he knew what a colloquium was. He certainly remembered that Westwood was in California, which was a definite violation of the dead chief's advice not to go south of Green Bay, Wisconsin. More troubling was the notion that trout season had just begun and he needed to check out certain streams north of Escanaba he hadn't fished since his youth. His favorite fly, along with the muddler, Adams, and woolly worm, was the bitch creek nymph, a name of ineluctable sonority.

"Where am I supposed to fish in California?"

"They got the whole ocean, you jerk-off."

B.D. had pulled up alongside the trail and Marten was itchy to get going. It was a scant half hour before first light.

"I don't think I could handle the ocean. It doesn't move like a creek. There aren't any eddies or undercut banks." Now he was feeling plaintive.

"There's a pond in a botanical garden that's chock full of orange carp." Marten jumped out of the car and turned on his flashlight, his back to the wind-driven rain.

B.D. got out shivering and remembered that for the five-hundredth time he had forgotten a warm coat just because the day had dawned bright and fair. The thin army-surplus fatigues were no good in this fucking weather, so there was no choice but to haul the bearskin out of the trunk. It sure as hell had kept a living bear warm, he thought, and now it's my turn. Marten fidgeted as he helped tie the bindings and then they were off into the moist and windy darkness, the small flashlight beam a puny comfort.

Day dawned, but not much of it. The clouds were nearly on the ground but the rain had stopped. B.D. was cozy in his wraparound bearskin while Marten jumped and flapped to keep warm, studying the windage for the slingshot. Through Delmore's spyglass B.D. dimly made out three tents, plus Shelley's Land Rover and a big black 4WD pickup down the hill about fifty yards. He also glassed the closest log road, about a half mile away at the end of a long gully, for the possible sight of a cop car. It seemed to be getting darker again and he looked up from the spyglass only to receive a big raindrop in his left eyeball. He flipped the bear head back over his own as Marten readied the first shot which would be an M-80. They knelt behind a huge white pine stump, B.D. flicked the Zippo, and Marten sent the first charge soaring toward the encampment, followed instantly with a succession of three cherry bombs. B.D. went back to the spyglass and saw a big man running down toward the pickup. Marten sent an M-80 in the man's direction and he hit the grass, rolling downhill and hiding behind a stump. The rain began in earnest again and B.D. put down the spyglass because the Zippo was too hot on his other hand. He took out a spare butane, then noticed Shelley sprinting toward them, following the coursing fuses as if they were tracers. She was about halfway to them, dressed attractively in bra and panties and screaming when she wheeled, hearing the three motorcycles and Fred's truck attacking the camp.

"B.D., you motherfucker!" she screamed, at a dead run again. Before B.D. could stop him, Marten sent a cherry bomb in her direction but it didn't slow her down. Marten grabbed the spyglass and studied the mayhem at the camp, still stooped behind the stump in case the big guy started shooting. It didn't look good for Fred. The big guy was clubbing him into the ground despite the fact that Rose was on his back, jerking at his hair. The motorcyclists were doing a fine job on the tents.

"B.D., you motherfucker!" Shelley screamed again. He was swept away, peeking over the stump, watching her nearly nude form running toward him in the rain. If only it were for love, he thought, jumping out at the last moment with a mighty howl. Her bare feet slipped from beneath her as she threw herself backward, her screams now in terror rather than anger. He was on her like a bear, crawling over her, growling and howling, giving her a very wet kiss.

"It's just me, your long-lost love," he whispered, before he felt Marten frantically pulling him off. She opened her eyes for a moment, then rolled sideways, covering her face with her hands. Marten was yelling something and when B.D. stood he could see the big black truck heading toward them, jouncing sky high on the rolling ground. B.D. trotted and hobbled back toward the culvert bridge, turning to see Shelley running off toward the camp and the pickup closing in on Marten, still kneeling behind the stump and lighting his blockbuster. He held the fuse just short of disaster, then pitched it onto the pickup's hood. The big man threw himself sideways, the bomb went off, and the driverless pickup crashed into the stump. Marten ran for it and when he reached B.D. they watched the big guy wandering back toward the encampment, still in his underpants.

A scant but speedy hour and a half later they had crossed the International Bridge at the Soo, and in a few hours were in a town on the Superior coast with the unlikely name of Wawa. B.D. had wanted to stop for breakfast which had astonished Marten, who had said, "We're on the lam, asshole." Back in the woods near Hawk Junction they slept for a while at the hideout cabin of a friend of Marten's, a Canadian Mohawk on the run from the government, then they traded the Lincoln Town Car even-up for a muddy, brown Ford Taurus station wagon with bald tires and ninety-seven thousand miles on the odometer. The Mohawk fried up a panful of venison which B.D. relished even though it tasted of cedar branches. The rule of thumb was that you never poached a deer before July Fourth when their bitter winter feed was out of their system. While Marten attached one of his fresh license plates to the Taurus, B.D. leaned against the vehicle thinking about how lovely Shelley looked in the rain. The worm began to turn. He doubted that she would ever forgive him but he knew she wouldn't forget him. They headed west.

Westward Ho

In Westwood Brown Dog recognized a cloud as one he had seen several years before over two thousand miles to the east out near Fayette on Big Bay de Noc. The cloud was sure enough the same one, no question about it. The question was what route did it take to California, to Westwood in particular? This cloud sighting was not remarkable in itself. In a lifetime in the woods he had witnessed three different birds (a raven, a red-tailed hawk, and a lowly robin) drop dead off their separate perches, and once while illegally pillaging a shipwreck in Lake Superior at a depth of a hundred feet or so, a very large passing lake trout had picked that moment to drop, wobbling slow and lifeless to the lake's floor. There was a moment's temptation to pluck it up and stow it in his diving bag with some brass fittings from the sunken ship, but then it occurred to him that the fish had achieved a peaceful death and it wouldn't be quite right to fry it up, douse it with hot sauce, and eventually turn it into a turd. As a child his grandfather was wont to say when B.D. was sullen or depressed, "Keep your chin up, Bucko. We all end up as worm turds."

The cloud passed away, replaced by blue. B.D. stretched in his nest beneath the immense leaves of the taro bush (*Colocasia esculenta*) in the U.C.L.A. botanical gardens, a bush, he decided, that was one of God's most peculiar inventions, so unlike his native flora in Michigan's Upper Peninsula as to be from another planet. But beautiful as his dome of vast green leaves was it did not help Brown Dog locate himself as was his habit on waking. This was to break the thrall of his vivid dream life, a spell that dissipated easily when you said, "I'm in the cabin where it's about forty degrees. The wind out of the northwest at thirty knots. November first and if I hadn't had the extra poke of whiskey I would have got up in the night and fed the stove and it would have been fifty in here instead of forty, a weenie-shrinking dawn." That sort of thing. How can you start the day without knowing where you are?

Or, perhaps more important, why? The answer to which is bound to be lengthy, imprecise, blurred by the urge to think that where you are is bound to be the right place on your short and brutish passage. Seven days ago he had been in the Upper Peninsula and now he was under a taro bush in Westwood in what is euphemistically called greater Los Angeles (what with lesser Los Angeles throbbing to be released on a moment's notice and frequently springing free).

Frankly, Brown Dog was on the lam, having flown the Michigan coop with Lone Marten, an erstwhile though deeply fraudulent Indian activist, after a series of petty misdemeanors and relatively harmless felonies. His original crime had been pillaging Lake Superior shipwrecks, even removing a Native body from one, a corpse he had eventually decided might have been that of his dead father, though this conclusion was based on circumstantial evidence. Like the proverbial collapsing dominoes, this first crime seemed to lead to others, though in his own mind he was altruistic because his abrasive brushes with the law had come from his efforts to protect a secret Indian graveyard, the presence of which had been betrayed in a pussy trance with a lovely young anthropologist. Concurrent with these legal problems was the fact that Lone Marten had abandoned him in Cucamonga two days before. Brown Dog had gone into a restroom to pee and when he came out Lone Marten was gone, and when Brown Dog had asked the attendant about Lone Marten's whereabouts because his precious bearskin was in the trunk the attendant had said, "Beat it or I'll call the cops," not a very friendly welcome. He persisted, asking directions to Westwood whereupon the attendant merely pointed west. Brown Dog was a bit transfixed by the attendant's large hoop earrings which seemed inadvisable if you were going to get in a fight. Your opponent had only to grab your earrings and you were dead meat, or so he thought as he set out for the west with a somewhat heavy heart but down a road with a comforting name, Arrow Highway.

The walk from Cucamonga to Westwood is some forty-seven miles, not all that far for a man often referred to in his home area as a "walking fool." It took Brown Dog a rather leisurely thirty-six hours, making way for short cheapish meals and naps which he accomplished with the true woodsman capability of dozing with his eyes open. This didn't seem the area in which you could safely close your eyes. When he had asked Lone Marten just how many people were in Los Angeles and Lone Marten had said, "Millions and millions," the amount proved mentally indigestible. Not since the student riots in Chicago that took place while Brown Dog was a very casual student at the Moody Bible Institute had he seen this many people going to and fro. It was apparent that there was a lot going on but he wasn't sure what. Another big crowd in his life had been the Ishpeming Bugle and Firefighters Convention a few years before but there the purpose had been quite specific. Brown Dog had stood in the garage parking lot waiting for the head gasket of his van to be replaced and had watched several hundred buglers take turns doing their best. This turned out to be more than enough bugling to last a lifetime.

A forty-seven-mile walk offers plenty of time to think things over but it is the walking rather than the thinking that calms the spirit. Brown Dog had none of the raw melancholy that the well educated often feel when first encountering Los Angeles. His frame of mind was a great deal more functional with the single purpose being to retrieve his bearskin and head back to the country, wherever that might be, though he had pondered Canada as a haven that might be safe from the arm of the law, and not the lovely strip club in the Canadian Soo where the girls got down to no clothing at all, but perhaps way up on the Nipigon River on the north shore of Lake Superior. Sizable brook trout were said to be plentiful there and he could always go back to the obnoxious job of cutting pulp.

B.D.'s last walk of this length had taken place a few years before when two Grand Marais girls he had driven over to Munising had ditched him there when he had drunk too much at the Corktown Bar and walked down a grassy knoll near the harbor for a snooze. He thought himself deeply in love with one of the girls, innocently named Mary, who originally hailed from Detroit and it was she with her own dark past who had hot-wired his van and taken off for a weekend in Iron Mountain. So deep was his grief and anger over this betrayal that he walked back to Grand Marais, taking a leisurely full two days, over forty miles and sadly, or so he thought in the present, about the same distance as Cucamonga to Westwood. But much of his Munising–to–Grand Marais hike had been cross-country and except for a stop at the small store in Melstrand to pick up a few cans of pork and beans he had not viewed another human being. It was mid-May and warmish with a big moon and by the time of his first campfire he had largely gotten over Mary. Frank, his true friend and the owner of a local tavern, had warned him that Mary was "fast," the evidence being the morning that B.D. had sunk himself in Frank's bathtub, the water to which had been added a potent anti-crab medicine. There weren't any fleas that far north and Brown Dog had been puzzled by a buggy feeling all over his body, even in his eyebrows. Frank had worked construction way down in Florida and made the expert analysis from experience.

A few hours out of Cucamonga he suddenly remembered where he had heard the name before. His grandfather had listened to the Jack Benny program on Sunday evenings on their battery-operated Zenith and Jack Benny himself had often traveled through Cucamonga on the train to Hollywood. Jack Benny's buddy Rochester would sometimes yell "Cucamonga" for no apparent reason and one summer evening when there was a very small bear rummaging in their garbage pit at the far end of the garden the bear had suddenly looked up on hearing Rochester's voice. He and his friend David Four Feet, who died in Jackson Prison, were full of envy at Rochester's voice though they were incapable of imitating it and when they tried Grandfather would yell, "Batten your gob."

The memory of Jack Benny lifted his spirits and B.D.'s vision expanded from the cement beneath his feet and the narrow tunnel in front of him that his emotions up to this point had allowed. Before Jack Benny he had been trying to remember the gist of the biblical story about Ruth among the "alien corn." During his brief period at the Moody Bible Institute in Chicago the pastor from the church back home had sent a letter about Ruth among the alien corn to assuage Brown Dog's possible homesickness. Unfortunately the church had mistakenly sent B.D. the entire tuition check rather than directing it to the institute and he had squandered the money on a black waitress. The expression "head over heels in love" had always puzzled him because, though love could be physically rigorous, it didn't seem quite that acrobatic.

As his vision widened somewhat his native curiosity, surely the most valuable thing one can own, took over and he began to observe this foreign country of Los Angeles more closely and certain things became clear. For instance, millions of new cars were supposedly sold every year but you saw few of them in the Upper Peninsula except on

Routes 2 and 28 during tourist season where they were collectively parked in front of the more expensive motels in the evening. Here in Los Angeles there were countless thousands of new cars which meant the locals must be making money hand over fist. But standing on an overpass stretched above the San Gabriel River Freeway and staring down at six lanes of jam-packed traffic going bumper to bumper in both directions, he wondered why the drivers on each side of the highway just didn't trade jobs and avoid the mess. B.D. also read the sign twice but couldn't find the San Gabriel River and there were no other pedestrians to ask the river's whereabouts.

Hours before he had stopped in a small park and had been rather amazed at the flora, none of which he recognized, though he knew the names of hundreds of trees and bushes in the Upper Peninsula. The birds were also a mystery and he wondered idly at God's messiness in inventing so many species, then decided it was the messiness of nature that gave it such beauty.

He tried to extend his pursuit by the law into a gentler region of his mind to avoid the sensation that he should be looking over his shoulder even though the scene of the crime was two thousand miles to the east. He had burned the tent of two evil young anthropologists to protect his Indian graveyard, also with Lone Marten had lobbed cherry bombs and M-80 firecrackers into a protected archaeological site, the graveyard, in an attempt to drive away the despoilers. This was scarcely a high crime but his probation had dictated he could not enter Alger County though the attack engineered by Lone Marten had strayed only a few hundred yards from Luce County into Alger. The point in Brown Dog's mind was that if only the law imitated the gorgeously messy aspects of nature the judge might say "Let bygones be bygones" or something on that order. And then he could go back home, assuming that he recovered his bearskin. Delmore had mentioned that a bearskin should never be taken away from the region in which the animal had been killed because the skin sometimes still contained the spirit of the beast though B.D. suspected that Delmore often made up Indian lore when it suited his purpose.

The biggest problem on the long walk had been water. They weren't exactly giving it away in this area. He had been charged fifty cents at a fast-food place for a large Styrofoam cup of water and hadn't been able to drink it because it seemed to contain some weird chemicals. The girl behind the counter had been sympathetic to B.D.'s startled look when he tasted the water and pointed out a cooler that contained quarts of the stuff at over a dollar apiece. It was a warm day and he had no choice. He wasn't quite prepared for this experience but recalled a quarrel in Frank's Tavern over the matter of bottled water that had recently entered the Upper Peninsula. At the time he had been struggling to hear his all-time favorites, Patsy Cline and Janis Joplin, on the jukebox and Ed Mikula, the chief of the local Finns, was hollering that God's own precious water was now being sold in bottles for more than beer or gasoline per ounce. Who was behind this crime was the question at hand? When asked his opinion B.D. said that water, gasoline, and beer were equally important but not interchangeable, and he was up to walking to any number of springs he knew of to get first-rate water even in the dead of winter, a fine notion though springs in Los Angeles were unlikely so he paid the full price for a quart of water that the label said had been shipped all the way from France, a boggling idea. He imagined some secret enormous burbling spring in far-off France and wanted to question the store clerk but she was now busy. There was the immediate notion that when he got back home he need only bottle twenty quarts of water from one of his springs to make a living wage. He had stuffed a fifteen-foot pole down in one of them and it had shot back up in the air from the force of the water. If you had a hangover you could just lie there on the soft green moss, drink plenty of the cold water, and after you were still for a while the brook trout would begin swimming around again.

After the first twenty-four hours of walking the map he had bought for yet another dollar at a service station had turned soft from his sweaty hands. He had passed the confusing place where César E. Chávez Avenue became Sunset Boulevard and had bought a black lunch bucket and a green janitor's uniform at a secondhand store, the lunch bucket to carry his water and any leftovers from his snacks. He was down to forty-nine dollars but then forty-nine was also his age so this collusion somehow appeared fortuitous at least for the time being. The problem was that he was beginning to stink and needed a place to suds off before putting on the clean clothes. The janitor's shirt had the name "Ted" stamped on a pocket but then he felt it was unlikely that he'd find a shirt with his own name on it. He made his way up to Silver Lake Reservoir, clambered over the fence, and had a short swim. A number of hikers and dog walkers had hollered at him because swimming was forbidden in the city's water supply but he ignored them. The objectors had withdrawn for the same reason that two unfriendly Mexican fellows had withdrawn back near Monterey Park when Brown Dog had asked for directions. First, to all he looked rather goofy, and second in modern terms he was quite a physical specimen from his lifelong work in the woods. He didn't have the big breasts of the many bodybuilders he had seen on the streets in their tight T-shirts, but he could unload a four-hundred-pound iron woodstove from a pickup all by himself and other men tend to notice those capable of such feats. But more important, B.D. lacked a single filament of hostility in his system. Even way back in his teens when he was a champion bare-knuckle fighter in the western U.P. he was not prone to anger unless an opponent poked him in the eye. Even his anger over the soon-to-be-desecrated Indian (Anishinabe) graveyard was directed more at himself for betraying the location. In addition, he had what used to be called a "winning smile," though that wouldn't be true as he drew near the Pacific and the more prosperous areas because two teeth were prominently missing.

Under his poi or taro leaf in the botanical gardens there were a number of things to take pleasure in. He had had enough sense not to discard the neatly folded garbage bag in his back pocket. "Just when you think you won't need it anymore you will," old Claude liked to say. Claude would get in his garbage bag when he was out in the backcountry and it began to rain, or if the wind was cold he would step into his, hunch down, and pull the drawstring and have a nice curled-up snooze. Claude insisted the garbage bag was one of the great inventions of modern man along with toilet paper and galvanized buckets. Brown Dog tended to agree but mostly when he needed one. The Westwood night was tolerably warm for a northerner but the laid-out garbage bag made a nice ground cloth to protect him from moisture. His pleasure was not diminished by the fact that Westwood didn't seem to have much in the way of woods, and just before dark he noted that the small pond with a feeder rivulet contained only a dozen or so lethargic orange carp. It might have been nice to cook one on a bed of coals but a fire would doubtless draw attention and the botanical park was officially closed for the night.

A good share of his pleasure under his leafy blanket came from his grandfather's notion that you had to make the best of it wherever you were, and throughout the long hike from Cucamonga he had been pleasantly boggled by all the colors of the people he had seen who must come from many lands. Way back in school he had never been quite taken with the idea of America as a boiling pot, partly because his grandpa had used a boiling pot to scald pigs at butchering in order to scrape off the hair. Despite his hard knocks he felt a specific pleasure in all he had seen, especially along the busy part of Sunset Strip as he had continued heading west late in the afternoon. There had been literally hundreds of beautiful women though they tended to be uniformly quite thin in his terms. Delmore liked to say that you should avoid women who don't enjoy their food because that means they have real problems, but even old Delmore would have had his head turned by this plenitude. To be sure, not one of them gave him a glance but he suspected this was because of the green janitor's suit and the black lunch bucket which had the good quality he noted of making him invisible to the many police he had seen.

In fact he had become quite invisible to everyone except for a few other menial workers who nodded in greeting. When he had made his way farther west into the swank residential area of Beverly Hills he fairly had to wave in the face of a girl selling star maps which he quickly perceived had nothing to do with the constellations. He repeated his question about the whereabouts of Westwood three times before she deigned to take notice. Her eyes focused past his neck as she said that a few miles farther on he should take a left on Hilgard. There was something distinctly familiar about her and he remembered that last winter when a tree he was cutting had kicked back and injured his knee, during his convalescence Delmore had rented him a video called *Butts Galore* and this girl sure looked like one of the "butts" in the film. He couldn't help but ask her and she replied, "Maybe yes, maybe no," but a slight tinge of blush entered her cheeks. He would have tried to continue the conversation but a carload of older tourists pulled over wanting to know where Fred MacMurray lived so Brown Dog moved on. You couldn't say *Butts Galore* was a top-drawer movie but it was certainly amazing to just get into town and meet an actress you recognized. The fact of the matter was that Brown Dog hadn't seen many movies. The closest theater in one direction was in Newberry and that was over fifty miles distant, and in the other direction Marquette's theaters were over a hundred miles to the west. Delmore played old westerns on his VCR because they were cheap to rent and he hated them which gave rise to a much needed emotional life. There was also the additional shortcoming to Brown Dog who lived on a subsistence level that a price of a movie was a price of five beers at Frank's Tavern. Once as an early teen he and David Four Feet had hot-wired a

Plymouth and gone to a drive-in theater to see what was advertised as a daring sex movie. Part of it was a cartoon showing a phalanx of sperm traveling up into the womb and David had hollered out the car window, "That's me in the lead," to much general laughter and horn beeping. The movie ended with a rather skinny woman giving birth in a rather frightening close-up that could not readily be distinguished from any of the farm animals they had seen giving birth. They both agreed they could have used the fifty cents apiece to see the genitals of a classmate, Debbie Schwartz, which is what she charged, a buck a look.

After finding his botanical-garden nest Brown Dog drifted through the greenery in the last of the twilight. There was a slight evening breeze from the west, clearing the air which had all day long resembled a sheen of yellow snot with the heat close enough to body temperature to emphasize the exudate nature of the air. B.D. found a patch of bamboo and lit a match to see it more closely, noting with pleasure that the bamboo was a giant version of the cane poles he had used as a child to fish inland lakes. This bamboo was a half foot in diameter and he supposed that it was capable of landing a fish the size of a Budweiser Clydesdale. The breeze picked up further and rattled the bamboo. He thought the breeze must surely come from the Pacific Ocean and his body fairly shimmered with delight at the prospect of seeing this body of water. He had spent enough time with maps, his favorite schoolbook being the world atlas in the library, and he remembered clearly what this ocean looked like on paper. While he arranged his Hefty garbage bag on the ground his thoughts of the Pacific wavered into the image of a girl getting out of a Mercedes convertible on Sunset, and as luck would have it he had been blessed with a clear view way up her legs to her pale blue undies and slightly visible fur pieces. She had trotted down the sidewalk and into a store and he had marveled at her grace of movement, the fluid lubricant that fills such a body and makes it move so beautifully. He whispered a very old song, "I'd like to get you on a slow boat to

China," something on that order, before he slept, quite unmindful in his ordinariness that his straits were dire indeed, or that some in this immediate area of a great university, not to speak of the film business, would mistake this ordinariness as extraordinary.

Those who sleep outside a great deal know that this sleep can't aspire to the comatose aspects of hibernation that so many seem to crave from night. You might wake up a hundred times for a moment or two, allowing your senses of hearing or smell or sight in the dimmish light to test your surroundings. This is unconscious enough not to deter from rest. Brown Dog was visited by a single curious cat for a short time, and also the stars which finally made an appearance as the ambient light of the city diminished. The few times he became conscious enough his thought processes settled on simple things such as he would not be able to continue spending seven dollars a day on water. The air was quite sweet in the garden, a wonderful contrast to the fungoid odors of the motel rooms he had stayed in with Lone Marten who was armed with a dozen phony credit cards. Brown Dog had suggested that a couple of cheap sleeping bags would cost less than a night in a motel and Lone Marten had called him a fool and a "blanket ass," a pejorative term for traditional Natives. Lone Marten insisted he needed a desk at night to work on the "colloquium" he would perform at U.C.L.A. Lone Marten called him a fool so often that in Laramie B.D. had to run him up the wall by his belt so that he flopped there while B.D. asked him to stop using the word "fool," that in biblical terms it was a terrible thing to call your brother a fool. Of course from his uncomfortable position Lone Marten agreed, thinking at the time that if he weren't David Four Feet's brother he might actually be in danger with this simpleminded fool who hadn't the sense to do anything to his own advantage.

About an hour before dawn a siren howled down Hilgard Avenue and through the foliage B.D. could see the flickering amber lights of an ambulance, the yowl the most ghastly of all human-produced sounds, which had barely subsided when a medevac chopper fluttered and whacked overhead landing on the roof of the medical center that adjoined the gardens. Rather than being irritated B.D. had the feeling that these local people had the wherewithal to immediately take care of their sick or injured. A few winters before a logger friend had had some of his ass literally frozen off when he had been trapped by a fallen log for about eight hours before help came. Of course, he reminded himself, he had seen a great number of the miserably poor on his day-and-a-half walk who might be advised to walk in front of a car for a change of luck. There was an owl with an unfamiliar call directly above him and moments later the first stirring of dawn birds which always brought on an hour or so of the deepest sleep the outdoor sleeper can have, maybe a genetic remnant from a time when the predatory enemy was always nocturnal and first light meant the sweet dream of security.

Having finally figured out where he was Brown Dog was on his knees neatly brushing off and folding his garbage bags when he was approached by two garden workers, a young man and woman, who told him he wasn't allowed to sleep there. "But I already have," he said, adding that it was a truly wonderful place. They were botany graduate students and the lumpish girl tried to give him a dollar which he turned down saying he already had forty-nine dollars. He asked a few questions about the flora which they referred to as "Pacific rim," a new term for him though in his mind's eye he could see the black ink outline of the ocean in the atlas. He also asked if there was a nice woods in the vicinity where he could camp out and they thought not, though the young man added that he might check out Will Rogers State Park farther out Sunset. A mountain lion supposedly lived there, right smack-dab in Los Angeles, also lots of coyotes, not to speak of rattlesnakes and birds. This information made B.D. think that this wasn't a bad place after all. He asked the whereabouts of the "Indian office" at the university in hopes of a starting place for tracking down Lone Marten. They only said that there might be one but they didn't know where it was. They said goodbye then and when they walked off with their pruning shears the lumpish girl had begun to look pretty good. B.D. thought they could sit naked together in the carp pool near the bamboo thicket and it would be like some old movie set in a tropical island. On the way out of the garden he looked at the top of a very tall palm tree and it reminded him of one of Delmore's favorite movies, *Sands of Iwo Jima,* which B.D. didn't care for because of the endless gore. The stealthy Japanese hid at the tops of coconut trees because, according to Delmore, their heads looked like coconuts. Delmore's own head looked like a beige bowling ball, size nine, in fact, on the top of a small wiry frame.

When B.D. emerged from the garden his heart jumped and his stride quickened. What luck! Right there across Hilgard, parked illegally, was the five-year-old dirty brown Taurus station wagon, Lone Marten's car, and a rumpled and burly man was unlocking the car. Brown Dog dodged the early-morning traffic with difficulty and when he looked back at the Taurus a squad car had screeched up behind it and the burly man was leaning against the car in despair. Brown Dog's momentum, caused by a leap to escape a yellow Ferrari, was such that he was nearly in between the burly man and the cop before he could stop himself. This was a collusion of fates that afterward would stun B.D. For lack of a better thing he opened his lunch bucket and swigged the last of his water, noting too late that it definitely wasn't Lone Marten's brown Taurus. Shit, he thought, as he smiled lamely at the burly man and the cop. At the very moment a half dozen U.C.L.A. coeds, definitely sorority girls, flounced up the sidewalk singing a merry tune, all with uniformly tan brown legs and trim bottoms. While the cop glanced at the girls the burly man winked frantically at B.D. and flashed a wad of bills from his pocket. The cop looked back at the man and then at Brown Dog with irritation.

"I think you were going to drive. I could take you in," the cop said.

"I was getting a manuscript out of the car while I waited for my driver, Ted. You really shouldn't arrest me for my supposed intention. Besides, Ted drives me everywhere."

"Get in the car and start it," the cop said and Brown Dog took the keys from the man and started the car, so obviously not Lone Marten's though it was even more of a mess. It didn't, however, smell of Lone Marten's main fuel, cannabis. The car phone, the first of his life, began to ring and the man jumped in the passenger side, saying, "It's the coast."

"We're already on the coast, fuckhead," the cop said and then demanded B.D.'s driver's license. "You're the driver. Where's your license?"

"Yes, sir," B.D. said, knowing with cops that politeness was the primary move. He was somewhat proud that he kept his driver's license current though in fact the renewal form constituted the only mail he ever received, not being a member of any organization or even owning a Social Security number. The cop appeared as if he were going to return to his squad car to check the license, then changed his mind saying that he was originally from Livonia which was part of Detroit and had been up deer hunting around Curtis which wasn't all that far from Grand Marais. The cop had also fished perch at Les Cheneaux and walleye near Rapid River, two species that bored B.D. though he didn't say so. B.D. asked him why he had moved to L.A. and the cop said he had always wanted to become an actor. As they shook hands the cop stooped and looked over at the burly man who was in the middle of saying on the phone, "If you think I'd do a rewrite for a hundred thou you can suck a Republican's dick."

"Bob, shut up and listen to me. Don't ever in your wildest dreams try to drive a car in this city again. You're grounded forever, Bob. You'd do a year minimum no matter what lawyer you got. If you so much as touch a steering wheel you'll be eating and shitting with beaners and jigs for three hundred and sixty-five days."

"You shouldn't talk to me like that, you blue-belt pansy. I was a United States marine," Bob said, hanging up the car phone.

"You were never a marine, Bob. We know your record. You're only a writer." The cop walked off as if he had won the day and B.D. turned to Bob wondering how he dared call a cop a "blue-belt pansy," so he asked him.

"The U.S. Constitution. Also he wants a part in a movie. He tried to get my last D.U.I. reduced but lower-echelon cops can't swing anything. I went over the curb on San Vincente onto the median because it was hot and I wanted to park under a tree for shade."

"What did you blow?" Brown Dog asked. Driving under the influence was a big-ticket item in the U.P., especially around Marquette and Escanaba.

"I blew a point two three which is slightly major." He gestured for B.D. to get moving and they headed north up Hilgard toward Sunset. "The name's Bob Duluth. Where do you want to go?"

Brown Dog said "the ocean" but the question was puzzling in that he had supposed Bob had places to go for meetings or whatever. There was also the unnerving idea that this was the most unlikely way he had ever gotten a job and there was the question of whether life should be changing this fast. He explained to Bob his theory about not driving over forty-nine and Bob said if you did that on the freeways you'd get your basic tailpipe up your ass. Bob's language was a strange mixture to B.D., half the low-rent vulgarity of pulp cutters and construction workers, and half the peculiar kind of elevated talk B.D. identified with woods yuppies, as they were called, richer people that built in remote places way up north in order to be close to nature. These were often nice enough folks but their conversational patterns were quite intricate. B.D. had cut firewood for a couple in their thirties who had had a top-rate crew come all the way from Minnesota to build them an elaborate log house. They overpaid him for firewood and he had tried to give them some venison (illegal out of season) in return, but they were devout vegetarians. This was quite odd to B.D., one of whose ambitions was to eat a porterhouse every day for a week if he ever had the wherewithal. The couple had even invited him to take a sauna with them and the woman was absolutely bare naked and a knockout at that. He feared he'd get an erection but then he had a hangover and they raised the heat level to an unbearable degree to "purify their bodies." They fed him a vegetarian meal with some vegetables and grains dressed up like meat which was pretty good though later in the evening he had one of Frank's special half-pound burgers. They had become distanced when he had run into the woman outside the I.G.A. grocery store and she had said, "I feel good about myself." B.D. had simply asked, "Why?" and she had totally delaminated and started screeching that he was a "thankless bastard" right there on the street which made the locals think he'd had an affair with her. Sadly, this was not true. Once when he had delivered firewood the couple had been doing their yoga exercises on the sundeck and the woman who was wearing a bikini had her heels locked behind her neck when she waved at him. He unloaded and stacked two full cords of beech while they were flopping around on the sundeck and he was quite amazed at their contortions.

Bob fell asleep in the car after using words as varied as "etiolate," "shitsucker," "fractious," and "motherfucker." Brown Dog turned off into the Will Rogers State Park out on Sunset just to check it out as he had a feeling the job might not last and he might need to set up camp. The park fairly made his mouth water as there were few people around and the hills looked endless. Just the idea that there was a mountain lion roaming around made all of the multimillion-dollar homes in the distance look rather toylike and puny. The yoga couple never had any houseguests at their "retreat," or so they called it, and the locals wondered why they had two bathrooms.

Before Bob dozed off B.D. had heard a few items from his past that seemed a bit jumbled and possibly fibs. Bob said that he initially meant to be a scholar of real old literature from England, had taught in Ashland in northern Wisconsin, then at the University of Wisconsin in Madison which he considered his home. His wife and the son and daughter attending college were all fatally ill. This raised a lump in B.D.'s throat though only moments later Bob said his son was a Big Ten gymnast and his daughter a long-distance runner who had placed high in the Chicago Marathon, and his wife ran her own landscape gardening business. B.D. tried to imagine them all plodding to their strenuous activities shot through with mortal illness. No matter how well they were doing Bob felt that it behooved him to make money to insure comfort in their doomed futures. In successive summers Bob Duluth had written three mystery novels that did very well that featured a midwestern professor who was alone among all men in sensing the true and pervasive evil in the world. For the past few years Bob had been in and out of Hollywood to make the vast sums of money required to pay for the treatment of his gymnast, runner, and businesswoman. He dared B.D. to ask how much and B.D. asked, "How much?" and Bob said, "Over a grand a day," an inconceivable sum to B.D. It was, however, in this matter and Bob's current occupation as a "screenwriter" that B.D. sensed the skunk in the woodpile. Back in high school there had a been a teacher fresh out of the University of Michigan, rather than one of the state's many teachers colleges, who was much disliked by the other staff for being too smart for his own good. This young teacher knew how everything in the world worked and, what's more, could explain it to his students. He cut up a bunch of movie film and somehow developed it, put it on a wind-up roller and spun it, showing how moving pictures worked. It was still as impressive to B.D. years later and the teacher hadn't made any mention of anyone writing the spinning film. Even though Bob Duluth said he only invented the entire stories for films he still seemed on thin ice. Unfortunately this beloved teacher had been caught tinkering with Debbie Schwartz on a woodland field trip, the same girl who made pin money showing her underpants. Debbie was fifteen at the time, though in most respects older than the teacher. The students widely protested the teacher's firing but the school board was adamant. Brown Dog and David Four Feet did their part by throwing dog shit and Limburger cheese in the blower down in the school's furnace room which evacuated the school. B.D. heard that years later Debbie and the grand teacher had been married and were living in a mansion near San Francisco, the teacher having invented new functions for computers.

As they continued on toward Malibu, Bob Duluth was still asleep, snoring in fact, with an unattractive bubble of sputum on his lips. B.D. figured the man must work pretty hard because there were bags under his eyes and he twitched in his sleep like Grandpa used to when he worked two straight shifts, sixteen hours, at the sawmill.

B.D. wasn't quite ready for one of the signal experiences of his life. He had been following a slow-moving green Chrysler driven by a blue-haired lady when he looked up on a rise in the road and there was the Pacific Ocean. He drove off on the narrow shoulder, got out, and leaned against the car hood, at first with his face in his hands and peeking out between his fingers because the view was far too much to be absorbed wide open. He felt choky as if there were a lump of coal beneath his breastbone and his body buzzed in a way not unlike the minutes before sex. If he had known Beethoven's "Hymn to Joy" he would have been hearing it, and the vast, rumpled bluish green water drew on his soul so that his soul only spoke the language of water, forgetting all else. He simply couldn't wait to touch it with his hands, so he jumped back in the Taurus and sped off with Bob Duluth opening one eye in careless nonrecognition Who is driving me and who cares? I've been up all night eating what's left of my heart, over an actress at that. A Brown Dog driving a brown car.

In Malibu, B.D. parked in the nearly empty lot of a restaurant, locked the car, and made his way down to the beach. He knelt and felt the water, colder than he expected, about like Lake Superior in May. A wave submerged his shoes with a delicious feeling, his feet, so unused to cement, still sore from the jaunt from Cucamonga. A big sailboat came by, its rail nearly buried in the water. B.D. waved and two folks in yellow slickers waved back, which gave him a good feeling about the human race. He sat on the beach for an hour in a state of total forgetfulness about his new job, watching seabirds that resembled the rare piping plover but were a bit larger, no doubt cousins. His mind was a peaceful blank other than thinking that after he retrieved his bearskin and before he headed back to Michigan to face the music, or better yet northern Ontario which was the U.P.'s cousin, he'd spend a couple of nights on the beach wrapped in his bearskin, and also a couple of nights on the ridge he had seen up in Will Rogers State Park. Of course there were many signs that said "No Camping" but then the world had become full of signs that said "No Something," so to avoid suffocation you generally had to ignore them. In the Upper Peninsula such signs were generally filled with bullet holes from those acting out of resentment or for convenient target practice. During the worst of the bug season, late May and June, when the mosquitoes and blackflies could be irritating, B.D. on breezy nights liked to sleep on a stretch of fifteen miles of deserted shore of Lake Superior, a different place each time, though most of the routine was invariable. First he'd get a loaf of homemade bread from an old lady he cut wood for, catch a few fish, buy a six-pack, start a driftwood fire, fry the fish in bacon fat in an old iron skillet, and eat it with the bread, salt, and the bottle of Tabasco he always carried in his old fatigue jacket, wrapped in duct tape so it wouldn't clink against his pocketknife. He'd finish the six-pack in the late twilight near the summer solstice that far north, nearly eleven in the evening, scrub the pan with sand, then get naked and scrub his body in the cold surf. A lady might come ambling along though this had never happened and it wouldn't do to be unclean.

When he reached the car and unlocked it Bob Duluth was still sleeping and now sweating profusely because the car was very hot in the midmorning sun. B.D. started the car but the air conditioner made a weird noise and wouldn't work so he opened all the windows. Bob had begun to make a keening noise in the midst of a bad dream and his hands flapped and clutched his face. At first B.D. couldn't think of what to do other than run for it, but opted for turning on the radio real loud. Luckily the dial was on a Mexican station and a woman's voice was full of passion and deep lyrical sobs, then she would lilt off into high beautiful notes. The music seemed to go with the wordless, verbless immensity of the ocean thought B.D., though not in that specific language.

"I was never the man I used to be," Bob said, opening his eyes and mopping his face with a handkerchief, looking out at the water. "When I die I will disappear at sea. A hot sea."

"In a boat?" B.D. asked, a bit unnerved by memories of choppy, rolling Lake Superior.

"I'm not at liberty to say. Let's have a beer. This fucking car is a steam bath. At a garage in Ensenada some fucker stole some parts from the air conditioner."

"It's not open until eleven," B.D. said, having checked the lounge door after his beach-beer reverie. B.D. followed Bob around to a service entrance where Bob banged at the door and gave a kid in dirty white kitchen clothes twenty bucks for two Tecates. B.D. was pleased to drink his first foreign beer while looking at the ocean.

* * *

"Feminine ambrosia. Seaweed trace. Nipple taste. A bit of tire," Bob said, tasting the wine.

"Oh Bob, you big dork," the waitress shrieked, tapping him on the noggin with her ballpoint.

The first beer seemed to have given them a certain momentum. B.D. thought other people might join them when Bob ordered five complete meals plus bottles of both red and white wine. B.D. stuck with Mexican beer, his wine-drinking career having ended young when he and David Four Feet had stolen a case of Mogen David which made them quite ill though they had drunk it all so as not to be wasteful. The very long lunch required seven beers which B.D. had always thought was a perfect number. Bob liked the number seven, too, noting that he had ordered five lunches rather than four because odd numbers were better than even. He had sworn, or so he said, during his impoverished youth never to get stuck with the wrong lunch which would leave you depressed the rest of the day. By ordering five you vastly increased the odds of getting something good to eat. B.D. raised the issue of the expense of this custom and Bob replied that his agent had negotiated a per diem of a thousand dollars a day which was peanuts compared to what certain actors and actresses required.

"We'll check the set tonight. We're night shooting. This bimbo actress has a hundred-foot trailer with a full Jacuzzi. She eats caviar on oysters which should only be eaten separately. Her hamburger must be ground from prime sirloin right in front of her eyes or she won't eat it. Her tuna fish must be made from scratch. She changes her underpants a dozen times a day, all at studio expense. I've heard that the best barber in Beverly Hills charges her five hundred bucks to shave her pussy because he's gay and doesn't like the job. Don't quote me on that because it might not be true."

This wasn't quite the kind of information B.D. was likely to quote though Frank back home might enjoy hearing it. His mind had been somewhat seized by the idea that this nutcase got a grand a day to live on and that before he ordered the food he had consulted his "food notebook," telling B.D. that he preferred to avoid eating food prepared the same way during the same year, adding that on New Year's Day the slate became clear again.

"What about eggs?" B.D. had asked.

"There are a thousand ways to cook eggs," Bob had replied, reeling off a manic string of egg recipes, many of them in French which B.D. recognized because he had met French Canadians over in Sault Ste. Marie. He rather liked the way they talked for the same reason he liked to listen to the older, traditional Ojibway (Anishinabe) talk, say when Delmore was speaking to a friend on the phone. Delmore explained to him that all that language was comprised of was agreed-upon sounds. And now he was listening to this batshit writer talk about his incapability of repeating meals within the same year. He wondered idly what his anthropologist lover, Shelley, would have had to say about it? She regularly visited her mind doctor for a tuning up and when Brown Dog looked at the wide array of food before them there was something crazy about it though it didn't deter his appetite. They ate Dungeness crabs, clams, oysters, and three kinds of fish, including sea bass and fresh yellowfin tuna.

"Can you offer me a recommendation for the job?" Bob asked, putting down his fork for a split second and taking a monstrous gulp of wine.

"Nope. I'm here on a secret mission. I didn't bring my paperwork." B.D. was pleased by his fib. No one could be expected to cart around all their paperwork though he, in fact, had none save the aforementioned driver's license and a twenty-nine-year-old selective-service card.

"I'd have to guess you were on the lam and trying to bury your identity in a big city," Bob said. "Don't forget that I write detective novels and am widely admired by professional criminologists."

"Tell it to someone who gives a fuck," B.D. said, studying the ornate carapace of the Dungeness crab, thinking that the creature carried around his or her house much in the manner of the way old Claude carried his Hefty garbage bag and taught him to do so. "I'm thinking of heading up to Oregon to cut timber, or maybe Chapleau up in Ontario. If you want to do a readout on me drive your own car and end up in the hoosegow playing with yourself."

"Calm down. I could easily jump on the computer and get your records."

"If you knew my name." B.D. took Bob's car keys out of his pocket and slid them past a bowl of *vongole* with a rich hint of garlic. Two women at a nearby table were eating lunch with their sunglasses on which seemed awkward to him.

"Chill out," Bob said, pushing the keys back toward B.D. and twisting a forkful of pasta and spearing a clam from the *vongole* bowl. "My own origins are unknown, even to myself."

"Mine too," said B.D., spooning up garlic and oil from the bottom of the bowl. Few tourists understood that a diet that included lots of garlic was useful as an insect repellent, though right now he was suddenly lonesome for his mosquito-infested home country, the lakes and bogs, the ceaseless cold rain, the pockets of snow in swamps that persisted into late May, the shelf ice buried in the sand and rock-strewn shores of Lake Superior that often lasted well into June. You could dig down and store your beer there and it kept wonderfully cold.

"I often pretend I'm a dark orphaned prince but the truth is my mother was promiscuous. It's brutal to accept that your mom was loose with her body." Bob was sad for a split second, then slurped down several oysters.

"I heard mine was too but I figured she must have had her reasons. Grandpa said we have strong bodies and can always earn our bed and grub, and sometimes women have to play it a little looser to get by. He might have been trying to save my feelings from anything I might hear when he raised me. You know, local gossip." B.D. felt that oysters were more interesting than the past.

"We left my dad and older brother who didn't look like me up on the farm near Cochrane north of La Crosse," Bob said. "We lived in Eau Claire, Fond du Lac, Oshkosh, and ended up in my high school years in Rice Lake, which incidentally has the best pizza in the world, a place called Drag's. Ever since I've not been much of a pizza buff. It's hard to step down. It's like going back to a waitress after sleeping with beautiful actresses and fashion models."

"I've always favored waitresses myself." B.D. had noted that the bones and meat of saltwater fish had a density that suggested they must work harder for a living than freshwater species. "Of course I don't know about magazine models much less actresses though I met one yesterday who starred in the film *Butts Galore.*"

"I've seen it. Intriguing but not much of a story line. Most of our porn is shot through with our collective tit fetish. If only the money spent on tit jobs around here was devoted to the five million children in America that go to bed hungry every night. Meanwhile, I grew up as a waif, moving from pillar to post, from dingy apartments in one Wisconsin suckhole city to another. But I was a bright lad and by dint of hard work became successful."

"What happened to your mother?" B.D. watched closely as Bob struggled a bit for an answer, B.D. recalling another radio program his Grandpa listened to after Jack Benny. It was called *Fibber McGee and Molly.* Fibber fibbed a lot.

"I support her lavishly in a posh retirement home in Milwaukee. My older brother and dad both wrote me notes to say that they didn't care for my detective novels. It hurt deep." Bob seemed pleased with this detail that should increase his credibility, or so he thought.

B.D. pushed himself back from the table, chock-full to the gills, and wondering why Bob never took note of the ocean right out the window in front of them. "Some of your lingo strikes me as far-fetched, Mister Bob. Maybe it just comes from the locale which doesn't seem like the rest of our country."

At this tense moment the waitress reappeared and asked if they needed anything more. Bob affected a heartfelt lust: "Only you, darling, can satisfy a need far deeper, far more basic than food. All this food we've eaten is dead. You're living food."

"Sure thing, Bob. Eat me and you don't get fat or drunk or have to spend an hour a day on the toilet." She slapped down the bill and flounced off.

Back outside they snoozed for an hour but with the car windows open, a sweet sea breeze wafting through the windows, keeping most of the flies away from their snoring mouths. They awoke on the same cue, a bit thick and grumpy. Bob opened the glove compartment and insisted they both take megavitamins, the capsules as big as horse pills, then directed B.D. to drive south to Santa Monica where he had a late lunch meeting.

"You mean you're going to eat again?" The thought of another bite made B.D. feel gaggy.

"Eating at its best has nothing to do with appetite." Bob took a small Dictaphone from his pocket and said, "Not call me a cab, but get me a cab," with the air of someone who had accomplished an important project. Bob then glanced over at the ocean for the first time and said, "Roll on thou deep and dark blue ocean, roll."

In Santa Monica they stopped at valet parking for Ivy by the Shore. Bob pointed at the pier on the other side of Ocean Avenue and told B.D. to be back in an hour, looking at his nonexistent watch as if puzzled.

B.D. was pleased to be out of Bob's range and have a chance to walk off the lunch which would only be justified by an eight-hour hike. There was the untypical fragile feeling in his mind, a fluttery sense that forbade him from getting his true bearings which, like the currently popular notion of "situational ethics," were not set in stone. The wanderer is vulnerable, and no matter that he hadn't been inside a church in twenty years except to mop up a flooded basement, certain almost religious feelings began to arise, the first surge caused by the overwhelming merry-go-round music coming from a big shed at the foot of the pier. Swank autos were parked in front and a group of natty chauffeurs were sitting in the shade. There was some kind of party for rich little boys and girls and their lovely mothers. B.D. stood there transfixed by the music which was just about his favorite kind, recalling all of his many trips to the Upper Peninsula State Fair in Escanaba though through the ornate shed's glass he could see that this was the most gorgeous merry-go-round in the universe. Once again he noted that because of his green janitor's suit he simply didn't exist in view of the others on the somewhat crowded pier. Three attractive nannies were around the corner smoking cigarettes and they looked right through the invisible B.D. He was pleased to have found the ultimate in disguises but if he was going to come across any affection in this town he'd better buy some extra duds.

The merry-go-round music had begun to increase a lump of homesickness in his chest, certainly a primitive religious feeling where the home ground is sacral, so that when you're on a foreign shore you recall the hills, gullies, creeks, even individual trees that have become the songlines of your existence. B.D. fought against the homesickness by looking north along the Pacific's shore up toward Malibu and the green hills sloping toward the ocean and the almost unpardonable beauty of the seascape. This place was not exactly the prison he was destined toward back home, or the Alger County jail where they couldn't scramble eggs at gunpoint and the sheriff cheated at cribbage. Not far from him in a moment of sheer good luck a lissome girl dropped her skirt though there was a bathing suit under it. The suit was drawn up a bit into the crack of her butt and she deftly used her thumbs to adjust the blue strap edges. His heart lurched as her hands gave her thighs a rub and when he sat down on a bench behind her he could see the blue ocean between her thighs. She reached playfully for a gull that flew swiftly by barely beyond her reach.

This vision was too much to deal with and B.D. moved farther out the pier where old men were fishing, turning several times to look back at the girl receding in the distance, unmindful of Nietzsche's notion that if you stare into the abyss too long it will "stare back into thee," but nevertheless feeling the admonition as a physical presence by the somber nut buzz in his trousers. Unavailability increases desire into the arena of dull incomprehension, and you can feel dowdy to a point that you may as well sit down, let out a sob, and eat your own shoes.

Despite all of this he was still capable of compassion both to others and himself. He did an abrupt about-face and hastily returned to the bench immediately behind the girl, picking up a stray newspaper and tearing a small hole in the crease. That way he could hold the paper up as if reading it and stare through the hole undetected. It was a counterspy technique he had read in a stack of old *Argosy* magazines in Delmore's woodshed.

The girl was now talking to a friend, a chunkier version of herself, and they were both sipping soft drinks through straws in plastic cups, making a noise that reminded B.D. of a very crude joke about a local woman back home who reputedly could suck a golf ball through a garden hose. He dismissed this witticism as unworthy of the vision through the hole in the newspaper, which already was producing an altered state, removing him from the mundanity of his problems. A great artist might be able to capture the ocean between her tan thighs, a distant swimmer's head bobbing through the frame. His concentration was absolute though it did not disallow certain thought of revenge against Lone Marten. This was only his second full day in town, and though he was currently feeling vaguely religious and lucky, he was mindful that his only other city experience in Chicago so many years ago was not exactly admirable. A fly landed and the girl twitched her butt like a horse shimmied a flank. A gay blade sat down on the bench a few feet away but the green janitor's suit repelled his interest. B.D. had to readjust his focus as the girl turned slightly sideways, a hand on her jaunty haunch. On their long escape drive from Michigan to L.A. they had stopped for a snooze beside the Wind River south of Thermopolis in Wyoming. B.D. had stretched out on his bear-skin rug but hadn't slept, watching the river transfixed, the smooth sheen of an eddy showing several dimpling trout rises. Now the girl was facing him with her slightly puffed "mons veneris" clear in the newspaper's hole. Suddenly two cups full of ice rained down on him and the gay blade quipped, "You've been caught, buddy."

B.D. dropped the newspaper and tried to smile. The girls laughed and gave him the finger. At least they had a sense of humor. He got up and bowed deeply, then made his way out toward the end of the pier where on a lower fishing deck he redeemed himself. An old, particularly wizened man had snagged his fishing rig on the bottom and whined loudly that it was his last rig. B.D. quickly stripped to his skivvies, made his way partly down an iron ladder, then jumped in after first telling the old man to hold on to his trousers and wallet. B.D. easily followed the taut fishing line down about thirty feet to the bottom. The visibility was poor and the water suprisingly cold, but he quickly untangled the old man's rig from a piece of rebar, cement reinforcing rod, jutting from a pier piling. When he came back up victorious from his charitable baptism a small gathering applauded, but there was Bob Duluth looking a little angry.

"B.D., you fucking moron, I've been waiting an hour. You could have drowned."

"Sorry, sir, just trying to help a poor old fellow out." He checked his own nonexistent watch as Bob had done earlier. "I'm an experienced diver."

"Fuck you, big shot," the old man said to Bob.

* * *

On the way east on San Vincente, a street B.D. found remarkable for its beauty, Bob had him pull over so he could point out the spot of his fatal D.U.I. There was nothing remarkable about the location except for the peculiar xenophobia of the one man showing it to another. Their stations in life couldn't be much further apart but Bob was from up in Wisconsin and B.D. from the Upper Peninsula, so that rather irrationally meant something to both of them as if they had together been cast up on the wilder shores of Borneo.

"Tell me about it, son," Bob said, at least affecting a stone-serious mood of concern.

"Tell you about what?" B.D. felt a little quavery when Bob used the authoritative "son" though Bob couldn't be more than ten years older.

"Tell me what you're running from. I'm sure I can help. Occasionally I like to alleviate suffering, to remove my venal blinders and do a good turn."

That threw the raw meat on the floor. They got out of the car, crossed to the wide grassy median strip, and talked under the very same tree where Bob had been rudely handcuffed, then hauled away. Somewhat in the manner of the ruthless interrogators created in his fiction Bob put B.D. through the exhaustive paces of his story, his three brushes with prison, the first when B.D. was a salvage diver and found the dead Indian in full regalia down in fifty feet of water for fifty years, perfectly preserved in the icy water of Lake Superior, then stealing an ice truck in an attempt to transport the body to Chicago for profit, followed by arson of the anthropologist's tent and camping equipment, all to protect his secret Indian graveyard from certain excavation, the only Hopewell site in the northern Midwest. B.D.'s so-called anthropologist girlfriend, Shelley, was right on the money as Eve in the original Garden, tempting the secret location of his graveyard with her body and that of her friend, Tarah, whose body was somewhat slimmer, a detail Bob drew from B.D. to get the whole picture, including the color of Tarah's undies. The third felony had been the recent attack on the site where a group of archaeologists and anthropologists from the University of Michigan were doing preliminary work. B.D. and Lone Marten had mostly lobbed fireworks from a relatively safe distance while the rough stuff had been left to Rose and a group of Anishinabe warriors. The main problem here is that B.D. had been enjoined from entering Alger County for a year to let the university people work without interruption.

B.D. tried to continue on with the flight west after swapping the hot Lincoln for a Taurus across the border in Canada, all engineered by the highly skilled criminal mind of Lone Marten. Bob held up his hand and rushed to the car to make a call. Out of sheer thirst they then went into a fancy Chinese restaurant in Brentwood where Bob was well known. Bob had a quick bottle of Puligny-Montrachet for a hundred bucks and B.D. drank three bottles of Kirin beer. Was there no end to the foreign beers available in this area? He did point out to Bob that L.A. lacked the wonderful bar life of Chicago where seemingly every street had its neighborhood tavern, or up in Wisconsin where apparently anyone could turn their home into a bar. Once over near Alvin when he had been fishing the Brule River he had sat drinking beer in such a house, took care of a pile of kids while the barmaid grandmother had cooked burgers for a crowd, and what's more, he had eaten four burgers for free for helping out, which included carrying the town drunk back to a shack over his shoulder like a two-hundred-pound sack of oats.

Bob wasn't listening. He was all business though B.D. reflected Bob could handle a bottle of wine as fast as an ordinary mortal could drink a beer. When Bob rushed out to fetch his I.B.M. laptop B.D. looked at the notes Bob had been making but they were scrawled in what must be a secret code. The Chinese waitress brought him another beer and bowed, so he stood up and bowed back which she found amusing.

"Welcome to our country," B.D. said, with what he hoped was a seductive smile. She was a real peach, as exotic as the flora in the botanical gardens.

"My family has been here since the 1870s. We came over to help build your railroads and mine your mines," she said with a twinkle. There was a slit in her skirt that ran halfway up her thigh. She didn't seem to mind the liability of his janitor's suit but he guessed that was because Bob was a high roller. With Bob's bankroll he probably got more ass than a toilet seat though there was the idea that it didn't seem to be doing him any good.

"Voilà!" Bob roared, rushing in with the laptop and tapping out some codes in front of B.D. Right there on the screen was the record prepared by Michigan State Police Detective Schultz on Marten Smith, a.k.a., Lone Marten, ex-member of the American Indian Movement (purged for embezzlement), expert at getting National Endowment funds for dissident films that didn't eventuate, wanted for credit card fraud, larceny by conversion, a dropped charge for manufacturing crystal methamphetamine, and having raised funds for a supposed Native radical group called the Windigos of which he was the only proven member, his main henchman a local fool with the unlikely name of Brown Dog, to be considered unarmed but nevertheless dangerous due to an early career as a bare-knuckle fighter.

Tears nearly formed at the sight of the word "fool." B.D. pointed out that Detective Schultz had been removed for illegally spying for political purposes which the state police had been forbidden to do. Bob countered that there had been the not so small item of sexual photos of Schultz and Rose, B.D.'s ex-girlfriend. A frame-up engineered by Lone Marten.

B.D. was amazed and disgusted that Bob had all of this information at his fingertips. Up until two years ago when he had met Shelley he had led a totally private life, mostly because, he now supposed, nobody was interested. There was a specific sorrow and yearning to find a truly remote deer cabin, and trade the off-season rent of it for some maintenance. He had reroofed many deer cabins, liked the smell of tar paper and shingles, and the bird-level view of the world a roof offered. Now tears of frustration actually did form which made Bob nervous indeed in this city where actual emotion is indeterminate.

"Stiffen up, bucko," Bob said, signaling the waitress for another bottle of wine. "We'll nail this miserable fuck to the wall."

"I just want my bearskin back."

"Of course you do. You didn't view Lone Marten as dangerous because he was the brother of your boyhood friend David Four Feet. Few of us will admit it to ourselves when our friends are evil, or maybe that all our friends are evil, including our parents such as my beloved though promiscuous mother, or all of our forefathers and foremothers back to page one in human history. You know the Bible, right? I've read the Gideon Bible in a thousand hotel rooms because television repels me except, say, Mexican or French television because I don't know what the fuck they're saying. Then it's okay. You tend to blame your erstwhile anthropologist lover, Shelley, for leading you astray but she didn't do it, your weenie did. Weenies and vaginas are the heart of the great mystery of life. They are our glory and our doom. Some eminent theologians have suggested that Adam and Eve didn't have genitals when they entered the original Garden but we must discount this as the thinking of dead-pecker old suits like we have in Congress. It's my contention that life as a whole might be much less than the sum of its parts and its most reliable content is evil. Right now we are sitting here having beverages in what may be thought of as the heart of the Evil Empire. Out here we stretch people's dreams and leave them only with stretch marks. Of course we're just making a living like anybody else, only more so."

Not surprisingly B.D.'s attention span had weakened though he affected concentration. The lovely Chinese girl was setting up tables across the room of the empty restaurant. The question was partly why people from all foreign lands, including America, looked so different. Frank had told him it was climate, referring to the hot sun in Africa, but B.D. was suspicious of that explanation. None of the Orientals he had run into in Chicago years back had looked yellow, nor did this girl. And none of the hundreds of Native Americans he knew looked red. A veterinarian from Charlevoix had told him in Frank's Tavern that if all of the dogs in the world were left in free concourse, down the line they'd all be medium-sized and brown.

Bob Duluth was waving his hands in the face of B.D.'s reverie, and sliding over the laptop for a closer view. A friend of Bob's at the L.A.P.D. had run a check on Lone Marten, and his local record was mostly concerned with wholesaling Formosan-made Navajo jewelry as the bona fide goods. This had pissed off the real Navajo. As a radical dissident Lone Marten was also under "light surveillance" in Los Angeles where it was also illegal. But hadn't these people taken over the empty prison, Alcatraz? There were also a number of addresses and phone numbers where he stayed when in the Westwood area, usually with other Native dissidents connected with the basketball powerhouse U.C.L.A. Bob suggested that he had an Italian friend named Vinnie who might retrieve the bearskin but Brown Dog said no. He'd do it himself. All of this stuff was going much too fast for his taste. Lone Marten would give him the skin if he hadn't already sold it.

Now the waitress brought a platter of ribs for a snack. Bob fell upon them but B.D. was capable of only a few, however delicious. Bob had claimed at lunch out in Malibu that he had pioneered the concept of multiple entrées, doubtless because he hailed from the Midwest where overeating is frequently regarded as an act of heroism. The waitress returned and asked Bob shyly if B.D. was famous? Her name was Willa and Bob said "definitely not" to her question. At the introduction B.D. dropped to a knee and kissed her hand, something he had seen in a movie.

* * *

They found B.D. a not so cheapish room between Westwood and Culver City at a place called the Siam, a motel with a modestly Oriental decor which made B.D. ponder the odds of getting Willa over for a visit. On the way out of the restaurant she had mysteriously refused to give him her Chinese name, much less her phone number. Bob said it was because he wasn't famous. They stopped at a convenience store and bought two cases of Evian for what Bob called B.D.'s "water fetish." When he drove Bob back to the Westwood Marquis, Bob told him to pick up some duds and gave him a five-hundred-buck advance on his salary which, though a great deal of money, didn't alleviate B.D.'s unrest.

Before he headed back to the Siam he took another quick walk in the botanical gardens. Bob had said one of the main secrets to his success was the nap he took every afternoon of a minimum of four hours duration. Deep in the foliage near the bamboo thicket he wondered if there were any possible secrets in his own life or was he simply an open, used paperback? This self-doubt quickly passed when he noted that the orange carp invariably swam counterclockwise in their miniature shaded pool. The carp were definitely more interesting to watch than the vagaries of doing a rundown on yourself. Like the rest of us B.D. didn't know what life was about, and now the lead carp made a graceful U-turn and slowly drew his school clockwise. That had to be one of the answers to the millions of questions life didn't really ask.

Before returning to his room at the motel B.D. picked up two nice outfits at a used-clothing store, colorful Hawaiian-style shirts and brown chinos, plus an attractive but dusty old fedora that reminded him of the hat his Grandpa wore to the fair and funerals. Bob had taught him how to use the car phone so he called Delmore back home and immediately wished he hadn't. Old Doris was in the Escanaba hospital with a heart attack and Rose was in jail for biting off the finger of a cop in the mayhem B.D. and the "evil" Lone

Marten had started at the graveyard archaeological site. Delmore was taking care of Rose's two children, Red and Berry, the latter, however charming to B.D., a retarded and unmanageable victim of fetal alcohol syndrome. Delmore had hired a full-time babysitter for the kids and he described the young woman as a real "peach," a white girl who wanted to devote her life to helping Natives. She even tried to get Delmore to eat yogurt. The upshot, though, was that B.D. must come home immediately and act the father for Rose's children. Rose would have to do a couple of years for the missing finger even though she claimed the officer had bruised her tits. "But how can I come home," B.D. asked, an unpleasant quaver rising in his chest. Delmore had a lawyer looking into whether B.D. was actually over the Luce County line into Alger when he lobbed the firecrackers. With the recent advent of laser surveying many county lines were in question, especially in this particular locale which was a dozen miles from any human habitation. B.D. insisted that he'd die of heartbreak in jail like Delmore had told him had happened to incarcerated Apaches. Delmore said that he could at least come as far as the Wisconsin border and call in for instructions. The conversation had all the disadvantages of the telephone where there's no time to digest the information before the next load arrives.

Back at the motel the desk clerk, a tiny man from Laos, was apologetic over the fact that the television in B.D.'s room didn't work and when he was told that was fine because B.D. hated television the man laughed long and hysterically. It was a morale raiser to tell a successful joke, even though you didn't know what the joke was.

In his room he chugged a bottle of water to try to tamp down the troublesome remains of the huge lunch. This was his darkest hour in most respects and he had only his twenty-three bottles of water for solace. He intended to try Bob's secret of success and take a long nap but first a shower was in order. Just before he turned the water on a slight noise caught his attention. He checked the door and peeked out the window at the parking lot blazing in the sun. There was a muffled scratching at the wall near his bed and the sound of a woman singing softly. It sounded like the French of the strippers in the Canadian Soo, all of whom came from Montreal. How nice, he thought, then returned to the shower. Five minutes later he heard the neighboring door slam and again peeked out the window, seeing a trim girl in a cream-colored outfit getting into a Mercedes-Benz convertible.

This did not help him sleep. He was outside of his tolerance in terms of time for lack of affection. Perhaps the new clothes, not to speak of the slick fedora, would help. The janitor's outfit was neatly folded on the dresser in case he needed to disappear again while stalking Lone Marten. The fact of the matter is that he felt utterly dislocated, a rapacious modern disease. The only familiar part of his surroundings was when he raised his hands from the bed, stared at them, and said "hands." The slump was a palpable weight on his chest and forehead. Grandpa used to say that life wasn't a bowl of cherries which was okay by B.D. because he didn't like cherries. Bob had flippantly asked him if he was afflicted with "dementia pugilistica," then explained the term by asking him if he was punch-drunk from his early fisticuffs. "Nope," B.D. had replied. He had rarely been hit in the face and that's why he always won. A good face blow disarms all but the most experienced. Now he flipped through a short list of assessments. Money. With about four hundred seventy bucks separated into several pockets and one sock for safety he was nearly as rich as he had ever been. Someday he hoped to buy a used yellow pick-up, a simple Ford 1500 would do. He would like a nice girlfriend but assumed so would everyone else. It really came down to the bearskin which was his single prized possession. Early in life Delmore had given up his bear medicine and turned to turtles, giving the skin to B.D. with ceremony.

He tossed and turned on the bed, ripping the thin sheet beneath him. They'd probably charge him an arm and a leg for the torn sheet. This was not the proper time but he was tempted to look at the nude photo of Shelley in his wallet for strength. A different kind of strength was needed for L.A. and it was scarcely a stiff pecker pointing at the snarling leopard lamp on the night table. Indeed, what power could the lonely wanderer summon that would be adequate for this vast tormented city sprawled around him, with its ten thousand laminae of sophistication and wealth, its venality and hatred, the million attractive women whose peculiar language he did not know? What he did know, though he had never collected his thoughts on the subject, which Shelley had him do on other matters, was that he was ill suited to leave the "back forty" as they used to call it. It had long ago occurred to him that the woods only prepares you for more woods. His expertise as a subsistence hunter and fisherman did not ready him for anything other than eating fish, venison, or grouse and woodcock. The end of that story was a full tummy and the memories of the splendor of the day.

In a way you didn't enter the woods, the woods entered you, and its presence did not make you more operable at the business at hand. Up until a few years ago game biologists had visited him to get the locations of bear and wolf dens in exchange for a six-pack or, in the case of wolves, a whole case of beer. He had given up this practice when Frank warned him that all the biologists were going to do was put telemetric collars on the animals so that they could keep track of them without effort like animal police. In other words, though Frank didn't say it that way, perhaps B.D. was betraying the creatures without knowing it. Naturally it was hard to turn down a six-pack or a case but he was full of enough remorse to meet all future biologists with a "get the fuck out of here" and a slammed door. And he had graduated in terms of human failing to gambling his knowledge on the Native graveyard for sex. It was certainly time to act noble but the training wasn't quite there, and perhaps nobility wouldn't help get back the bearskin.

Jesus H. Christ, he thought, hearing the roar and beeping of rush-hour traffic. How can they live with this fucking racket? He got off the bed and tried the radio built into the broken TV and had a thrilling moment when it worked. He tuned in some Mexican music loud enough to drown out the traffic noise. The yoga couple with whom he had had the parting over questioning why the woman felt good about herself possessed hundreds of records they played day and night, drowning out the birds and coyotes, and even a possible wolf. She was a tad thin for his taste but back in bed he recalled how pleasant she had looked when he had taken them on a day-long hike at their request. They had become a little lost on a series of ridges above a swamp that formed the headwaters of the Two-Hearted River and her husband, who had been irritated all day over the fact that the cellular phone attached to his belt didn't work in this location, totally lost his composure. B.D. claimed that they weren't lost, they just couldn't find their vehicle and said that he had happily wandered around a couple of days in this sort of situation. He knew the area well in May before all the foliage was out, and October when most of the leaves were down, but now the thickness of the greenery and the dull overcast hiding the sun's true position had made the route difficult.

On the bed B.D. realized why the experience had come to mind, first discarding the beauty of the woman's butt in her pale green trousers. It was because he feared falling apart now in L.A., delaminating as the man had done that day, including falling back and eating the rest of the sandwiches they had intended to share, hogging all the remaining water so that finding a creek or spring was immediately more important than finding the vehicle. The man's five-hundred-dollar custom hiking boots were turning his feet to purple jelly and late in the afternoon he had burst into paranoid sobs, claiming that B.D. and his wife were trying to kill him so they could become lovers and get his money. All of this on a simple ten-hour walk, B.D.

had thought, quite puzzled, though amazed that the wife remained curious about the flora and fauna and had pretended by midmorning that her husband didn't exist. They were a full two hours from the car when B.D. figured out the specifics of where they were but he didn't let on, wanting to stick it to the guy for his bad behavior. When nearly out of the woods the man had thrown his cellular phone out into the middle of an algae-laden pond covered with the white and yellow flowers of lily pads. "How ugly of you to throw your phone into the beautiful pond, darling," the wife had said. A scant hundred yards from emerging the man had clutched his head and yelled, "I hear a roaring," which was only a log truck on the road just ahead. Afterward the man had acted self-righteous rather than embarrassed, blaming the whole thing on an organic purge he had taken the day before to clean out his system. His wife and B.D. had watched in amazement as the man hogged nearly all the remaining water in the car and stuffed down two high-energy bars from the glove compartment without offering them a bite. For B.D. it was an incredible lesson on how you don't want to act in your brief time on earth. She had dropped B.D. off at his tar-paper deer hunter's shack, pressing a sweat-dampened fifty-dollar bill in his hand while her husband snoozed and moaned in the backseat. "Thanks for the wonderful day," she had said, staring straight ahead as if windshield wipers were the most interesting things in the world. B.D. had eaten a three-pound canned pork shoulder for dinner, then hoofed it the five miles to town in the twilight. The carburetor in his van was on the fritz and he was a little weary, but who could resist Frank's tavern when you had fifty bucks free and clear?

The upshot of the memory was something biblical on the order of "gird up thy loins," that is, stop your quavers and act like you know what you're doing. Anyone could become a slobbering asshole, even a guy who could do yoga and owned a hundred-grand log cabin with two bathrooms. He had been on a seven-day fandango, covering two-thirds of the country, and it was high time he get his bearings. He didn't know, of course, that by the time you truly felt the heartbreak of dislocation it has become the deep itch of getting better. And as the ceiling above him, speckled mauve, grew foggy and distant he entered sleep and the largely ignored arena of dreamtime wherein the simple little carp pond in the U.C.L.A. botanical gardens gradually became a mighty river on which he was floating on a log. Evil men in black uniforms followed in a boat shooting at him and forcing him toward an immense waterfall. At the last moment before being pushed into the thunderous cascade his body lifted up and he could hear the heavy creaking and flapping of his wings, his neck craned outward. He felt very heavy but maintained altitude and his flight pattern took him downstream far above the raging torrents. His wings became tired and heavy and he descended, landing at great speed but somehow clutching a large white pine tree at the edge of the river. Puzzled by his escape he looked down at his body and saw he was half bear and half bird.

The phone rang and it was a paw that lifted it clumsily from the cradle on the nightstand. "Hello," B.D. said in a throaty growl.

"What the fuck's wrong with your voice? It's Bob reminding you that you're picking me up at eight, about an hour from now. You got it?"

"Of course. I just finished my yoga and I'm doing my hair," B.D. said, clearing his throat of any bear remnants.

"You're fucking kidding. You're doing yoga?"

"Yoga and a gallon of yogurt a day keeps the doctor away," B.D. said, thinking about how Shelley and her friend Tarah lived the life of health, though they had had a weakness for cocaine and champagne.

"Cut the bullshit. Just be here. We have to go to the set. We're night shooting."

"What set?" B.D. asked, looking at his erection and wondering if there was bear power in it. Bears were notorious for endurance fucking.

"Just be here you goddamned fool." Bob sounded a bit speedy.

"Use the word 'fool' again and I'll give your Taurus to a poor person of color."

"I'm sorry. I apologize. Anyway I got Lone Marten pinned down to a speech he's going to make tomorrow evening. I'm hoping that they'll find out where he's staying. It's better if the showdown isn't public."

"Thanks, Bob. I better get my tux on."

"Don't wear a tux for Christ's sake."

"Okay." B.D. hung up, still feeling strongly the power and insouciance of his dream. Who's going to fuck with you if you're half bear and half bird?

In the lobby of the Westwood Marquis both guests and staff nodded and smiled at him under the careless assumption that he might be an important rock musician, many of whom stayed at the hotel, while B.D. was confident that it was the combination of the tropical shirt and his natty fedora. When he found Bob in the lounge drinking a martini out of a beer mug Bob looked at the hat and said, "Nifty." The hat had the extra advantage of hiding his stiff and unruly hair. During his childhood visits to the barber for his twenty-five-cent haircut the barber would whine that it would take a quarter's worth of Brylcreem or butch wax to mat down B.D.'s hair.

The hardest thing for a rural stranger in a huge city is to figure out the relationship between what people do for a living and where they live. On home ground you can drive down a street and say butcher, baker, candlestick maker as you pass successive houses. In Los Angeles, of course, you immediately give up to the nagging grace of incomprehension, as you do in New York City, with its layered oblong onions of life, its towering glued-together slices of separate realities held together by plumbing pipes and brittle skins of stone. In New York you can at least imagine you are way up in a childhood treehouse and those far below are not woodland ants but asthma-producing roaches. But then a pretty girl walks by with nine goofy dogs on tethers and you can get the feeling that these folks know what they're doing. In Los Angeles any sort of comprehension is out of the question for the initiate, though after a number of visits there are certain buildings, streets, and restaurants that become comforting landmarks. This is also true of the locals, most of whom become quite blind to their surroundings, like, say, the citizens of Casper, Wyoming. The sophisticate, the student of cities, soon understands that Greater Los Angeles resembles the history of American politics, or the structure of American society itself. The connection between Brentwood and Boyle Heights is as fragile as that between Congress and the citizenry though the emotional makeup of both resembles the passion and power of the *Jerry Springer Show*.

Thus it was on the way between the Westwood Marquis and the Sony Studios in Culver City that Brown Dog could bark out fondly on passing the Siam Motel, "That's where I live," to Bob Duluth who had his nose in his brightly lit laptop computer.

"Ah, yes, the wonderful Siam. Beware of a faux-French girl who lives there. That means she's not actually French. She's from Redondo Beach. Real French girls find it impossible to get green cards, you know, permits to get work. I was deeply in love with Sandrine for about three days. I introduced her to a couple of friends from Paris and they were amazed. They thought Sandrine was more French than the French with an impeccable Auvergne accent to boot. Whenever any filmmakers have a bit part for a French girl Sandrine gets the call. Her scam is to plaintively ask a gentleman to help her get a green card. Of course I tried. A lawyer charged me a grand to look into the matter for ten minutes. The immigration people told him that I was the thirty-seventh person trying to help Sandrine get a green card. Be careful about your wallet if you meet her."

"Not if you keep your money in a sock," B.D. quipped.

"A sock is an obvious place to hide money. Ask any girl in Vegas. She checks the socks first."

"I mean the socks you are wearing. You tend to limp a little so you don't wear out the money."

"What if you need to buy a hot dog or a drink?" Bob closed the computer top. His mind thrived on doses of inanity.

"You keep a little spare in your front pockets. It's close enough to your weenie so no one can get at it. It's a real sensitive area. My old girlfriend Shelley told me it's like my religion but she was dead wrong. I keep my religion secret."

"Not a bad idea, I mean secrecy in this town. With actresses I recommend talking about religion as a sexual ploy. Just ask them what God's specific purpose was in creating the movie business, and I don't mean it cynically. Stay earnest and a bit above the idea of sex. Probe for their deepest hopes and fears and tie it into the higher purpose, whatever that might be."

"Is my neighbor Sandrine religious?" B.D. wanted to bring it closer to home.

"She claims to be a French Huguenot. That's where the Arcadians, or Cajuns, come from. More to the point, she doesn't allow entry which at first made me think she was a transvestite. A closer look told me no. She seems to deeply enjoy sixty-nine, though I think she uses a thin plastic liner in her mouth. Once when she was in the bathroom I saw a packet of them in her purse."

"You don't say." B.D. was a little unnerved by this information. It smacked of the *Twilight Zone* repeats that Delmore occasionally watched at dinnertime. "You mean you snooped in the poor girl's purse?"

"Just checking for a pistol or switchblade. I have trouble performing the sex act if I feel threatened in any way. We grow up haunted by the tales of easy sex that don't eventuate. If you're in Eau Claire they tell you all the girls in Oshkosh fuck at the drop of a hat so you drive your old Plymouth to Oshkosh where they say it's Milwaukee, and in Milwaukee they say the college girls in Madison will leap on your head if you whistle, but in Madison you're assured that Eau Claire is stuffed to the gills with dumb secretaries who will fuck you silly for a three-course meal at McDonald's."

"You just went in a circle," said B.D. who was a student of road maps. A cabin owner had given him an old Rand McNally and B.D. had spent many an evening studying it.

"That's what I mean. Now I offer girls modest scholarships which keeps it on a higher plane. Before I forget, don't admit to anyone you're my driver. It has to do with labor relations. The teamsters might slit my tires."

"What will I say I am?" B.D. pulled up at the Sony security gate which protected Tri-Star and Columbia from Greater Los Angeles.

"*El don Bob,*" said a Mexican security officer poking his face in the window.

"*Qué pasa,* baby?" Bob waved. "Give my aide-de-camp here a badge for the set."

B.D. pinned on his "VIP" badge, not quite remembering what it meant. Also "aide-de-camp" seemed a step up in the world from "driver" which he had also done for Lone Marten in the semi-hot Lincoln Town Car which they swapped even up for their escape vehicle, the brown Taurus.

At the set, the front of a fake small hotel, Bob was met by the director and producer and he handed over a paper with the new line. B.D. was standing close enough to hear the director summon over the star actor who was darkly tanned but looked a bit like a bloated peanut. Now instead of the actor saying to the doorman "Call me a cab," he would say "Get me a cab." The reason behind the change, Bob was explaining, was because the actor was a distraught and impulsive lover and would not be in the mood to be polite to a hotel doorman. It didn't seem a very interesting point to B.D. but both the director and the producer liked the idea and

Bob beamed. The actor wasn't quite sure but after an initial frown he prepared himself emotionally for the next take.

B.D. was amazed at the hundred or so people working on the set, the grips and gaffers, makeup people, continuity girls, assistant directors, wardrobe ladies, and a few important studio executives who stopped by for a few minutes before driving home from work. Everyone seemed to greet Bob as if he were a big shot, and smiled at B.D. as he drifted toward the caterer's table, as if the VIP badge might mean something. Bob, still beaming, slapped him on the shoulder, "All in a day's work," he said, grabbing B.D.'s arm as he reached for a hot dog and soft drink. "Save your appetite for dinner, plus we got work to do." Another fucking food bully, B.D. thought as Bob led him to the entrance of the fake hotel. Shelley had been like that, forcing him to eat a big bowl of Tibetan boiled grain that you had to chew on a long time like a cow does its cud. Don't eat a hot dog kiddo, it will rot your insides out.

The next shot would be in a mock-up of a hotel room, Bob explained, stepping over tangles of cables and wires that looked dangerous to B.D. who always felt nervous over something so simple as plugging in a lamp. This was doubtless due to all the ranting his Grandpa had done about the destructive powers of electricity and automobiles. B.D., however, was pleased when a gaffer said, "Great hat" and a makeup man screeched "I *love* that hat, darling." It was a little disappointing, though, when he found out that the actress they were about to meet wasn't the one who demanded that her hamburger be ground before her very eyes, and had her parts exhaustively shaved. This one was named "Shoe" which seemed odd, but then he had gone out with a barmaid over in Neguanee whose last name was Foot who was first-rate, if a bit on the hefty side.

And there she was sitting on a rumpled bed in a bra and a half-slip, a bottle of whiskey and a full glass of the precious amber liquid on the nightstand beside her. While she talked to the director a makeup girl further tousled her blond locks. She stood up and gave Bob a peck on the cheek, nodded at B.D., and said, "What an adorable hat." He flushed deeply and bowed, then stepped backward toward the door, well behind the huge million-dollar camera, at least that was the price Bob put on it. Bob and the director and Shoe were discussing the upcoming scene and then went through the actual paces. She stood grief-stricken at the window as her lover drove off in the cab, came back to the bedside where she tossed off a glass of whiskey, screamed, "Goddamn you, Richard," then threw herself sobbing on the bed. B.D. quickly made note of the idea that movies were made of discouragingly small pieces and also, what kind of stupid shit could walk away from this woman? His eyes bugged in alarm when she tossed off the full glass of whiskey in rehearsal and the assistant cameraman whispered that it was tea. It was beautiful indeed when she threw herself on the bed and her sobs were so convincing that you wanted to rush to her side and comfort her. The slip nudged up the back of her legs so far that you could almost see her fanny and a smallish lump arose in his throat when he realized that such beauty was not for the likes of him.

After five of the eventual nine takes of the scene B.D. drifted back outside because the hot lights caused sweat to trickle down his back and legs and from beneath his magic fedora. The hundred or so employees were still milling around outside and when he emerged from the hotel several of them asked him how the scene was going. He said, "Swell" as he stared out over the assembled crowd from the foot-high vantage of the hotel's steps which he noted were not real cement though they looked like it. Oh sons and daughters of man, under the vast and starry night though the stars are invisible, what are you doing here while your histories moment by moment trail off behind you like auto exhaust, he thought though not quite in those words. What wages did they draw to endure such torpor, though he couldn't say they looked more miserable than most hardworking folks. At least they could feel there was glamour in the end product, which was hard to envision cutting pulp on a cold snowy day, somewhat stunted third-growth timber that might very well end up in a newspaper after being extruded from the mill. Maybe these workers felt like those in an absolute assembly line in an auto factory and though they were remote from the end product they were confident that out would pop a Cadillac. Cast in the best light, B.D. decided, this work could be likened to his years as an illegal-salvage diver, bringing up antique booty from the depths. Some people would pay top dollar for a binnacle brought up from an old freight schooner resting in peace in the depths for over a hundred years.

Brown Dog stared out at the crowd for a long time with the nonconceptual attentiveness of a child. In terms of local social mores such stillness was extralegal and many in the crowd found themselves staring back. Was this fucking goof really important they wondered? They all knew from common gossip that the screenwriter, Bob Duluth, wasn't dealing from a full deck, didn't have both oars in the water, but they were bright enough to also know that he was the origin of their employment. In the parlance of the industry, screenwriters were an unfortunate necessity, or "just writers" as the executives tended to refer to them.

Finally a very large black security officer approached B.D. and asked him if he needed anything and B.D. whispered, "A beer, sir." Off to the side, but fairly near, two wardrobe girls were skipping rope and smiling at him as they went through intricate, hyperathletic moves. They must be more accessible than a famous actress he thought, recalling the intimidating beauty of the woman as she glugged her whiskey tea and, after the shot, wagged her butt at Bob and the director.

The security man returned with a beer enclosed in his big paw. B.D. stared at the label. St. Pauli Girl all the way from the land of Germany. He wondered if they could come up with a Goebbels' or a Stroh's from Detroit. Probably. He thanked the security officer who followed B.D.'s line of vision to the wardrobe girls skipping rope.

"Watch out for those two ladies. They're not twins but they're known in the business as the Terrible Twins. There are no snakes in the world as dangerous as those two, not even the dreaded fer-de-lance of my home country."

On further conversation it turned out that the security man, Harold, came from Belize, and his crisp elocution was explicable because he was not a victim of our educational system. Harold gave B.D. his card in case he needed any after-hours "protection," then withdrew with a slight bow when Bob reappeared mopping his face with a handkerchief. When they had shaken hands it had occurred to B.D. that Harold was as large as the federal officer that had arrived in Grand Marais to arrest three men for shipping illegal otter skins across state lines. When the officer, who was also black, got out of his car "he just kept on getting out" an old Finn had said. He was at least six and a half feet and about three hundred pounds, wore a cowboy hat and a silver-plated long-barrel .44 on a hip holster. The trappers had offered no resistance.

Bob waved a hand in B.D.'s face to catch his attention at the same time the wardrobe girls, the Terrible Twins, approached wondering if they wanted any after-work company? Bob said that he and B.D., who was given yet another card, were booked solid for the rest of their lives. The girls gave him the finger and strutted away.

"Gee whiz, Bob, they're cute." In addition to being real hungry the twins had given B.D. a nut buzz just by standing there. One of them wore soft cloth trousers that pulled right up in the fold of her genuine article.

"A grief too deep for words," Bob said. "There's a lot wrong with me possibly but I'm not some sort of toe-freak masochist."

On the way to the club on Santa Monica Boulevard Bob's dialogue was rather manic and B.D. turned him off, his hunger pangs now so severe that his mind flitted to and fro between other great hunger situations in his life, say the time he was lost from dawn to dark on a cloudy day while deer hunting and when he reached his battered old van there was a precious can of emergency Spam in the toolbox. His cold hands shook and he struggled to open the can, dropping the contents when he cut his finger. He had hastily and unsuccessfully tried to scrape pine needles, leaf fragments, and his own blood off the meat before cramming it in his mouth. It lasted three bites and there was nothing to wash it down with except a few ounces of banana-flavored schnapps in a dusty bottle, given him because it was too repellent for the purchaser. In the ensuing indigestion he felt the inventor of banana schnapps ought to have his ass kicked. Spam alone, however, was a reliable staple for the weary white trash of the northern forests, or that was what Shelley called them.

"Did you ever notice how often you look at the clock and it reads eleven-eleven," Bob asked loudly to get his attention.

In truth B.D. had never noticed this but quickly figured it only happened twice a day and said so.

"It's not reality but our perception of reality that counts," Bob said, finishing off one of those little two-ounce bottles of airliner booze. "When you ride first-class for thousands of extra dollars they give you these free. Maybe it's because eleven-eleven is when I get up, and when I eat dinner."

It had just turned eleven and B.D. was wondering why there was so much traffic. In most places night and day aren't so different in emotional content and rather rigid patterns are followed. There were long lines and youngish people outside of clubs, and a movie theater playing something on the order of *Fungoid Fat Guys Must Die*. He didn't realize it was Friday night since what day it was never had any importance in his life. His mind wavered back to his hunger and Grandpa's contention that even saltines were a feast for a hungry man. It didn't take all that many years for him to figure out that Grandpa was frequently full of shit, sitting there before the woodstove eating stinking Liederkranz cheese and pickled bologna with his saltines, talking grandly about how much hemp they had smoked at the government-sponsored CCC camps during the Depression in order to save their pathetic pay for beery weekends. Now this same hemp, B.D. thought, could get you locked up real tight for a long time.

When B.D. pulled up in front of the club he asked if Bob might send him out a sandwich, say liver sausage, sharp cheddar, with a thick slice of raw onion, plus a Budweiser if possible.

"I'm a liberal Democrat with populist roots. You're coming in. I've already figured out your meal. I just hope you love spinach."

"I can handle it with pork products," B.D. quipped, handing the keys to the dirty car to the reluctant valet, who then grinned when Bob got out and handed him a twenty.

Inside the club the air was thick with smoke what with smoking being the main reason the private club existed. On the way to their table Bob explained quickly, if loudly, that since the politically correct fascists in California had banned smoking even in bars, certain intelligent radicals had joined together to form clubs in honor of freedom. B.D. thought that the swank club wasn't exactly reminiscent of the Chicago radical explosion but then he wasn't in a critical frame of mind over such matters. He only smoked when drunk but that was because cigarettes had become too expensive. Throughout the club folks were puffing away with panache. They were the nattiest group B.D. had ever seen in one place, all gathered in rebellious smoking friendship.

When they reached their booth blood rushed to B.D.'s face. Bob's date, Sharon, whom he had mentioned earlier in the day, turned out to be a junior high girl, or so he thought. Sharon sprawled in the red leather booth in a short pink dress, white anklets, and black patent leather shoes known as Mary Janes, looking thirteen at the outside. She batted Bob with the Sherman Alexie novel she was reading when Bob slid into the booth beside her and cupped her ass. B.D.'s mind spun, thinking it was odd that California banned smoking and then allowed this sort of thing. He sat down hesitantly at the scene of yet another crime and on a closer look figured she might push eighteen but was dressing real young for private reasons. Bob chuckled at his discomfort and said that Sharon was a recent graduate of Radcliffe on the East Coast, which raised in B.D.'s mind the image of a building on a cliff above the stormy Atlantic.

"You're real lucky to go from one ocean to the other," B.D. said, shaking her small soft hand which made him quiver.

"I've never thought of it that way." Sharon was wondering if this asshole was for real or putting her on. "Bob talked about you on the phone. I have great sympathy for you and the plight of your people."

"The road is both long and short. I have my hopes in my heart." B.D. was a little confused by a woman in the booth behind Bob and Sharon whose monster tits were literally falling out of her blouse. She flashed him a dizzying smile.

"Well put," Bob said. "The struggle is both in the moment and in the long term." He grabbed the arm of a passing waiter. "Why don't you miserable fucks bring us some drinks?"

"Do many Natives wear such wonderful hats?" Sharon ignored Bob's impatient anger, not being an alcoholic herself though she was mildly wired on Zoloft.

"A few of us in the brotherhood," B.D. said, wondering at the same time why he was spilling bullshit. Sharon was like Shelley who seemed to demand it. If he had had a pencil or pen he could have used the old trick of dropping it on the floor to look up her legs but then, however pretty, she was a tad scrawny. Bob, who had just gotten up to track down drinks, must be trying to recapture his youth or something like that, but then again he might just be trying to help Sharon out.

"Bob's a swell guy," Sharon said, glancing across the room at Bob at the bar demanding service. "I just worry he's going to blow his tubes with booze like my dad did. Sure, he's a good writer but ninety-nine point nine percent of all writers are forgotten within a month after their last book."

"Why would anyone want to be remembered?" B.D. asked. "We're all worm chow." He felt cozier watching Bob approach followed by a waiter with a tray containing two bottles of wine and a martini, the other hand holding an ice bucket with three Buds.

It wasn't really a swell evening except to B.D. Sharon only picked at a plate of two oysters, two shrimp, and two cherrystone clams on a bed of radicchio while Bob had a double order of veal chops and pasta. Lucky for B.D. Bob's spinach joke was only a side order that accompanied a prime New York strip that weighed nearly two pounds. He had noted it on the menu but then it cost thirty-eight dollars so he had settled on spaghetti and meatballs which only cost the astounding price of eighteen dollars. There was a restaurant in Iron Mountain where the same dish was only four dollars and a single meatball was the size of a baby's head and a side order of half of a roasted chicken was only two bucks. Bob stepped in and insisted B.D. have the steak saying that in L.A. a man requires power food. Sharon's pathetic dish irritated Bob so much that he began choking. B.D. agreed on the idea of power food, describing the sense of well-being he felt after eating five deer hearts. Sharon impolitely pointed out that they were both full of shit.

"Only partially full, darling. But then so are you. From birth to death the primate colon is never completely empty." Bob's voice carried strongly and two couples at a table across the aisle from their booth didn't seem happy.

Sharon giggled and playfully lifted a leg and kneaded Bob's ample tummy with a shiny, patent leather shoe. As B.D. worked methodically on his steak, eating the delicious fat first, he noted Sharon was a pretty smart gal. She and Bob had a high-minded argument about whether the media, *in toto,* was in reality the main weapon of mass destruction in the world since it irretrievably warped the minds of the collective citizenry. According to Sharon TV, the movies, newspapers, and nearly all books were actually a nerve gas dumbing down the world. Bob countered by asking, "Then why do you want to enter the movie business?" Naturally, she said, "To improve it."

"You lame fucks from New York and your itty-bitty art films," Bob said. "You xenophobic dweebs think that New York is the world. Everything is cold and sooty and everyone shivers in leather jackets at dawn. You see a bridge, buildings, and pigeons. Then more bridges, buildings, and pigeons. Throw in a dog or two and a Chinese restaurant and a bum picking his nose." Bob was carried away but not so far that he neglected his meal.

"You liberal romantic novelists come out here thinking you're going to do good work and what do you come up with?" Sharon talked so softly you had to stop chewing so your mandibles didn't drown out her voice. "You think you can apply your lame sensitivities across the board to every situation and what do we get? Shooting. Everyone shoots everyone. You think that the paradigm of life is crime. You fall back on your limp penises which take the form of guns. Bang. Come. Bang. Come." Sharon wiped her spotless lips with her napkin, a prim gesture. She pouted at B.D. who had finished his steak and was loving the spinach which swam in olive oil and garlic. "What do you think, Mister Noble Savage?"

"I was thinking that this was the best steak of my life and that I want to get my bearskin back." He eyed her uneaten cherrystone clams and she pushed them over. This was another adventure in the making because he had never eaten a raw clam. "I know I'm missing out a lot where I live but I don't have a TV, the movie houses are far away, and I don't care for newspapers because the pictures are in black and white and the world is in color." He felt weak in the face of her onslaught.

"But sweetheart, you get the nerve gas in the discourse of everyone you know." She stuck her tiny foot out under the table and gave his pecker a polite nudge.

Just then Bob's cellular buzzed and he portentously lifted it from the belt holster. He said, "Yes. No. Yes. No. Great," writing down an address from his jacket-pocket notebook and clicking off the phone. He eyed B.D. and affected the voice of Joe Friday. "I've got Lone Marten's address. We should move in now." He was clearly in his cups and smirked with a sense of mission, picking up a veal-chop bone and gnawing at a difficult piece of gristle.

"It would be better to move out at dawn," B.D. said, sensing that caution might be a better tack.

"Tomorrow is Saturday which makes dawn around noon, at least in L.A. Bob always sets his alarm for eleven-eleven sharp." Sharon turned to Bob who was staring blearily at the bar then waved at a couple.

"It's Sandrine and her big-shot NBC stiff. He saddle-soaps her boots with his tongue. I can imagine what that might do to your taste buds. Take it from me, your palate is a big part of your future. Once your palate goes the rest of your sensory apparatus dries up like a cow pie in the noonday sun, under which only grubs and maggots can thrive—"

"Oh for Christ's sake, Bob, shut up." Sharon nudged him so hard that only superior balance in such matters saved his glass of wine.

"Sandrine de la Redondo, this is your neighbor Brown Dog at the Siam," Bob said, ignoring the TV executive in his English bespoke suit and amber steamed glasses, and very clean ears, when they approached.

"*Êtes-vous célibataire*?" Sandrine asked, placing her hand cheekily on his neck. B.D. stared deeply into the bare midriff of her outfit, smelling the pleasure of lilac bushes on a May morning.

"That means, Are you a celebrity?" Bob translated.

"It means, Are you single?" Sharon corrected.

"*Pouvez-vous venir prendre un verre chez moi ce soir?*" Sandrine asked, running her little finger behind his ear which made him shudder.

"She wants to know if you'd like a drink later." Sharon yawned.

"Yup. Don't mind if I do." He figured if this woman were immediately interested in him there must be something seriously wrong with her. Just what it might be was the intriguing question. If she wanted a green card he'd promise her one by dawn. He waved a bit limply as Sandrine and her limp boyfriend departed.

"She wants a part. Everyone wants a part of some sort. Including me. I'll take him home. We're stopping by a very important party where he's going to introduce me to people who might give me a job." Sharon shoved Bob out of the booth with her heels, straightening her legs made strong by tennis and whatever. Bob merely signed the bill and tossed a C note on the softening pats of butter on which a single fly was mired.

Nothing, for the time being, could be other than it was, B.D. thought, stretched on his bed at two AM back in his room at the Siam. He thunked his drum-tight tummy. Perhaps late in the evening was too late for a two-pound steak? On the way home he had bought a six-pack of Grolsch for ten bucks with a devil-may-care attitude to tamp the steak down while he listened to Mexican music. There were apparently only so many parts and jobs in the movie business and a lot of people wanted them, but then he recalled that when United Parcel Service had had an opening in Escanaba over two hundred men had applied. There were a lot of *benefits*, everyone said. If you stayed on the menial level you could avoid this mad struggle. If you needed some dough you showed up with your chain saw, a can of gas, and a few quarts of oil and you could always cut pulp. If you needed a place to stay there were hundreds of deer cabins in the Upper Peninsula you could stay in for doing some fix-it work. Through his friend Frank at the tavern he was always in demand. He'd live-trap the porcupines and red squirrels that were damaging a cabin and let them loose near another, say at the cabin of the yoga couple to see if the critters liked expensive dwellings. The present was hard enough to deal with so that you couldn't very well handle the notion of the future. He had noticed that it arrived in daily increments without any effort. The more central struggle in life was between water and beer. Too much beer, he knew from many years of experience, tended to be hard on the system. The yoga couple had told him that Elvis Presley need not have died had he consumed enough water. All of Presley's pain and drug taking were due to constipation caused by bad diet (cheeseburgers and grilled peanut-butter-with-banana sandwiches) but mostly by a failure to drink a lot of water. B.D. had been concerned about his love for Frank's cheeseburgers and the yoga couple had given him a ballpark of four twelve-ounce glasses of water per cheeseburger. You had to get up and pee a lot in a cold cabin but luckily there was a window near his cot. He ultimately did not scorn these wood yuppies because, at this moment, they would obviously better know how to deal with Los Angeles than he did. He found it hard to counsel himself against impatience though he had only been there two days. And the third day looked like it would bear fruit, as the Bible people say.

Sandrine knocked at his door at three AM adding a muffled French greeting. B.D. was ready with a rule that she had to talk in American. He had also dispersed his four hundred and seventy dollars in a half dozen places, including a fifty in each sock. Someone said that you had to give a little to take a little, the kind of confusing homily life is built on. Sandrine's room was very pleasant indeed, papered with French posters that included a sublime river gorge in the Midi that might hold lunker trout. I should be back home fishing at this very moment, he thought, because timewise it was six AM in Michigan and he could imagine dawn mist curling on the surface of this favorite beaver pond that had yielded a three-pound brook trout on a No. 16 female Adams with a soft yellow belly. Sandrine had decided B.D. was at least a minor rock musician, though never on the cover of *Rolling Stone,* from his absurd outfit and because she knew that Bob wouldn't be hanging out with nullities. When they smoked a joint as an alternative to a drink B.D. saw problems coming, in that it was by far the strongest pot he had ever experienced. It miffed him when she turned on the television but she said, "The walls have ears" and that the immigration people were hot on her trail. In France she had lived in a château but in "Amerique" it must be the Siam for concealment from the neofascist government. She was incapable of dropping her entire disguise, and her central motive, rather than the green card, was getting the thousand bucks Bob owed her for a sexual favor. Perhaps B.D. was gentleman enough to cover his friend's debt for a poor girl? "Let me think it over," he said, speaking into a clenched fist as if it were a microphone. The pot smoke had begun to swirl around his brain pan and the yoga couple's advice to "listen to your body" was at the moment not very attractive. Right in front of him Sandrine had changed into something more comfortable, a soft cotton shift leaving her legs bare to the midthigh. His tummy beef became restless and began to moo. She took off his fedora and leapt back as if hit by a cattle prod, proclaiming his hair to be the ugliest in the cosmos. Luckily for him she was an experienced cosmetologist. She led him to the bathroom, had him bend over the bowl, and sheared off close to the scalp his bristly skullcap, a matter of no importance to him though when he saw the lid of water covered with his hair he thought of biblical Samson being shorn by Delilah. When she flushed the toilet the swirling vortex of hair looked like a cow's ass. She finished his head off with a bluish rinse at which point he recalled Delmore's portentous dream that he would return home with a weird haircut! My God, but life was mysterious. They embraced in front of a large bathroom mirror with Sandrine releasing his weenie from captivity. It seemed far away as it prodded her warm cotton outfit seeking out the bull's-eye. "*Non, non, non,*" she whispered, heading for the bed. They flopped into the age-old upsy-downsy position, a practice Bob had advised she preferred. In his pot haze anything was fine by him and this delightful lass had obviously been there before. Without the stealthy effects of beer, steak, and marijuana it would have been over in a trice. The world seemed dark so he opened his eyes and there between the two orbs of her bottom he could see Vincent Price on the television. It was the very old horror movie about parachutes that didn't open, an apt metaphor for his life. Delmore had complained that modern airliners weren't equipped with parachutes. She thwacked away at his chin and he felt her hands run up his calves and shins to the only thing he was wearing, socks. Her hands played over his insteps as Vincent's airplane cradled through the clouds between her butt cheeks and she gargled, "A present for Sandrine, *merci*." At his moment of release she shrieked, "You fucking cheapskate," having peeled off the socks and found the two fifties. She leapt up with tears in her eyes, shaking the paltry bills that he hadn't exactly given to her. While he quickly dressed she threatened to call the Mafia which he had only dimly heard of, though post-dope paranoia had set in and any harm was possible. Up until this point, and he was well into his forties, he did not believe that the aftermath of sex could depress him. When he pulled on his trousers she grabbed for his wallet which he had wisely left in his room and they tumbled backwards onto the bed. While she kicked and emitted fake sobs on her belly he stood and decided hers was actually the top fanny of his life which did a lot to lift his momentary depression. When he reached the door and took one last look she held out a hand imploringly for more cash, every bit as winsome as the divine actress earlier in the evening. Back in his room he drank a quart and a half of his valuable stash of water and went to bed without a single thought.

The phone rang at eleven-twelve in the morning. B.D.'s eyes were already open and he was thinking of Frank's wise saying "No matter where you go, there you are." How could anyone quarrel with the depth of this statement.

"We have a rendezvous with destiny. I feel great. How about you?" Bob said loudly enough on the phone that B.D. had an ear buzz. After Frank's wisdom he was trying to think of what the yoga couple had told him to the effect that all over the body are hands and eyes, or throughout the body are hands and eyes, which means there are a lot of resources if you want to use them. The couple were big on quotes. They had them tacked and taped up all over the place.

"B.D., are you there?" Bob could hear breathing but that was it.

"Yup. I was lost in thought."

"Did you get together with the lovely Sandrine?"

"In a way. Do you believe in evolution?"

"Everyone does if you watched *Planet of the Apes*, but what the fuck are you talking about?"

"I was wondering if you could be descended from a bear rather than an ape?"

"I don't think so but then science is not my long suit. Are we still on?"

"Yes. If it's okay we move out at dawn. Sharon said that's in a half-hour hereabouts."

"Come up to the room and we'll strategize. I'll order breakfast."

When B.D. washed the sleep from his face he was startled by his haircut and its bluish cast. All the more reason to own a fedora. That Sandrine was a real pill. His socks felt deeply the lack of the two fifties so he redistributed his three hundred seventy. At this rate blow jobs were going to get priced out of the range of the common man and inflation alone would insure marital fidelity, assuming you had a wife.

As an afterthought before getting into the car B.D. slid a crisp dollar under Sandrine's door as a teasing tip, affording her one-third of a cup of coffee to meet the day which showed signs of a terminal smog alert. His eyes and nose itched like they did around a dump fire where tires were burning, but then perhaps it was the right kind of weather for the mission. The yellowish sky looked ominous and he ran a finger along his badly chapped lips remembering the source of the ailment. Frank had told him that before Native warriors entered battle they liked to say "Today is a good day to die," but that seemed a bit much for the current situation. A modest injury would be appropriate but he didn't want to bite the big one, as they say. Not that he wanted another go at the brunette bombshell Sandrine, at least not at that price. For a hundred bucks you could get by a whole winter month if you were careful. A couple of old World War II veterans at the tavern had told him that in war-torn Europe or Japan a fellow could get sex for a candy bar but that hadn't seemed like an admirable transaction. The least you could do is fry up a chicken and make mashed potatoes for the poor girl, bake up an apple pudding with brown sugar and lots of butter.

Up in Bob's room B.D. was impressed with the setup in that there was a living room and two bedrooms with one full of books and used as a study. It hadn't occurred to him that this was possible in a hotel. In the living room beside the table full of food there was a telescope on a tripod aimed down at the swimming pool. There was the question of if you wanted to see the ladies why not go down to the pool and take a look but Bob said, "It's safer this way." B.D. was a bit played out on women and focused the telescope on a flock of pale green parakeets in a flowering tree. He was disappointed when Bob didn't know the name of the tree, also when Bob said that the hotel was trying to get rid of these lovely birds because they sometimes shit in flight on guests around the pool.

"What are they supposed to do? Birds don't have toilets." B.D. was irritated. These birds were as pretty as orioles.

"The manager thinks they're doing it on purpose."

"I hope so." B.D. sat down at the amply laid table. The steak had now left quite a hole in his stomach.

"I ordered you country ham, country eggs, and country fried potatoes. The menu doesn't say if the toast is country, maybe suburban."

"I could use some gravy but I'm not complaining. Catsup will do." B.D. fetched his Tabasco from a pocket and quickly learned that it burned his chapped lips. He speared a piece of Bob's smoked salmon and judged it not bad. As a joke Bob had ordered B.D. a large glass of carrot juice which he poured in the toilet when Bob went to his bedroom to dress. The carrot juice wasn't pretty in the swirling toilet any more than his hair had been the night before. At least Bob had been kind enough not to laugh at the blue haircut. Bob just said, "You're in Rome and you have done as the Romans would." When Bob came out of the bedroom he wore a nifty camo T-shirt under his Italian sport coat in honor of the mission.

"Sharon said that we keep trying to paint the world with our own colors when it already has its own," B.D. said.

B.D. took one more look through the telescope, having noticed a non-birdlike movement beneath the parakeet tree. It was a woman in a white string bikini and adjusting the telescope he could see a hint of short hairs emerging from one of the greatest non-bran muffins in the kingdom. Bob took a peek and said that it was Nina Coldbread, the Italian television mogul, set to give her skin a good scorching. When Bob had offered her a villa for her company she had only yawned and burped, or so he said. While Bob looked overlong through the telescope B.D. sensed that he had been given an overexposure to beauty, that in the Great North a lifetime could pass without seeing such a woman, and if it happened it would become a precious memory. Perhaps a man was better off if his experiences were more limited, and did not even include the velvet battering ram of the night before that made his face sore and tender. Perhaps the experience had knocked some sense into his head, perhaps not.

* * *

Bob became more than a little nervous when B.D. pulled their vehicle up to a security gate off Benedict Canyon, the address where Lone Marten was supposedly staying. Bob knew from some alcohol-suffused memory that it was the home of a studio honcho which would fill any screenwriter with fear but he couldn't remember which one. He rattled off a list of studio names, then remembered Universal and was relieved because he had already burned his bridges there with a not very exciting project, *Some Called It Tuesday,* about the sexual adventurism of a Republican wife. Bob had B.D. hit the buzzer and when a voice asked, "May I help you" Bob yelled out, "We are of the people" and the huge gate magically opened. Bob told B.D. that the woman of the house was active in civil rights specializing in Natives. They drove through a brick-lined tunnel, the ultimate in security from God knows what, and emerged onto a large green sward in front of an English Tudor house. In the middle of the huge lawn but near the driveway a woman in a lilac peignoir was playing croquet with three obvious Natives, all with long black ponytails. Another man was sleeping beneath a pine tree.

"Irony scratches her tired ass. Redskins playing croquet," Bob chuckled.

"Not really. The Ojibway invented croquet though they only used balls hand-carved from the boles of a diseased oak that had been struck by lightning." Under pressure B.D.'s mind had become antic. He knew that the man beginning to sit up under the pine tree was none other than Lone Marten.

They got out of the car and the woman rushed over saying, "Bob, Bob, Bob, welcome aboard." Bob flushed with pleasure that she remembered his name but then he realized she might not have a memory suffused in alcohol. They embraced as is the custom of the area and she made a bow to B.D. whom she took for a Native, but B.D., intent on his purpose, was already striding through the wickets toward Lone Marten. A large Lakota, at least that's what it said on his T-shirt, stepped in B.D.'s path when Lone Marten screeched and began climbing the pine tree. B.D. eyed the Lakota's general musculature, then looked over the big shoulders at Lone Marten still screeching up in the tree.

"I have no quarrel with you, chief. He stole my bearskin. At one time I was the best fistfighter in many counties. I haven't forgotten it all."

"He stole your bearskin?" The Lakota turned to stare at Lone Marten up in the tree, then back at B.D. "I saw the bearskin yesterday. I think he might have sold it."

"My Uncle Delmore gave it to me. His was bear medicine and he gave it to me because after he moved south he had to go over to turtles."

"We never got along with you Chippewa people which is putting it mildly, but times have changed. Even nowadays you can't be stealing a man's bear medicine." The Lakota nodded and stepped aside, though by now everyone had followed B.D. to the pine tree. B.D. picked up a couple of croquet balls and hefted them, firing the first into Lone Marten's ass which was hanging over a branch. Bob tried to grab B.D.'s arm but without success. The Lakota and Bob explained the problem to the hostess who was wringing her hands in horror at male anger, something she had seen in her husband though in a more subdued form. She grasped B.D.'s arm as he was ready to fire the second croquet ball at Lone Marten's head.

"Lone Marten, I can climb up and tear you out of that tree like a bear would!" he yelled, though he turned politely to the woman grasping his arm.

"Lone Marten sold the bearskin to Lloyd Bental at our fundraiser here yesterday. He's going to donate half the proceeds to the cause. If that's not good enough I can pay you for it." She took the cellular from her gossamer waistband and shrieked, "My checkbook please."

"No you can't." B.D. slumped to the ground with his face in his hands, not noticing that on hearing the name Lloyd Bental Bob had shrunk back, his face becoming as pale as dirty snow.

An impasse had been reached. The Lakota and the two other Natives sat down on the far side of the tree from B.D. and were eventually joined by the woman who assumed there was something sacramental going on and she should probably join in. Her maid came running with the checkbook and was shooed away. Meanwhile, Bob had returned to the car where to his dismay he could only find three little airline booze bottles. The very name Lloyd Bental, by far the most powerful producer-director in Hollywood, shrank all his blood tubes with fear. If you crossed Lloyd you'd never work in Hollywood again. No one had dared count how many writers had been sent back East with jellied brains and shriveled nuts.

Finally Brown Dog stood up, raised his chin, and stared hard up in the tree at Lone Marten who now felt like a fired writer sent back East. For the first time in his life Lone Marten knew he had gone too far. When the chance had come to sell the bearskin to the mogul he had known it was the wrong thing to do just as he knew it was wrong for poor dumb Brown Dog to let the fucking *wasichus* know the location of the graveyard. But then Lloyd Bental had been accompanied to the fund-raiser by two young actresses who had made Lone Marten's skin steam and itch, not to speak of a roll of hundred-dollar bills that would choke a pig. White women and money, not to speak of drugs, had always wrung his smallish petty-criminal heart.

"Lone Marten, if you don't help me get my bearskin back I'm going to track you down and tear out your heart." With that not very ambiguous statement B.D. walked slowly back to the car, using a sleeve to wipe away his tears. The woman followed him to the car and asked where he was staying and when he said "Siam" she naturally thought of Yul Brynner and Anna. She patted Bob, who was a slobbering mess, through the window, and she really didn't mind when B.D. did a U-turn in the yard, digging up long divots as he sped off. This was real emotion.

It was his darkest hour and his hands felt numb on the steering wheel. Traffic was tied up on Sunset due to an accident and B.D. felt poignantly the utter crush of civilization. An eighty-year-old Finn he had known well had flown out this way to see his son and had warned B.D. that "the world is filling up." No shit. B.D. wanted to turn turtle like he did when he and Lone Marten had driven through the profound ugliness of Las Vegas, and where he simply raised his shirt collar and sank into its dark confines, preferring his own rank air.

It didn't help that Bob was in his bibbety-babbety-boo state, blabbing away about Lloyd Bental's seven Oscars, his hundreds of millions of dollars, his homes in Beverly Hills, Palm Springs, Palm Beach, Acapulco, his brownstone in Manhattan, his grand apartment in Paris, not to speak of the beach house in East Hampton. These details wavered B.D. a bit from the purity of his righteous anger wondering if the guy had the pipes drained to avoid freezing up when he moved from place to place and the way the fixtures within unused toilets tended to seize up. Then the phone rang interrupting Bob's interior and exterior monologues and it was as if Bob didn't recognize the phone so B.D. answered it. It was the croquet hostess who called to say that she had gotten in touch with Lloyd Bental but that he was unwilling to give up his rug which, even at the moment she had called, he was stretching out on because it made him feel spiritual. She had also phoned her husband, waking him up in London, but he was calling the head of the prop department of his studio and a bear rug would be delivered to the Siam. B.D. was on the verge of telling her to go fuck herself but a dimmish idea began to emerge so he only said, "Thank you, white woman, and let me say you looked good in that lilac gown." Despite his anger at the time he had made a record of her attractiveness.

Meanwhile, Bob had continued rattling on and the upshot was that he could no longer help B.D. try to recover his bearskin because if he were caught crossing Lloyd Bental he would "never work in this town again."

"You could work in Nebraska," B.D. said lamely, eyeing the traffic congestion ahead for an escape route.

"He'd have me followed there, buddy. His vengeance is sure and swift. He even takes it out on animals. A few years ago, someone gave him a wolf hybrid as a pet. She shit on the floor as animals will do. Lloyd had her dyed solid pink and she expired from embarrassment. The Humane Society was called in but even they were frightened of Lloyd Bental. I've got a family to support, a sick wife and two sick kids. They need groceries and milk. I need to send home five hundred grand a year."

"What about your promiscuous mother?" B.D. asked, without irony.

"Her too. She's in her midseventies but she's probably still hitting the streets. Mind you, my heart's with you."

"No car?" B.D. could see a life on foot returning. Walking anyway cleared the mind.

"No car. My car's my trademark. Everyone in town knows my car, especially the cops. I could rent you one." His voice trailed off into bleating.

When B.D. parked at the hotel Bob was racked with sobs of grief and fear. They embraced in front of the puzzled doorman and Bob stuffed some more money in B.D.'s pocket. He turned away as Bob tripped up the steps and walked kitty-corner over to the botanical gardens, needing a big dose of nature to gather his thoughts. A little dose would have to do.

B.D. hoofed it back to the Siam in an hour. In the garden there had been an Oriental in a white suit sitting by the carp pool and since he had his heart set on it B.D. sat there too. After about a half-hour of mutual silence the Oriental smiled and got up. They talked for a few minutes and B.D. learned that the guy was composing himself to do an eight-hour brain surgery on a little girl. B.D. wished him good luck, thinking of Rose's little girl Berry, back home, whose head was severely cross-wired, which came from Rose's heavy drinking when she was pregnant and now the condition was hopeless. All the way back to the Siam B.D. felt the peculiar, damp heaviness of homesickness swelling in him. He actually craved to get bitten by mosquitoes and freeze his ass off on one of those cold summer mornings when the wild huckleberry crop was in danger and he had gone out to pick a few to make pancakes. He always used way too many berries so the pancakes were a mess but, nevertheless, good. Afterward a beer would cut the sweetness of the maple syrup and then he'd take a stroll of a few hours or go fishing.

Back at the Siam he had a shower, throwing his fancy Hollywood clothes aside with disgust. It was time to return to the cool, level-headed humility of his janitor's suit with the unknown Ted's name on the pocket. With his ear to the wall he could hear Sandrine singing, certainly the most noteworthy experience he had had in town though the reviews were mixed. The view had anyway been wonderful despite the occasional intrusiveness of Vincent's dour face between the smooth cheeks. He had barely finished a quart of the expensive water when there was a knock on the door. He took the precaution of peeking through the curtains and there stood Lone Marten holding a bearskin rug with a green felt liner. He opened the door and the rug looked even more pathetic than it had through the window with a slight cinnamon phase to the fur and rubber nonskid gizmos on the liner. It might not be possible but the skin looked like it belonged to a very gay bear.

"This car I borrowed cost a hundred thirty grand," Lone Marten said, gesturing at the Mercedes convertible behind him.

"Tell it to someone who gives a shit." It did occur to B.D. that the amount probably surpassed his lifetime income. "That bear rug looks like it came from the prop department at Universal."

"How did you know?" Lone Marten looked quizzically at the rug in his arms.

"I have my ways." He swiveled to see Sandrine peeking from her door wide-eyed.

"Lone Marten!" she exclaimed.

"Sandra, the French girl! How strange to see you in humble circumstances, including B.D."

"Sandrine's the name, kiddo. I bet you thought of fencing that car in Tijuana for a lot of bucks. I live here because it's free rent. I can't live with a man because you guys are the spawn of the devil, maybe worse."

It turned out that her NBC exec boyfriend had taken her to the fund-raiser up Benedict where he had bid on some ersatz turquoise jewelry.

"Sandrine, darling, I need a pair of scissors." Everyone seemed to use the word "darling" and he might as well join them. He took the bear rug into his room, intending to somehow sneak into Lloyd Bental's house and switch the rug for his bearskin. He'd probably end up dying in a California prison but so what? Maybe they'd let him out in a couple of winters so he could go home and hear the delicious sound of crunching snow beneath his feet.

Sandrine and Lone Marten sat on the bed smoking a joint while B.D. cut loose the lining with the scissors. Lone Marten discussed several ways he might help B.D. get his bearskin back, including the highly creative way of blowing up the house with a ton of nitrogen fertilizer, some kerosene, and blasting caps. Sandrine yawned when she heard Bental's name.

"Think smarter and try to remember that I'm otherwise going to tear out your heart." B.D. had finished with the rug noting that someone had shampooed and softened the fur and given the bear marble-blue eyes. There is no end to blasphemy, he thought.

"I know Lloyd Bental real well," Sandrine bragged, which really got their attention. "I've blown him a few times. I won't fuck him because he's not a star, only a director and producer."

It hadn't been real hard to strike a deal for Sandrine's help. Lone Marten started at five hundred bucks but she held out for the usual thousand, glaring at B.D. and reminding him of the measly two fifty-dollar bills in his socks. Lone Marten took out a wad and peeled off the ten one-hundred-dollar bills, explaining plaintively that this was the people's fund-raising money and now they'd lack money to repair their leaking tepees. Sandrine made a fake yawn and went to get Lloyd's number from her five-inch-thick alligator-skin personal phone book. The moment she left Lone Marten whispered to B.D. that the money was bad counterfeit he'd bought for twenty bucks for a thousand, useful in such occasions. B.D. agreed and when Sandrine returned she said that Lloyd only had a thirty-minute "window" at nine before going to dinner so they had to be on time. That meant they had two hours to stew in their juices. Sandrine was hungry so Lone Marten took her out for something to eat, tooling out of the Siam parking lot with unbelievable speed. B.D. requested that they bring him back a liver sausage on rye with onions, cheddar, and hot mustard but wasn't too hopeful they'd succeed. This was as close as he could come to power food from back home. A deer heart or liver would be more proper to ready himself for the momentous night ahead but either of them would be hard to find in the neighborhood. A number of times hunters had given him and Frank bear meat, wanting to keep only the hide. They quickly discovered that you had to get all the fat off older bear or there was a predominant flavor as if you had mixed axle grease and saddle soap. Younger bears, especially female, had fewer purines in the blood and on slow nights in the kitchen of Frank's Tavern in late October they'd make some experimental bear stews using lots of garlic and red wine, but sometimes varying the recipe with garlic, hot pepper, and dark rum which Frank said is how they cooked old goat down in the sunny Caribbean. The downside of bear meat for Brown Dog was that it always caused remarkably vivid bear dreams. It was pretty frightening to make love to a sow bear even in a dream, and the male bears, the boars, made Mike Tyson look like Mary Poppins. Delmore had teased him that in the old days it wasn't unknown for a man to become a bear if he ate too much bear meat or generally fooled around with them too much. Down near the headwaters of the Fox River one evening while fishing he had sat with his back against a big white pine stump and a sow bear had come along and sat down no farther than twenty feet from him. It was a real attention getter and they both averted their glances, knowing that in the natural world a direct stare is considered at the very least impolite. Even ravens don't like to be stared at and if you look off to the side a bit they're much more likely to stick around.

The slam of a car door jogged him from his bear trance which had only served to increase his homesickness. His heart leapt at the idea of his liver sausage sandwich and he sniffed the air as he opened the door. It was Sharon driving the brown Taurus with Bob snoring away beside her. Now she was in adult clothes, a tank top and Levi's, rather than a pink dress and shiny black shoes. She leaned against the car door with an attractive twist to her hips and her nipples were perky beneath the tank top.

"Bob insisted I drive him over to apologize to you and now he's asleep."

"Let sleeping dogs lie," B.D. said for no reason at all.

"Don't be too hard on him. He's just a big kid."

"I'm not. He's got his own problems. It must be pretty hard when your whole family is sick, not to speak of your mom loose on the streets."

"Oh, that's all bullshit. Our families are friends from way back and there's nothing wrong with his wife and kids except the usual neuroses, dope, and alcohol."

"You don't say." B.D. couldn't figure out if he was startled, surprised, or just plain diverted for a moment from his own problems. "I thought you were his lady friend."

"I admit I have to lead him on a bit. I really want a career in the movie business and after last night's party I think I might have a job with the great Lloyd Bental. He reminds me of a pear with lipstick but I liked him a lot. He quoted poetry to me in five languages."

"Well, congrats to you." Now B.D. was startled. Within this big town there was obviously a small town. The last thing he was going to do was tell Sharon he was forming a plot against the versatile Lloyd.

"Did anyone ever tell you that you're weirdly attractive?" Sharon had glanced over to make sure Bob Duluth was still asleep.

"Can't say that it never happened." Their eyes fixed deeply on each other unlike what's permitted in the other part of the animal world. B.D. bowed and swept an arm in a gesture to his motel room door. Sharon entered with a pronounced blush. Not a little while later he would have a perplexing moment thinking about how fucked up the relation between time and people can be. He and Sharon had fairly collided behind the door. Her jeans were half down and he was kneading her bare bottom while she yanked a bit roughly on his weenie as if starting an older-model outboard motor. Their tongues were sweetly entwined when Lone Marten screeched up outside yelling, "Liver sausage from Nate and Al's." It was simply heartbreaking, so near but so suddenly so far. Injustice spread around him like an elephant fart. He quickly cinched his pecker under his belt and went outside, followed by Sharon who for some reason whistled "The Colonel Bogie March."

"Here it is, blood brother, and with double meat." Lone Marten handed him the lunker sandwich just as his pecker fell in his trousers like the reverse of the famous Hindu rope trick. He turned abruptly, hearing an audible hissing. Sharon and Sandrine were faced-off a mere foot from each other spitting out their words.

"Trying to cop another of my boyfriends, you string-bean Ivy League bitch," Sandrine shrieked.

"I'll kick you in the cunt, you gold-digging faux-French street slut," screamed Sharon.

B.D. leaned against the passenger side of the Taurus, looking down in embarrassment at the sleeping Bob. This range of female anger horrified him. He took an enormous bite of his sandwich, feeling the possibility that since he had just been cheated of sex, it was also possible to lose his sandwich. Lone Marten moved quickly between the women and in perfect unison they both slapped him for reasons of their own. Sharon stalked to the Taurus and B.D. reached in the window and patted Bob on the head. Bob woke up smelling the sandwich and quickly took an offered bite. B.D. had to jump as Sharon backed up.

"Goodbye, old pardner." He waved. Bob looked something like a wizened child who had fallen asleep after a tantrum.

Zero hour. Sandrine drove the car expertly up Beverly Glen, what with her NBC boyfriend owning the selfsame vehicle. The front seat was rather small and Lone Marten had to sit on B.D.'s lap. Imagine paying that kind of money for just two seats, B.D. thought, noting that Lone Marten's bony ass lacked the charm of either Sharon's or Sandrine's. The plan was that Sandrine would go into Lloyd's house and before she did her job she'd leave the door ajar, presuming she could divert him from whatever room held the bearskin. This was less than a guaranteed plan and when Lone Marten said something about "giving it the old college try" it meant nothing to B.D. who was irked that Lone Marten and Sandrine were sharing yet another joint so strong that the secondhand smoke addled him.

"Je suis ici," Sandrine warbled, pressing Lloyd's gate button, *"Je suis là."* There was an immediate mellifluous, baritone "Goody" from the other end, and gates as large as those in a prison movie began to open. B.D. and Lone Marten slid down until they were out of sight. Sandrine slapped at Lone Marten as he lifted her short-cotton dress for a peek. B.D. couldn't help but feel a little smug over the time he had spent in Sandrine's nether regions notwithstanding the now permanent image of Vincent Price. Just as she stopped the car he grasped the substitute bearskin which felt feminine, albeit dry. Sandrine got out and he heard her throaty laughter, and her saying something more in French and the man's hearty laughter which sounded something like the Escanaba newscaster's on TV when some tourist insisted on watching the news at Frank's Tavern. B.D. couldn't help but take a stealthy peek out the car window. The man wore a short yellow robe and did look like a pear with lipstick as Sharon had described him. B.D. had to admire how fast he worked because he already had Sandrine's skirt above her waist. B.D. was thrilled to see that after they walked up the wide, palatial steps she was able to leave the door slightly ajar. Above the ticking of the Mercedes engine B.D. listened for her voice which would call out "Moola" if she managed her intent of getting Lloyd out the side door and into a rose garden, or into a bedroom, anywhere at a safe distance from the bearskin should she be lucky enough to note its location. Lone Marten looked a bit glazed and drooling under a bright mercury-vapor light above them. And then B.D. heard the high clear call of "Moola" and eased himself out of the car, the cinnamon skin with blue marble eyes in hand. When he reached the steps he turned and saw that Lone Marten was following him like a zombie. B.D. grabbed him, carried him back, and threw him into the car, looping a seat belt around his neck. He would have to go it alone.

And it was easy as pie, though he was first diverted by the splendor of the home, thinking it must be the kind of place where the king of the world would live. He tried to run silently on his tiptoes which proved unsuccessful, but then he quickly found the bearskin which was predictably on the floor of a den lined with hundreds of photos and testaments to the greatness of Lloyd. B.D. swiftly folded his bearskin and stuffed it into the black garbage bag that was still handily in the back pocket of his green janitor's trousers. He carefully arranged the ersatz skin, looking up for a moment at the line of Oscars on the fireplace mantel and suspecting they must be pure gold. The only close call was when he heard a female voice with a Mexican accent calling out, "Mister Lloyd, is that you?" but by then B.D. was in the foyer near the front door and at that moment the great Lloyd himself groaned out mightily from the garden, "Mom, Dad, success," which made B.D. pause a split second while tripping down the steps to the car. He recalled one night in Munising while making love vigorously to an actual lawyer's wife he had slapped his own ass and yelled out, "Ride 'em, cowboy," and she had crossly jerked his ear.

Lone Marten was sitting upright dead asleep and B.D. shoved him down, climbing on top of him and pushing him into a ball on the passenger-seat floor. He decided not to take another peek when he heard Sandrine and Lloyd calling out their melodious *au revoir*s. He was unnerved by the thumping of his own heart and fear that Lone Marten would let out another movie-Indian *Ugh!* He searched out Lone Marten's face and firmly pressed a foot against his mouth. And then Sandrine was in the car which roared to life and he could not help but press his own face against her lap and give her a hearty kiss. Her fingers tapped a rhythmic tattoo on his neck as he pushed up her skirt. She sang a little French ditty and there was grace in not knowing what the words meant.

The only real reason to go back to the motel room was the full remaining case of expensive water plus a few spare bottles. He had debated whether to head to the airport or a bus station but then at least four days on a bus would increase the chances of someone stealing his prize. He felt he probably had enough money for a plane ticket, at least partway, though no specific figure offered itself. He asked Sandrine if he might have a loan if he ran short on ticket money and her *no* was explicit.

"I went down on you all the way from Beverly Hills to Santa Monica and you won't pony up a cent." He found this discouraging.

"Here's the buck you slid under my door, asshole." She smiled.

They stopped at Sandrine's exercise place in Santa Monica so she could pay her bill with her earnings from Lloyd. Lone Marten wandered off to buy a five-buck cup of coffee and there was the question of borrowing some counterfeit but that seemed touchy. He had never been on a plane before except a small Cessna with a logger checking out territory and it hadn't been too pleasant other than seeing the bottoms of rivers and lakes from the air. Now he stood looking into the open front of the gym with growing amazement. The rock music was quite loud and there were rows upon rows of exercising women following the movements of a sleek, young black instructor. B.D. did a little body count and figured not one out of fifteen women needed exercise and here it was shortly after ten in the evening and they were pumping and jerking themselves into a froth. Would the wonders of this place never cease? He noticed again that those passing on the street utterly ignored him in his green janitor's suit. Earlier there had been a temptation to pick up both the water and his fancy Hollywood outfit but where would he wear the outfit up home?

When Lone Marten returned with his quart of coffee he seemed hyper. B.D had previously wondered how whatever the man put in his mouth always caused some immediate effect. This time Lone Marten had also scored some speed at the coffee place and was offended when neither Sandrine nor Brown Dog wanted any. All the way to LAX they wrangled about one thing or another centering on Lone Marten's idea that they fence the expensive vehicle in Tijuana and then he and Sandrine could fly off to a South Sea island with the proceeds.

"I have to live in this town," Sandrine said, rather righteously.

"Maybe I could use you in a documentary I'm going to do for the National Endowment for the Arts about Cheyenne dancers," Lone Marten suggested.

"What's the part?" There was a trace of interest in Sandrine's voice.

"You'd be a lamprey eel in a wig that sucked out men's souls through their peckers," Lone Marten shrieked with laughter.

"Cut that shit out. This lady helped us." B.D. placed a hand firmly at the back of Lone Marten's neck.

On the car phone Sandrine had found out there was what she called a Northwest "red-eye" from L.A. to Minneapolis leaving at midnight, which didn't sound all that encouraging to B.D. but then he sensed that fate was beginning to be kind to him. When she dropped him off B.D. walked around to the driver's side to kiss her goodbye.

"Goodbye, darling. You're fab. Come see me again," she said. It was nice to end it on a high note.

While sitting at the gate and waiting to board B.D. rehearsed his airport troubles. The attractive woman at the ticket counter was at the same time so daffy and crisp he figured that she too must be trying to get into show business. It was Memorial Day weekend and the only seats left were in first class which would take nearly all of his money, about nine hundred dollars which included what Bob Duluth had kindly stuffed in his pocket. There would be no money left to take the feeder flight to Marquette. Or he could take his chances at the gate with *standby tourist class*, which would also entitle him to the flight at seven in the morning. There was a real ugly sound to *standby* so he turned over all of his crumpled money except eleven dollars, reassured by Delmore's dream of picking him up in Minneapolis with what Delmore had called a "weird" haircut. It was clear that one should try to fulfill a mentor's dream.

There was a worse mess at the security check when the bear skull showed up on the monitor screen and a black woman in a nifty tight uniform screeched, "What's that?" Two security agents took B.D. aside and there was the question of whether he had the proper papers for the bearskin as required by United States Fish and Game. This was a real impasse but luckily the shift was changing, the agents didn't want to be involved, and B.D. used a line Frank had used when the cops had pulled them over on the way home from the Seney Bar. "I fought in Vietnam to keep this country free. My body looks like someone went over it with a big leather punch. We took a lot of incoming mortars on the Mekong Delta which really fucked up the fishing." That was enough and he proceeded to the gate not knowing that only the most ardent officers want to deal with a crazy.

When he called Delmore from a pay phone the news was mixed, but tending toward the median strip of the good side of life, except for old Doris who was still in intensive care. To B.D.'s surprise he hadn't wakened Delmore at the late hour in the Upper Peninsula. Delmore had been chatting with a man in Uruguay on his ham radio and described it as an "up-and-coming country." Delmore demanded that Brown Dog come home immediately, not only to see Doris before she "cacked" but to take over the raising of Rose's children, Red and Berry. The erstwhile white nanny who loved Natives only lasted three days because Berry had done such things as put a baby snake in the girl's cereal and had eaten hamburger raw with salt and pepper. There was still some controversy over whether B.D. was actually in Alger County when the fireworks were lobbed at the archaeological site. The real crime still garnering news was the fact that Rose had bit off a police officer's finger, though a feminist lawyer had come up from Lansing to help because of Rose's contention that the officer had manhandled her tits.

Whether B.D. liked it or not Delmore and his lawyer were working on a deal for which Delmore had signed an affidavit claiming B.D. to be the true father of Rose's kids. Since the new prosecutor was a Republican who believed in family values he wouldn't want to put the father in prison too, which would cost the county a fortune in foster care. Raising the kids also had the virtue of keeping B.D.'s "nose to the grindstone," not really an appealing idea but anything was better than confinement behind iron bars. B.D. had never felt that Frank's idea that we all spend our lives in a cage included him. Finally B.D. told Delmore that he better start driving now because the plane would arrive at six-thirty in the morning in Minneapolis and there wasn't enough money for the Marquette flight. "I told you this would happen, you goddamn numbskull," Delmore crowed, adding, "Be at the curb. I don't want to pay no parking charges."

When B.D. took his seat near a window at the front of the plane he stowed the bearskin under the seat in front of him, then took off his shoes so he could place his stocking feet against the fur, making it impervious to theft. A prominent Minneapolis businessman sat down beside him and was obviously unhappy to do so. The man wore a tailored pin-striped suit and made B.D. feel more invisible than he had felt before which was some pretty stiff competition. When the stewardess came around for drink orders B.D. asked for the price and was delighted to find out they were free, though later he figured out the nine drinks he consumed in the night were actually a hundred bucks apiece. His composure was pretty firm except for the improbable land speed of the takeoff and the ungodly noise of the engines. Soon afterward his skin prickled at the beauty of all the lights of Los Angeles, drawing their vision within as an uncritical child does. And later, when the altitude reached over thirty-five thousand feet he had to say to his seat partner, "We're seven miles up in the air, the same distance so I'm told of the deepest part of the Pacific Ocean." The man quickly closed his eyes, feigning sleep.

And later yet, far below, he could see small thickets of lights that marked villages and cities that blurred into lovely white flowers.

When the snack of a seafood salad was served B.D. quickly determined the food wasn't of the quality of Bob Duluth's Malibu restaurant, took his bottle of Tabasco from his pocket, and turned the contents of the plastic dish into an appealing pink. The man then looked at him longingly and B.D. passed the hot sauce.

"How bright of you," the man said.

"Can't say anyone ever called me bright," B.D. said, savoring his burning tongue.

"Fuck 'em, you're bright." The man had finished his third drink and was warming up.

It turned out the man had done some rather fancy kinds of hunting and fishing and was quite pleased to find someone to listen to his self-aggrandizing tales of salmon fishing in Iceland and Norway, duck hunting in Argentina, dove hunting in Mexico where in one fabulous afternoon he had shot three hundred white-winged doves. Coming down to earth he also admitted to simple grouse shooting up near Grand Rapids, Minnesota, where Judy Garland had been born and not all that far from Bob Dylan's birthplace. The man took out his computer and showed B.D. moving pictures of his two Brittany bird dogs and the dogs actually barked rather loudly which turned the heads of passengers who were trying to sleep. Since men are men, whatever that means, the man also showed him several different photos of his Los Angeles girlfriends. He traveled to L.A. and back once a week and though he was happily married, attested by earlier computer photos of his wife and children who came right after the dogs, the road was a lonely place and a hard-working man deserved affection. If B.D. hadn't dozed off for a few minutes he would have seen the photo of a poor French actress the man was helping to get a green card. B.D. also didn't take note that during the entire four-hour flight the man hadn't asked him a single question about his life. The final transfiguration was the shimmering dawn on the greenery far below. "This is the shortest night of my life," B.D. said too loudly. Even time herself didn't stand still in a way you could count on.

Nine drinks is quite a bit on earth let alone in a cabin pressurized to a mile high, a dangerous height for drinking in volume. When the plane landed on a cool, wet, and windy Minneapolis dawn the other first-class passengers gave the prominent businessman and Brown Dog meaningful glares which were not recorded. The businessman conked a fancy lady on the head while dislodging his briefcase from an overhead bin, tried to kiss a stewardess goodbye, and brayed he was now headed for work in his brand-new Land Rover. The copilot, peeking out from the cockpit with a tired smile, chided the stewardess for giving the asshole too many drinks. Even B.D. dimly knew that it was time for their friendship to end and let the man go ahead while an older woman across the aisle told B.D. that he was an "enabler."

He was well down the long corridor and emerging into the main terminal while clutching his full garbage bag to his chest when he stopped to ask himself why the ground, the endless carpet and now the hard floor, felt so strange beneath his feet. He had forgotten his shoes and when he turned to retrieve them he saw that he would have to go through security again which was definitely a bad idea.

Outside he sat on a bench near the curb and was soon wet and cold but dared not retreat for fear of missing Delmore. Finally he unwrapped his bearskin and enshrouded himself in it, violently hung-over but warm. Two eco-ninnies fresh out of Boulder, the kind that piss off left, right, and middle, stared down at him with anger from the height of their elevator Birkenstocks but he was nonchalant, safe and secure in this citified version of the north country.

Finally, after more than an hour, Delmore beeped his horn repeatedly from a scant five feet away and B.D. roused himself from a beautiful dream where he and Sandrine were whirling through the universe attached tails to teeth like Celtic dogs. He opened the car door and spread out his skin.

"I got the bearskin back," B.D. said, near tears.

"I didn't know you lost it. It's a good thing you got those clothes because I forgot to tell you on the phone there's a chance you can get Rose's old night job sweeping the casino. So help me navigate out of this goddamn suckhole." Delmore passed B.D. the map but he was already asleep, having heard nothing at all.

They were halfway across northern Wisconsin on Route 8 when Delmore stopped the car at a roadside park that abutted a lake east of Ladysmith. He had bought a loaf of bread, mustard, and a can of Spam as a welcome-home lunch for Brown Dog who still hadn't awakened. The sun was out now, and though it still was only in the high fifties Delmore felt warm and good to have his relation back even though the simpleminded fool wouldn't wake up. Delmore made the sandwiches, set out an ice chest with a six-pack for B.D. and iced tea for himself. He became a little irritated, went back to the car and turned on a Sunday morning Lutheran church service at blasting volume. B.D. sank deeper in his bearskin and Delmore opened a beer and dribbled some on his lips. B.D. fumbled for the door, got out and fell to his knees, got up and took the can of beer from Delmore. He drank deeply, blinking his eyes at the landscape, rubbing his stocking feet on the soft green grass, drained the beer and handed the can to Delmore, then half-stumbled down through a grove of poplar, cedar, and birch to the lake where he knelt in the muddy reeds and rinsed his face in the cold water. On the way back up the hill he took a longer route through the woods, half-dancing through the trees like a circus bear just learning his ungainly steps, slapping at the trees and yelling a few nonsense syllables, dancing back to the picnic table where he popped another beer and picked up his Spam sandwich, looking out at late spring's deep pastel green with the deepest thanks possible.

The Summer He Didn't Die

PART I

What is life that I must get teeth pulled? Brown Dog thought, sitting on a white pine stump beside the muddy creek with a swollen jaw for company. It was late April and trout season would open in two days. Brown Dog was a violator and had already caught two fine messes of brook trout, not in contempt for regulators but because he was hungry for brook trout and so were his Uncle Delmore and his stepchildren, Red and Berry. Despite this Brown Dog put the highest value on the opening of trout season which meant the end of winter, though at his feet near the stump there was still a large patch of snow decorated haphazardly by a sprinkling of deer turds.

Here I sit in the Upper Peninsula of Michigan, one hundred eighty pounds of living meat with three separate teeth aching and sending their messages of pulse, throb, and twinge to each other, their secret language of pain, he thought. Brown Dog was not what you call a deep thinker but within the structure of aching teeth mortal thoughts tended to arise in the seconds-long spaces between the dullish and the electric, the surge and slight withdrawal. Sitting there on the stump he blurred his eyes so that in his vision the creek became an immense and writhing brown snake emerging from the deep green of a cedar swamp. Until the autumn before the creek had run clear even after big rains but the bumwads from the County Road Department had done a sloppy job on an upstream road culvert and now the water was the color of an average mud puddle.

Brown Dog knew that teeth were simply teeth and they shouldn't be allowed to repaint the world with their troublesome colors. When he had gone into Social Services the week before more than curious about finding help for his malady, he was not allowed to immediately see his ally Gretchen but first had to pass the foamy gauntlet of the Social Services director Terence Stuhl who always reminded Brown Dog of the suspicious water of the Escanaba River after it had been sluiced through the local paper mill. Stuhl was more bored than mean-minded and began chuckling the moment he spotted Brown Dog in a mirror on the far wall of his office that reflected anyone entering the lobby of his domain and was stuck there temporarily dealing with the purposeful hostility of the receptionists to whom anyone on any sort of dole was up to no good and must be tweaked into humility. Along with his relentless chuckling Stuhl sucked on a dry pipe sometimes too deeply, whereupon the filter stem would hit his uvula and he would begin choking and then draw on a bottle of expensive water paid for by the taxpayers of Delta County.

Stuhl, however, was far from the biggest asshole Brown Dog had to deal with in life. Stuhl merely drew Brown Dog's file, really a rap sheet, from a cabinet and chuckled and choked his way through a recitation of Brown Dog's low crimes and misdemeanors: the illegal diving on, stealing, and selling of old sunken ship artifacts in Lake Superior, the stealing of an ice truck to transport the body of a Native in full regalia found on the bottom of Lake Superior, the repeated assaults on the property and encampment of University of Michigan anthropologists who were intent on excavating an ancient Native graveyard, possibly the northernmost Hopewell site, the secret location of which had errantly been divulged to a very pretty graduate student named Shelley while Brown Dog had been in the usual ill-advised pussy trance. There were also small items like a restraining order keeping him out of Alger County, the site of the graveyard and his former home in Grand Marais, a lovely coastal village. Another charge of flight to avoid prosecution for a trip to Los Angeles had been dropped through the efforts of Brown Dog's Uncle Delmore, a pure-blood Chippewa (Anishinabe). Delmore had managed to keep Brown Dog out of jail by arranging the marriage to Rose, a cohort in the attack on the anthropological site. Unfortunately Rose in a struggle had bitten off part of the finger of a state cop and had another year and a half to serve which seemed to be a long time, two years in all, but then her court-appointed lawyer, a dweeb fresh out of Lansing, far to the south, had claimed the photos showed that Rose had also blackened the cop's eyes and ripped his ear after he had touched her breasts. Rose had also intemperately yelled during the trial that the judge was welcome to kiss her fat ass which brought titters from the audience and angered the judge, especially when Rose had turned, bent over, and showed the judge the ample target. Brown Dog had regretted missing this proud moment but he had been on the lam in L.A. with Rose's older brother, Lone Marten. Rose's other brother, David Four Feet, had died in Jackson Prison and had been Brown Dog's best boyhood friend. Rose had behaved poorly in detention, so that when Delmore, Brown Dog, and Rose's children, Red and Berry, had driven to the prison near Sault Ste. Marie the children hadn't been permitted to witness their mother's marriage. Rose hadn't even kissed B.D. through the heavy metal screen. She only whispered, "My heart and body still belong to Fred," another cohort in the attack on the anthropologists. On the long drive home Brown Dog reflected that the only marriage of his forty-nine years hadn't been very imposing but was better than being in prison himself. The deal Delmore had made with the prosecutor, thus allowing Brown Dog to return from the not so golden West, was simple enough: marry Rose and assume full responsibility for raising her children, Red and Berry, whose separate fathers were indeterminate, and save the county a bunch of money. Red was fourteen years old and no particular problem while Berry at nine was a victim of fetal alcohol syndrome, a modest case but debilitating enough to prevent any chance at what our society clumsily defines as a "normal life," a concept as foggy as the destiny of the republic itself. As a purebred and an enrolled member of the tribe Rose had a few benefits, and along with some help from Social Services and what he made cutting pulpwood for Delmore, Brown Dog got them by, with the only sure check being the fifty dollars a week Gretchen and Social Services had helped extricate from Delmore after a tree kicked back and crushed Brown Dog's knee.

In truth domesticity is an acquired talent and up until his prison wedding Brown Dog had not spent more than moments a day devoted to it. So much of his life had been lived in deer cabins where he traded his handyman services for rent. He was fairly good at laying out new but cheap linoleum, reroofing, shoring up sagging bunk beds, fixing disintegrating woodstoves, and cutting firewood that he was never without a place to stay. This scarcely qualified him to raise two children but then Rose's mother, Doris, though quite ill had helped him right up until Christmas morning when she had died, an event that was the reverse of Dickensian expectations. Delmore's cabin back in the woods was hard to heat by the beginning of November, and too far to the road for Red to catch the school bus, so Delmore had bought a repossessed house trailer which was placed a hundred yards from the main house. Brown Dog had pickaxed frozen ground to dig a pit for an outhouse. There was electricity, and a propane cooking stove and a heater, but water had to be hauled from Delmore's in a big milk can on Berry's sled. The sled broke and he had to buy a new one plus a toboggan for the water, all of which had cost him two full days of wages.

In her last waning days Doris had been moved from the trailer into Delmore's house where he had patiently nursed her. They had been friends since they were children, over seventy years in fact, keeping in touch during the long years Delmore had worked in an auto factory four hundred miles south in Detroit, and had become wealthy by default having bought a small farm during World War II on land part of which became the wealthy suburb of Bloomfield Hills.

Back at the creek Brown Dog sipped some whiskey from a half-pint, then stuffed three fresh wet camphor patches against his teeth, a patent-medicine nostrum for toothaches, the relief offered of short duration. He was tempted to take the ten bucks in his pocket straight to the tavern and drink it up but he needed it for dinner groceries for the kids and himself. Gretchen at Social Services had given him *Dad's Own Cookbook* by Robert Sloan as a present and he was slow to admit that he had come to enjoy this duty more than going to the tavern after a day cutting pulpwood. There weren't any tourist women to look at in late fall, winter, and early spring, just the same old rummies, both male and female, talking about the same old things from bad weather to frozen pipes to late checks to thankless children to faithless wives and husbands. Since the arrival of the cookbook Delmore had taken to strolling down to the trailer around dinnertime sniffing the air like an old bear ready to gum chickens. He would carry a Tupperware container for a handout because he had a short fuse for Berry's errant behavior, especially when Red was late coming home from school, Brown Dog was cooking, and Delmore felt defenseless in the onslaught of Berry's affection. Brown Dog thought of Berry's mind as being faultily wired so that if she peed out of a tree, took a walk in the night, or sang incoherent songs it was simply part of her nature while Delmore always wanted the lid of reality screwed on real tight. He loved Berry but craved a safe distance from her behavior. Delmore had overexposed himself to the *Planet of the Apes* movies on television and liked to say, "We're all monkeys only with less hair" and Berry was a further throwback to ancient times. Brown Dog had noted a specific decline in Delmore beginning at the time of the death of Doris nearly four months before. On her sickbed he had sung to Doris, "I'd like to get you on a slow boat to China" nearly every day which Brown Dog had thought an odd song to sing to a dying woman though Doris had enjoyed it and joined in. The evening before when Delmore had showed up for a serving of spaghetti and meatballs he had intoned, "As a reward Prince Igor received as a gift his choice of dancing girls. More sauce, please." Delmore listened to Canadian radio with his elaborate equipment and Brown Dog guessed that certain things Delmore said came straight from a program of high culture. Delmore liked the idea that Canadian radio gave a lot of Indian news and referred to them as "our first citizens." When Doris was on her deathbed and Brown Dog tried to get information on his own parentage Delmore had turned the radio way up so no one could think straight. It was a gardening program about the care and planting of perennials, but then Doris was unlikely to give him information anyway. Genealogy was the last of her concerns. Delmore had been somewhat miffed when Doris had given her medicine bag to Brown Dog to keep for Berry until she was old enough but to hide it away so Rose couldn't sell its contents for booze when she got out of prison. Doris had shown him her loon's head soapstone pipe that was made about the time of Jesus, or so she said.

On his way back to the car Brown Dog detoured up a long hill, a place he favored when his heart and mind required a broader view of life than that offered by the pettier problems that were mud puddles not the free-flowing creeks and rivers he cared so deeply for. You could sit on a rocky outcropping and see the conjunction of the West Branch and Middle Branch of the Escanaba River miles away and in a thicket on the south slope there was a Cooper's hawks' nest and a few hundred yards away a bear den, both of which were used every year he could remember. It was a hill that lifted and dispersed sadness and when he had nearly reached the top it occurred to him that while his teeth still ached the pain had become more distant as if he were a train and the discomfort had receded to the caboose. When he reached the top he did a little twirl on the ball of one foot which he always did to give himself the illusion of seeing 360 degrees at once. There had been a brief spate of late April warm weather but enough to cause the first faint burgeoning of pastel green in the tree buds. He sucked in air to balance the arduous climb and felt he was sucking in spring herself, the fresh earth smells that were the remotest idea during winter. Rare tears formed when he saw the back of the Cooper's hawk passing below him. If you hung out long enough in the area the local hawks and ravens grew used to your presence and resumed their normal activity though it was fun to irritate red-tailed hawks by imitating their raspy whistle. He dug under the roots of a stump and drew out a metal box that contained marbles, arrowheads, and a seminude photo of Lana Turner he had owned since age twelve. He didn't take a look but dug deeper for a leather pouch that contained a half-full pint of peppermint schnapps from which he took a healthy gulp then lay back for a session of cloud study. Delmore had told him that way out west in northern Arizona there was a tribe that lived in cliffs and thought the souls of their dead ancestors had taken up residence in clouds. It was pleasant to think that his mother who he couldn't remember lived in that stratocumulus approaching from the west, and maybe the father he had never laid eyes on had joined her in the cloud. His grandfather who raised him had loved lightning and storm clouds and would sit on the old porch swing and watch summer storms passing over the northern section of Lake Michigan. Brown Dog didn't give a thought to his own afterlife, the knowledge of which would arrive in its own time. At the moment as the Cooper's hawk passed overhead for a quick study of the prone figure Brown Dog thought heaven would be to live as a Cooper's hawk whose avian head was without the burden of teeth.

Coming down the hill after a brief snooze and another ample sip of the schnapps he paused for a moment of dread, mere seconds of understandable hesitation at the idea of returning to a domestic world for which he had had no real training. The option of at least a full year in jail reminded him of his grandpa saying, "Caught between a rock and a hard place." When he had visited arrested friends jails were smelly, and full of the clang of gates and doors closing. The food was bad, there was no place to walk, no birds. His old girlfriend, the anthropology graduate student Shelley, had told him that way back whenever in the Middle Ages hell was thought to be a place totally without birds. Jail was also a place without women, an equally dire prospect, and more immediately punishing. Brown Dog was greatly drawn to women with none of the hesitancy of his more modern counterparts who tiptoed in and out of women's lives wearing blindfolds, nose plugs, ear plugs, and fluttering ironic hearts. One warm summer morning when a damp sheet was wrapped around the knees of Shelley's nude body Brown Dog had gazed a long time at her genitals and then began clapping in hearty applause. She was a little irritated to be awakened thusly, then warmed to the idea that this backwoods goofy thought a portion of her body about which she had some doubt was beautiful.

When Brown Dog reached his car, a '72 Chevelle, the force of his aching teeth made him quiver. He took four ibuprofen with a swig of water from his canteen. Delmore had gotten the car in payment for a bad debt from a cousin over in Iron River, not remembering that the old brown sedan was powerful with a 396 engine, what Red from the backseat called "kickass," so that when Brown Dog stomped the gas pedal to see what would happen it was a neck snapper. Delmore was amused saying the Detroit cops used Chevelles for chasing miscreants. Brown Dog was appalled. Rose had wrecked his beloved old Dodge van in a stupor, and after that had come the Studebaker pickup with no side windows. On his grandpa's advice he habitually held his speed at forty-nine which, by coincidence, was also his favorite temperature.

On the drive home he found his irritation at Delmore rising. That day after making his way through Social Services past the frothy Stuhl and reaching his ally Gretchen's office he had poured forth his tooth pain but found her less responsive than usual. Rather than her usual abrasive self Gretchen was morose. Since they were long acquaintances, almost friends, Gretchen confessed she had lost her lover of eight years' standing, a "marriage" of sorts that had begun her senior year at Michigan State University. Despite her grief she arranged for Brown Dog to have a free consultation with a dentist friend of hers. There was no public money available for actual treatment. Gretchen was sure, however, that she could find a way to get the money out of Delmore by bringing up his failure to adequately cover Brown Dog's accident when a tree bucked back and shattered his knee. She could also legally force Delmore to install full plumbing in the shabby mobile home. Delmore loathed Gretchen, huffing and referring to her as a "daughter of Sappho," an old-fashioned term of opprobrium for lesbians. Rather than listening to Gretchen's invective Brown Dog had drifted off remembering the diner waitress he had made love to on Gretchen's living room floor when he was supposed to be painting the walls yellow. The waitress had one short leg but he had decided many mornings at breakfast in the diner that this short leg had become attractive in its own right. He hadn't realized that Gretchen's lover was upstairs, presuming her to be at work. From snooping in Gretchen's undies drawer and finding photos, Brown Dog knew that lady was a real looker. Sad to say that on hearing the love racket downstairs she had called Gretchen's office and

Brown Dog had been caught in the saddle, though in fact he was underneath. This event had cooled the friendship which gradually warmed up, mostly because Gretchen liked this preposterous fool, so unlike her father and his cronies. She'd grown up in a modestly posh suburb of Grand Rapids where all the men were middle or higher management in Steelcase (purportedly the world's largest producer of office desks, file cabinets, and folding chairs) or Amway, a super version of the old Fuller Brush Company. She actually loathed her bully father, not to speak of his friends and their veiled but implicit condescension to all things female from the Virgin Mary to cats and dogs. If they were to fish with female worms the worms would be chuckled at with the curious sense of superiority many males in this culture feel their weenies entitle them to.

Brown Dog cooled his heels for a full hour in the office of Gretchen's high-end dentist chum. The waiting room reminded him of fancy hotels in Chicago though he had only looked through the windows of such places. There were three women and two male patients also waiting who were clearly members of what Delmore called Escanaba's "upper crust," though that designation might also include successful car dealers and their wives. None of the others returned B.D.'s friendly nod but he thought perhaps they were also in pain and therefore uncivil. He did note that the pine sap on his trousers had stickily attracted dirt and that the Mexican chicken stew he had made from *Dad's Own Cookbook* the evening before had splattered a goodly amount of grease on his camouflage T-shirt, a discontinued item from the back corner of a discount supermarket, twelve of them in fact for a dollar apiece. He did recall that in his earlier days rich people greeted poor folks on the street and were now less likely to do so.

The dentist was chunky indeed with a mottled beige complexion but B.D. couldn't help but feel thrilled during the cursory examination when her green-smocked pelvis brushed against his knees. She was genuinely appalled when she learned he had never in his life been to a dentist. He was embarrassed enough to try to change the subject by asking her why she wore the thin latex rubber gloves. "AIDS prevention, you goof." She was not so much angry as dumbfounded by his dental neglect. Besides, Gretchen had used the term "goofy" when referring to B.D., saying also that she had heard around town that he was quite the lover. The dentist, Belinda Schwartz, had found slim pickings among the men of her own social set, the "upper crust" as it were, including Stuhl, Gretchen's boss, who was an implement freak, two car salesmen, and an alcoholic who worked for the newspaper who had shit his pants after collapsing in her bathtub. Belinda who had a decided nonresemblance to fashion models had taken to driving north to Ontonagon on weekends where her randy spirit had easily won the affection of a number of young Native men, two Finnish miners, and a mulatto logger who had sent her to body heaven. On questioning, Brown Dog had admitted his career as a bare-knuckle fighter early in life and she advised that this was the reason his teeth were permanently loosening from their deadened roots outward. Before leaving she gave him a few dozen Percodans and Percocets recognizing his pain, and then, as advised, called Gretchen to say she would need a deposit of three thousand for starters. Gretchen called Delmore with the news and the threat that she could force him to install proper plumbing. Delmore called her a "vile rug muncher" and she, unfazed, merely said, "I'm going to win this one, kiddo."

Two weeks later, the pain drugs long gone, Brown Dog's sore teeth were still being held hostage to the war between Delmore and Gretchen. When he had returned from the dentist late that afternoon he expected a shit monsoon but instead Delmore wept quietly on his porch swing, then was kind enough to offer B.D. a drink of his rationed Four Roses whiskey. When B.D. patted Delmore on the shoulder Delmore said he was weeping for the youth of America. This surprising announcement was allowed to stand alone in the coolish April air for at least five minutes. B.D.

had heard most of the "youth of America" material many times before but was attentive to new additions. On the way home he had taken a Percodan with a warm can of beer found under the car seat which had made him as impervious as a stone Olmec head to Delmore's caterwauling about the toughness of the cinema hero John Wayne in *Red River*, the manliness of the football coaches Woody Hayes and Vince Lombardi to which B.D. always replied, "It's easy on the sidelines," at which point Delmore added Bobby Layne, the old Detroit Lions quarterback, and the brave young men at Iwo Jima and on Pork Chop Hill, not to speak of the Ojibway warriors, Delmore's own ancestors, who had repelled the Mohawk invasion in the eighteenth century in a battle in the eastern Upper Peninsula.

The upshot of Delmore's mournful speech was that in the old days when "men were men" they pulled their own teeth rather than spend someone else's hard-earned money. B.D. knew this was true having watched out a back window as his grandfather pulled his own molar. He also knew that Delmore had full dental insurance in his retirement from the auto factory negotiated by the AFL-CIO. The next day Delmore had brought home new GripLock pliers and a fresh quart of whiskey as a further challenge, a bargain compared to the cost of dentistry, or plumbing for the house trailer.

The stalemate had continued with one long evening spent in the woods with the pliers and whiskey, but when the coolish metal of the pliers touched a sore tooth he recoiled. There was a profound sense of body attrition so that when he took out his weenie to pee he addressed it: "Someday you'll wear out, old friend." But not yet, of course.

When Brown Dog confessed Delmore's pliers and whiskey ploy to Gretchen she delaminated, irrationally calling the county prosecutor to see if there were any criminal ramifications which there weren't. She got a casual Republican chuckle and the information that self-dentistry was a holdover from the "good old days" when "men were men." She fairly howled over the phone, "You fucking moron," at which the prosecutor hung up with a "Tut, tut, cutie."

Gretchen looked out her office window at B.D. who was evidently talking to a crow at the top of a young maple and the crow seemed to be listening attentively. She called Belinda and struck a deal for the worst of the three teeth. Gretchen would front the money though her ex-girlfriend had cleaned out their joint account. Despite love people like to set aside secret money and Gretchen had a stash that would cover the first tooth. Gretchen was abrasive indeed but was a woman of wide social conscience and had read everyone from Simone Weil to yesterday's freshest social alarm. Her five-year-old Subaru had a longish bumper sticker that read 5,000,000 AMERICAN CHILDREN ARE HUNGRY. She took a hidden cigarette from a desk drawer having put it there for such an occasion. This would be her first cigarette in three full weeks plus two days but she was needy.

Brown Dog was a little startled when Gretchen came out the back door of the Social Services building. He was swimming in a murky sea of seven Motrins but his senses were alive to the forsythia blooming in the reflected heat of the sunlight on the east side of the building, also the crow that had fled when Gretchen had come out the door. He was sure he recognized the crow from the woods behind Delmore's house and both he and the crow were wondering what the other was doing in downtown Escanaba. It was nearly lunchtime but it was hard to take his stomach anyplace interesting that his teeth were capable of following save chicken soup. Gretchen in her habitual gray skirt and black turtleneck suggested an unattainable alternative. He took her hand and kissed it in the manner of the old movies Delmore favored. Delmore would crow that Charles Boyer got more ass than a toilet seat.

"We're going to the dentist," she said.

"I'd go anywhere with you." He bowed.

"Stop it. I mean now."

He followed Gretchen to her car thinking he caught ever so slightly the sound of her compact butt cheeks squeaking. There also was the scent of hair spray and Dial soap. His organ fluttered like a nesting grouse though he knew making love to Gretchen was less likely than his becoming the pope or president. He was disappointed when she merely dropped him off at Belinda's office rather than coming in and holding his hand.

Belinda was a clear-cut trencherwoman and was irked that she was giving up most of her lunch hour to yank a tooth. She'd have to settle for a couple of hurried Big Macs or Whopper Juniors rather than the hoped-for Chinese Buffet, all of which would defile the diet she had begun the evening before after a mayonnaise frenzy, an addiction she blamed on her parents who had taken her to France when she was twelve and where near Arles at a restaurant called Paradour she had discovered aioli and had never slowed down. She made her own and after devouring it with any other foodstuff handy she was invariably in tears.

While waiting for the nitrous oxide to take effect on B.D. Belinda for the hundredth time wondered how Gretchen's attractiveness went to waste. She was surprised when she turned from her equipment tray, cursing her assistant who was on lunch break, and discovered her patient had an obvious growing erection in his trousers and was smiling. Normally men were far more frightened in the dentist's chair than women. She took a protective smock from a cabinet and brought it up slowly so her hand touched his protuberance before she attached the smock. B.D. greedily kissed her hand leaving a little slobber on her latex glove. She stepped back with her pliers trembling. If you bought him some clothes he would be more than acceptable and the way his sexuality overcame the fear of pain made him a hot number. She felt a tingle herself as she leaped toward his mouth like a tigress and pulled all three of the bad teeth after which she led him to the small recovery room with its cot and vase of forsythia blossoms mixed with pussy willows. She then trotted across the highway for her Big Macs, deciding at the last moment to add a small order of fries. The very idea of sex made her ravenous.

Getting up from her desk after her first very large burger bite she took a peek in at her patient who tried to smile seductively though blood was leaking from his mouth. Belinda patted his mouth dry then couldn't help herself and gave him a hug, massaging his strong shoulders and letting a hand stray down toward his fly. He nuzzled her breast leaving a telltale smear of blood, but their love was not meant to be, at least for the time being. Belinda was thinking of hoisting a leg over the cot, no mean feat for her, when a buzzer went off on the office's front door which meant her assistant was returning five minutes early from lunch, a rare event. She quickly composed herself and told Brown Dog to be at her house at nine PM sharp, then left the recovery room only to see it was Gretchen who had come to fetch her client. Gretchen glanced at the red smear on Belinda's breast without comment, noting that her friend was breathing as if she had jogged up a ski slope. Love is certainly where you find it at this latitude, she thought.

"I jerked three for the price of one," Belinda said in a croak.

"Thank you." Gretchen counted out five hundred bucks on Belinda's desk.

"We agreed on seven," Belinda said coming back to real life. "I got a car payment."

"I'm tapped out." Gretchen glanced disapprovingly out the window at Belinda's black Mercedes convertible, an SL500R, and doubtless the only one of its kind in the Upper Peninsula, a vehicle of ghastly cost bought at wholesale through an uncle who was a dealer in Detroit. Given Belinda's sexual habits she would have been better off with a Chevrolet Suburban with a water bed in the cargo space and black satin sheets with stirrups purchasable through sex magazines. Gretchen quelled her unkind thoughts. After all she had got three extractions for the price of one. Belinda was a good egg though it was unfortunate that she was shaped like one.

B.D. emerged from the recovery room beaming with a wad of pinkish gauze against his mouth. "My head feels a pound lighter," he slurred. In truth his spirit soared. His mouth was now without the throbs he'd felt for over a month and he was looking at an afternoon off. The sun shone, it had to be nearing fifty degrees, trout season was open, and though his mouth was sore indeed, the fact that his throbbing pain had dissipated made him childishly happy as it does for everyone in the human race. On the way out Belinda slipped him a card with her phone number and home address and "9 PM" scrawled at the bottom. Gretchen caught this exchange and found herself admiring Belinda's vitality, her ability to close the deal. Unlike former President Carter "lust in the heart" was a piddling abstraction. When Gretchen turned on the sidewalk and saw B.D. kissing Belinda's hand she felt no urge toward the film rights of the coming escapade, quite forgetting that ninety-nine percent of the people making love on earth aren't particularly pretty, and if we are to believe Hollywood alien couplings are even less winsome.

The difference between physical and mental pain was not a matter that Brown Dog had pondered greatly. The exhausting reality of physical labor each day tended to winnow the diffuse nature of mental pain into smallish knots in the psyche, thus when cutting pulp, felling trees to be trucked to paper mills, the pain of Shelley's betraying the secret location of the Indian graveyard to the academic predators at University of Michigan isolated itself to the size of a dried pea in his brain and could generally be avoided like most bad memories. It reminded him of the fifth grade when on a cold dark winter morning after peeing on a snowbank he had caught his pecker in the zipper of his trousers. His best friend David Four Feet had flopped around in the snow howling with laughter. When David's crippled legs tired he would scamper along like a chimp so when he received his true ceremonial name it recognized his permanent infirmity. The tribal shaman had forecast a great future for David but he died in a fight in Jackson Prison at age twenty-five. B.D. supposed that every boy at one point or another had zipped up his weenie but when Doris had told him of David's death he had simply fallen to the ground in a whirling nexus of grief, his heart curdled. A month later over in Sault Ste. Marie an acquaintance who was half Chippewa and a prison guard had checked on the matter and discovered that David's opponent had also died of stab wounds which meant eventual vengeance was out of the question, leaving B.D. to question the usual galaxies when he slept outside on summer nights.

Twenty-five years later while gathering his fishing gear on an early May afternoon he knew he was going to fish a stretch of creek that was favored by him and David Four Feet as a camping spot. The troubling idea arose when he looked into the darkness of his creel that we are mostly alive in each other's minds and that we're only dead when we're dead to ourselves. This notion understandably made him reach for the schnapps bottle under the car seat. The liquor stung the three holes in his gums where teeth had once been but the sensation was tolerable in view of the coming desired effect.

There was a dreaded gravel crunch behind him and he turned to see Delmore standing on the county road some fifty feet from the mobile home looking pensive which meant yet another request for brute labor was coming. B.D. decided on a preemptive strike.

"Look. I pulled my teeth at no cost to you," B.D. announced pointing at his own gaping mouth.

Delmore nodded as if this feat of moral strength was small potatoes. What he wanted at the moment was for B.D. to transplant four birches and three cedars to a place behind the house as a small grove within which he would bury the urn of ashes that had once been Doris. B.D. readily agreed and added a spade to his fishing equipment withholding the information that cedars would only survive in clumps. He was in a hurry to go fishing and consent was the best tactic for escape.

"Charlton Heston says the government is going to take our guns," said Delmore, trying to prolong human contact.

"Take them where? I didn't know you owned one."

"Be that as it may I have a right to own one," Delmore huffed.

B.D. shrugged and got into the car but Delmore hung tight to the window continuing the usual blather. B.D. pointed out that Delmore could hide his nonexistent pistols and rifle in a hollow log. After all, the local police and rescue squad had been unable to find the kid down the road the summer before when he was supposedly lost in a forty-acre piece of swamp. While watching the situation B.D. had noted that four of the cops in separate squad cars were mostly talking to each other on noisy radios, and the rescue squad guys were doing the same on walkie-talkies so how could they hear the kid if he called out? B.D. knew the parents who were slovenly boozehounds well beyond his own questionable level of behavior. Just before dark when the collective rescuers broke for dinner B.D. called out, "Ralph, fried trout" and the boy emerged from the swamp green with algae-laden water and a face swollen by bug bites. When B.D. took Ralph to Delmore's for dinner Delmore called the boy's grandfather up in Baraga after seeing the bruises from the drunken beatings received from parents. After Ralph was fetched in the morning by the grandfather, B.D. drove Delmore down to the parents' trailer where Delmore quietly told them they would go to jail forever if they tried to take back their son.

On approaching a brook trout stream or beaver pond Brown Dog invariably got the jitters despite having trout-fished on several thousand days of his life. He had reflected on the idea that these tremors were not unlike those preceding lovemaking wherein the heart quivered, the mouth dried, and the surroundings became diffuse. To calm himself he decided to first dig up the small cedars and birches, wrapping the roots in the pieces of wet burlap he had brought along to protect the tiny root hairs that drew in their food. While he dug he was diverted by thoughts of his impending date with Belinda that evening. The fact that she was a tad burly did not lessen the intensity of his fantasies, the idea that they might mate like bears in the moonlight of her backyard. He hoped he had a clean shirt left because Belinda was pretty high class though his experiences with the rich anthropologist Shelley had led him to believe that love could conquer his shabby wardrobe.

Brown Dog was intensely wary and attentive in the woods except when in a pussy trance, thus he failed to see a man leaning against an olive SUV, and glassing him with binoculars two hundred yards down the road. B.D. put the trees in the trunk leaving the lid up but binding it to the back bumper with a bungee cord. He stepped back in alarm as Dirk the game warden swerved up, then jumped out with his hand on a holster. Game wardens in the Upper Peninsula had been especially careful since one had been murdered on the Garden Peninsula a few years before.

"Dirk, it's me," Brown Dog whispered. Pistols frightened him, designed as they were for punching red holes in people.

"I see it's you. It could have been someone who looked like you," Dirk said, taking his hand away from the holster. "Anyway, you're under arrest for stealing from state property."

They both looked at the forty acres from which B.D. had dug up the birch and cedar saplings. The land had been pulped in the winter and no self-respecting hurricane or tornado could have done a better job of laying waste to forty acres of woods. There were piles of tops strewn about and water-filled trenches dug by the giant tires of the log skidder. Many of the younger trees had been fatally scarred by the falling older trees when they had been cut.

"It's the law," Dirk added.

"The law sucks shit through a dirty sock," B.D. offered.

"Be that as it may I've already radioed in the offense. I have to take you in."

"You want me to spend a year in jail for digging up a few saplings? I'm already on probation. I got eleven teeth pulled this morning." B.D. pointed at his widely opened and still bloody mouth at which Dirk recoiled. "Red and Berry will be sent off to foster homes. Remember after Thanksgiving and just before she croaked Doris gave you a pound piece of chocolate cake? Delmore gave you a bone-handled knife and an eagle whistle his great-grandfather made before the Civil War. Last week Berry showed your wife a place to see all the spring warblers. We're an American family and now you're pissing in the whiskey? I even bought a fishing license this year in your honor."

Dirk was stricken, shuffling his feet in a clumsy two-step. Being a game warden could be real hard. In March he had chased a drunken snowmobiler who had hit a bump and when his outflung leg struck a light pole guy wire the force had torn the leg nearly off. Dirk had stupidly opened the snowmobile suit and once again discovered how much blood a body contained. He had gone without dinner. And then there was Doris who had been his favorite old woman on earth including his mother who was still a virago docent at the local hospital. Doris told him wonderful stories about the old days, how in the Depression when deer were scarce she and her brothers had helped their father dig up and kill three denned bears for food and how consequently the family had been afflicted with bear nightmares so severe a Midewiwin shaman had to be called in to purge them. Doris had added that a cousin over near Leech Lake in Minnesota had been so hungry he ate a trapped wolf and the next day had torn out his own dog's throat with his teeth. Her cousin had never recovered but had disappeared north hopping on one snowshoe. Doris had finished the story by telling Dirk, "You have to be careful what you eat."

A compromise was reached. Dirk helped B.D. replant the trees back in their holes with the burlap intact so that B.D. could retrieve the saplings without too much labor after he fished and Dirk was in another part of the county. When finished they both looked at their surroundings without comment. Nothing man does to nature is very pretty, or adds rather than subtracts, and though B.D. earned his livelihood cutting pulp the immediate ugly results singed his brainpan. Of course within a year or two the land would begin to repair itself with new growth but the purpose of paper for newsprint, cardboard boxes, sacks, shiny sheets for magazines seemed suspicious at best.

While Brown Dog floured and seasoned the dozen brook trout he rehearsed the catching of them. The first four had come from a cloudy eddy with worms and a Colorado spinner for visibility, the next five were caught on a Taiwanese bumblebee imitation, and when that delaminated in the manner of cheap flies from Taiwan he caught the last three trout in a tail-out with his favorite fly of all, a No. 16 female muddler with a tiny yellow tummy that he regarded as his most stable girlfriend. In another large black skillet, an iron Wagner of his grandfather's, he made Sloan's "Home Fries Supreme" from *Dad's Own Cookbook* with potatoes, onion, green pepper, garlic, and a little paprika. Red and Berry insisted on these potatoes often and they had the grace of being easy to make compared to the special-occasion spaghetti dish that involved frying up a whole chicken plus Italian sausage which was then added to a marinara sauce. Like any working housewife Brown Dog got home tired so did a lot of his cooking prep work the evening before. For instance he had already started a pot of "Dad's Own Chili" for tomorrow because his hot date with Dr. Belinda was coming up, the thought of which palpitated his loins.

He turned from the stove and saw that Berry was playing with her largish pet garter snake on the table of the trailer's dining alcove. She was actually trying to feed the snake a browned garlic tidbit, originally a product of a cooking accident that he liked to snack on though not as much as Berry who would devour a cupful. Berry's teacher in "special education" had sent a note home asking, "What is this young woman eating?" and B.D. called the teacher to explain the passion.

B.D. sat down with Berry who gave him a hug. She would never be able to read, write, or actually talk but B.D. communicated with her perfectly. At the Christmas program for her special education class Berry had held up pictures of fifty different birds and imitated the songs of each so that it sounded like the birds were in the Christmas tree behind the podium. When he had taken Berry and Red walleye fishing over on Big Bay de Noc Berry had confused the gulls with her imitations so that they had followed their boat in a huge flock, driving B.D. crazy until Berry sent the gulls packing with a goshawk shriek. All birds were frightened of goshawks. Berry liked to eat raw slices of walleye with salt and Tabasco but Red wouldn't touch it.

"You better put the snake away, dear heart. Delmore and Red will be here for supper in a minute." After school Delmore helped Red with his homework and now Red was getting mostly A's. He was also the captain of the seventh-grade football and basketball teams which was pretty good for a mixed-breed boy.

While he watched Berry put the snake away in its arranged nest in her dresser B.D. felt a blurred pang for his former undomesticated life. In one deer camp he had reroofed for rent between hunting seasons there was a big garter snake that hung out coiled around the pilot light of the propane cookstove for warmth. When B.D. would put down a skillet for breakfast the snake would vacate for the day, slithering out a burner, down the counter to a place behind the breadbox that was near the woodstove. When the days were warm enough the snake would crawl to a corner mouse hole that led to the outside world. Tavern tarts visiting for the night were horrified by the snake except for a 4-H girl from Germfask who sat by the woodstove rehearsing "He's Got the Whole World in His Hands" on the saw for the talent show at the county fair. The snake seemed charmed by the musical saw which was wavering and querulous as if it were a metal loon. The girl was too young at seventeen for B.D.'s taste but she avoided sexual contact in high school to maintain her reputation. B.D. didn't mind the saw music. It wasn't something you wanted to hear every day but at least this girl Rhonda didn't screech at the poor snake.

He turned to see Berry jumping straight up and down as high as any seven-year-old in far-off Africa. He had promised her a puppy after they all went down to Antrim County for the long Memorial Day weekend to pick morel mushrooms with some Pottawatomie friends of Delmore's. Watching Berry made B.D. angry at Rose. Her mother, Doris, had described Rose as "a big rock on a narrow shelf." You stay drunk when you're pregnant and you got a baby girl maimed in the head. Berry's teacher said they were lucky as far as fetal alcohol syndrome usually went because Berry was a happy child enclosed in her own world, a woods nymph whose curiosity made the natural world an endless source of pleasure while most victims of the infirmity were uncontrollable and sullen, sensing their difference from others. The teacher loaned him a book by Michael Dorris but B.D. couldn't read it because each page gave him a heavy heart. He was at least halfway through a copy of *One Hundred Years of Solitude* a tourist had given him ten years before. He never read more than one page at a time but the book made him want to head down that way, noting on the map that there was plenty of water in Colombia and doubtless the fishing was pretty good. The trouble was he wouldn't be going anywhere until Rose got out of prison. He couldn't forgive Rose for Berry but then she was scarcely asking his forgiveness, or God's for that matter. Larger questions led his thoughts to crawl toward a vision of Dr. Belinda in a garter belt. He turned up the heat and flipped the brook trout for the extra skin crunch the kids liked.

* * *

After dinner and a lukewarm dribbly shower from a hot- water tank recovered from a junkyard Brown Dog emerged to find Delmore playing Chinese checkers with Red and Berry who hadn't the foggiest notion of what was going on but loved the game. Delmore and Red were tolerant as long as Berry didn't throw or swallow the marbles. Delmore was impressed that B.D. was going off to seduce a "professional woman" and had suggested that if he did a good job Dr. Belinda might take a budget look at the kids' teeth. They were spending the night with Delmore because of their stepfather's hot date and Red was already protesting that they might have to watch John Wayne's *Red River* for the hundredth time. B.D. had kissed the kids good night and was at the door when Delmore remembered and handed him a letter from the school district that said that in the coming September Berry was to be transferred to a public boarding school down in Lansing that specialized in her kind of infirmity. Locally they were at their wits' end with Berry, plus their budget was being severely cut by the state but they were confident that Berry's "socialization skills" could be increased in Lansing and one day she would find her place in society. This is a translation of the dreadful "education speak," a language as otiose as legalese.

Brown Dog paled and handed the letter back to Delmore. As he opened the car door he looked up at the stars beginning to gather in the spring twilight and howled at the heavens, "NO GODDAMNED WAY!," then gave the thumbs-up sign to Delmore who was peering from the doorway with Red and Berry beside him. Berry returned B.D.'s howl with her patented whippoor-will imitation, the melancholy musical plaint of a rarely seen avian creature, a twilit sound that introduces us to the coming dark that we forget during the day.

Belinda, dressed in a fuchsia peignoir, answered the doorbell at nine PM sharp. She lived in a development called Nottingham Hill though there was no hill in the immediate area and Nottingham itself was some five thousand miles to the east. After her scruffy student days in Ann Arbor and dental school in Detroit, she wanted not only the new-car smell but the new-house smell. She wanted something charmless but efficient which wouldn't further exhaust her after a full day spent with her hands in people's mouths. Dental care wasn't a high priority in the Upper Peninsula, an economically depressed area dependent on mining, logging, and tourism, and of late she had dealt with some toothy horror shows, including Brown Dog, who now stood on her doorstep looking more concerned than lustful.

"Come in, darling."

"Don't mind if I do." Passing through the foyer it occurred to him that he couldn't recall ever having been in a new house. Above the odor of Belinda's heady perfume the house smelled like a new car that he had recently sat in out of curiosity at the Chevrolet dealer's. There was low music that resembled the muffled harmonies he had heard in Belinda's dental office.

"Is something wrong?" she blurted, having expected some kind of brazen gesture. "Do you want a drink?"

B.D. accepted a glass of whiskey on the rocks and quickly told her of the threat against his stepdaughter, Berry, all the while staring at a far corner of the ceiling as if it might hold an answer.

"They can't do that. My cousin's a big-deal lawyer down in Detroit. We won't let it happen, kiddo." Belinda meant to change the emotional texture of the evening.

B.D. finished his drink and looked at Belinda through tears of gratitude. He had found an ally and they fairly collided in the middle of the living room before falling to the carpet which he thought might be made of cat hair because it was so soft.

When B.D. left at dawn he felt at one, or maybe two, with the loud profusion of spring songbirds, his skin pricking at the warble of warblers. Of all the nights of love in his life Belinda had proven the sturdiest combatant. He aimed to take a bedroll with his chain saw to the woods because he knew that exhaustion would set in at some point. During a halftime break they had eaten some cold roast chicken with mayonnaise that smelled and tasted like garlic. He told Belinda of little Berry's affection for toasted garlic. It seemed obvious that females who like garlic might have some sympathy for each other. They danced naked in a circle to mysterious music that Belinda said was Jewish. True, the spectacle wasn't ready for film but it was nonetheless joyous.

Rather than wake the kids Brown Dog slept a couple of hours sprawled in the backseat of the car wondering if there might be a salve appropriate for his sore weenie. He put a stray jacket of Berry's over his face to protect himself from the loud whining of mosquitoes. He had invited Belinda for dinner and supposed she might like the chicken-and-sausage recipe favored by the kids and Delmore. She likely wouldn't be impressed by their humble trailer and maybe Delmore would consent to dinner at his house though he had an aversion to messes. The main thing was to get Belinda interested enough in Berry to help out against the government, a shadowy monster the nature of which Brown Dog had never been able to locate. B.D. thought it would be nice if there was a simple recipe book that explained the government to innocent citizens interspersed with good things to cook including photos. It seemed a raw injustice that he had only been Berry's father for six months and now the government was bent on taking her from him, a problem that couldn't be resolved by a few hours of fishing followed by drinks.

PART II

With an eye toward free dental treatment Delmore had welcomed the idea of having the dinner for Belinda at his house. On getting out of her spiffy car she had made a faux pas by saying that the unsightly, abandoned trailer just down the road should be hauled away which Brown Dog corrected with "That's where I live with the kids." To get off the embarrassing hook Belinda had taken Red and Berry for a spin in her Mercedes convertible. Brown Dog and Delmore were left in an actual cloud of dust standing there next to the mailbox on the country road.

"I admire you," said Delmore.

"I doubt that." B.D. had noted that Delmore was less mentally solid than in former times but figured that with increasing age he had dropped all barriers that might impede his self-interest.

"Don't doubt me, nephew. That is a lady of substance. Her ass is an axe handle wide."

"Am I your nephew?" B.D. was stunned. Delmore had never called him nephew before and though it was no longer a large item in his life at age forty-nine, he was still curious about his own ancestry, the possible line of which had been purposely blurred by the grandfather who raised him, Delmore himself, and the pure-blood Doris whose passing at Christmas had left him missing what he thought of as a beloved aunt. B.D. had detected that he was a mixed blood but then so were tens of thousands of others in the Upper Peninsula. When the loggers and miners swept through the area on the path of conquest their sexual energies naturally sought out what was available, and that included Ojibway (Anishinabe) women. But then so what? Delmore had once said that people willingly jumped into the Mixmaster of sex and the product was likely improved by the variety of ingredients. "If you keep breeding beagles to beagles you'll get dumb beagles." This had been after a day of unsuccessful rabbit hunting when the beagle had disappeared into a swamp near Rapid River and had been found two days later some twenty miles to the west sucking eggs in a farmer's henhouse.

Dinner went fairly well with Belinda loving the chicken-and-Italian-sausage dish laden with what she called "the spice of life" which was garlic. By the time he had dished up ample portions for Belinda, Delmore, Red, and Berry, B.D. found himself with two wings but waxed modestly philosophical over the idea that a father must first provide for his family. Belinda had also done quite a job on the venison salami he had put out before dinner. The good news was that she would take a free look at the teeth of Red and Berry. The possible bad news was that she had had lunch with Gretchen and there was not much that could be done about Berry being sent off to school in Lansing in the coming September. It turned out that despite having married the incarcerated mother, Rose, to keep out of prison himself B.D. didn't as yet have what constituted "clear title" to the children. There was a probationary period of a year which was only half over. He was obligated to provide for Red and Berry but Social Services and the educational system still held authority. Belinda said this would be very expensive to fight in court and Delmore choked on his single remaining strand of spaghetti.

While B.D. washed the dishes Delmore showed Belinda around the farmhouse bragging that nothing much had been changed since he had fixed the place up after coming back north in the 1950s. The linoleum was original and he had hung the floral wallpaper with his own hands. Belinda was dubious about the anteroom filled with Delmore's ham radio equipment, but then Delmore startled her by saying that like computers the process was more interesting than the content. Delmore put on his earphones, flicked some knobs, and quickly discovered that his radio friend in Mexico City had lunched on pork and vegetable soup, taken a two-hour siesta, and was dressing to go back to his dry-cleaning shop. When Belinda shrugged Delmore ominously warned her that in a time of worldwide crises it would be ham radio operators who would save the day.

B.D. was finishing the dishes and watching Berry do expert cartwheels in the backyard when Belinda said goodbye with a "You going to visit me later, cutie?" He was tempted but had to turn her down mostly because of a profoundly sore weenie from last night's sensual acrobatics. Belinda admitted that she was also "saddle sore" and B.D. had a momentary and unconvincing glimpse of himself as a mighty stallion like a horoscope drawing of a half-man, half-horse.

There was an hour left of daylight so B.D. took Berry back to the creek partly to get her out of the hair of Red and Delmore who were playing chess. Delmore had *Red River* on the VCR and Red knew this was to throw him off his chess game. At age twelve Red was a child of his times with a fascination for the space program and all things technological and the cornball, lugubrious cowpokes of *Red River* filled him with a mixture of spleen and boredom. Even as a burgeoning star athlete Red had no tolerance for the mythology of "manly men." Coaches were a necessary evil. He was pleased that his stepfather, Brown Dog, was a kindly fool, utterly without the silly macho characteristics of the Escanaba male population who affected total heartiness for hunting, fishing, and watching professional sports. Red listened to U2 while laboring over his homework with complete pleasure after which he would read a book by Timothy Ferris on astronomy. He had scant interest in his own purported father who was rumored to be a wandering botanist from Michigan State University his mother, Rose, met while berry picking. Before she died at Christmas his grandma Doris told him that he must be gentle about his mother's energetic affection for the male sex. "Some of us gals are just like that," Doris had said.

Back at streamside B.D. and Berry sat on a grassy swath watching the water for signs of brook trout activity. Berry had the trembles so B.D. put his hand gently on her head to calm her down. Berry was a regular fish hawk who could see into the water far beyond B.D.'s capacity or anyone else's for that matter. She pointed to a riffle corner beneath a dense overhanging alder and it was a while before he could see the trout sliding back and forth in the varying shapes of the current. With a hand on her head he wondered, What does she know and what doesn't she know with a head full of short circuits? What will become of her in a world that has so little room for outcasts? Why does the government have the right to take her away? She's a woodland creature as surely as the little year-old bear she had spotted sleeping against a stump on a walk a few weeks before. At first to B.D. the shape of the bear had only appeared as a black peppercorn in the pale greenery of spring.

He got up and deftly caught the fish with a fly called the muddler. Berry, meanwhile, quickly plaited and braided marsh grass, forming a small green sack to carry the fish home which the only father she knew would cook her for breakfast. She had thrived with her mother in prison. One winter when she had peed her bed and Rose was drunk on butterscotch schnapps Berry had been thrown naked out the back door into a snowbank. Now when her brother,

Red, chewed on his favorite butterscotch candy Berry fled the immediate surroundings. The scent of butterscotch clearly presaged evil in her neural impulses.

Saturday dawned windy and cold, with rain driving in sheets against the mobile home which rocked in the gale on its cement-block foundation. Brown Dog watched the rainwater ooze through the cracks around the aluminum casement window above his head, noting the ghastly cheapness of the construction. Aluminum had to be an enemy of civilization. He lay in his cold bed remembering his grandpa's "joke": "It's darkest before it gets even darker." His sleep had been interrupted several times by worries about Berry though he was consoled by the idea that he had four months to resolve the problem. The government already had the somewhat justified idea that he was a total miscreant and there was nothing to prevent him from taking Berry and making a run to Canada in August. Doris had liked talking about her relatives in Wawa on the east end of Lake Superior, and also her dear cousin Mugwa who trapped up on the Nipigon. Mugwa was a U.S. citizen but had flown the coop to avoid the Vietnam War, rare for an Ojibway who like the Sioux farther west were always ready for a good fight even when it was on the behalf of their ancient enemy.

By seven AM, the appointed time, they were all ready for the trip to the Boyne City area to pick morel mushrooms. Berry had decided to wear her best red dress over her trousers and she and Red were sitting in the back of the Chevelle. Delmore was in a snit because he had intended to make Spam sandwiches to avoid the expense of a lunch stop but the Spam had disappeared from the pantry. They had been through this before on outings and B.D. knew Red was the guilty party because Red hated Spam and liked the luxury of a restaurant hamburger. Red was an inquisitive boy and knew that Uncle Delmore carried hundreds of dollars in his wallet and thus his tightwad nature was inscrutable.

Three hours later they were at the Straits of Mackinac with the wind whipping over the water so strongly, say upwards of fifty knots, that semitrucks were prevented from crossing the Mackinac Bridge, known widely as the "Mighty Mack," the largest suspension bridge in the world until the building of the Verrazano in New York City. Brown Dog had never met anyone who had seen the Verrazano, the idea of which was ignored by the locals who preferred to think of their bridge as the biggest.

They stopped at Audie's in Mackinaw City for lunch and B.D. reflected again on how once you crossed the straits the women looked different, not exactly scrawny, but definitely more slender. You went over a five-mile-long bridge and suddenly women looked more like they did in magazines. Their waitress was so attractive that Red blushed. B.D. sat at such an angle that he could see back into the kitchen where the waitress squatted down on her haunches to retrieve something from a drawer. She swiveled and said something he couldn't hear and he had a momentary glimpse up her pale green waitress dress. His heart perked and his bollocks twinged. There was enough of his early religious phase left in him that he could again give thanks for the mystery of female beauty, her graceful butt protruding like a barnyard duck's. A little badge on her chest gave her the soft name of Nancy and she was doubtless the type that took a shower and changed her underpants every single day. His mind drifted back to his schoolboy days when the lyrics of "Four-Leaf Clover" had been changed to "I'm looking under a two-legged wonder ..."

"Pay attention," Delmore barked at him. "I've been trying to tell you that the price of cheeseburgers has gone up twenty cents from two years ago. Inflation's eating up my savings."

They hit the mother lode pronto a few miles north of Thumb Lake. Rather, B.D. and Berry hit the mother lode because it was still raining and Delmore and Red wouldn't get out of the car. Delmore was engrossed in his morel mushroom notebook in which he had logged his mushroom locations since he was a boy while Red was reading about galaxies.

B.D. and Berry managed to pick a little less than a bushel in an hour by which time they were dripping wet and Berry had uncontrollable shivers. She was an ace mushroom picker what with being closer to the ground in height and picking at a trot. She would whistle when she found a good group among the miniature fiddlehead ferns, wild leeks, and trillium. B.D. also pulled a bushel of the leeks to make vinegar as Doris had done where you boil the leeks with white vinegar which added a fragrant and wild taste and then you got to eat the pickled leeks which could save a dish as dull as the meatloaf he made for Delmore who said the dish firmed up the wobbly backbone of America.

Delmore, meanwhile, was brooding in the car. He had decided against visiting his relatives over between Petoskey and Walloon Lake. Some of these relatives were fine, especially the older ones, but the younger tended to be low-rent chiselers with a fondness for narcotics and rock and roll. The Berry worries had also struck Delmore hard. Berry reminded him of his own sister who had run off to Milwaukee at age fourteen and had never been heard from again. Delmore had ample funds from the sale of his small farm near Detroit and his UAW pension, plus Social Security, but couldn't resolve his old man's tremulous worries over his remaining family, Brown Dog, Red, and Berry, not counting Rose in prison or the phony activist Lone Marten. There were also numerous cousins beyond his sphere of interest. He felt responsible for B.D., Red, and Berry but B.D. had to be kept on the shortest string possible. B.D.'s legal scrapes had cost him a pretty penny, and a possible court case over Berry was a nightmare source because you could pay all that lawyer money and still lose. It was as bad a bet as loaning money to relatives which at base was the reason he didn't want to head toward Petoskey. Delmore as a child of the Great Depression had an ocean of empathy within him but it was only allowed to emerge in trickles or else it might run dry. The memory of boyhood dining on beach peas, soft turnips, withered carrots, and moldy shell beans did not urge him to openhandedness with money.

When Brown Dog and Berry returned to the car with their leeks and morels they were in high spirits despite being cold and wet. There is something inscrutably satisfying about finding a good patch of morel mushrooms that travels far beyond their excellent flavor, perhaps a trace of the glad hearts of hungry earlier gatherers in the long weary path of evolution. To Brown Dog, success in fishing, hunting, or gathering always reminded him of when he was a teenager and his grandpa who raised him was mortally ill in August and had made a request for venison on his deathbed. A half hour later B.D. was skinning an illegal doe in the pump shed and fried up the liver for dinner. A young doe liver is better than calf's liver and Grandpa said that the doe offered him another month of life, in actuality three weeks.

Berry took off her clothes and Delmore wrapped her in his warm flannel shirt and jacket and put her in the front seat directly behind the blower to the car heater to warm up her legs. While Delmore was preoccupied B.D. slid out a pint of schnapps hidden under the seat and took a healthy pull in the ditch with his back turned as if he was peeing. When he turned back to the car he was startled by the thinness of Delmore's arms in his undershirt. Delmore used to be a muscleman and now time had begun to enshroud him.

To the surprise of B.D. and Red, Delmore then suggested they take a spin to Lansing for a look at Berry's upcoming school to see if it was acceptable. Lansing, the state capital, was about four hours to the south.

"It's Saturday. Won't it be closed?"

"You can find out everything by just looking at a building and its grounds. Are there bushes and trees and flower beds? Is there a thicket for Berry to visit? Is there a creek or river nearby? You're a country bumpkin. You don't know your basic buildings. If you were ever in Wayne County headquarters you'd fall to the floor in a dead faint." Delmore liked to affect the "man of the world." B.D. was pleased because it meant he wouldn't have to save Berry's life by himself.

Red piped up that since they were headed that way he'd like to take a look at Michigan State University where he intended to enroll down the line. This irked Delmore who said that Bay de Noc Community College would be good enough. Michigan State was too expensive.

"I can get a scholarship as a member of a disenfranchised minority," Red said, returning to his book. He put his arm around Berry to calm her down. Berry always sensed the slightest quantity of tension in conversation which would make her tremble and her skin buzz. When old Doris died Berry had wrapped herself in one of Doris's worn housedresses and lay in the corner for several days. B.D. had brought her back to life by driving up to Shingleton and spending a day's wage buying her a child's pair of snowshoes. A few days later she had returned from a snowbound trek with a dog collar with a license attached. He had called the owner who said the dog had run away several weeks before. This mystified B.D. so he followed Berry at a secretive distance taking along Delmore's war-surplus binoculars. She always headed for their favorite brook trout creek which emerged from an enormous swamp, some seven by nine miles in size. A group of feral dogs lived there which a local sportsman's group had tried to exterminate several times because the dogs killed deer for food not unlike the men themselves. Brown Dog sat on a hillside a half mile distant and glassed Berry in a clearing beside the creek. She was sitting on a stump with a half dozen of the normally unapproachable wild dogs milling around her. There were also a few ravens in the trees above that shared the dogs' deer meals. It was at that moment that B.D. decided it would be better to get Berry her own dog.

By the time they got south of Mount Pleasant the weather had turned fair and warm and B.D. reflected again on the brutish climate of the Great North where it had cost the town of Ishpeming an arm and a leg to replace pipes frozen eight feet in the ground after it had stayed below zero thirty days in a row.

It was easy to find MSU because of a convenient highway sign. B.D. noted the campus was a pussy palace with college girls in summer skirts or shorts in full frolic, running, jumping, dancing. This clearly cast a different light on education and he offered himself a tinge of regret that he had barely made it through the eighth grade. A coach had beaten him nearly senseless before the pain made B.D. respond whereupon he had cracked the coach's jaw with a short uppercut. Were it not for fifty witnesses on the ball field B.D. would have gone to reform school for this illegal act. Many coaches like to slap boys around from their position which offers impunity but this coach was a hard puncher.

Navigating Lansing, the state capital, was a near disaster. Delmore insisted he knew Lansing like "the back of my hand" from visiting a girlfriend in the late 1940s but fifty years later they seemed to have changed the city. One-way streets, unknown in the Upper Peninsula, were an especial problem. Delmore fumed but then in the very shadows of the state capitol building, imposing except for what went on inside, a kindly and apparently gay policeman gave them directions. When they sped on Delmore said, "That fellow is light in his loafers."

The school and residential quarters were a stunning disappointment. The buildings virtually squatted in a cement-covered field beyond a cyclone fence. Beside the entrance were two starved maples in wooden planters. Off to the side a gaggle of children mooed and moaned on teeter-totters and swings. Delmore covered his face in his hands and Red said, "This place sucks." B.D. remembered his early Bible studies well enough to think of the heap of beige bricks as the abomination of desolation spoken of by the prophet Daniel. He squealed the tires to get away and Berry waved at a little boy bleating and spinning in circles by the fence.

They were a full hour north of Lansing headed home before anyone said anything about the school.

"I wouldn't send an Arab to that goddamned place." Delmore's voice fluttered with anger.

The lump in B.D.'s throat had gradually dissipated through the grace of a sex fantasy about Belinda and now Delmore's anger delighted him. Delmore had the wherewithal to give him a grubstake if he had to cut and run with Berry. B.D. wasn't partial to television thinking of it as a time-gobbling machine but he had noted that when criminal types laid plans for escape they always headed south so he would confuse any authorities by making his way north. Belinda had referred to Berry as "mentally challenged" and so did Gretchen at Social Services. B.D. wondered idly who had come up with such a phrase which struck him as lame as a dead worm. In his terms a challenge preceded a fight and Berry didn't seem to be quarreling with her mind but rather living with it in a separate world possibly more similar to that of an especially fine dog. It was clearly time to go to the humane society and get her some companionship.

They got home around midnight and found Belinda asleep upright on Delmore's porch swing.

"You got your work cut out for you," Delmore guffawed and tottered off to bed.

Brown Dog took the kids over to the trailer. Red was asleep on his feet and when B.D. opened the door to Red's tiny room, normally strictly off-limits, there was a line of garish photos from *Penthouse* on the wall above the bookcase of abstruse titles in the sciences. Gretchen had told him that he would have to give Red a chat about the birds and the bees because the school was "woefully lacking" on sex education. She had given B.D. a booklet on the subject that included unattractive and complicated diagrams of male and female plumbing as if they had been sliced in half sideways. B.D. figured that it would be better to use a naughty magazine which would offer up the beauty the subject deserved.

B.D. walked back to Delmore's where Belinda still snored softly on the porch swing, her head atilt so that moonlight shone down dreamily on her cheek. B.D. quivered in thanksgiving. His luck hadn't run good in years but now before him was the gift of this great big girl who also happened to be a top-notch dentist. If he hadn't abandoned his religion he would have knelt there in gratitude. He knelt there anyway and soon enough Belinda slid off the swing so they could go at it like love-struck canines unmindful of the noise they made. Soon enough Delmore appeared at the screen door and flicked on the porch light.

"Jesus, I thought some animal was getting killed," said Delmore, looking away in modesty.

"We got carried away," Belinda said demurely from her hands and knees. B.D. had collapsed on her back, his face buried in her hair.

"Have fun, kids." Delmore turned off the light and retreated.

B.D. rolled off Belinda's ample back with a thump on the porch boards. Her butt glowed mysteriously in the moonlight but he was plumb tired from mushrooming, the very long day, and the six-hundred-mile drive. He was fast asleep in a trice and Belinda covered him with an expensive comforter from her car trunk that had been used for less satisfactory assignations. She tingled all over with her good fortune at finding this wonderful backwoods nitwit. She had told Gretchen that B.D. filled her with an "inner glow," which she'd regretted when Gretchen had looked off with melancholy having recently lost her own lover.

All too bright and early Berry woke up B.D. on the porch with a fat, fresh garter snake wrapped around her arm. They were having a Sunday morning open house at the humane society and he knew it was time to fetch a pup after picking up Delmore's Sunday *Detroit Free Press* which, despite the fact that Delmore had been out of the area for half a century, was read with exhaustive intensity. None of the contents meant anything to the rest of the family but Delmore liked to read aloud before Sunday dinner. "Five in Dope Gang Found with Severed Heads," "Rouge River Catches on Fire," "Road Rage Starts Fatal Fistfight." In the relatively newsless area like the U.P. where "Old Finn Walks Twenty-five Miles to See Brother" made the headlines (when asked he said, "I don't have no car"), the news from Detroit was as garish and unbelievable as anything on television.

They were early at the humane society, a visit to which is to encompass a miniature Treblinka where neglected creatures awaited the gas chambers except for the few lucky enough to be selected as pets. To get a female spayed often meant half a week's pay. Growing up in the waif category and having spent time in jail on several occasions put Brown Dog in a state of double emotional jeopardy. The elderly male attendant offered them tepid lemonade and a store-bought cookie from a card table festooned with yellow crepe paper. B.D. had seen the attendant, a retired schoolteacher, shuffling around town with his own three mutts on leashes. Off to the side at the end of the small building a large brindle dog was barking and Berry rushed over.

"I don't recommend that pup for a young lady," the attendant said, taking B.D.'s arm.

This naturally made B.D. curious and he walked over to where Berry stooped beside a cage. The female was a large three-legged mixed hound, a bear dog that had lost a limb in an encounter. The pup, about six weeks, had a walleye and big feet. The attendant muttered on about the irresponsibility of bear hunters who hauled hounds north then lost or abandoned them. He guessed the father to be a wild half-Lab, half-Catahoula wild-hog dog a farmer had shot for killing a calf that April. The mother growled at B.D. and the attendant while she licked Berry's proffered fingers as if she were a long-lost puppy. The mother had been owned by a pulp cutter who had given her up after she ate a dozen of a neighbor's laying hens. The female pup was still and taciturn in the cage and then raised its head and began howling.

B.D. lost himself in thought. How could you separate a mother from the pup? Not having had one of his own B.D. had a weakness for the idea of motherhood. Two dogs would complicate life but then life was always complicated. Berry had entered the cage and was holding the pup who had stopped howling. The mother licked the pup and Berry hugged her large head. B.D. certainly didn't know the word but the mother could best be described as "baleful" as she neared the end of the long hunting life for which she had been genetically designed. Bear dogs are at best canine guided missiles who, once they learn the scent of their prey, are forever fixed on pursuing bear of which the U.P. had an abounding population. B.D. figured that since the mother was reduced to three legs she shouldn't be too hard to handle. With the pup it was simply a matter of banishing interest in bear and deer and fixing its predatory interests on harmless species such as red squirrels, chipmunks, and rabbits, or even the local raccoons who had prevented Delmore from raising sweet corn in his garden.

"What's their names?" Brown Dog knelt down by the pen and Berry led the mother over for an introduction. She sniffed his hand and perceived the connection to the girl.

"The mother's name is simply Bitch which of course you'll change to something suitable for the young lady," the attendant huffed. "The pup is nameless."

"Ted," Berry said, one of the few words she could say. She seemed to pick up about twenty percent of any adult conversation and Ted was the name of her favorite brown-and-black teddy bear. The fact that the puppy was female was meaningless to B.D. and Berry but not the attendant who was nonplussed. Berry carried the pup toward the car and Bitch followed wagging her tail as if she knew her liberation was at hand.

"Is your daughter O.K.?"

"Nope. The mother drank too much schnapps when she was carrying her."

"She should have her butt kicked. Can you offer a contribution?"

B.D. had seven dollars and gave the attendant five because he had to keep two bucks for Delmore's Sunday paper. There went his Sunday six-pack. He'd have to grill the pork steaks without a beer. Delmore did most of the grocery shopping and was always on the lookout for meat bargains. He usually bought less than enough but excepted Sunday dinner from his penurious impulses. A black crony from his years at the auto factory in Detroit used to barbecue him pork steak cut in two-inch slabs and fifty years later still sent along jars of his private sauce. His name was Clyde and he visited once a year usually around July 4th. B.D. was amused at the way the ancient black man and the old Anishinabe would sit on the porch swing mixing Guckenheimer whiskey (the cheapest extant) with lemonade arguing about religion, race relations, and politics. Clyde was deeply Christian while Delmore remained proudly heathen which was fodder for quarrels far into the night.

After finding some change on the car floor and buying the paper B.D. had enough left for a single beer. Berry sat in the backseat fairly glowing with the puppy asleep on her lap and the mother curled beside her. A man emerging from the store came close to their car and Bitch rumbled like a distant thunderstorm.

On the way home the idea of grilling without beer overwhelmed B.D. and he detoured toward Belinda's to borrow enough for a six-pack. He heard a whimper and turned to see if it was Berry or the pup. The pup was hungry and Berry had parted her blouse to let the pup nurse at her barely existent breasts. It was startling but being a new parent B.D. hadn't any idea what to say. He stopped on the road's shoulder by which time Berry had placed the pup against its mother's teats. This girl is a lot smarter than the school people think B.D. once again decided. Berry smiled broadly and B.D. reached back to squeeze her hand. Bitch growled at the gesture as if she had decided that Berry was also her pup.

His ignorance on how to be a parent did not stop B.D. from seeing Berry in himself as many parents note in their children when certain actions cast them far back in their own past. He became suddenly teary when he remembered his grandpa bringing home a mongrel pup they named Bud who grew up a tad feisty. Bud was thought to be a boxer-terrier mix and once when he and David Four Feet who was crippled and couldn't run crossed a pasture to fish, a dairy bull had given them a hard time. Bud had leapt up and grabbed the bull's ear which had changed the bull's malevolent intentions. One of the few books B.D. had read as a child was *Brave Tales of Real Dogs*. Bud could go halfway up an apple tree to catch a squirrel which was somewhat less than heroic as was his tendency to make love to a garbage can.

Just as they reached Belinda's B.D. became unsure if it was proper to borrow from a new lover to buy a six-pack. Delmore was late on his pay for cutting pulp, also the fifty bucks per week he had coming for the shattered knee the year before. He never understood why Delmore delayed his pay so that he felt like he was sitting in a dentist's chair. He had gone so far as to refuse to make Delmore his favorite macaroni and cheese covered with a thick lid of fatty bacon until he coughed up the money. Delmore would then set up the card table in the parlor, put on a pair of dime-store reading glasses and a visor he didn't need, and count out the musty ones, fives, and tens from a coffee can.

It wasn't until he turned into Belinda's driveway that he saw her leaning against the back of an expensive gray Toyota Land Cruiser with an arm around a burly man in a khaki outfit who seemed to teeter on a pair of ornate cowboy boots. There was a rusty twinge of jealousy in B.D.'s heart and a flash of knowledge swept through him in microseconds, a talent of our neural impulses that is either good or bad depending on the situation. His first thought was, Another one is gone. He tended to lose women in their mating age when their biological subconscious rang a buzzer and told them he wasn't future material. They could be drawn to him sexually but then he knew it was on the order of Ripley's famed *Believe It or Not.* He tended to have brief forays with women like Belinda or Shelley, the anthropology graduate student, or with tavern tarts who were drawn to men who worked in the woods. The middle range of women with upward fantasies considered him invisible. His purest love was for the social worker Gretchen who was beautiful and intelligent but also a devout lesbian. Once when painting the interior of her house he had seen her backside in undies while she made morning coffee and his knees had wobbled so that he had to grab the doorjamb for support. That was love! Recently when he had had a drink with Gretchen to discuss Berry's predicament he nearly brought up the idea that he could dress up in women's clothing and she might find him temporarily acceptable. He only held his tongue because she said, "Life sucks" so loudly it drew the attention of everyone in the tavern. There were tears in her eyes from the loss of her long-term lover which he noted seemed the same as straight folks getting a divorce. When she took his hand in her grief an electric jolt went to his heart and also helplessly to his weenie.

All of this passed through his mind with the speed of a full-length movie accelerated to a screen time of seconds. He turned off the ignition and tried to glare at Belinda and her affectionate friend who was a big sucker but with jelly around the waist. They advanced with smiles and she introduced her friend as Bob, a prominent writer who was doing a piece for a national magazine on the rural poor of the great north. Bitch had become unglued so B.D. got out of the car. She didn't seem to mind Belinda so it was easy to see that Bitch would be a bit slow with men. She hung her head out the car window and growled until they withdrew to Belinda's porch. Bob and Belinda had lived together in a communal house in Ann Arbor while attending the University of Michigan. Bob had covered war stories in Yugoslavia, Afghanistan, and different parts of Africa, but had recently married and decided stateside was a safer bet for a man who hoped to raise a family. B.D. couldn't help but ask him about why all these warriors in foreign lands shot their automatic rifles in the air in celebration. The question was, didn't they know that the bullets had to land somewhere and might kill innocent people? B.D. was mindful of this because once he and David Four Feet had shot arrows straight into the air and an arrow had stuck in David Four Feet's head. When David had started screaming Bud the dog had bit him in the leg. Bud didn't like loud noises and whenever possible enforced this aversion.

"They don't care if they kill innocent people," Bob said with an air of such ineffable melancholy that B.D. regretted the question. "How much did you make last year if I may ask?" Bob continued, taking out a notebook.

"I made about five grand cutting pulp for my Uncle Delmore but then you have to add in fifty bucks a week I get for an accident which pulverized my knee. A tree kicked back on me."

"Kicked back?"

"The branches hit another tree which kicked back the one I was cutting. Sort of like getting kicked in the knee by a big plow horse."

"That amount is the same as a first-class ticket from Chicago to Paris," Bob said to Belinda with a sigh.

"I wouldn't know, I fly business. But the flight's ten hours and he makes that in a whole year," Belinda said irrelevantly. Belinda caught B.D.'s longing glance at the refrigerator and fetched him an imported beer which B.D. noted cost as much for a single bottle as his discount six-pack preference. He then sipped his beer and listened carefully to a quarrel develop between Belinda and Bob about the usual social engineering in which creatures like B.D. were referred to as "the people." The radical patois was unfamiliar to B.D. though he remembered a few phrases from his time with Shelley who had gone to the same college. Gretchen had told him that rich people always presumed to know how the dirt poor should live their lives. B.D. was aware that Bob's deluxe SUV out in the yard had set him back fifty grand which would require the entirety of seven years of B.D.'s earnings, though that assumed that you spent nothing on food and shelter.

"I'll pay you five hundred dollars if you drive me around for two days to see the poor," Bob said, then paused as if waiting for B.D. to bargain.

"You should be able to do it in two days. It's not like you're overhauling an old Plymouth without the parts." B.D.'s mind virtually swooned at the idea of five hundred bucks. Red wanted these special athletic shoes which were expensive because they were named after an NBA basketball player, and Berry needed a new winter coat because she had wrapped hers around a dead deer down the road from the trailer. An early April snowstorm had concealed both coat and deer and by the time B.D. discovered them in the melting snow the coat was odiferous. He would also secrete a few bottles of schnapps here and there in the woods for a rainy day, also buy a big ham to cook as Delmore was always coming home with a small smoked pork shoulder. Other items trailed off, like boots that didn't leak and Red wanted a subscription to a magazine called *Scientific American.*

Bob and Belinda sat there idly thinking about the relationship of the poor and overhauling an old Plymouth. Bob offered two one-hundred-dollar bills as a down payment for which B.D. signed a receipt. Bob suggested that they start "at dawn or a few hours thereafter" which puzzled B.D. so they settled on eight AM.

Out in the yard Berry played with Bitch and Teddy. Bitch got along pretty well what with missing a hind leg. Belinda served her a pot of chicken soup after quarreling with Bob over whether or not to warm it up. B.D. noted that they quarreled like old lovers over matters as remote as whether they had taken five or seven hits of LSD before a Detroit rock concert. Bob wandered off in some ornamental bushes and sipped from a flask he took from his back pocket which meant he was a not-so-secret drinker. When he said goodbye and got back into the car B.D. was momentarily puzzled over what Bob was after in the local poor. Did he just want to look at them and describe them in the written word? Who would want to read about these people among which B.D. numbered himself? Who were the folks that found this interesting and why? His friend Danny had lost a leg the year before when his crushed foot had caught an infection and he couldn't afford a hundred and fifty bucks for an antibiotic. B.D. had seen Danny's foot which looked like a red-and-gray catcher's mitt and stunk to the high heavens. What was the point in reading about Danny's foot? B.D. reminded himself to ask Gretchen about this matter.

When B.D. arrived back at Belinda's house at eight the next morning Bob looked a bit rough with pinkish eyes and ultraslow movements. He was leaning against his SUV's fender speaking into a Dictaphone: "I am embedded in Michigan's Upper Peninsula, a little-visited area of characterless landscapes, of impenetrable forests and vast swamps laden with algae and densely populated with virulent flying pests of every description. On a hike at dawn I was lost in a local swamp and my face is now puffy and ravaged by bug bites ..."

Bob went on and on and B.D. looked at the tiny slough at the back of Belinda's yard and figured that was how Bob had gotten his pants wet to his knees. Belinda had already left for work and B.D. stood there gnawing on a messy chunk of leftover pork steak he had brought along and listening to Bob continue with the Dictaphone: "... and on this rutted dirt road which reminds me of the Mississippi Delta are the tar-paper shacks of pulp cutters who supply logs to the local paper mill which may very well supply the paper for the magazine you now have in your hands, gentle reader. Must our forests be cut for this purpose? Advanced environmentalists think magazines should be limited to the Internet while paper companies point out that the trees are going to die of old age anyway and thus loggers can be thought to be merely euthanizing our forests. Meanwhile whole families live in these tar-paper hovels and beat-up trailers where the children are poorly clothed and fed and education is paltry within this ancient triage of survival."

B.D. was confused because Belinda's home was smack in the center of Escanaba's most expensive housing development, but then he figured it was not for him to question the procedures of a famous writer though he was irked by Bob's final Dictaphone sally: "I am being escorted today by a big, rawboned Indian logger who looks like he could make mincemeat out of Mike Tyson. He has been clearly brutalized by the hardest labor possible and is functionally illiterate. You who live on the Mary Poppins playground of the eastern seaboard are in for a tough ride as I offer you material to soil your lily-white left- and right-wing hands ..."

B.D. was pissed because to his mind only Indians were Indians, those who practiced the life and religion like the Chippewa people he had met at the winter powwow including the mysteriously traditional Midewiwin tribal members. Even Uncle Delmore barely made the cut though Aunt Doris had certainly fit the definition. B.D., despite the high probability of his mixed blood, simply thought of himself as a backwoods workingman. He was also irritated at being described as illiterate because every few years he took an evening off to write down his thoughts and he had read all of his grandfather's library of Horatio Alger, James Oliver Curwood, and Zane Grey. Alger had advised "hard work and pluck" though pluck seemed to be a hard-to-define item. He had also spent idle time in the past decade reading over half of *One Hundred Years of Solitude* a rich cottager had given him when he delivered a couple of cords of firewood. B.D. knew he couldn't last a minute with Mike Tyson who could knock down a dairy cow with a body punch. It was clear that Bob didn't know the first thing about the sport of boxing.

Their workday continued poorly with a visit to Doris's cousin Myrna up north of Gladstone. Myrna lived near a shabby rural enclave but her own cabin was as neat as a pin. Myrna served them a slice of blueberry pie and Bob seemed disappointed that she owned a computer and was well versed in the lawsuit against the BIA over unpaid or lost royalty moneys. Myrna was steamed because she had knitted four hundred pot holders for a homework company and never got paid. Bob swiftly offered to look into the matter but Myrna seemed to doubt his effectiveness and said that the company had a Chicago address and a nephew was a steelworker in nearby Gary. The nephew intended to look into the matter armed with a ball bat just like in *The Godfather* which she thought was a wonderful family movie. When Bob began to quiz her on the life of poverty Myrna was less than cooperative though she said that she had started paying her own way at age seven and since she was currently seventy-seven she had worked nearly seventy years in what she called the "free-market economy."

The local tribal council had bought her the computer so she could e-mail relatives. Myrna felt lucky she had been smart enough to make a living. She said it was harder in the old days when one winter there were few deer and her family had had to eat their plow horse.

When they left Myrna's cabin Bob and B.D. had a modest squabble over Bob's desire to meet someone who was more of an "Indian Indian" and B.D. said that Indians were just people and didn't go around acting Indian all day long. Their conversation further declined when Bob whined that he had had to devour three Viagras during his night with Belinda to "achieve parity" with her rapacious sexual needs. Back in their university days other young men in their communal household had barred their doors while Belinda stalked the halls looking for an angry sex fix. B.D. had long since ceased to judge women as sexually promiscuous as himself but this news about Belinda hurt a bit because he felt they were still on the first flower of their love. There was the question that he had become so domestic what with raising Red and Berry and trying to make a living that he was no longer a lover known far and wide (in the U.P.) for his considerable bed energies. A select few women like Belinda required extra effort and he had fallen short.

This maudlin mood kept getting interrupted by Bob working his cell phone and his OnStar phone at the same time. Bob talked to people in New York and D.C. while B.D. drove the fancy Land Cruiser, the dashboard of which reminded him of the gizmos in the cockpit of the plane when he had had his own jet trip. Rather than seeking out the poor Bob kept having him drive up high hills for better phone reception. At one point he was impressed when Bob shouted, "Tell *National Geographic* to kiss my ass."

B.D. had assumed that they might share a six-pack on their journey but Bob insisted that alcohol even in its slightest form could steal the incentive for the work at hand. This was after B.D. had driven into the yard of a casual half-breed acquaintance known as

Larry Big Face and they were met at the fly-covered screen door by Larry's old mom who had a goiter under her chin as big as a football. She heated them up some beavertail stew but when Bob started asking questions all she would say was "Fuck you, white boy" which Bob found discouraging. Her son Larry was in jail for throwing someone out through the window of a bar up in Ishpeming. Bob offered her his hip flask and she downed its contents in seconds but still wouldn't answer any questions. "Mind your own fucking business," she screeched. They left in a hurry when her pet, a vastly overweight raccoon, waddled snarling out of the bedroom. Out in the yard Bob said he suddenly had to go to the toilet and B.D. pointed to the outhouse over near a pen that contained a furious billy goat.

B.D. doubled back from Sagola over through Crystal Falls to Iron Mountain so that they could have lunch at Fontana's and hopefully a beer. Bob was talking on his cell phone when they walked into the back of the restaurant and he collided with a doorjamb but seemed not to notice. B.D. had observed that when cell phones weren't working properly people would hold them up and stare at them in betrayed puzzlement.

In the restaurant their workday effectively ended when Bob noted a locked cabinet of expensive wine, then sniffed the air and smiled his first smile since arriving in the great north. B.D. ignored him and chatted with a foxy waitress he had bedded years before during a women's bowling tournament in Escanaba. B.D. had visited the restaurant several times when flush and had always ordered the "Roman Holiday" which included a meatball the size of a baby's head, a big link of Italian sausage, plus gnocchi and spaghetti all drowned in an excellent but not very subtle tomato sauce. In the old days you could get a side dish of half a garlic-roasted chicken for two bucks if you were really hungry.

After washing up in the toilet B.D. paused extra long for an unwise, critical look in the mirror. He tried very hard to ignore a twinge in his jaw which might mean yet another tooth had armed itself and was ready to attack its owner. He was also worried about a local news item on the radio he had heard while Bob was in the outhouse wherein a fishing friend Marvin, also known as Needle Dick, had been apprehended on his motorcycle with a female passenger going 120 miles per hour in a 25 miles per hour speed-limit area up in Marquette. Marvin had resisted arrest by throwing the cop over the top of his squad car and would miss Christmas this year.

"I've designed a meal for us," Bob said when B.D. arrived at the table. B.D. thought, There goes my Roman Holiday, but then in the darkish corner of their banquette he saw three opened bottles of wine and Bob was starting with a martini. The alcohol embargo had been lifted and what's more Bob slid three hundred dollars across the table.

"I'm having to cancel us until a later date. I'm headed for Afghanistan on a fifty-grand story." He was pounding the table with his cell phone for emphasis then gestured at the wine. "I haven't had a decent meal in nearly two days. We're celebrating by trying out a lot of the menu."

What a day. What a night. They were frazzled after lunch and slept for a while in the car in the restaurant parking lot. B.D. judged the meal as wonderful indeed until halfway through and two bottles of wine, which Bob drank like beer or cool water, when Bob began to cry. Bob had been in Rwanda and told B.D. that he had no idea what it was like to see thousands of men, women, and children who had been hacked to pieces. B.D. agreed, but that didn't close the matter the descriptions of which scarcely jibed with the marinara on the gnocchi. B.D. thought, The man has been on the go for a decade and though he's thirty-three he looks like he's pushing fifty and when he eats it's as if the substance is far greater than the food mixed with his falling copious tears. Delmore had spoken of his nervous crack-up before leaving Detroit and B.D. figured that was what Bob was experiencing. B.D. made bold and asked if this was the right time for Bob to return overseas. "I've spent all my earnings on wine, women, and song in the capitals of Europe. Now I have to feather my nest. My wife, Tanya, likes five-hundred-dollar scarves and shoes." B.D. was working on his T-bone and couldn't digest Bob's information. The T-bone was aggravating his newly sore tooth though Bob's word paintings of the outside world made his own life appealing.

It was just before dark when B.D. dumped Bob off in Belinda's yard. Bob had bought and drank an additional two bottles of wine for the drive home. Belinda didn't want him carried into the house because he had pissed his pants. It was a muggy evening so she covered him with a pink sheet to protect him from mosquitoes.

"I was unfaithful to you with Bob," she said, shaking with tears.

"I know it." B.D. gave her a hug. It had been since Christmas and the death of Doris that he had seen anyone cry and now even educated people were falling apart.

"That asshole told you, that fat-assed motormouth. Now you probably think I'm a catcher's mitt," she sobbed.

"I've never once thought of you as a catcher's mitt, darling." He held her tightly while watching Bob roll over in his pink cocoon. It was hard to get a clear view of what was going on in his life.

Delmore was miffed when B.D. got home. He said he had prepared a fine dinner but Red and Berry had given their portions to Bitch and Teddy who had taken up residence under the porch rather than in the brand-new doghouse Delmore had bought. B.D. glanced at the wastebasket beside the kitchen counter and noted the three empty cans—one had contained a popular beef stew, the others corn and tomatoes. The fact that the kids steadfastly refused to eat Delmore's "secret recipe" did not prevent him from trying it again. B.D. figured you didn't have to be a great cook, just passable. In between sexual bouts at Belinda's they had watched her favorite programs on the Food Channel and B.D. realized he would never be able to chop onions like Bobby Flay or the burly, red-haired Italian.

"The daughter of Sappho called. She says she needs you badly. To mop her floor or what?" Delmore's dislike of Gretchen was boundless.

B.D. called Gretchen who was capable of only sobs and hiccups, then said good night to Red and Berry who were watching the kind of contemporary horror movie where a monster shoots out of a woman's bare chest and bites off the head of her fatally startled lover.

"We must learn to accept our losses." Gretchen's voice was slurred. There was a bottle of Canadian whiskey on the kitchen table before her and she wore a loosely wrapped violet-colored robe which bespoke spring in B.D.'s heart. This was the rarest of all occasions when he didn't feel like drinking. He had been well behind Bob in the wine sweepstakes at lunch but still had had enough to want to avoid a "doubleheader" which is what getting drunk twice in one day was called in the U.P.

In truth B.D. was being thrown about Gretchen's kitchen like a ping-pong ball by moral ironies. On the one hand Gretchen had always admired his great talents as a listener which centered itself in actual curiosity about what people said, a rare claim in itself. While he sipped his whiskey and she gulped hers she compared her loss of her lover Karen to his coming loss of Berry. This made B.D. bilious with anger so that he finally downed his drink in one gulp. Gretchen's Karen had written her a taunting and cruel letter from New York City where she was ensconced with a soap opera starlet.

"But then life is a soap opera," Gretchen choked. She went on to describe her last-ditch efforts to at least secure Berry one more year at home. She had been told to mind her own business which

Gretchen had always done and a nasty squabble had ensued. She then came home and found the letter from Karen.

"They're not taking Berry from me. They'll have to pry my cold, dead fingers from my rifle first." B.D. couldn't remember when he had heard the catchy phrase. "I'm smuggling her into Canada and that's that."

"You'll be gone from me forever," Gretchen sobbed.

"You could go along. We'd get married and raise Berry," B.D. suggested hopefully.

"Cut that shit. You know how I loathe you men and your silly peckers." Gretchen poured herself another drink, half of which missed her lolling mouth.

"I'm not saying we would have to go all the way. Berry needs a mother." It was here that the moral ironies intensified. B.D. had been fiddling with his car keys and impulsively shoved them off the table. One part of him felt high-minded about saving Berry but the other half, perhaps more, was intent on catching a glimpse of Gretchen's bare legs. He bent down for the keys and the view was more than he had hoped for. The bottom of her robe was fully open and she wore no panties. While he was bent thus the blood pumped into his head and both his sore tooth and weenie felt the ancient rhythm of his heart. He tarried a bit long as if in a trance.

"You asshole!" she said, kicking out a foot and narrowly missing his head.

He reared up dizzy from forgetting to breathe. He covered his face with his hands while struggling to prepare a suitable defense but when he peeked through his fingers she was asleep. This presented another satanish temptation but he knew it was time to be noble. Grandpa had told him to never take advantage of a drunk woman unless you were drunk yourself. He picked up Gretchen and carried her to her bedroom. He felt it wasn't fair to himself to avert his eyes so he didn't but it would have to stop with looking. He remembered way back in Horatio Alger when villains were called "craven" and he didn't want to be that. He placed her gently on the bed and drew her robe ever so slowly together resisting the temptation to play peekaboo with the robe flaps. Her body was the loveliest he had ever seen and somehow looked educated. Oh how he craved to plant one little kiss on target but he didn't. He wrote on a tablet on her nightstand, "No greater love has man than me for you" and left. Out in the bracing midnight he felt brave, strong, and good, qualities he would need in the coming months.

PART III

The summer came and went quickly which is the nature of summer for people who are not children, those lucky ones to whom clocks are of no consequence but who drift along on the true emotional content of time.

After Brown Dog's exhausting day with the educated class—Bob, Belinda, and Gretchen—he and Delmore settled down in their own humble War College, the farmhouse and trailer on Berkutt Road, named in honor of the nineteenth-century timber predator who sheared the Upper Peninsula of its virgin forest like an insane barber. B.D. and Delmore were trying to come up with an early and tentative plan to save Berry from the government. They would sit at Delmore's dining room table for their skull sessions with Delmore putting on his money-counting visor and making notes on a law tablet. The pressure on them was such that B.D. was excused from pulp cutting on Delmore's timber leases. With Berry in specific peril Delmore became curiously older, melancholy, and less scroogelike. B.D. felt himself in an odd twilight zone of unexperienced mental activity and insomnia because he was no longer physically exhausted every evening. Delmore was in full contact with Canadian relatives fixing on a nephew of Doris's whom he had previously thought of as a draft-dodging malcontent who lived on the Nipigon River to the east of Thunder Bay. B.D. talked to the man on the phone but was not encouraged when he sounded more than a little like Lone Marten, the radical Indian activist who had gotten B.D. in so much trouble previously. This Canadian nutcase called himself Mugwa, which meant Bear, which Delmore regarded as "dangerous medicine." B.D. and Mugwa arranged a meeting in the Canadian Soo though B.D. was a felon and not welcome in Canada, and Mugwa would likely be imprisoned if he entered the United States. B.D. would have to count on entering Canada as one of the thousands of innocent fishermen who invade Ontario every summer. The idea of being camouflaged as what you already were intrigued him.

The morning after his abortive swoon over Gretchen B.D.'s sore tooth pulsed erratically like Gene Krupa on his first drum set. At dawn on his narrow and shabby bed he thought he might levitate with the pain which exceeded that of his crushed knee the year before. You could somehow keep knee pain at a mental distance but the toothache embraced his consciousness so that he hoped he would be lucky enough to have a semitruck run into his face. His remnants of youthful religion were neither very broad nor deep and it hurt to talk but he found himself silently praying, "O God of heaven and earth heal this toothache." Nothing much happened except that he remembered his baptism by immersion as a teenager and how a girl named Evelyn emerged from the tank in a wet white dress and you could see the whole works. The preacher had always prayed that the congregation be free of lust but that had seemed a dead-end project. He waited until six AM to call Belinda who said she had been up much of the night talking to her rabbi in Detroit about her sexual addiction. B.D. stared at the phone as if he were hearing information from outer space. Belinda told him to come in just before noon and in the meantime to indulge in ibuprofen and whiskey.

"Your bicuspid is on the fritz," Belinda said. "I'm going to have to jerk it."

B.D. stroked her bottom through her crisp green dentist's smock as she slapped the gas mask on his face. When lunch hour was in the offing Belinda worked with greater energy and since this was Thursday the diner down the street would be offering meatloaf with generic gravy. B.D. had developed a courageous erection and she was amused to feel it wilt under the power of nitrous oxide. A girl had to love a man who caused so little work. Despite her two-hour chat with the rabbi she wasn't fool enough to think her preposterously strong urges would dissipate overnight. The rabbi had put her in touch with a sexual- addiction encounter group up in Marquette less than a hundred miles to the north. She thought that the encounter group would doubtless be populated by people from the local university, the kind that were forever finding something wrong with themselves or others and frequently both at the same time. The most exhilarating aspect of living in the Upper Peninsula, unlike Ann Arbor, was discovering how slow the people were to complain about life's brutal vagaries. The working class didn't complain about hangovers because if you had enough money to get drunk in the first place you were in fine shape.

Belinda jerked B.D.'s bicuspid in a trice, perhaps prematurely, but then she was anxious to meet Gretchen for lunch and it was hard to forget the time she'd arrived at the diner late and they had sold out the meatloaf special. When she had recently reached the age of thirty she had developed a taste for food not unlike her mother's inept cooking. Gone were the days when she lived a block from Zingerman's deli and the world's best food was in immediate reach. Now she had to wait a whole day for FedEx. Only that morning she was dipping into her Vacherin cheese when Gretchen stopped by for a Percocet for her hangover. She once again lectured Gretchen on limiting her affections to one woman even though she admitted that her own versatility left her emotionally awry. There was always the chance she would meet Mr. Right in the sexual-addiction group.

The girls were almost done with lunch when B.D. showed up with a cheek full of gauze and stupidly had a spoonful of Gretchen's meatloaf gravy before Belinda could hoover all of it. The salt in the gravy soaked through the gauze and B.D. was left kicking the air. Bertie, the owner of the diner and an old friend of Delmore's, brought over a water glass of schnapps from a secret kitchen stash. B.D. sipped it through a straw wedged well back in the good side of his mouth.

"You didn't do anything to me last night, did you?" Gretchen teased.

"Nope. I'm not that low," B.D. muttered.

"Yes you are. The last thing I remember was when you shoved your keys off the table to look up my legs. Then I blacked out so you missed your chance if you're being honest. I woke up and my robe was wide open and I thought, Oh no, have I committed a heterosexual act in my drunkenness?" She and Belinda laughed heartily while B.D. hid his face in his hands so that they couldn't see his actually emerging tears. Had he tripped over his temporary nobility just because he had obeyed Grandpa's dictum of not making love to a drunk woman unless you're drunk yourself? Would a single kiss on the mons veneris have been amiss? Such ethical questions brought only despair and he drew deeply on his schnapps straw. He looked at Gretchen in her pale blue sleeveless summer blouse and his heart fibrillated. He wanted to say, "I know our love is never to be but why tease me?" Sometimes women were too vicious for words. It was like a Valentine where you got shot through the heart. Before coming to town that morning he had seen Bitch catch a woodchuck, then play tug-of-war with the carcass and Teddy, and then they sat down and ate the woodchuck including the feet.

B.D. felt like the woodchuck and brushed away his tears. Belinda and Gretchen looked at him with uncertain sympathy and both reached out a hand for his. Despite their cruelty he trembled with either love or lust but then they seemed to be inextricably entwined.

B.D. waited until the Fourth of July weekend for his reconnaissance trip to see Mugwa in Canada. Delmore had become more traditional referring to Mugwa as "Frank" so as not to enrage the bear spirits. B.D. noted that Delmore had begun to use more and more Chippewa phrases remembered from his youth. Red was snarky and embarrassed when Delmore began praying and burning some cedar branches at dawn but then Red had won a scholarship to a science camp and went away for three weeks. Berry was lonely for her brother who treated her with uncommon kindness for an obnoxious teenager. B.D. had some doubts about leaving Berry alone with Delmore but figured that the weekend of the Fourth was best for the Canadian trip. He'd have to buy a new shirt and trousers and perhaps a fly rod because his old one was so wrapped with duct tape it made him look low-rent. It amazed him to see how expensive fly rods had become but then he hadn't owned a new one in over twenty years. New clothing was even more problematical until on a side street he found a fly-by-night shop featuring "discounted items" including everything from plastic dishware to tires to vitamins to clothes. He felt lucky to buy a khaki fedora with a fishing theme, an embossed trout leaping for a bumblebee, and a Hawaiian shirt with a print of young folks in an old Ford convertible riding down a road under palm trees. At first he resisted the five-buck price tag on a green polyester sport coat that had the added advantage of making him invisible in a thicket but then bought it when the diminutive olive-skinned clerk assured him that he would look "swell" in it. Also it was the same shade of green as Gretchen's bikini when they had taken Berry on a swimming picnic on the shores of Lake Michigan the week before. They were afflicted by sand flies and B.D. got to rub some bug dope on Gretchen's back while she took care of the rest. She'd laughed when his hands had trembled. After they had eaten their fried chicken and deviled egg picnic Gretchen had slept on the blanket for a while and B.D. had brought his head very close to her body and fluttered his eyes in order to take hundreds of mental photos of her body. He paused overlong on her belly button as if to parse the mystery of birth reflecting again how he'd never known the woman out of whom he had popped. He felt blessed when Gretchen turned over and he was able to take frameable mind shots of her backside. His heart swelled and he waved away Berry who was trotting from a path of beach grass with a large black snake wrapped around her arm. He was uncomfortable with his tumescence and slow to admit that Gretchen might as well be another species. Ever since Belinda had joined the sexual-addiction encounter group he had come up short on the lineaments of gratified desire. The group had agreed Belinda should limit herself to twice a week which didn't quite do the job for either of them. She had also become angry at him when he'd laughed at her melancholy story of an English professor who masturbated relentlessly over a student he loved. New rules were in force making it illegal for a professor to have an affair with a student so the girl had given the poor teacher nude pictures of herself in order that he might abstractly consummate their love. Belinda had tried to help the man but his taste was limited to small, skinny females. B.D. had thought this very funny and Belinda had shoved a large cinnamon roll in his face. Professors were in the same boat as he was with Gretchen.

The road to Sault Ste. Marie lifted his spirits. In a lifetime noteworthy for its lack of domesticity the last nine months had nearly crushed him. He had developed an intense sympathy for all of the ordinary folk who had followed the nesting imperative and spent so much energy raising another generation. It simply enough filled their lives like it did his own and there were no longer those thousands of hours indulged in the dimension of stillness, the fishing and hunting and directionless wandering with the only route offered by curiosity, living in borrowed deer camps which he'd fix up for rent. Not counting beer money you could live on a few bucks a day. A can of Spam, a can of beans, and a head of cabbage filled your tummy supplemented by fish and venison and berry picking. Once in the fall a hunter had given him a bear heart which he had slow-roasted but the night had haunted him with bear dreams. That was what worried Delmore about his Canadian relative they had chosen to help save Berry. If you owned bear medicine it was to be treated with total secretiveness and modesty or you were asking for trouble. It seemed proper, however, to have a nephew with a blood connection be central to the project.

Canadian customs passed B.D. through with a few questions and a wave. "I'm here for the lunkers," he said, meaning large trout, adding he was headed up to Wawa and maybe the Nipigon. On the other side of the barrier the line of Canadian cars trying to enter the United States was massive. Delmore had explained that ever since the disaster of September 11 the U.S. had tried to tighten its borders but the three-thousand-mile line shared with Canada was an improbable task. Delmore claimed that he could drive a herd of elephants from Canada into Minnesota unnoticed. To be sure terrorists could cross Lake Superior into the U.P. but Delmore questioned what they would find worth blowing up. B.D. strenuously ignored the news. With little solid knowledge but possessing a large imagination the idea of killing thousands of innocent people was far beyond his ken to be stored with the other immense question marks life so generously offered.

When B.D. pulled into the parking lot of the Black Cat Strip Club he guessed that the large round man sitting on an old Harley was Mugwa. The man had a shaved head except for a long pigtail and was shirtless with a dirty leather vest. Driving closer B.D. could see an amateur RED POWER tattoo on his shoulder which was massive at close range.

"That's a dumb-looking hat, cousin," Mugwa said in greeting.

"I'm disguised as an American fisherman." B.D. took off the hat and stared at it. He was startled when Mugwa embraced him.

"I kept telling Delmore on the phone that Mugwa is my actual name. I tried to steal a bear cub when I was a boy and got mauled." He turned and lifted up his vest revealing the scar tissue of claw marks which were whitish against his brown skin.

"Delmore doesn't listen too good," B.D. said.

"You're supposed to say, 'Delmore doesn't listen too well.' Bad grammar is just another excuse white men use to hold us down. I was a bouncer here for two years. I still get a discount on drinks." He lit a joint and took a mighty suck in the broad daylight of the parking lot, then handed it to B.D. who took a small polite puff. "This shit keeps me from getting drunk." Mugwa then made a gesture toward an alley and three more large Natives came toward them on motorcycles. "Our brothers. They're involved in the plan."

Inside the club and after two beers it occurred to B.D. he had never felt safer in a drinking establishment. Delmore had told him that when he was a boy on Beaver Island they once got a thousand pounds of lake trout and whitefish in their net on an overnight drop. Unlike many tribes in the U.S. they rarely suffered a protein shortage. Mugwa's three "brothers" said nothing though one offered B.D. a big piece of moose jerky that was delicious with cold beer.

"It's a nothing muffin. We'll pick you and the girl up on Whitefish Point and run you over to Batchawana Bay or up to Wawa, and then you can stay with me until this blows over. We'll run an American flag on the fish tug. I went a step further than Delmore and talked to my cousin Rose in prison, your so-called wife. She signed her permission to have Berry carted off to Lansing. She's a drunken bitch and doesn't want to take care of her own daughter when she gets out next year. She told me that she's going to rob banks when she gets out. She always was a pissant. When we were little she beat my tricycle to pieces with a ball bat."

B.D. was agitated. They had finished their business but the dancing girls weren't due to appear for nearly another hour, at five PM. Delmore had demanded that he come back that evening if humanly possible whatever that meant and now B.D. was facing a four-hour drive without an ounce of hoped-for stimulation.

Mugwa guessed the source of B.D.'s unrest, went backstage, and retrieved a stripper still in her street clothes.

"This is Antoinette. She's from Quebec City and won't speak English for moral reasons. She's going to give you a grand deluxe fifty-buck lap dance."

Antoinette moved a chair free from the table and gestured B.D. over. She wore a white blouse and a loose summer skirt and looked like an especially irritated coed. B.D. felt a smirk rising on his body and bowed to Antoinette who glanced away in boredom and said something in French to Mugwa.

"The rules are you can't touch her. Keep your hands at your sides," Mugwa explained.

B.D. ducked when it looked like Antoinette was going to kick him in the head. She slowly raised a foot high above her own head and lowered it softly on B.D.'s She slipped her skirt and blouse upward in this precarious position and threw them in B.D.'s face. Now she stared into his eyes as if with evil intent like Faith Domergue in Delmore's favorite old movie, *Kiss of Death.* Her body was similar enough to Gretchen's to further unnerve him. She slipped out of her bra and panties and put them over his head and around his neck in an aggressive parody of strangulation, then flopped onto his lap writhing then suddenly yawned and pretended to sleep. He caught her scent of moist lilac and despite his swoon he reminded himself to keep breathing. If only it were Gretchen! Antoinette deftly swiveled until she was crouched yowling like a lust-maddened female cat with her bare butt in his face. He was achieving a permanent memory. His warrior friends at the table laughed in unison with her feline yowling, and then B.D. began to black out forgetting to breathe. Mugwa jumped forward and caught him in midfall. B.D. stood there dizzily. Antoinette kissed his cheek then snapped the head of his protuberant penis under his trousers with her fingers as if it was a large marble. She flounced toward the backstage door letting off one more feral yowl that shivered what was left of B.D.'s timbers.

"I made love to her once and afterwards I spent a whole hour in the St. Marys River before I resumed my human shape," Mugwa said. The warriors nodded sagely.

B.D. reached home just after darkness fell parking at the trailer in case Delmore and Berry had gone to bed early. The road home had stretched his nerves thin, with the warm confidence engendered by Mugwa and his warriors disappearing in the frightening performance of the stripper. When they all had parted in the parking lot they'd stood in a circle holding hands and making shattering war whoops except for B.D. who could only manage a screech. To B.D. these guys were "old-timey" Indians who did not fit under his easygoing social umbrella of hard work, poverty, alcohol, cooking for the kids, gathering enough firewood for two homes for winter. They had an extra inexplicable feral edge not totally unlike the stripper. All women were potential members of his fantasy life but if Antoinette walked up to one of the many tar-paper hunting shacks of his life he'd have to climb through a window and run for a swamp. There had also been a close call on reentering the United States when an INS officer started barking at him and he was saved by another INS officer whom he used to talk to about fishing at the Elks Tavern on the American side of Sault Ste. Marie. This brought up the question of if he escaped to Canada would he ever be able to return? He had a hard enough time in America let alone a foreign country though the U.P. and nearby areas of Ontario surely looked the same. This brought up the immediately unsolvable question of why they were different countries. Delmore liked to listen to CBC on the radio and it took a while to determine specific differences. Canada certainly carried far less of the attitude of the world big shot.

Walking down the dark gravel road B.D. was struggling to remember the words to the national anthem when he thought he perceived an orange blur of flame at the far front corner of Delmore's house. He broke into a short run but then saw two shapes around a campfire half-shrouded by the lilac grove. Coming closer he saw it was Berry roasting marshmallows and Delmore sleeping sitting up wrapped in his bearskin. Berry waved a burning marshmallow at him and grinned. She was wearing Delmore's old fur-collared bathrobe which Doris made for him. According to Doris turtle clan people were always cold like their amphibian counterparts. B.D. was embarrassed to see the contents of Doris's medicine bag spread on Delmore's lap. He didn't know much about such matters but the bag had been willed to Berry and needed to be protected from Rose if she ever returned after getting out of prison. He had heard about the soapstone loon pipe that was said to be a thousand years old. There was also Berry's dried umbilical cord, a few bear claws, turtle scales, and an eagle-bone whistle sent by a cousin of Doris's out in Frazer, Montana. A hunting party of Chippewas had gone west out of curiosity and the U.S. government wouldn't let them return to the U.P. so they had to stay in Montana. Some were Windy Boys who had relatives in Peshawbestown, north of Traverse City. B.D. had no idea what to do so he settled on worrying about Berry and her marshmallows and how all that sugar was liable to keep her up late into the night whistling her repertoire of birdsongs. It wasn't bad listening but you kept waking up thinking it was early morning.

"I had this dream," the waking Delmore said hesitantly, "that you and Berry were in a cabin up on the Nipigon with that chiseler social worker."

"I doubt that. She told me that when she was a girl this Canadian schoolteacher tampered with her so she's not warm to Canada." When B.D. had tried to find out exactly what the teacher had done Gretchen had demurred with "just what men do" but then that seemed to cover about everything.

"I'm only telling you what I dreamt not offering you a bone of contention."

Berry offered them each a blackened marshmallow which might be as close as she ever came to cooking. They ate with relish.

Suddenly it was August and a letter came from the school in Lansing enumerating the things Berry would need when she came south in September. It was two pages long and included everything from three toothbrushes, three pairs of shoes and a pair of rubber boots, six skirts and seven blouses, and so on to the question, "Has this child received sex education?" Berry was playing Chinese checkers while her pet snake slept curled up on the game board. B.D. and Delmore glanced over at Berry before Delmore touched a match to the list and threw it off the porch. Bitch and Teddy came out from under the porch, looked at the burning paper and then up at Delmore for an explanation. He was upset with Bitch who that morning had crushed a mud turtle in her strong jaws. B.D. had struggled to get the turtle away from Bitch and Delmore buried it out by the ashes of Doris near the clump of red cedars.

The letter from Lansing had stated that they must deliver Berry by three in the afternoon the day after Labor Day. Delmore said that that meant they would have to get up at five in the morning assuming that they obeyed the letter which they weren't going to do. Such errant thinking had distressed B.D. who already had too much on his tin plate. Life had been easier when he was cutting pulp ten hours a day. He was inexperienced at thinking ahead. For instance, a few days earlier Delmore, who had been in communication with the people who ran Red's science camp, had announced that he was sending Red off to Cranbrook, a private school in Detroit, in the fall. Brown Dog was stunned by this news but then Delmore reminded him that he would be hiding out in Canada with Berry. Delmore explained that Red was "the future of the family" and couldn't very well live with a back-road geezer like himself. B.D. was embarrassed that he had forgotten to make any plans for Red but chalked it up to his love problems which were the lack of love in nature. One night after a prodigious romp on Belinda's carpet she had announced that the affair was over. She had convinced the English professor in their encounter group to try a woman in a larger package and they were headed to Las Vegas for a week's vacation together. She said she needed a "real boyfriend," one that she could introduce to her parents.

"I'm not real?" B.D. had said and she had burst into tears of class-conscious shame then assured him that he and his stepchildren still had a lifetime of free dentistry ahead of them. Immediately feeling good about herself Belinda reminded him to bring in Berry for a teeth cleaning before she went off to Lansing. B.D. had wisely not disclosed his Canadian plans to Belinda whose emotional volatility spooked him. One late evening over a post-love snack (bagna cauda) she had questioned his feelings about her Jewishness and he had said he didn't have many which upset her. People like Belinda with her lifelong exposure to the media and the educative process couldn't comprehend the airy lacunae in the minds of someone like B.D. For instance, he knew Jesus was a Jew who had been executed by the Romans. Delmore had said that Americans were the new Romans so B.D. had imagined that prominent local businessmen might string up a rabble-rouser like Jesus. The itinerant life he had led in the great north simply enough hadn't exposed him to Jews, or blacks for that matter. Thirty years before during a few months at a Bible college in Chicago he had fallen in love with a black woman and several times had eaten blintzes at a Jewish delicatessen and considered the blintzes a considerable step up from Christian pancakes.

Berry's teeth cleaning had gone poorly. B.D. had been in the waiting room reading about emperor penguins in *National Geographic* and how the males suffered tending the eggs while the female was off feeding on krill whatever that was when he heard Belinda scream. The problem was that after a few minutes in the torture chair Berry had waited until Belinda's back was turned, shot toward the open window, pushed out the screen, and was gone. B.D. and Belinda gave chase without knowing what direction to go. Belinda stopped at Social Services to get Gretchen to help out. B.D. headed for the marina figuring Berry's love of water might take her there. Berry never got lost in the woods but then he was unsure if this fine sense of direction applied to the city of Escanaba. The sensation of looking for Berry was even more desperate than the week before when he badly needed a six-pack and had spent three hours looking for the car keys which he finally found in Berry's tiny bedroom in a dresser drawer with her pet snake. The snake clearly understood B.D. wasn't Berry because it bit him in the finger when he retrieved the keys.

He was searching the marina area when Gretchen joined him breathless and crying. He tried to calm her down by saying that he was sure Berry would show up but it turned out that Gretchen had gotten another venomous letter from her ex-mate so that two events together had sunk her graceful ship. B.D. put an arm around her shoulders feeling in his arm and hand the same shimmer and buzz he sensed in Berry when she was grief-laden or frightened. It was then he heard the untender cry of a goshawk, a sound that frightens every creature the size of or smaller than a snowshoe rabbit. He heard it again and was thinking of the profound irritability of the goshawk when he suddenly wondered what this reclusive hawk was doing in Escanaba? He looked up and there was Berry at the very top of a tall fir tree where she waved and started down. Gretchen caught her in her arms on the last branch, hugging the only living soul that made her feel motherly.

* * *

By the end of the first week of August Delmore had begun marking the days on the calendar, "just like they do in the movies," he said. Red was home from science camp and terribly excited about going away to a good school. They didn't see much of him because Delmore had relented and bought him a budget laptop which made Red oblivious not only to them but to the world at large. Berry could sit beside him for a full hour watching the screen. B.D. had taken Red into his confidence on the Berry rescue plan.

"I'm proud of you, Dad" was all that Red had said before returning to his computer. B.D. had felt a lump in his throat and went out on the porch. He couldn't remember a single time in his life when anyone said they were proud of him. Of course he admitted to himself that he hadn't given anyone an occasion for such an emotion.

Tick-tock, tick-tock, time went barreling along. In mid-August Gretchen was still in a state of despondency over the unfairness of love and B.D. for obvious reasons was deeply sympathetic. He invited her out to the house for dinner so that they could plan a camping trip up to the shores of Lake Superior where the renowned poet Longfellow had gotten his secondhand information for his doggerel poem "Hiawatha." Delmore pretended to be huffy about having Gretchen in his home since she had cost him money enforcing certain regulations concerning B.D.'s crushed knee, plus the plumbing and heating in the trailer. That evening, though, the heart had gone out of his cheapskate anger. After all, his dream had presented Gretchen as an ally. Once again B.D. had cooked the chicken-and-Italian-sausage concoction from *Dad's Own Cookbook* and once again he was left with two wings for his own portion. He didn't mind because he was concentrating on Gretchen's morale without probing too deep. The unworded question was why she bothered opening mail when the consequences were so ugly. The only mail B.D. received was every few years he got his driver's license renewal form sent to the Dunes Saloon in Grand Marais, thus escaping the ill tidings that pursued Gretchen. She told B.D. that at least once a month her mother would write begging her for a grandchild despite problematical sexuality. B.D. had naturally offered his services for a nickel which she thought quite funny questioning whether he thought of himself at the top of the genetic heap. "Yup," he had said. B.D. only knew about genes because of Delmore prating about his theory that all of the world's problems were caused by notions of ethnic virtue and that if marriages were limited to interracial lovers there would be peace on earth.

There was the boon, balm, elongated serenity of three days of camping east of the outlet of Beaver Lake in Beaver Basin. They never saw a single soul except a park ranger who harassed them just as they were leaving on the last evening. The uniform made B.D. nervous as he was still on probation and had four more months before he was legally allowed back in Alger County. Gretchen in her green bikini easily diverted the ranger's interest in B.D. by saying that their camping permit was in the parked car five miles distant in a Jiffy bag with her lipstick, mascara, and vibrator. The ranger reddened and scooted off down the beach.

The days were warm and clear and the nights resplendent with their deep throw of stars which, without ambient light, were a creamy blanket of glitter above them. Gretchen remembered a line of Lorca's from her college Spanish class, "the enormous night straining her waist against the Milky Way." B.D. thought it over and said, "He got it right."

Gretchen and Berry slept in a small mountain tent with a cloth floor while B.D. rolled up in a blanket near the driftwood fire he enjoyed tending through the night. He felt they were lucky because Lake Superior had been uncommonly surly throughout the summer. One especially blustery day the marine forecast had predicted winds of sixty knots and waves of twenty to twenty-four feet, weather to be expected in October and December but not usual in the summer.

The second morning at dawn B.D. had awakened Gretchen and Berry so they could see a sow bear and two cubs bathing far down the beach, and that night while watching the grandest northern lights he could remember they had heard a single wolf howling to the southwest. B.D. was amazed because he didn't know of a den in that area—there were two dens closer to Grand Marais—but then a conservation officer had told him that a dominant male might walk seventy-five miles in a night patrolling his territory.

To B.D. the only mildly sour note was all the packets of freeze-dried food Gretchen had packed along. He caught a few coasters, lake-run brook trout, off a creek mouth and that helped. They picked enough blueberries for one enormously thick pancake B.D. made in his iron skillet which they ate with spoons, squatting around the pan. Gretchen only suffered two emotional lapses which weren't helped by the fifth of schnapps B.D. had brought along. A few gulps of schnapps and Gretchen would begin sniffling and Berry would pet her as if she were a dog.

"How can I endure you and Berry taking off for Canada and leaving me behind?"

"You're welcome to come along. We could be like old-timey pioneers," B.D. offered.

"And give up my career?" Gretchen kept reminding herself to toughen up but these silent admonitions weren't panning out.

B.D. noted that every time he said something to Gretchen of late she turned it around. This didn't used to be so. As a social worker she had been helpful over the years. He remembered the golden day when he was broke that she got him snow-shoveling jobs and he made seventy bucks. He had desperately wanted to make her feel better but knew he was flunking the job. Looking across the campfire where Gretchen had her arm around the snoozing

Berry B.D. couldn't think of a thing to do except maybe take a bus to New York City and drown Gretchen's ex-lover.

Gretchen, however, was sitting there wondering just how she came to be camping in the wilderness with this mixed-breed pulp cutter and his brain-damaged stepdaughter whom she couldn't help but love. Of late she had been profoundly sunken in what she perceived as the accidental nature of life. If she hadn't gone to that stupid sorority mixer a decade ago she would never have met Karen. When Gretchen had brought the subject up with Belinda she felt a sense of mutual misfortune akin to looking for solace in chaos theory. Now before the fire there was this intriguing nitwit who didn't resemble anyone in her upbringing and the dear little girl who, in addition to being herself, struck Gretchen as an apt metaphor for the human condition. For instance, that morning she and B.D. had watched Berry way down the beach chatting with a flock of ravens which had struck Gretchen as far more interesting than talking to her fellow workers or fundamentally hopeless clients. Of course when she and B.D. approached Berry and the ravens the birds had flown away.

"Delmore told me this woman got pregnant standing on her head using a bulb baster. Maybe you should have your own personal baby if you can't be Berry's mother." B.D. bravely continued trying to think up solutions for the life of the woman he adored.

"That seems a little abstract." Gretchen appreciated his caring nature. Did she really want to live and die a social worker with no one to love her? Was having a baby a solution?

When Gretchen dropped off B.D. and Berry in the midafternoon there was a firm sense of zero hour closing in. The dining room table was covered with topographical maps and navigational charts. Delmore played the general to the hilt and even mentioned Rommel's invasion of Egypt referring to James Mason in the movie rather than a historical text. Red showed B.D. a number of e-mail exchanges between Delmore and Mugwa, most of them reassuring Delmore that Berry and B.D. could safely be transported to Canada by a souped-up fishing tug that could outrun the local Coast Guard launch. Cigarettes cost three dollars a pack more in Canada so Mugwa by exploiting tax-free cigarettes through the Bay Mills Reservation had been running loads to Canada and making thirty bucks a carton on a thousand-carton load. B.D. was amazed by this and wondered why he himself had come up so short on earning a solid dollar. This questioning over his lack of venal talent quickly passed into the real complications of cooking the extra-thick pork steaks Delmore had arranged in their raw state. By sheer luck a bear had killed two of a cousin's pigs up by Trenary and one of them was salvageable though messy indeed. When Delmore had reached the farm the day before the bear had returned to his second carcass and had been shot at twilight by Delmore's cousin Clarence. They were both distressed that the bear was very old, hairless in places, and his teeth ground down into dark stumps.

"He's us, Delmore," Clarence had said and Delmore had felt his old body shudder.

The pig meat, however, looked lovely to B.D. after his freeze-dried camping trip. Delmore sat on the porch and watched the barbecuing critically. He didn't like the idea that he'd have to go back to his own cooking when B.D. flew the coop. Like nearly everyone else Delmore was from the school of why do something if you can get someone else to do it. Sitting on the porch steps with Bitch leaning affectionately against him he wondered what could possibly become of his nephew. That morning a mailman had hit a raccoon down the road which Delmore had skinned, boiled, and fed to Bitch and Teddy who now looked at Delmore like a boy does a sexy aunt.

"Whatever do you do with that left-wing lesbo?" Delmore asked teasingly as B.D. sauced the pork.

"A gentleman never tells." B.D. recalled the line from a Cary Grant movie Delmore favored.

"I suppose your horse doesn't exactly jump out the barn door anymore," Delmore continued to tease.

B.D. suspected that Delmore had had a drink from his secret stash of whiskey and demanded one for himself. Despite exhaustive searches he had never found this whiskey which was hidden inside a piece of ham radio equipment. While Delmore fetched him a drink B.D. sipped his discount beer and wondered if there was a better smell on earth than sizzling pork fat. Gretchen's neck. He turned and Gretchen was coming down the road and stopped out near the mailbox where Berry was bathing her pet snake in ditch water. Gretchen was wearing her heartlessly seductive blue shorts the soft material of which outlined her sacred muffin. The shorts combined with the pork made B.D. feel faint but the largish glass of whiskey restored him. While he finished the barbecue Gretchen and Berry were on their hands and knees playing with the pup Teddy and Gretchen's arched butt seemed to be aimed at his heart. His lonely penis moved in his trousers as if awakening on a lovely May morning. She turned and flashed him a bright smile over her shoulder. He would never know that when she had reached home from their camping trip that afternoon she had clocked her menstrual cycle on a calendar to check for the prime dates for conception. She was of more than two minds about the matter but sensed that evening that this mortal decision shouldn't be precipitous. While eating her pork barbecue she looked across the table and met B.D.'s eyes wondering if she could make love to this absurdly endearing man. Maybe if she got real drunk, she thought. She seemed to be recovering from her crack-up over lost love and the timing for actually losing her virginity seemed all wrong.

Delmore ended the evening by ceremonially handing B.D. and Berry the passports he had secured, then taking them back. You didn't need a passport for Canada but Delmore proudly defined how far ahead he was thinking. If the authorities were in hot pursuit to retrieve Berry for their "Nazi"-inspired school B.D. would simply fly with her to Mexico where Delmore's ham-radio friend would look after them.

"My people have been harassed by the white devils since they got off their crummy boats. I am making my stand," Delmore said toasting the air and B.D. "You must act with the courage of your forefathers."

B.D. was startled. He had always considered himself as primarily white. Gretchen raised her can of beer with enthusiasm so B.D. joined in with a tremor because her lips were smeared attractively with barbecue sauce. Love by definition need not be requited to be endlessly fueled and the patch of barbecue sauce concentrated in the corner of her mouth exceeded in beauty the fabled Gesmina biting a rose in ecstasy.

Red, meanwhile, was pondering why his no-nonsense uncle Delmore was talking more and more like a movie Indian. It was as if Jeff Chandler was in the wings feeding Delmore his lines. Sensing a softness Red had pointed out to Delmore that his budget computer might not be adequate. As a practical joke he had accessed the *Penthouse* Web site and Delmore had sat there fidgeting in disbelief. Red's campaign for an Apple might have to be delayed until Christmas which would be lonely without Brown Dog and Berry.

Early the next morning B.D. and Berry went off to catch brook trout for lunch. B.D.'s sleep had been haunted by a set of emotions known as "cold feet" that had wrestled him ceaselessly until dawn when it occurred to him that he could at least ask Gretchen for a few of those nude photos of her and her lover Karen he had found in her dresser drawer a few years before when he had painted the interior of her house. How could she say no when he so badly needed a memory of her to carry to a foreign country? His cold feet warmed a bit but there was still a remnant in his gut of unrest over fleeing his native land. One of the photos had shown Gretchen splayed on her back on a blue blanket reading a book called *The Well of Loneliness* which is exactly how B.D. felt at dawn when Berry had appeared at his bedroom door with a fresh can of worms for fishing.

Bitch and Teddy tagged along on the hike back to the creek and when Teddy got tired on her short legs Berry would carry her over her shoulder. B.D. could remember clearly when his life had been as splendid as this joyous pup's. Even her three-legged mother flounced in the underbrush with the glory of the woods though she was indeed looking for the scent of a creature to chase, kill, and eat.

They pushed on farther than usual to a beaver pond upstream, on the creek. Berry climbed a fir tree on the edge of the deep pond and pointed out locations of trout she could see from her aerial position. B.D. waded in his trousers because both his waders and hip boots had leaks that exceeded the abilities of duct tape. It was a warmish morning and there was the additional great pleasure of late-August fishing without the hordes of airborne biting insects. He tried a fly called a Bitch Creek Nymph but it didn't work so he tied on a cone-nosed rubber bugger a resorter had given him and soon had eight fine trout for lunch. While Berry plaited and wove a grass basket for the fish B.D. sat on a stump where he kept hidden a pint of schnapps for his fishing expeditions in the area. Strange to say he didn't feel like a morning drink. His thoughts drifted to the old days when at the first signs of trouble he would simply run away as far as a tank of gas would take him, maybe only to Bruce Crossing where he'd fish the Middle Branch of the Ontonagon and sleep in his battered old van. What happiness! Sitting there on the stump he was visited by a wave of incomprehension. The sun in the sky wasn't problematical but who could have imagined water? Berry rolled her eyes when Bitch ate a fat black snake with Teddy pulling on the snake's tail for a portion. Berry was reason enough not to run away. She could talk with her eyes. Far in the distance they could hear the horn of the Chevelle beeping and headed for home.

Delmore, Gretchen, and another woman were standing beside a black Ford sedan with a state insignia on the door panel when B.D. and Berry emerged from the woods tattered, wet, and dirty. Gretchen was more than a little nervous and said that the woman, Edna by name, was here to make sure that they were prepared to take Berry to Lansing this coming Tuesday after Labor Day. Gretchen stooped to look at the trout Berry was displaying. Edna wore a billowy peasant-mother print dress. Delmore was smiling but his eyes said he'd like to gut her like a hog.

"Of course we're ready. I was never late for anything in my life."

"America has given your people a hard road." Edna spoke in a soft lilting voice that still somehow grated. "And now we want to help you by lifting the burden of caring for the poor child so that you can go forward with your lives. We can't heal Berry. Medical science can't heal Berry but there will be a sense of healing for her at school where she'll be with other learning-impaired children who will love her as much as you do. She'll be in an environment of learning, loving, and laughter. She'll be able to come home for a week at Christmas and you'll be amazed at the miracle of change in her. She lives in a dark country now and we're going to turn on the lights for her."

Delmore gave Gretchen a side glance that said, "Get this nutcase bitch out of my yard." B.D. was boggled trying to understand just what the woman was saying while Berry honked like a goose and went over to the porch, took out her jackknife, and began cleaning the fish. Gretchen gave B.D. a kiss on the cheek and she and the woman drove off.

"That should remove any tiny little doubt we might still have. They ought to air-drop her into Russia where she belongs." Delmore turned to B.D., his face askew with rage. B.D. patted him on his bony shoulder.

The last weekend raced, dipped, and flew by them like an evasive nighthawk. On Saturday afternoon Brown Dog stopped by Gretchen's house and discovered her in her yoga outfit. She served him a glass of red wine which was a bit sour for his taste and when she left the kitchen for a moment he added a teaspoon of sugar. The label said the wine was from France and he recalled when he was young how World War II veterans would brag that in France and Japan right after the war you could make love to a girl for a candy bar. They never said what kind of a candy bar was a sure thing.

"I knew you liked these shorts." Gretchen came back into the kitchen. She had changed out of her yoga clothes into the blue shorts and danced a brief hootchy-cootchy. "Part of me wishes I was going along with you and Berry."

"Which part?" B.D. asked and then immediately put his face in his hands realizing his stupidity. He peeked through his fingers and was relieved to see that she was shaking her head and grinning. Better to strike while the iron was hot.

"Years ago when I was painting your bedroom I happened to peek into a drawer and notice some beautiful photos of you. I was thinking I could use one to take along to Canada for a good memory."

Gretchen paused only a moment. The photos were buried under her seventy-seven pairs of panties and she had forgotten them. What better way to help break the thrall of her ex-lover Karen than to give this big goof their skin photos?

"Take your pick," she said returning with the photos and tossing them on the kitchen table where he sat.

"Can I have two? You have a front and back." B.D. pushed aside the photos of the saucy Karen whom he considered the spawn of Satan. He picked three. "You also have sides." There was a noble full-length profile of Gretchen looking at a seagull.

Gretchen was going off to a rock concert in Marquette with Belinda but would come over the next day for the last evening's supper. At the door she hugged him tightly. "If I ever decide to have a baby I'm picking you to do the deed."

He couldn't quite feel his legs when he walked down Gretchen's front porch steps and sidewalk. It was like a hundred songbirds had been let loose in his hollow body. Hope was not a regular part of his emotional vocabulary but now it ricocheted through his human shell on the wings of birds.

Sunday was full of the morose and disconnected act of packing, wandering around in a light rain, cooking Delmore and the family a large pot roast in Doris's ancient Dutch oven. Berry sensed something was up with the packing of her little red suitcase into which she had snuck her snake. Her mind wasn't too dim to remember her mother who had thrown her out in the snowbank. B.D. noted her tension and showed Berry his duffel bag which he placed next to her suitcase near the front door. He kept her busy peeling garlic and onions and scraping carrots and then they went out and played a long game of tag in the rain with Bitch and Teddy.

Even Red was distraught until he spied Delmore out a side window dancing in circles around the grove of cedars. Delmore was caped in his bearskin and shook a stone-headed war club Red himself had made in Cub Scouts at the heavens as if threatening the gods. Red called to B.D. and Berry who were drying off in the kitchen and the three of them stood at the window watching Delmore's dance. B.D. put an arm around each of his stepchildren. None of them had a specific idea of what Delmore was up to in his dance but they sensed it was a good thing. Berry raced out and joined the old man. She did a dance which was an imitation of a raven, hopping and flapping in a circle next to Delmore. B.D.

found himself sniffling with the grace of what he was watching. Red stared at the ceiling as if it were an admirable direction, then back at the dancers. "Cool," he said.

It was at this point that Brown Dog's cold feet totally disappeared. At breakfast Delmore had claimed that Ontario was also Chippewa territory and now B.D. felt that even though that category might not include himself it was fatally necessary to get Berry to this safe place. Delmore insisted that everything was led by spirit and that her spirit would surely die in Lansing.

By late afternoon there was a blustery northwest wind so that the sky cleared and the sun shone by the time Gretchen appeared with her car washed and carrying an overnight bag. According to Delmore they should leave before five AM in order to meet Mugwa's fish tug on the money so that neither party would be loitering. The newest e-mail from Mugwa told them not to worry. He was sure that the Coast Guard would be resting up Labor Day morning in order to get ready for the last of the drunken holiday boaters that afternoon. Just to be sure he was having a friend radio in a Mayday from the southern part of Whitefish Bay which would distract any patrol boat. All B.D. and Berry had to do was walk out the dock behind the fish market and hop aboard at "800 hours," a term B.D. didn't understand.

"Dad, that's military for eight AM. Don't you know anything?" Red said.

"Not much," he admitted, putting the peeled potatoes into the oven to brown with the pot roast.

Dinner was fairly quiet except for discussing a plan to all meet in Thunder Bay for a week at Christmas. Playing against type, it was Red who was overcome and fled for the comfort of his computer.

"That young man will go far," Delmore said. "His mother is dumb as a post so his dad must be top-drawer."

B.D. and Gretchen took a walk down the gravel road in the glittery, clear twilight with the north wind turning the silvery undersides of the leaves of birch, poplar, and the alder in the rim of the swamp. Bitch and Teddy took off after two deer that crossed the road in the distance and Gretchen sprinted after them for pure fun. B.D. was amazed at her speed and the way her fanny and thighs pushed her along so quickly that her feet barely touched the ground. She returned breathless and smiling.

"What're the odds on you trying to have a baby?" he asked with a foiled attempt at diffidence.

"I'm not sure but probably ten to one against."

"Does that mean if we were together ten days I'd strike it rich one of the days?"

"That's not the way it works, dipshit." Gretchen punched his arm and ran back to the house.

When B.D. got back to the house Gretchen had started doing the dishes and Red was fast-forwarding a videotape of *The Misfits* to the place where Clark Gable was struggling with the horse, a scene Delmore loved though to him the rest of the movie was incomprehensible. Red rewound and played the scene three times until B.D. wished that the horse would stomp Clark into the ground.

"Fifty years ago a bunch of Detroit women thought I looked a bit like Clark Gable," Delmore said. He was sunk in the easy chair so that he looked half-gnome, half-turtle. The possible resemblance was a far reach.

Berry lay sleeping across Gretchen's lap, the virgin pale white and the child brown. B.D. and Gretchen looked at each other listening to Delmore's snores while Red quickly changed the television to a West Coast NFL game. B.D. was surprised that he had forgotten to have a drink and poured them a whiskey but Gretchen declined hers. It was time to go to bed but the lump of impossible love was growing ever larger beneath B.D.'s breastbone. It was very much like being lost in the woods with little chance of getting out before dark. Gretchen brushed back Berry's hair and ignored his dog-pound puppy glance. Finally she said it was time to go to bed. He lifted the still-sleeping Berry and Gretchen kissed him on the cheek and went into Delmore's spare bedroom. B.D. carried Berry down the gravel road to the trailer, a little startled when Berry woke up and responded to a whip-poor-will. Her call was so accurate it seemed like the bird was on his shoulder.

Gretchen rapped on the trailer door a little after four AM. B.D. stumbled out of bed in his skivvies thinking it was the police. He had been dreaming about the stripper Antoinette in the Canadian Soo, really a nightmare because she was jumping so high that when he jumped up toward her his outstretched hand only touched the sole of a foot. He turned on the light and Gretchen came up the steps looking at his penis half-escaped from the fly of his undies.

"How silly," she said, holding a bag of pot-roast sandwiches and a thermos of coffee. She had slept poorly with both Delmore and Red waking her to talk over the sadness of departure. Delmore felt poorly and wasn't coming along. Red would stay behind to keep an eye on him. They ate their alfresco breakfast with relish though B.D. added a thick slice of raw onion to his sandwich.

"I can't believe you're eating raw onion for breakfast."

"It wakes up my head. Sometimes I have trouble getting outside of dreams. Sometimes it's not until noon." B.D. was trying to imagine that they were a married couple while Gretchen woke up Berry.

They were two hours into the drive over between Newberry and Hulbert when Gretchen screeched and drove off the road. She had forgotten to put B.D.'s duffel and Berry's red suitcase in the car. It was a beautiful dawn with the tops of the trees tossing in the cool wind and rumpled marsh willows swaying back and forth. Gretchen started crying and B.D. had the acute pleasure of putting his arms around her and comforting her.

"I won't miss my sky blue toothbrush," he said.

Berry was awake in the backseat and caught on to the difficulties. She looked stricken and made a snake motion with a hand. B.D. and Gretchen drove off Route 28 onto a two-track in a swampy area. Berry jumped out and within minutes returned with a small garter snake. She zipped it up in a pocket and grinned widely at them. Gretchen dried her tears and drove on with B.D. reassuring her that Delmore had given him a bunch of money and that there must be clothes to buy in Canada, but then he moaned that he had forgotten his fly rod and flies. Gretchen was wearing her patented black turtleneck and gray skirt and tugged the skirt up to divert him from his grief. He boldly pretended he was tired and curled up on the front seat with his cheek resting on her thigh.

"You're pushing it, kiddo," she hissed, patting his cheek and tickling his ear.

B.D. closed his eyes and felt her turn north on Route 123. It seemed altogether right to him that they would drive through the small village of Paradise. It would be hard to find someone less demanding of life than Brown Dog and his current position was beyond his most strenuous ambitions.

The fish tug was just pulling into the dock with their arrival. Gretchen pinched B.D. awake from his phony sleep already having noted that his eyes were open to a slit for the view. He sat up with his face slack and moony.

"I love you," he whispered with the wind buffeting the car.

"Go, for Christ's sake." She jumped out and drew Berry from the backseat, kissing her and pushing her toward B.D. who stood outside looking at the choppy waters of Whitefish Bay. He turned to the boat at the end of the dock and saw Mugwa waving, his pigtail whipping in the strong wind, and his three warriors beside him.

"Go," Gretchen yelled in his face, then gave him a quick open-mouthed kiss. B.D. took Berry's hand and they trotted down the dock to the boat with Berry making loud seagull cries so that the local gulls responded.

It was a very rough five-hour trip with the wind coming down the full four-hundred-mile fetch of Lake Superior. Within an hour out B.D. was hugging the commode and almost wanting to die but the memory of Gretchen's thigh gave him mental balance. Berry, meanwhile, was jumping up and down with the pleasure of the trip, wearing a yellow slicker to protect her from the back-hatch spray. Mugwa scratched B.D.'s head when they rounded Cape Gargantua and surged on toward Wawa.

"You're only an hour from a six-pack, buddy," Mugwa growled.

B.D. peeked out the hatch and over the top of the furious waves at the steep green forested hills and granitic outcrops of Canada. Berry came over and tried to help him to his feet.

Brown Dog Redux

PART I

Brown Dog drifted away thinking of the village in the forest where the red-haired girl lived. When she had served them pie and coffee at a diner and a chocolate milk and cookie for Berry he had teased her by saying, "Cat got your tongue," when she didn't respond to his flirting. She had gestured to her mouth indicating that she was mute and when he hid his face in his hands in embarrassment she had come around the counter and patted his head and laughed the soundless laugh of a mute.

Now he was waiting for Deidre in a very expensive coffee shop in downtown Toronto in which he felt quite uncomfortable. He was nursing a three-buck cup of Americano, more than a six-pack of beer back in Escanaba where in some places a cup of coffee was still a quarter. He much preferred the diner with the red-haired mute girl up near Gamebridge where a kindly social worker had taken him and Berry for a Sunday ride in early March so that they finally could have their first trip out of the city in months. They had a fine walk on a snowmobile trail through a forest while Berry had run far and wide as fast as a deer over the top of the crusty snow. Berry's legs were getting longer and when they visited nearly every day the lovely winter ravines in Toronto she'd run far ahead of him.

Now it was early April and he was getting an insufferable case of spring fever. The proprietor of the coffee shop, a big strong woman, was staring at him as if he was a vagrant. He avoided her glance by eagerly looking out the front window hoping to see Deidre, though his errant mind was back at Moody Bible Institute in Chicago thirty years before where in a dark hallway there was a painting called *Ruth Amid the Alien Corn*. At the onset the painting irritated him because it was obviously wheat, not corn. Ruth, however, was lovely and fine-breasted looking into the somber distance with teary eyes. Once while he was looking at the painting one of his devout teachers, Miss Aldrich, had happened along and explained that Ruth had been exiled and was terribly homesick thus the wheat or corn was *"alien." Brown Dog in Alien Toronto* didn't have a ring to it but it was on the money.

Finally Deidre appeared at the window and waved to him. Brown Dog was startled because she was talking to a man he recognized as her husband. They had all met two weeks before at the Homeless Ball, a fund-raiser for the indigent. The man, Bob by name, had a peculiar shape what with being thin from the waist up with a silvery goatee, and quite large down below with a big ass that even now forced the tail of his tweed sport coat out at a sharp angle. The question was, why was he here? He sat himself down at a table twenty feet or so away and glared at B.D. with the usual sullenness of a cuckold.

Meanwhile Deidre sat down all flash and bustle with the usual merry smile and began to unwrap her ten-foot scarf. When she ordered her double-decaf soy-milk latte with a pinch of sassafras pollen, B.D. momentarily forgot the glowering husband thinking that he would get stuck with the bill which would equal a good bottle of whiskey. The coffee fetish that was sweeping North America left him restless and puzzled. Like his uncle Delmore, B.D. would often use the same grounds for two pots.

Brown Dog was wise enough to understand that the presence of Bob meant that their two-week affair with a mere four couplings was over. He wasn't really listening to Deidre as his mind rehearsed the four: once in his room while Berry was at speech therapy, twice in a modest hotel, and once in a snow cave he and Berry had carved into a hillside in the Lower Don Parkland. They screwed while Berry was running in the distance. The snow cave had been awkward because B.D. had to back in first and then Deirdre backed partway in and pulled down her trousers. There was very little room to maneuver and she was a big strong girl so that he was driven breathlessly into the narrow back wall of the cave freezing his own bare ass.

"Are you listening?" She waved a hand in front of his face. "I was saying that I think I must have taken an extra Zoloft by mistake. Bob made me a gin fizz before putting his salmon soufflé in the oven. Suddenly I became dizzy and weepy and just plain spilled the beans. Of course Bob was outraged and wanted the details. He thought it was strange that I was fucking a proletarian which is his professor language for a workingman. Anyway, we had it out and when we were finished the soufflé was ready to eat, an odd coincidence, don't you think? You could use a shower."

"I've been shoveling snow since seven this morning so I worked up quite a sweat in nine hours." There had been a few inches of dusty snow and B.D. had wandered the streets of a wealthy neighborhood near the curling club. He would shake a little cowbell and those who wanted their walks cleaned would come to their front doors. This system had worked well the entire winter and he had made enough money to support himself and Berry in their ample-sized room in an old Victorian mansion in an area gone to decay.

"I have the distinct feeling you're not listening to me," said Deidre in a huff.

"You're saying that our love is not meant to be," B.D. said seeing a wonderful piece of ass disappear into the usual marital void. He could feel her heat across the table. She was a real burner and in the ice cave he had marveled at the heat her bare butt had generated during its strenuous whack-whack-whack. She seemed fit as a fiddle though she claimed to have allergies to peanuts, dairy products, and latex so that she carried nonlatex condoms for emergencies in a secret compartment in her purse. One afternoon they were at a sports bar watching football and he had eaten free peanuts while she went to the potty and when she came out she shrieked, "You could kill me." If he so much as touched her arm, with peanut oil on a finger he could kill her, or so she said. His uncle Delmore was always watching the *Perry Mason* repeats on television at lunchtime and this peanut thing seemed like a good plot though B.D. regarded Perry as one of the most boring fucks in Christendom.

Suddenly Bob was at the edge of their table and B.D. slid his chair back in case the dickhead made a move. "You cad," Bob said, grabbed his wife's arm, and then in a miraculous act grabbed the check for the Americano and the double-decaf soy-milk mocha latte with a pinch of sassafras pollen (two bucks extra). Despite being called a cad which he thought might be an old-timey swearword B.D.'s heart soared when Bob picked up the check which meant that he and Berry could eat out rather than cooking something in the electric fry pan in the room. How could he be a cad when it was Deidre who'd instigated the affair after they had fox-trotted in a dark corner at the Homeless Ball and she had been delighted when his wanger got stiff as a rolling pin?

On the way out of the coffee shop he discovered that someone had stolen the snow shovel he had left tilted against the building near the doorway. Maybe this was a good omen, a sign that it was time to somehow leave Canada? The blade was made out of plastic anyhow and didn't make the old-fashioned grating noise on cement. After Deidre had slumped forward steaming in the snow cave she had said, "It's so primeval," and B.D. had began quoting Longfellow's "Evangeline." "This is the forest primeval. The murmuring pines and the hemlocks..." As a high school teacher Deidre had been impressed but then B.D. told her the story of how in third grade he and five other skins, three mixed and two purebloods, had been forced to memorize the first pages of the poem for the school Thanksgiving program but on stage his friend David Four Feet had made loud farting noises instead. The assembly fell apart, laughing hysterically, and the teachers and principal ran around slapping as many students as possible. David Four Feet was severely crippled and got away with murder because none of the teachers wanted to beat up on a cripple. Since B.D. was David's best friend he offered an alternative for their anger.

B.D. waited outside the lobby door until Berry's speech therapist appeared with Berry leaping down the last flight of stairs crouched like a monkey. The therapist was terribly skinny and B.D. had the fantasy of fattening her up to a proper size. There was the old joke of getting bone splinters while screwing a skinny girl. He doubted that this was an actual danger but it was easy to see that this young woman was about thirty pounds on the light side. He thanked her profusely even though Berry hadn't learned a single word. Berry was his stepdaughter and the victim of fetal alcohol syndrome due to her mother's voluminous drinking of schnapps during pregnancy.

They made the long twilight walk to Yitz's Delicatessen with growing hunger. More than ever before Brown Dog felt on the lam. Five months before, their entry into the safety of Toronto had been nearly jubilant. Their contact, Dr. Krider, who was a Jewish dermatologist, had taken them to lunch at Yitz's and B.D. had eaten two corned tongue sandwiches plus a plate of beef brisket for dessert while Berry had matzoh ball soup and two servings of herring during which she made her perfect gull cries as she always did when eating fish. The other noontime diners were startled but many of them applauded the accuracy of Berry's gull language. Dr. Krider for reasons of historical and political sympathies was an ancillary member of the Red Underground, a loose-knit group of activists on both sides of the border and extending nominally to Native groups in Mexico. In recent years any action had been made complicated by Homeland Security to whom even AARP and the Daughters of the American Revolution were suspect. Dr. Krider had found them their pleasant room and had B.D. memorize his phone number in case he was short of sustenance money. B.D. had assured the good doctor that he had always been able to make a living which was less than accurate as this often meant the forty bucks he could make cutting two cords of firewood which he would stretch out for a week of simple food and a couple of six-packs in Delmore's drafty trailer. The escape from Michigan into Canada had been occasioned by the state authorities' impending placement of Berry in a home for the youthful mentally disabled in Lansing. B.D. and Delmore had made the eight-hour drive south from the Upper Peninsula to Lansing only to discover that the home and the school in which Berry would be stored was profoundly ugly and surrounded by acres of cement, an alien material, and thus the escape plan was made. Gretchen, B.D.'s beloved Sapphic social worker, had driven them over to Paradise on Whitefish Bay where they had boarded a Native fishing boat, a fast craft that was sometimes used to smuggle cigarettes into Canada where they were eight bucks a pack. In the coastal town of Wawa they were met by a kindly, plump middle-aged Ojibway who was traveling to visit a daughter and drove them the two days to Toronto in her ancient pickup. The woman named Corva had drunk diet supplement drinks all the way and B.D. and Berry had subsisted on baloney and white bread because Corva had been forbidden by the Red Underground to stop for anything but gas. Since they were used to eating well on venison and trout and illegal moose and the recipes from B.D.'s sole printed volume, *Dad's Own Cookbook,* they were famished when they reached Toronto, and Yitz's was their appointed meeting place. It wasn't until they passed the Toronto city limits that Corva turned to him and asked, "Are you a terrorizer?" and B.D. replied, "Not that I know of." The few members of the Red Underground he had met in Wawa were terse and rather fierce and it had been hard to feel what Dr. Krider had called "solidarity." Dr. Krider had said to him, "The weather has beaten the shit out of you," and B.D. had replied that he had always preferred the outside to the inside. It was so pleasant to walk in big storms in any season and take shelter in a thicket in the lee of the wind. Once he and Gretchen had taken Berry for a beach walk and a violent thunderstorm from the south on Lake Michigan had approached very quickly so that they took shelter in a dogwood thicket. Berry had what Gretchen called "behavioral issues" and kept running around in the storm despite Gretchen calling out to her. Lightning struck very close to their thicket and in the cold and wet Gretchen came into his arms for a moment. She said, "How can you get a hard-on during a lightning strike, you goofy asshole?" and he didn't have an answer though it was likely her slight lilac scent mixed with the flowering dogwood plus her shimmering wet body, the thought of which drove him sexually batty.

Now the air was warmish in a breeze from the south in the twilight and walking through a small park Berry incited a male robin to anger by making competitive male calls. B.D. held up his hand to protect them from the shrieking bird and said, "Please, Berry, your dad is thinking," which was not at all a pleasant process. As they neared the delicatessen, he remembered two rather ominous things. In their goodbyes Corva had said, "Don't hurt no innocent people. You're with a rough bunch." And Dr. Krider had told him, "Since you entered Canada illegally you'll have to leave Canada illegally. You don't have any papers so you're limited to odd jobs." The latter part of the admonition didn't mean much because all he had ever done was odd jobs except for cutting pulp for Uncle

Delmore, a job abbreviated when a falling tree bucked back from the spring in its branches and busted up his kneecap.

This hard thinking made B.D. hungry so he ordered both a corned tongue and a brisket sandwich plus a plate of herring and potato salad for Berry. Berry refrained from her gull calls waiting for this old man to enter wearing his Jewish black beanie. They would spend a few minutes across a table from each other exchanging different birdcalls. The old man was some kind of retired scientist and tricked Berry by doing a few birdcalls from a foreign country which at first puzzled her but then made her laugh. B.D. watched them at play pondering the obvious seventy years' difference in their ages. He wondered where the word "Yitz" came from because he associated it with one of the best things in life, good food. It wasn't like one of those Michigan diners with a barrel of generic gravy out back connected by a hydraulic hose to the minimal kitchen which heated up grub from a vast industrial food complex named Sexton. B.D. could imagine the actual factory with cows lined up at a back door waiting patiently to become the patented meat loaf and their nether parts stewed into the barrels of gravy.

It was at three AM that his destiny changed. He awoke with an insufferable pain in his lower unit accompanied by a dream in which he had been kicked in the balls by a cowboy as he had been so many years before in Montana. As life would have it things suddenly began to happen. Since he was moaning when he turned the light on, Berry was hovering over him and started singing one of her verbless songs. Her words were not quite words but were always pleasant.

He couldn't stand up straight but managed to slink down the stairs and drop Berry off with Gert, the landlady, a horrid old crone who, however, adored Berry for playing by the hour with her two nasty Jack Russell terriers. The dogs loathed everyone including their owner but liked Berry whom they perhaps regarded as an intermediate species.

Luckily the closest hospital was a scant five blocks away and B.D. trotted through the night bent over from the waist in the manner of a Navajo tracker. He tripped over a couple of curbs with his eyes closed in pain soaking himself in a puddle from yesterday's slush. It was not in his nature to be fearful and he had anyway guessed a kidney stone as the grandfather who'd raised him experienced a kidney stone about once a year whereupon he would take to bed with a fifth of whiskey which he quickly drank. Grandpa would howl, roar, and bellow in a drunken rage and then after a few hours of this would fall asleep and on waking act fit as a fiddle.

The emergency room was fairly crowded and B.D. was out of luck because he didn't have a Canadian health card with a photo ID. He also made a mistake by acting manly despite the pain which made his eyes roll back in his head. This faux manliness was typical of some men in the Great North who pull their own bad teeth with the aid of whiskey and grip-lock pliers. He was slumped in a chair in a far corner pondering his lack of options when a diminutive young woman in a gray dress and white hat stooped beside him. She had been near the front desk and had overheard his ID problem and asked him if he knew a private doctor. He said no but then remembered his Red Underground contact Dr. Krider who was a skin doctor. He had written Dr. Krider's number on the back side of a photo he had begged off Gretchen, hoping for a nude though he knew it was unlikely. Instead he got a photo of Gretchen on the beach in a two-piece blue bathing suit, a towel wrapped partly around her hips, but clearly showing her slightly protuberant belly button. This photo and his Michigan driver's license and an old brass paper clip to hold cash were the sole contents of his pockets except for a lucky Petoskey stone with its pattern of ancient invertebrates. Unlike most of the rest of us except the homeless, B.D. had no Social Security card, draft registration card, credit or insurance cards.

Despite her miniature size Nora, his immediate savior, drove a large Plymouth station wagon, sitting on a stack of cushions to see out the windshield. B.D. slumped on the seat beside her, tilting sideways until his head rested against her thigh. Despite the near delirium of his pain he was always one to take advantage of any possible physical contact with a woman. He looked up at the passing streetlights determining that Nora's scent was wild violets. Another surge of pain prevented him from trying to turn over so he could be facedown on her lap, since his teens a favorite position.

When Nora pulled to a stop at Dr. Krider's home an immense man appeared and carried B.D. inside the house, impressive B.D. thought since he weighed one-ninety. He also noted that he was in the posh neighborhood of his snow shoveling. The huge man lowered him to a sofa at which point B.D. could see that he was an Indian with a pockmarked face and a bushy ponytail. Dr. Krider poked and probed B.D.'s lower stomach and bladder, determined that he had a sizable kidney stone, and administered a shot of pain-killing Demerol. Nora had retrieved a warm washcloth and had bathed B.D.'s face and now he had it buried in her neck, a vantage point from which he could see down under her blouse to a single peach-shaped breast. Krider had pushed up his shirt and pulled down his trousers and as the Demerol slowly took effect B.D. was embarrassed that he was wearing wildly colored Hawaiian underpants which Gretchen had sent him for Christmas as a joke. He was also chagrined that the peek at Nora's titty had given him a boner.

"I can't believe that a man passing a kidney stone is tumescent," Dr. Krider chuckled, "but then I've seen geezers in hospitals minutes from death still trying to pat a nurse's ass."

Nora blushed and snapped B.D.'s dick with a forefinger, wilting it. This was a well-known nurse's trick to control excitable patients.

"Nora! That was unkind," Dr. Krider said. "Surely a penis isn't a threatening object to you?"

"Bitch!" said Charles Eats Horses, the big Indian who was a Lakota.

"You could make it up to me later," B.D. squeaked in his drug trance as Nora rushed from the room in tears.

B.D. dozed for a few minutes then lapsed back into pain. The stone was making its determined way down his urethra, propelled by satanic forces. He flapped his hands wildly in the air as does a dying grouse its wings. He crooned a song of pain which resembled Berry's verbless melodies. In short, he flopped and writhed. Dr. Krider gave him another quick shot and Charles Eats Horses put on a CD of Mozart's *Jupiter* Symphony. Charles had heard his oldest sister die giving birth in a remote shack on the Rosebud Reservation and the savagery of B.D.'s personal sound track was close to home. B.D. himself was sure that he was giving birth to an unadorned concrete block and if a river had been available he would have gladly rolled into it in a fatal winter swim.

Finally the stone emerged, rough-hewn and the size of a smallish marble.

"I'll have this set in a ring for you," Nora joked washing away a splotch of blood.

"Will I ever love again?" B.D. croaked.

"It might be a few days," Krider said, yawning.

B.D. fell asleep wonderfully without pain for the first time in half a dozen hours. Dr. Krider and Charles went back to bed and Nora settled in at the far end of B.D.'s sofa with an afghan throw after covering him with a duvet. To be sure this man's penis was decidedly more ample than her boyfriend's. He wrote book reviews and everything else in the catchall category for the Toronto *Globe and Mail* and she felt lucky indeed that he was a compulsive oralist who also sang in an Episcopalian choir. Only last week he had started singing "A Mighty Fortress Is Our God" while going down on her. A former boyfriend with an XXL wanger had caused her discomfort and she had dropped him like a spoon when the smoke alarm goes off. As her eyes closed she tried to erase the vision of the half dozen silly-looking penises of her past in favor of a cinnamon sticky bun at the airport. The mind can become so tiresome when it comes to sex and the man at the far end of the capacious sofa mystified her until she remembered the louts up on Manitoulin Island when at thirteen she had gone to the cabin of a friend's parents. She and her friend had been sunbathing on the cabin's deck and a mixed-blood had brought a cord of wood in a battered pickup and when stacking the wood had said, "How about a blow job, cuties?" They were shocked but then laughed when her girlfriend replied "Beat it, jerk-off." The man had swarthy good looks but at the time she couldn't imagine herself ever following through on such a request.

B.D. slept for an hour or so waking at the first peek of dawn through an east window when he felt the toes of his right foot touch what was obviously smooth skin toward Nora's end of the sofa. He was instantly alert enough to be cautious, squinting in the dim light and noting her soft feminine snore and answering with his fake snore to show her if she awoke that anything was an accident of sleep. The drugs had worn off and his hardening dick was painful but then one must be brave. The hurt reminded him of his early teens when he and his friend David Four Feet who was crippled and walked like a crab would have off-the-cuff masturbation contests and on the way to school would mysteriously yell, "Four times," "Five times," or less. B.D.'s record was seven and it had caused the kind of pain similar to the passing of the kidney stone.

Now he moved his toes lower until he encountered the magic area and it felt like his big toe was touching a mouse under a thin handkerchief. He snored louder in a proclamation of innocence. Dare he wiggle his toes to offer her pleasure? he wondered. She stopped snoring and pushed her vulva against his talented toes. From the other room a clock alarm rang. She stopped moving but he didn't, his destination now dampish. They heard Dr. Krider's padding feet in the hallway and she moved well back into her corner of the sofa. His friend David Four Feet used to say, "Drat it, foiled again," when one of their pranks went awry. B.D. never gave time much thought but it occurred to him that if Krider's clock had delayed itself ten minutes she could have been slowly spinning on his weenie like a second hand. Time is a bitch, he thought, his right toes feeling absurdly lonely. He continued to fake sleep until he dropped off listening to Nora and Dr. Krider talk. She said something about visiting Berry to tell her that her daddy was okay.

When he woke again there was only Eats Horses offering a breakfast tray of a bowl of oatmeal pleasingly piled with sausage links to counter the banality of oats. B.D. was still morose about his lost opportunity with Nora and the obvious healing power of a good fuck. Now that the white people were gone Eats Horses dispensed with the Indianness of his speech, the peculiar way our characters offer people what they expect.

"We have to get out of Dodge pronto," Eats Horses said.

"Why?" B.D.'s first thought was, Why leave an area with such fine pork sausage?

"We're both illegal and Dr. Krider is too valuable to the movement. He could be busted for harboring illegals. We have to leave Canada."

"I can't figure out how," B.D. said. "Trout season starts in two weeks and here I am high and dry." He had finished the sausage and now the oatmeal looked real ugly.

"Fuck your trout season. First you trade in illegal shipwreck artifacts, then you try to sell a frozen body, then you violently raid an archaeological site. You become a phony Chip activist and befriend a convict named Lone Marten. You steal a bearskin from a fancy home in L.A. You smuggle your stepchild out of Michigan in defiance of state laws. A criminal like yourself is no help to us."

"How do you know all this shit?" B.D. was appalled.

"Until a year ago I was a cop in Rapid City and when you got here I had a buddy on the force check your rap sheet. You're poison. That's why we never got in touch with you. I quit being a cop and went into the house-painting business with my cousin but we were going to paint a shed and got caught with seven gallons of red paint and Homeland Security entered the picture. For years the Lakota have been threatening to give those presidents on Mount Rushmore a dose of blood-red paint. We'd bought ours in Denver to escape the hassle. The paint store in Denver must have tipped the cops off. Anyway I was accused of plotting a terrorist act but after a month in jail the ACLU bailed me out. I made my way here but now I have to leave. Your uncle Delmore made a contribution to the movement so the leadership instructed me to take you and your stepdaughter along."

"Were you, in fact, going to paint a shed?" B.D. was suddenly thinking of Delmore watching the *Perry Mason* reruns and thus he asked a Perry-type question.

"None of your business," Eats Horses said.

"How come you're called Eats Horses?"

"Many years ago in the time of my grandparents the rez got cheated out of its government-allotment food and people were dying of starvation so some started eating their horses."

"Why go back if we're only going to get arrested?" B.D. was horrified at the idea of jail having been there a number of times. He'd also heard that you could no longer take Tabasco with you to jail so how could he eat jail food?

"I have a new identity and I think Krider is arranging one for you. I'm going to be security and a bouncer at a strip club in Lincoln, Nebraska. I got a poet friend Trevino Brings Plenty who says, 'Alive in America is all we are.'"

Eats Horses lapsed into a melancholy silence and B.D. joined him. They were clearly homesick men on the run.

"When I was a kid I told my grandpa who raised me that I wanted to be a wild Indian when I grow up and he said, 'If you do keep it under your hat.' I guess I'm only about half anyway."

"I'm three-quarters and that doesn't make it easier. If my brain was white my ass would only be in a different kind of sling. A white friend got his house foreclosed and I said, 'At least I don't have a house.'" Charles Eats Horses laughed hard so B.D. joined him while thinking of the five-hundred-buck trailer he had lived in with Berry before escaping to Canada.

The phone rang and it was Nora. She was sending a cab for B.D. because she had to be at work in an hour or so. Berry was fine and playing with the terriers. A letter had come from someone named Gretchen.

While B.D. dressed he thought how dramatic life had become. He had never ridden in a cab and there was a letter from his beloved Gretchen whom he hadn't heard from since Christmas. He dressed hastily still feeling spongy from the drugs, the railroad spike in his bladder having become a thumbtack. While waiting at the door Eats Horses told him to get packed up as they would be leaving in a few days and B.D. replied that since they owned practically nothing he could pack in minutes.

It was a fine glittery late morning with a specific warmth in the sun not felt since the autumn before. In the cab B.D. had a rare sense of prosperity sniffing the air which had that new-car smell. The driver was from far-off India and was nearly as small as Nora. They didn't understand each other but that was fine. The driver pointed up through the windshield and said, "Sun," and B.D. said, "You got that right."

Up in the fourth-floor room Nora was kneeling sideways on a kitchen chair, her body halfway out the window, watching Berry far below leading the terriers around with grocery string for leashes. B.D. couldn't help but make contact with Nora's jutting butt which she wiggled a bit.

"I feel bad about snapping your weenie so go ahead if you wish. I have a boyfriend so I'll pretend it's an out-of-body experience."

He felt like the luckiest man in the world as he lifted her skirt. Her rump was so pretty his skin tingled. There was a song he should be singing but he couldn't think of what one. He pulled down her delicate panties and planted a big wet kiss on target and then stood remembering that in his narcotic haze early in the morning Nora had drawn a small vial of blood while Dr. Krider watched.

"Why?" he had asked.

"To check your PSA, your prostate."

"You don't have one," he'd said, a little smug in this rare piece of knowledge.

"I've got other stuff," she'd laughed.

"I'm aware of that," he had said dreamily.

B.D. liked this kind of confab, this banter or repartee, a word he didn't know, because it meant the world was going along okay. Now he began to do his job admirably, staring down at the sacred mystery and beauty of female physiognomy, trying to divert his enthusiasm so he wouldn't come too quickly. His mind started singing a song they sang in fourth grade, "A Spanish cavalier stood in his retreat and on his guitar played a tune, dear." The kids sang this loudly though the meaning of "Spanish cavalier" was in question. Nora began to furiously rotate her butt counterclockwise and that was that. B.D. was in no way prepared for the pain caused by his urethra so abraded by the kidney stone. He yowled and fell backward on his ass, the passage of the sperm raising the image of the hot liquid lead Grandpa poured into molds to make fishing sinkers.

"I could have told you the last part wouldn't be fun but I was looking out for number one," Nora said, looking down at him with a merry smile.

"I forgive you," he said, jumping up at hearing Berry climb the stairs. He recalled a magazine article in the office of his ex-lover the dentist, Dr. Brenda Schwartz, that said, "No gain without pain." "I just pray we get another chance."

"This was a one-shot deal, kiddo." Nora let Berry in the door and embraced her, then left.

The blues descended lower than his sore dick with Nora's departure. Never in his life had he been attracted to a small woman and the idea that it was a "one-shot deal" left him bereft. He was nearly irritable with Berry which was unthinkable. When she had nothing else to do she would jump straight up and down in place and in the year this habit had begun she had acquired the ability to jump astoundingly high. "Too bad she'll never make a living out of her jumping and birdcalls," Uncle Delmore had said.

B.D. took a large package of pork steak from the mini-fridge and decided to cook it all in his outsized electric fry pan. Once the pork began to brown he opened Gretchen's letter with a bit of dread. Delmore maintained that no one in the United States complained as much as those who'd graduated from college and that sure was true of Gretchen. Despite her beauty and good job as a social worker she was often lower than a snake's ass, B.D. thought. Once a week she'd drive all the seventy miles up to Marquette just like Brenda the dentist to see a psychoanalyst. Brenda went for what she called her "eating disorder" and she had wept hysterically when B.D. had said, "You're fine, you just eat too much." Gretchen on the other hand was lithe and beautiful but beginning with her Christmas letter she'd said she was discovering in therapy that she was sexless and it was driving her batty. After college she had discarded men as "horrid" and B.D. remembered poignantly her nitwittish young woman friend who had discarded Gretchen. Once when he and Gretchen had had a couple of drinks in her kitchen he had asked about the mechanics of Sapphic lovemaking and she only said, "You're disgusting." Now in her early thirties Gretchen was thinking about having a baby and was seriously considering

B.D. as a sperm donor. He was proud as a peacock but couldn't understand why she would refuse him the pleasure of slipping it in for a minute rather than an artificial method.

While chopping a head of garlic to add to the pork steak, B.D. meditated on the letter. Gretchen's analyst had said that her sexless nature was "rare but not unheard of." Once when they had taken Berry swimming Gretchen had fallen asleep on her huge flowery beach towel and B.D. had slowly studied her body from the vantage point of an inch distance trying to memorize it for recall on cold winter nights. She had awakened and looked down under her sunglasses and thought he was on the verge of probing her pubis with his nose.

"What are you doing?" she'd shrieked.

"I'm memorizing your body for cold winter nights. Turn over because I'm missing the butt side."

"You asshole," she'd said, raising her foot and pushing him away. Her soft warm insole against his neck was one of his most cherished memories.

Berry nudged him to remind him not to burn the garlic. She used to like burned garlic but now she wanted it softened. They ate the entire pan of pork steak with a loaf of the French bread he bought daily from a bakery down the street, the likes of which was unavailable in Michigan's Upper Peninsula. The bread was so delicious it mystified him. They were always passing stupid laws, why not make it a law that this sort of bread be available everywhere in America?

B.D. began to doze in his chair from his long uncomfortable night and full stomach. Berry was making a variety of birdsongs and he knew she was begging for an afternoon walk. She also made a couple of guttural mutters, a struggle for the "b" consonant that might mean she was on the verge of saying "bird" after nearly four months of speech therapy. Berry loved the teacher which led B.D. to the obvious fact that Berry at age ten needed a mother and the sadder fact that her own birth mother would be in prison a couple more years for, among other things, biting a thumb off a cop when a group of malcontents had raided an archaeological site. The therapist had pointed out that Berry hadn't felt an urgency toward speech since B.D. was basically her only current human reality and they communicated perfectly well. B.D. had nervously confessed that he had whisked Berry out of Michigan rather than subject her to a state school and the therapist had said Berry would still need "socialization" with kids her own age in some community. B.D. had thought of moving her over to the Sault Ste. Marie Tribe of Chippewa Indians rez near Sault Ste. Marie but he was persona non grata in the Soo area for reasons of past misdemeanors.

He dozed for a few minutes while she brushed his hair and brought him his coat, and then they headed out for the Lower Don Parkland. Outside, B.D. wasn't sure of reality because the long night of pain and narcotics made the world uncommonly glittery and vivid. There was also a brisk southwest wind and suddenly the temperature was in the low seventies. It was Saturday afternoon and the streets were full of nearly frantic walkers trying to shake off the lint and cobwebs of a long winter. Younger people, say under twenty, were moving into dance steps as they walked and kids were jumping up and down a bit envious of Berry's jumping power. It all reminded B.D. in his floating body of those musical comedies from the forties that Uncle Delmore loved on television. Delmore's highest admiration was saved for Fred Astaire. He would say, "Just think if Fred had learned Indian dance steps and showed up at the Escanaba Powwow!" B.D. admitted it would be quite a show. Delmore also loved Gene Kelly who could run up a wall, do a flip, and land on his feet. It would be fun to do that in a tavern, B.D. thought when he saw the movie.

When they reached the area Berry ran up the gully to their snow cave. B.D. followed slowly noting that the snow and ice had collapsed part of the cave and if he had been in there with Deidre when it happened they might have been suffocated or, more likely, he would have pulled an Incredible Hulk move and burst upward through the snow and ice saving his true love. Only she wasn't much of a true love. She and her turd husband were going to a place called Cancún to renew their vows. At least Nora, who had also removed herself from the list of possibles, wouldn't die if she touched a peanut butter sandwich. Nora had said she was a gymnast in high school and could move her butt like a paint mixer in a hardware store.

B.D. sat on a big rock while Berry called in groups of crows, not a difficult thing to learn to do as the Corvidae are curious about why humans might wish to talk to them. What's the motive? they wonder. Soon enough, though, Berry had attracted a massive number of crows and a group of bird-watchers, those cranky coup counters known as twitchers to the Brits and some Canadians, made their way up the gully and scared the birds away. Birds have finely honed memories for people and they were familiar with Berry from the dozens of trips into this part of the Lower Don Parkland. Berry was irked and crawled into what was left of the cave.

As B.D. dozed in the sun his half-dream thoughts turned to Deidre's heat source. A thousand Deidres making love in a gymnasium would melt candles. He opened his eyes to the departing birds not knowing that their raucous cries were his Canadian swan song. In his view far too much had been happening and he craved the nothingness of the Upper Peninsula, a feeling he shared with the ancient Chinese that the best life was an uneventful one.

They walked. And walked and walked. Because of his tough night B.D.'s feet were marshmallows which nonetheless dragged him along. Berry teased the bird-watchers along the paths by hiding in thickets and making the calls of dozens of northern songbirds that had not yet arrived from their winter journey south. A man with thousand-dollar binoculars told B.D. that Berry could be a "valuable resource" and B.D. agreed, lost in his diffuse homesickness for brook trout creeks and the glories of snowmelt time when the forest rivers raged along overflowing their banks, and bear fed happily on the frozen carcasses of deer that had died of starvation, and icebergs bobbed merrily in Lake Superior on huge waves often carrying ravens picking in the ice for entombed fish. On this afternoon Toronto seemed vividly beautiful, a characteristic in the perceptions of those who had endured extreme pain and survived it. The world, simply enough, became as beautiful as it does to many children waking on a summer morning.

By late afternoon Berry had shown no signs of tiring while B.D. was barely shuffling along. He saw a young man taking a Tums and asked for one.

"My fried pork lunch is backing up on me," B.D. said, explaining himself.

"I had pizza with too many red pepper flakes," the young man said in a strange accent. They spoke for a few moments and it turned out that he was a country boy from near Sligo in Ireland. B.D. had been amazed by how many of the foreign-born he had met in Toronto and had often wished he had recorded the nationalities in his memory book which, of course, he didn't own. Geography had been his best subject in high school but he had found to his dismay in Toronto that someone had changed many of the names of countries in Africa after they gained their independence.

He was asleep on his feet by the time they reached Yitz's for supper. He settled for a bowl of beef borscht while Berry had three orders of herring and a serving of French fries which she ate at a back table with the children of a couple of waitresses who were kind to her. B.D. in his semi–dream state was thinking that it was only ten days from trout opener in Michigan which seemed so fatally far away. The first week of the season he often visited a daffy hermit north of Shingleton who was a fine angler but had some peculiar ideas. One of the theories the hermit mourned over was that there was a hidden planet in our solar system that contained an even million species of birds but we would never be allowed to visit them because of our bad behavior as earthlings. The hermit painted watercolors of these birds and one that B.D. especially liked was a huge purple bird with an orange beak that had three sets of wings. Who was to say it didn't exist? B.D. had never cared for the naysayers of the world of which there were far too many.

They took a cab home after they proved to the driver that B.D. had the estimated ten-buck fare. Berry was frightened of the driver who was angry over the war in Iraq and decidedly anti-U.S. B.D. was helpless to say anything but "It's not my fault."

B.D. fell asleep in his clothes while Berry danced for an hour or so to country music which she did every evening. He drifted off to Patsy Cline singing "The Last Word in Lonesome Is Me." It was a full seven hours but seemed only moments when there was an alarming knock on the door, startling because it was the first time there was a knock at the door in their five months of residence. B.D. heard Nora's voice and his heart took flight as he turned on the lamp. She had obviously returned for more of the same and in his pleasant drowsing head he had a vision of her delightful paint shaker doing its sacred job. But no, when Berry opened the door it was not only Nora but Charles Eats Horses and a sturdy Indian woman in her fifties who wore a business suit and was introduced as the Director.

"We move out at dawn," said Eats Horses. "I heard that line in a movie once and always liked it." Eats Horses was wearing a leather jacket with beaded lightning bolts and looked ominous. Berry who was wary of strangers went to him and took his hand. He picked her up. "We're going home."

Nora and the Director helped them in their hasty packing. B.D. was miffed when they said there wasn't room for his big, used electric fry pan which had set him back five bucks. The Director also shook her head no when he tried to put the last remaining beer from the fridge in his jacket saying that no alcohol was allowed on the "tour bus." B.D. was confused and picked up Gretchen's letter and sniffed it for signs of life feeling an ever more insistent tug of homesickness. Nighttime wasn't his time for clear thinking. In troubled times B.D. tended to cut way back on alcohol to avoid feeding the fire of chaos but at the moment he felt the need for a double whiskey because Nora was sniffling at the door and bounteous tears were falling.

"You poor redskins. I love you."

"I can't be more than half. I'm just a mongrel," B.D. said, embarrassed.

"My great-grandmother was married to a Jewish peddler in Rapid City in 1912. There aren't hardly any Lakotas with a streak of Jew," Eats Horses joked.

"I'm a mean-minded, ass-whipping pureblood," the Director said, embracing Nora.

It took only minutes to arrive at the arena parking lot a dozen blocks away. B.D. was irritated because the Director beat him to the front seat where he had fully intended to feign sleep and let his head fall onto Nora's lap.

The tour bus was an immense affair with THUNDERSKINS painted in large red letters on the side surrounded by yellow lightning bolts, all on the black metal skin of the bus which was lit up like Times Square and ready to go. The Director explained that the Thunderskins was a Lakota rock-and-roll group with only two more stops on a month-and-a-half tour, one in Thunder Bay, on the north shore of Lake Superior, and the last in Winnipeg, after which they would head south to Rapid City and Pine Ridge to drop everyone off, "everyone" being the usual assortment of roadies and soundmen, both skins and whites who were now outside drinking from pints and perhaps dragging at joints before entering the bus where the Director manned the door like a guard dog. The four stars of the band would fly on a plane to Thunder Bay and the Director explained to B.D. that the plane wouldn't work for him and Berry and Eats Horses because of the tight security at all airports. B.D. noticed that the small crowd of employees all nodded to Eats Horses and then averted their eyes.

"They think I might be a *wicasa wakan* but I'm not," Eats Horses whispered to B.D. who was even more confused not knowing that *wicasa wakan* meant medicine man, often a somewhat frightening person like a *brujo* in Mexico.

Eats Horses took over the door frisking while the Director showed B.D. and Berry to a small compartment at the back of the bus across the aisle from her own. There were two cots, an easy chair, a miniature toilet, and a window looking into the night. Before B.D. fell back to sleep after a cheese sandwich and two cups of strong coffee he wondered how so obvious a bus was going to smuggle himself and Berry back into the United States. He was diverted by seeing Nora drive away and how when they'd kissed goodbye she had rudely pushed his hand off her ass when only yesterday at high noon she had allowed him to grip her hip bones like a vise. Berry was sitting on her cot looking frightened and B.D. held her hand but the Director came back and got Berry saying she needed some mothering. B.D. fell asleep to the wheezing of the big diesel engine beneath him as the bus moved north on Highway 400 toward the landscape he called home, dense forests of pine, hemlock, tamarack, and aspen surrounding great swamps and small lakes that had wonderful fringes of reeds and lily pads. There were creeks, beaver ponds, and small rivers where B.D. would always find complete solace in trout fishing. He was observant of the multiple torments people seemed to have daily and felt lucky that he could resolve his own problems with a couple of beers and a half dozen hours of trout fishing and if a female crossed his path whether fat or thin, older or younger, it was a testament that heaven was on earth rather than somewhere up in the remote and hostile sky.

B.D. had a head-and-chest cold, an infirmity he only experienced every five years or so and which he blamed on his kidney stone exhaustion. He slept most of the day and a half it took to reach Thunder Bay, waking now and then to study the passing Lake Superior Provincial Park south of Wawa and the Pukaskwa National Park farther north along the lake. There were an unimaginable number of creeks descending from the deep green forested hills down to Lake Superior which tingled his skin despite the irritation of coughing and blowing his nose. He felt much better the second morning when they had stopped at a bar and restaurant and with several of the crew had drunk his meal in the form of three double whiskeys with beer chasers, a surefire cold remedy. Two of the Lakota crew members not realizing that B.D. was local to the other side of Lake Superior warned him that they were in "enemy territory," the land of the Ojibway, the dreaded Anishinabe who had driven the Sioux out of the northern Midwest.

B.D. had never been more than vaguely aware of rock and roll and was ill-prepared for the spectacle that would meet him in Thunder Bay. He knew it mostly as the music heard in bars favored by young people in Escanaba and Marquette but then he had never owned a record player in its varied forms and had certainly never fed a jukebox with any of his sparse beer money. He couldn't recall understanding a single lyric of this music except "You can't always get what you want" which he viewed as the dominant fact of life. He was back asleep from his liquid lunch when the tour bus pulled into the arena parking lot. He awakened to an oceanic roar and screech that reminded him of a ninety-knot storm on Lake Superior hitting the village of Grand Marais. In the bright afternoon light out of the window thousands of young people, mostly girls, were jumping straight up and down in the manner of Berry and screaming, "Thunderskins, Thunderskins, Thunderskins!" Within minutes of leaving the bus it occurred to him that he should have taken up a musical instrument, say a guitar, when he was young and learned how to sing. The Director had put a small laminated card around his neck reading "Backstage Crew" and the frantic girls stared at him like kids looking at a gorgeous ice cream cone on a hot day. He felt a little embarrassed, actually unpleasant at this sense of power, quite uncomfortable over the way he was encircled by the most attractive females looking at him imploringly. He had always had more than a touch of claustrophobia and recalled his panic at nineteen when he had been caught up in a big Labor Day parade in Chicago and had run for it a few blocks down to Lake Michigan where he could breathe freely. When looking at the *Tribune* the next day he had figured out that there were many more people involved in the parade than lived in the entirety of the Upper Peninsula. Now it occurred to him that one girl was enough but thousands screaming like banshees made you crave a thicket.

"Hey, B.D., they just want a fucking backstage pass," one of the Lakota crew yelled at him, noting his puzzlement.

B.D. made himself busy helping the crew unload the sound equipment, then when he found he was getting in the way drifted off toward the waterfront to get back in touch with Lake Superior which would likely calm his rattled brain. He was pleased to find Charles Eats Horses down near a pier sitting on a park bench.

"This water reminds me of the sea of grass in the Sand Hills of Nebraska south of Pine Ridge."

"If I had a good boat I could head straight south to the Keweenaw Peninsula and be fairly close to home but then I don't have a good boat and storms come up real sudden."

Eats Horses explained to him that Berry would be staying in a nice hotel with the Director who had to watch the rock stars carefully. One of them was her son and he was crazy as a weasel in heat. B.D. felt mildly jealous about Berry but since he had grown up without a mother himself he figured Berry needed the company of a female. Looking out over the water toward his homeland he felt his homesickness become as palpable as a lump of coal in his throat.

PART II

Dawn in Thunder Bay. The two AM announced departure of the tour bus was delayed by a snowstorm but by dawn the wind had shifted to the south and the snow turned into an eerie thunderstorm so that Brown Dog peeking out the bus window was startled by a lightning strike glowing off white drifts in the parking lot. He had a somewhat less than terminal hangover and could easily see the dangers of life without the immediate responsibility of looking after Berry. It was quite literally a "blast from the past" what with B.D. not having had a hangover in his five months in Canada, certainly the longest period since age fourteen when he and David Four Feet had swiped a case of Mogen David wine from a truck being unloaded in an alley behind a supermarket in Escanaba. The aftermath had been a prolonged puke-a-thon in the secret hut they had built beside a creek outside of town.

B.D. lay there in his bus compartment watching the rain that had begun to lift so that he could see far out into Lake Superior to the water beyond the shelf ice. He diverted himself from the memory of last night's mud bath by pondering the soul of water.

He had meant for a couple of years to enter a public library and look up "water" in an encyclopedia but doubted that any information would include the mysteries of water that he so highly valued. Life could kick you in the ass brutally hard and a day spent fishing a creek or a river and you forgot the kick. Now, however, with no fishing in sight he could vividly remember the wonderful whitefish sandwich in the bar, and then meeting the two girls in their late teens who had spotted his "Backstage Crew" badge. The concert was sold out and they had no tickets. He was sitting there with a Lakota nicknamed Turnip who thought the girls "skaggy" but B.D.'s mouth was watering though one of the girls was a tad chubby and one very thin. B.D. thought that if you put the two together the weight issue averaged out. Playing the big shot he got them in a side door of the concert which was far too loud for him to endure and the flashing lights were grotesque. Berry was up on stage jumping straight up and down batting at a tambourine and looking very happy. The girls jotted down their address and phone number and said they'd see B.D. at their apartment after the concert. He left feeling smug about his worldliness. Back at the bar after having more drinks and playing pool with Turnip, who looked a bit like a turnip, he saw that the streets were filling up with the concertgoers so it was time to make a move. Unfortunately after walking around in the snowstorm and stopping at another tavern B.D. gave the slip of paper to a bartender who said there was no Violet Street in Thunder Bay and what's more the phone number only had six digits. Turnip thought this very funny while B.D. was morose.

"I bet they're backstage with the stars. We could check it out. Those guys get more ass than a public toilet seat," Turnip said.

B.D. waded through the snow to his lonely bed with the honest thought that women in general were as devious as he was.

When they reached Winnipeg early the next afternoon he was having an upsetting discussion with the Director about Berry and couldn't quite separate the conference from a wild series of dreams he had just had during a nap. He had confused the roar of the bus engine with that of a female bear he used to feed his extra fish when he was reroofing a deer cabin. He had cut twenty-two cords of hardwood to get through the winter and when April came and the bear emerged from hibernation she was right back there near the kitchen window howling for food. Tim, a commercial fisherman, had given him a twenty-pound lake trout no one had wanted so he cut off a three-pound slab for dinner and tossed the rest to the bear who ate it in a trice then took a long nap in the patch of sunlight out by the pump house. One night when he heard a wolf howling down in the river delta the bear had roared back. She was simply the most pissed-off bear he had ever come across so he named her Gretchen.

"What are you going to do when Berry hits puberty in the next year or two?" the Director asked.

"The court appointed me to look after her," he answered irrelevantly. He was still caught up in the dream where he was down on the edge of the forest on the Kingston Plains and he and Berry were chasing two coyote pups who dove down into their dens under a white pine stump and Berry suddenly became as little as the pups and followed them which was impossible.

"What are you going to do when she reaches puberty?" the Director persisted. "I talked to your uncle Delmore on my cell and he's obviously senile. He said he contacted Guam on his ham radio. What the fuck is that supposed to mean? I talked to your friend the social worker Gretchen. She lives twenty miles away in Escanaba and only sees you two on weekends if then."

"Berry would have died at the school. It's all cement around there." B.D. was becoming irritated with the Director and wished he knew how to retreat to his dream state where when Berry came back out of the coyote den they had driven to his favorite cabin and fried up a skillet of venison.

"What I'm saying is that you got your head up your ass. Time moves on. Berry is going to be nicely shaped. What are you going to do when boys and men come after her for sex?"

"Kick their asses real good." B.D. felt a surge of anger that accompanied the beginning of a headache. The Director reminded him of an interrogation with the school principal he and David Four Feet had undergone in the seventh grade when they had thrown chunks of foul-smelling Limburger cheese into the fan attached to the oil furnace in the school basement. All of the girls in the school had run screeching into the street while the boys had merely walked out to show that they were manly enough to handle a truly bad smell.

"Well, I have a friend in Rapid City who runs a tribal program for kids with fetal alcohol syndrome and when we get there she's going to look at Berry."

They were both diverted by the bus pulling into the arena parking lot in Winnipeg. There were even more hysterical fans than there had been in Thunder Bay. It was a mystery to B.D. because this horde of fans must know that the stars were arriving by plane. It reminded him from way back when, of a geek kid in the eighth grade who claimed that his cousin in California had seen the Disney star Annette Funicello in the nude. Boys would gather around the geek to hear the story over and over. This was about as close as anyone in Escanaba was ever going to get to the exciting life of show business. B.D. figured that to these thousands of fans the Thunderskins bus without the stars was better than nothing.

In truth he found the noise of the fans repellent. The only loud sound he liked was a storm on Lake Superior when monster waves would come crashing over the pier in Grand Marais or Marquette. He also liked the sounds of crickets and birds, and a hard rain in the forest in the summer with the wind blowing through billions of leaves.

The Director stood up to leave and B.D. shook her hand hoping that she would believe his heart was in the right place in regard to Berry. She gave him a hug and he held her as tightly as possible. A spontaneous hug from a woman always filled him with the immediate promise of life. Sure enough his pecker began to rise and she pushed him away laughing.

"I'm fifty-nine and it's been quite a while since anyone got a hard-on over me."

"My friendship is there for the taking." B.D. wanted to say something proper far from the usual "Let's fuck." In truth she was more than ample and most would think her dumpy but he craved to get at her big smooth butt. She escaped all atwitter and he turned to see female fans staring in the window and he thought if the window would only open he could pop it in that brunette's chops making sure to avoid her big droopy nose ring.

The ride through western Manitoba into eastern Saskatchewan had increased his homesickness to a quiet frenzy. Creeks, rivers, and lakes were everywhere in the forested landscapes. To a lifelong fisherman even a large mud puddle presents a remote possibility and the water he saw was overwhelming. Once when the bus slowed for a logging truck hauling pulp to make paper he saw an American redstart in a white pine, a wildly colored bird that he often saw near his favorite stretch of the Middle Branch of the Escanaba near Gwinn and seeing the bird enabled him to smell the river and the forest in that area which tingled his skin.

In Winnipeg the Director checked B.D. and Berry into a room that adjoined her own in a fancy hotel which added a different kind of tingle as B.D. assumed that at some point he might be able to pull off a quick one with the Director. He had hoped to take Berry to the zoo but by the time they got settled in and had a room service bite it was midafternoon and Berry and the Director had to go to a rehearsal. This was the last stop on the Thunderskins's tour and they wanted to go out in a firestorm at the huge sold-out arena. Berry beat on her tambourine every waking hour but B.D. found it oddly pleasant since she did it so well which made him wonder about the intricacy of the rhythms she heard in her limited brain. Once in high school he had driven with a couple of pureblood friends way up to a powwow in Baraga and was amazed at how good it felt to dance for hours and hours, a state of being carried away that reminded him of the pleasure of being half-drunk rather than fully drunk.

While the Director and Berry were getting ready two of the stars dropped by but as with his other brief encounters their eyes passed over him as if he didn't exist. B.D. figured this was what happened when you were around far too many people like when he had gone to Chicago at nineteen or more recently in Toronto. The only way people got along was by largely ignoring each other, a far cry from the Upper Peninsula where if you avoided the downtowns of Escanaba and Marquette you were never surrounded by people and on the rare occasion he saw another human in the backcountry he always hid until they passed from sight.

At present he was sick to death of people and decided to stay as far as possible from the music folks. He set off on a long walk mostly enjoying the vast railroad yards because there were no high buildings around to block out the late-afternoon sun though there was the troubling question of who could keep track of so many trains? He was somewhat disappointed that the fabled Red River wasn't red and when headed back to the hotel he saw in the distance Charles Eats Horses enter a building he followed. It turned out to be an art museum with a large display of Inuit work. He was pleased with himself that he remembered that the Inuits lived up in the Arctic and were what most people thought were Eskimos. He noticed that when Eats Horses passed an attendant several rooms ahead she averted her eyes. She was, however, friendly to him and he took her short, round figure to be Inuit.

"Were you born in an igloo?" he asked.

"Were you born in a tepee?" she joked. Her smile was so glowing he felt the usual tremor. He wanted to tell her something interesting but she turned away to explain some whalebone and walrus-tusk carvings to some elegant old ladies. The art was so striking to B.D. that he felt hollow in his head and chest and he did not hear Eats Horses walk up behind him.

"I just knew you were an art lover," Eats Horses said, half seriously.

"I heard it's all in the wrist," B.D. answered, a little embarrassed at the strength of his emotions.

Eats Horses put a heavy hand on B.D.'s shoulder. "I want you to listen carefully about Berry. I know kids like her and they don't turn out well."

"Yes, sir. All I know is that she has to walk in the woods every day." He squeezed his eyes shut so tightly that he felt a little dizzy and when he opened them to regain his balance Eats Horses was gone. B.D. doubted that Eats Horses was the ex-cop and house painter he said he was. Once over near Iron Mountain back near a beaver dam in the woods B.D. had run into this Crane Clan Midewiwin guy that he had seen years before at the Baraga powwow. It was generally thought that this man flew around at night and ate whole raw fish. The man was pleasant enough but when he reached under a submerged stump and caught a brook trout with a single hand B.D. had left the area.

On the walk back to the hotel he rejected the idea of the five double whiskeys he felt a need for and instead stopped at a diner for a fried T-bone. The Director had passed on a gift envelope from Dr. Krider with five hundred bucks in twenties which B.D. figured was the third-highest amount of money he had ever possessed. If you have five hundred bucks a ten-dollar fried T-bone seems less of a luxury. The meat was only fair but the potatoes were pretty good with catsup. The waitress was a sullen, bony young woman who never met his eyes. It seemed to him that young women were getting more sullen every year for undisclosed reasons, all the more cause to keep the Director in mind as a possible target if Berry went to sleep. Grandpa had the theory that you should never go after a female with a bad father because they're always pissed off. However mediocre the meal was B.D. figured it was better than the catered backstage buffet before the concert which, though it was free, featured food he didn't recognize. Once Gretchen had served him a tofu burger that tasted like the algae that formed pond scum. Gretchen had mentioned dozens of times how awful her father was and also that an older cousin had tinkered with her pussy when she was eleven. There seemed to be no end to the problems that could arise in life. When he was eleven there was a neighbor girl who would show you her butt for a nickel but if you tried to touch it she'd smack the shit out of you. He'd heard that now she was a school principal up in Houghton.

Back in the hotel room he recognized that the quivery feeling was due to the idea that if things went well he would be back in the United States of America, more exactly North Dakota, in less than eighteen hours. He opened the minibar where he'd seen the Director take out cans of orange juice for herself and Berry. This was the first minibar of his life and he was amazed at the rack of top-shelf shooters on display. He went "Eeny meeny miney moe" and took out a small bottle of Mexican tequila which went down easy as pie. He snooped in the Director's room and saw a rather large pair of undies she had washed out and hung up to dry on a towel rack. He felt a twinge of lust which he knew couldn't be resolved. He sat down with the clicker and shooters of Johnnie Walker and Absolut vodka noting a sign on the television that first-run and adult movies were available at twelve dollars a crack which seemed outrageously expensive but then when would he ever stay in a fancy hotel again? Even the glasses were glass rather than cellophane-wrapped plastic. He was never allowed to touch the clicker for Uncle Delmore's satellite television so he was very wary about its operation and it took some time to get it working. It was easy to reject *Teenage Sluts on the Loose in Hollywood* as porn made him feel silly and he had never regarded sex as a spectator sport.

You simply had to be there with the raw meat on the floor as they used to say. The slightest peek up Gretchen's summer skirt would set him churning but neither film nor the Playmate of the Month did the job. Unfortunately he selected a film called *Pan's Labyrinth* because of the unknowable mystery of the title. It took a total of ten shooters to get through the film and he was frequently either frightened or in tears. He assumed that the film was a true story and he thought of the little girl as Berry and he was the satyr trying to help her get through life. By the time the film ended he was drunk with a tear-wet face. If this could happen in the world it was no wonder that he craved to live in a cabin back in the woods. He had done poorly in world history in high school but was aware of the twentieth century as a worldwide charnel house. His teacher who was a Democrat from the working-class east side of Escanaba had told the students that there were at least ten million Indians when we got off the boat and only three hundred thousand left by 1900. Now in the hotel room, however, the fact that this evil Spaniard had murdered the little girl, the Berry equivalent, sent a sob through his system and he finished his last shooter, arranged the bottles in a circle, and fell asleep in his chair.

He awoke at four AM to pee and in the bleary toilet mirror he saw that there was a note pinned to his chest. It was from the Director and only said, "Shame on you." Soon after daylight Berry and the Director were having room service in the other room when he came fully awake and examined his mind for vital signs. Berry came in and kissed his forehead and headed into the bathroom with her armload of rubber snakes which she always played with in the tub. On this morning the two-headed cobra didn't look good to B.D.

"Are you up for it, Lone Ranger?" the Director asked standing in the doorway of her room.

"Come to think of it I am," said B.D. squirming slowly out of the easy chair. During even minor league hangovers sudden movements cause sudden pain, the physical equivalent of a blowing fuse.

They had to arrange themselves near a dresser to keep an eye out the nearly closed door of Berry's bathroom. The Director's butt was large indeed but as marvelously smooth as B.D. had hoped for. In his not limited experience Indian women had the smoothest butts though this was a Lakota, the ancient enemy of B.D.'s half-Chippewa blood. Let there be peace in the valley he thought. The only drawback was the mirror over the dresser. He certainly didn't want to see himself what with being the least narcissistic of all modern males. The Director let out a few muffled yelps and he hissed, "Sssh" and then it was over and a sharp pain descended into his noggin from the heavens.

He pulled up his trousers and quickly moved to the room service table for some lukewarm coffee, cold sausage, and sodden toast.

"It's so like a man to go from fucking to eating in a split second," the Director giggled, rearranging her clothes.

"What was I supposed to do?" B.D. said with a full mouth.

"You're supposed to say 'Thank-you ma'am' and give me a heartfelt kiss."

B.D. swallowed a mouthful of food, choked a little, and gave her a passionate heartfelt kiss, dipping her as one does a woman on a dance floor. Lucky for her he was strong.

Shortly after noon the tour bus followed by the equipment semi turned off on a gravel road south of Boissevain. The moves were well planned and the crew unloaded two big ceremonial drums and hoisted them onto the long luggage rack on top of the tour bus. The Director took the tambourine away from Berry and B.D., Berry, and Eats Horses went up the ladder and Eats Horses got under one drum and B.D. and Berry under the other. Two crew members beat tentatively on each drum with Lakota wails and laughter. For some reason Berry responded with the chirping of a cricket until B.D. said no, mourning the effect of the drumbeats on his hangover.

The bus took off hitting the border of the United States near the Turtle Mountain Reservation in North Dakota. The drumbeats softened while the Director talked to the customs agents whom she knew from other crossings there.

"You know my boys are clean. No drugs or alcohol on the bus or they get their asses kicked off." The customs agents were eating their lunch sandwiches and were quite bored with trying to catch putative terrorists who were unlikely to come their way.

The bus roared off and the drummers beat hard and wailed loudly as they entered the promised land which had been less than wonderful to the Lakota in recent centuries. A dozen miles south in a cottonwood grove the rooftop passengers climbed down the ladder and the Director returned Berry's tambourine which made her happy. B.D. was a little dizzy and nauseous thinking that seven shooters would have been adequate rather than ten, and slightly disappointed that North Dakota looked identical to Manitoba but it might have been due to the way one hangover resembles another. Nothing helped until he had pork liver and onions and two beers in Rugby which was supposedly the geographical center of North America. Out in the restaurant parking lot he lamely tried to figure out how they'd determined this. He also wondered how he would protect himself from his excesses if Berry went under the Director's care for a while. The answer was to live so far back in the woods that you only went to the tavern once a week. Maybe twice. When he got back on the bus the Director teased him in a whisper about his short "staying power" then punched him so hard in the arm it went numb. He reflected from experience that you never quite knew if an Indian woman would make love or beat the shit out of you.

At nightfall the tour bus was camped at the site of Wounded Knee. Charles Eats Horses went off and spent the night sitting up wrapped in a blanket. The crew started a fire to cook the steaks the Director had bought along with a case of beer to celebrate the end of the tour. B.D. was mournful that a single case only offered two apiece, scarcely enough to wet your whistle. As much as possible he avoided remembering when he was sixteen and Grandpa had given him a lecture on the dangers of liquor saying that it had killed B.D.'s mom and dad. No more information on them had ever been forthcoming from Grandpa though B.D. had heard that his mom, Grandpa's daughter, had danced for a while in a strip club in Escanaba. Since Grandpa was mostly Swede and Irish the skin blood had come through his dad who had taken off for Lac du Flambeau. Right now at Wounded Knee he surely didn't care if he was part Indian or in his private thicket on the edge of the Kingston Plains where he could watch breeding sandhill cranes. Uncle Delmore was always watching horror films on television. Berry liked them but B.D. had an aversion to being frightened. He had peeked in from the kitchen during a werewolf film and decided he would a lot rather be a werecoyote assuming they existed.

He was washing up in his compartment when he heard the Director enter. She looked out the window at Berry and two crew members dancing around the fire.

"I'm going to make that girl into a fancy dancer. She's real good."

"That's a wonderful idea," B.D. said patting the Director's ass and hoping to redeem the idea that he had no staying power.

"Back away, dickhead," she chortled at him and made for the door. "You remind me too much of my husband. He was drunk and the police clocked him at over a hundred miles per hour outside of Chadron before his pickup flipped about twenty times."

She had left in a virtuous huff and B.D. remembered a conversation when he and Berry and Delmore were eating Sunday dinner at Gretchen's. Delmore had taken Berry for a ride down to the harbor and B.D. had whimsically asked Gretchen why no woman had ever asked him to marry her.

"You're a biological question mark," she had said. "Women in general want some romance but when they look for a mate they most often estimate the man, at least subconsciously, as a provider.

You present yourself as a fuckup but the reason you can get laid is that you intensely like women without irony."

B.D. had reminded himself to look up "subconscious" and "irony" in Delmore's dictionary. Gretchen had been wearing pale blue fairly tight shorts and when she vigorously mashed potatoes at the stove her butt cheeks jiggled so attractively that B.D. felt tears arising. He had stopped well short of persisting on the marriage issue because Gretchen could be a little cruel. Years before, she had used her authority to thoroughly review his school records and discovered that his intelligence was well above average which made her question him sharply.

"Why live like you do? You're smart enough to do otherwise."

"I just slid into it," he had answered nervously.

"Well, you flunked English literature but you aced geometry."

"Geometry was real pretty."

It occurred to him then that she would never understand the deep pleasure of spending a whole day in the company of a creek. If he could make a subsistence living repairing deer-hunting cabins, cutting firewood or pulp why should he do more? He spent the rest of his time wandering in the woods and following creeks to their source. When Gretchen had said that he was frozen in place at age twelve he had reflected that that had been a good year. He had caught his first brook trout over three pounds on a beaver pond north of Rapid River, he owned a little terrier that rode in his bicycle basket and could occasionally catch a flushing grouse, and he had gotten to screw a beered-up sixteen-year-old tourist girl down on the town beach. The accusation of being frozen at age twelve did not seem to be a serious charge. Once when he got winter work at about age twenty as a janitor at a bowling alley he didn't think these fully employed men at their weekly bowling league were having all that much fun trying to break 200. They mostly had fat asses and when they jumped up and down they didn't jump high.

Now out the tour bus window it was pleasant to watch Berry and Turnip dancing at top speed. Turnip always looked ungainly but turned out to be a fine dancer. B.D. left the bus and moved hot coals off to the side and arranged the grill face so that it was well balanced on rocks, electing himself as the steak cook. Not so far off in the moonlight he could see Charles Eats Horses sitting in the cemetery with his hands pointed up toward the sky. The Director sat on a lawn chair guarding the beer and B.D. decided to drink his share of two real fast to acquire a modestly good feeling. The meat was real fatty rib steaks, his favorite cut, and the bone made it possible to eat with your hands rather than struggling with plastic knives and forks. Everyone was so tired that they ate fast and went to bed. When he went into the dark to pee B.D. was thrilled to have Turnip pass him a pint of schnapps for a couple of deep swigs. Berry continued to dance in the firelight without drums, banging on her tambourine, until the Director led her off to bed. Up home Berry tended to avoid all strangers but B.D. admitted to himself that she was having a good time with these people. She seemed to love music just like she was enchanted with birds. The Director had said that there were a lot worse things than being mute.

They got an early start in the morning and B.D. was upset when saying goodbye to Charles Eats Horses who was still sitting out in the cemetery but seemed to be in some sort of trance though he hugged Berry. The tour bus stopped in Pine Ridge and dropped off three crew members including a very strong young man named Pork. B.D. had learned that Pork had gotten his name when he had run away to Pierre when he was twelve. He was very hungry and went in to the supermarket to steal a pound of hamburger to eat raw but had grabbed a package of pork sausage by mistake. Ever since then Pork had had an affection for raw pork. He seemed fairly smart and said at one time raw pork could be dangerous but trichinosis was a thing of the past. Out the window in Pine Ridge, which was a dreamy place surrounded by beautiful country, B.D. saw Pork embrace his wife and son and get into a fairly new Chevy pickup.

On the way up toward Rapid City, B.D. sat up front with Turnip who invited him to stay at the condo he had inherited from an aunt who had been a school principal and a successful horse trader. Turnip said the group of condos shared a heated pool and when the weather was warm he would sit by the pool in Vuarnet sunglasses with a hand-tooled leather briefcase a rich white woman had given him down in Santa Fe, New Mexico, when the band toured there. Pretty girls and women would come up to him at the pool and chat because he looked like a big shot. He would tease his neighbors because the briefcase was full of R. Crumb comic books. He showed one to B.D. who thought it was the best comic book he had ever read.

They stopped at a country gas station for fuel and coffee and in an adjoining field two girls were practicing barrel racing with their quarter horses. B.D. was appalled at the speed at which the horses were running and turned to the Director beside him.

"They could die if they fell off."

"They don't," she said but then she yelled at Berry who vaulted the fence and ran toward the girls who now were taking a break. Berry went past them doing a top-speed figure eight around the barrels and then she stopped by the girls and petted the horses while she cooed like a dove. B.D. told the Director that he didn't think that Berry had ever been near a horse. They crawled through the fence and made their way to the girls. Berry was rubbing her nose against the nose of one of the horses who seemed to like it.

"She ain't right in the head," the girl said to the approaching B.D. and Director.

"That's true but she's a sweetheart. How about giving her a ride? She's never been in the saddle before," the Director said.

The girl gestured to Berry who leapt on with one flowing move.

"That's quite a trick," the girl said leading the horse by the reins then handing the reins to Berry. "I bet she can handle it."

The horse took off for the far barrel and B.D. covered his face with his hands and peeked through his fingers. Berry was pasted to the saddle and neck of the horse like a decal but when the girl whistled and the horse ran back toward them abruptly stopping Berry slid forward and hung there with her arms around the horse's neck. She was all aglow and crooning. B.D. reached for her and she dropped into his arms.

"Now she's both a dancer and a cowgirl. All is not lost," the Director said.

B.D. paused halfway crawling under the fence watching Berry grab a post and vault over the top wire the same way he used to do when he was young. Way too much had been happening in this life and there under the bottom wire he was suddenly trying to focus.

"How am I supposed to get back home?" he asked almost plaintively.

"Well you can't fly because the computer at the airport might pick up the Michigan warrant. They might not still be looking for you but we can't take a chance. The jail in Rapid City is full of drunk Indians. Your uncle Delmore is sending someone out to pick you up. He says you'll owe him big."

"He always says that," B.D. said thinking he'd have to find a good hiding place back home. Delmore had plenty of money but like many old people he was fretful about it. "During the Great Depression I couldn't afford the hole in a doughnut," he would say.

B.D. pretty much sat for two full days on a cement park bench on the grounds of the Rapid City hospital. He packed along sardines, cheese, crackers, and Bull Durham. He was rolling his own cigarettes from Bull Durham and though there was a mysterious sign saying "Smoke-Free Zone" he couldn't imagine anyone would object on these warm windy days of early spring. He was wrong.

A security man approached and said he could be arrested which caused a quiver of fear. B.D. played dumb when the security man pointed at the sign ten feet away.

"Can't you read?"

"Not too good," B.D. said as if trying to parse the sign.

The Director was running Berry through a battery of tests. B.D. had tried to give the Director the five-hundred-dollar gift from Dr. Krider but the Director had refused saying, "You can't give me all your money. Are you stupid?"

This seemed possible. He hadn't been able to reach Uncle Delmore or Gretchen on the phone and her answering machine said she would be away for a week. Turnip had dialed the numbers for him on his cell phone and when B.D. worried about the expense Turnip said that he got a deal for three thousand minutes. B.D. wondered how they could possibly keep track of such things at the same time thinking that Delmore rarely answered the phone because bad news always came over the phone. He didn't watch television news because he said he didn't need to know all of the bad news in the world in ten minutes. Delmore listened now and then to Canadian news on his big powerful radio because things didn't seem to be going so bad up that way.

B.D. hung out on the bench in front of the hospital because the medical tests made Berry so unhappy that she cried which she never did normally. She was so sad that when she and the Director came out for a break from the tests she didn't even make gull cries when she shared sardines with B.D.

"Sardines have gone up from nineteen cents to a dollar in my lifetime," B.D. reflected. He was remembering his youth when toward the end of the month Grandpa's pension money ran low and they would eat five tins of sardines and boiled garden potatoes from the root cellar. It was their "dollar meal," better in the summer with added onions, radishes, and tomatoes from the garden.

"Christianity might be bullshit but I heard a priest say that greed was the Antichrist." The Director hugged Berry who was trembling.

"Berry's mom used to throw her naked out in the snow when she peed the bed. Back then Berry was always trembling but she lucked out when her mom got sent to prison."

"I'd like to slit that cunt's throat," the Director said matter-of-factly.

Berry began to cry again when the Director led her back toward the hospital. B.D. wasn't feeling well having had one too many with Turnip and his anger over Berry's trials exacerbated his discomfort. He had stayed two nights in a sleazy motel because he hadn't wanted to stay at the Director's because she wouldn't allow alcohol in her home and Turnip's condo made him too nervous. Turnip had had some young lady neighbors in for drinks in the late afternoon when they got home from work. They were dressed slick and neat and were professional women working in real estate and one was a teacher "looking for something better." The problem was that B.D. couldn't get a fix on what they were talking about and Turnip had put on loud rock-and-roll music. They fawned over Turnip but let their eyes pass quickly over B.D. They were technically real pretty but he didn't feel a true-to-life nut itch over a single one of them. When they entered a tall one name Deedee had approached him.

"What do you do?"

"Cut logs. A little carpentry when I can find it."

"You Indians are so devil-may-care," she giggled chugging her Budweiser.

"I'm not a real Indian like Turnip. I'm just a mixed breed like most dogs." He was tempted to tell he was a wanted man on the run but she had quickly turned away.

Turnip had made them a batch of margaritas and winked at B.D. when he poured most of a bottle of tequila into the shaker.

"I'm sending these bitches to the moon pronto. We're in for some C-minus fun," he whispered.

B.D. took a couple of gulps of tequila and then when the rest of them went out to see someone's new leased car he slipped out the back door and headed for the scrungiest side of town where he had a fry bread taco covered with hot sauce. After dinner he bought a pint of McGillicuddy's schnapps to settle his stomach, then headed back to his motel room where there was a big photo of Mount Rushmore. He tried to imagine Charles Eats Horses pouring a gallon of blood-red paint down along George Washington's nose. Every movie on cable TV seemed to involve people shooting each other and he wasn't up to being a witness to malice of any sort. Finally on the National Geo channel he found a documentary on Siberia which seemed a totally wonderful place, the kind of country he'd learn to love in three minutes flat. He sipped out of the 100 proof bottle disliking plastic glasses because years ago one had sprung a leak and left a last drink on his wet lap. There was an improbable surge of homesickness and he made do by reliving a long trek west of Germfask in search of a rumored beaver pond which was actually in a federal wildlife area where it was illegal to fish, the smallest of considerations because on the sparse two-tracks you could hear the rare federal vehicle a half mile away and merely step into the brush. At the beaver pond he hooked what he thought would be the largest brook trout of his life but after a prolonged struggle the fish turned out to be a pike of a half dozen pounds. He would have preferred it to be a brook trout but gracefully accepted its pikedom. It was June and pike are quite tasty from the cool waters of the early season. By the time he got back to the car it was nearly dark, after ten this far north in June. He drove over to near Au Train where an old Indian lady he knew lived far back in the woods in a tar-paper cabin. His grandpa and this woman were sweet on each other and when he was a boy he'd fish a nearby creek while the two had their monthly assignation. When he arrived just before midnight with the pike her cabin was dark and it scared the shit out of him when he heard a growl from a nearby thicket. She was playing a joke on him after she had been out night walking. She cooked up the pike and they ate it with bread, salt, and some elderberry wine she had made the autumn before. She sang along with the country station from Ishpeming and was particularly good at duets with George Jones and Merle Haggard.

The reverie put him in a fine mood though the Siberian program segued to heart surgery on a zoo elephant and he turned off the television not wanting to know if this elephant failed to make it through the operation. The heart was red and huge and its beating was tentative. B.D. recalled that once when Grandpa was telling his World War II stories there was one about a whale seen in the North Pacific that had a heart big enough for a man to sleep in.

He managed his second long day of vigil fairly well. The Weather Channel predicted a storm by evening but the day had a warm breeze from the south. The hardest part was when the Director and Berry came out and Berry closed down and became stonelike. Due to some blood test she wasn't even allowed to eat the Big Mac with extra onions he had bought her. Berry's only sign of life was to point straight up at the tiny specks of hawks making their spring migration.

"She's not looking too good for a normal life," the Director said.

"I already knew that," B.D. said, his gorge rising.

"So did I but they have to figure out what's possible. She won't ever be able to talk but she's physically coordinated, strong, and agile."

"I already knew that." The anger was a knot in B.D.'s throat so that he couldn't swallow.

"These are specialists in this infirmity, B.D., so you'll have to be patient. We'll be finished by three and then I'm going to take Berry out north of Sturgis toward Bear Butte to see some baby buffalo. You got a big surprise coming about that time."

A doctor walked by and Berry shoved her head into B.D.'s jacket. He patted her back and her muscles were tight as a drum.

"I don't want no surprise. I want to head home with my daughter."

"You can't. We're already processing with the state of Michigan for the change of guardianship. Her mother has consented. Eventually the state of Michigan will withdraw the charges against you. Her mother got another five years for biting off a guard's ear. You know this is best. What would you do when she got pregnant at age twelve by whomever?"

"Likely kill whomever."

"Then she would have no one. She's going to live with my cousin's family north of here. They got cows, horses, and dogs and she'll go to this special school part-time."

B.D. began to cry for the first time he could remember. The Director hugged him and dabbed his tears with a good-smelling handkerchief and Berry came alive enough to hold his hand. They left and he quickly finished the bottle of schnapps, reached into his pocket, and rolled a cigarette and lit it. Suddenly the security guard was in front of him.

"I'm going to have to call the police, I warned you."

"It would be the last number you ever dialed," B.D. said levelly.

"How come you're crying?" The security man shrugged, not wanting to get his ass kicked.

"They're taking my daughter away from me," B.D. said.

"That's an awful thing to have happen," the guard said and walked away.

B.D. saw a black dog out in the parking lot. He whistled and the dog trotted over with its long rabbit ears and ungainly body what with its front rather slender compared to its big back end. B.D. unwrapped Berry's Big Mac and was amazed when the dog ate the burger in polite bites rather than gulps. The brass collar said that her name was Ethyl, a fine match he thought between name and this peculiar beast. Here Ethyl was out on a stroll and lucked into a burger. The basis of a friendship having been made Ethyl hopped up onto the bench, circled a few times, and nestled in for a snooze. From her somewhat distended teats it was apparent that Ethyl was a mother and B.D. mentally bet that she was good at it as he stroked her long floppy ears. Turnip had said that the Director had raised five kids, the last being a member of the Thunderskins. How could I know how to be a mother when I didn't even have one myself, he thought. He knew he was better than Berry's criminal mother Rose but that might be like comparing cat and dog turds. He leaned forward trying to prop his elbows on his knees for a little snooze. There was a chance of falling on his face if he fell asleep but that might be fun compared to the rest of what had been happening. He was not under the illusion that most of us are that he was in control, that he was in the driver's seat, as they say. And a wide streak of the dour Lutheran ethos of the Great North said that it is always darkest before it gets even darker. His last hope was to get home and have a life that the ancient Confucians thought was the best life, one in which nothing much happened.

He did doze and he did fall over but only scraped one palm on the cement. The Director and Berry came back out for a few minutes and Berry was a tad cheerier, especially with Ethyl to pet.

"Your surprise is getting closer. I just gave directions," the Director said grabbing Berry's hand and walking swiftly back toward the hospital. Ethyl tried to follow but there was a shrill whistle from a block away out beyond the parking lot. Ethyl took off toward the whistle and B.D. had the maudlin thought, Now I've lost my dog, but then he saw something that made his heart jump. Out in the parking lot a woman looking like Gretchen got out of a car that looked like Gretchen's. Unable to believe this B.D. swiveled around until he was looking back toward the hospital. His skin prickled.

"B.D., it's me," she called out. "I'm here to drive you home."

It was as if the sun had risen in the middle of a stormy night. He didn't dare turn around and then a kind of paralysis seeped into his system. She sat down beside him and took his limp hand.

"I know it's been a hard time for you."

"You could say that."

"Everything is for the best. We've got to haul ass. It's Friday afternoon and I have to be to work Monday."

They all had a goodbye lunch at a plastic picnic table outside a McDonald's. Gretchen and the Director sipped sodas and ate granola bars while shuffling papers. B.D. and Berry ate with Berry sitting on his lap. She was fairly happy having perceived that she didn't have to go back to the hospital. B.D. and Gretchen were quite overcome and plans were discussed to come back to South Dakota around the Fourth of July for a visit.

Gretchen drove B.D. to the sleazy motel to pick up his bag and he had this idea that they should rest up because he had already paid for that day and night.

"Just get your bag, you nitwit," she laughed. She was wearing a blue summer skirt that thrilled him to the core.

PART III

"I was hoping to take a look at this Corn Palace." B.D. had been dozing but it seemed like every time he opened his eyes there was a billboard for the Corn Palace, a building constructed out of ears of corn. Since he had worked often as a carpenter he couldn't imagine corn as a building material. It was probably like cheap brick facing. "Why would they put up a building made of corn?"

"So that geeks like you will stop in Mitchell, South Dakota, and spend money. The weather is shit anyway and I'm tired and hungry."

It was sleeting and the thermometer in her Honda Accord had dropped to freezing from forty in the last hour. She steered downtown encircling the Corn Palace which indeed was made of full corncobs though they were the only tourists and downtown was pretty much closed. Gretchen chose a higher-end motel back out by the interstate because there was a restaurant attached and she didn't want to drive any farther.

"We've been talking all afternoon but I can't stop thinking about intrauterine pollution."

"What's that?"

"Chemicals from the environment get into the womb and affect the baby's teeth. I live too close to that stinking paper mill."

While she checked them into the motel B.D. reflected on her endless monologue on possibly having a baby. Since he was to be the sperm donor he first had to have a physical checkup to make sure he wasn't diseased.

"I'm thirty-three. I have to come to a decision," she had said.

"That's the age Jesus was when he died," B.D. had said lamely.

"What's that supposed to mean?"

"Nothing. I'm confused about being a sperm donor."

"It's easy. I don't want to do it in a doctor's office so it will happen at my house. After your checkup you'll whack off into a syringe bulb and I'll inject it you know where."

"I have my dignity," he had said, copping the line from one of Delmore's *Perry Mason* reruns.

"You'll get over it."

"Why can't I just put it in for a few minutes?"

"The idea is repellent to me."

While she was in the motel office it occurred to him that he associated repellent with the insect repellent he smeared on himself, especially in June when blackflies and mosquitoes were active in the trillions when he was fishing.

"You could drink a bunch and take one of your tranquilizers," he suggested.

"I'm a victim of anhedonia which means my neutrality is probably an organic response to trauma."

"I don't get it."

"I'll explain it over dinner."

Their two rooms were adjoining but when B.D. opened his side he noted that hers was still locked.

"Your door is locked."

"Yes, it is."

She took a quick shower and he got a hard-on just listening to the water run. He would have perished from lust if he hadn't found a two-ounce shooter of Canadian whiskey at the bottom of his duffel.

At dinner her soapy smell made his tummy quiver. So did his Seafood Medley for $9.95 for different reasons. It was all deep-fried and tasted like it had spent a lot of time on the bottom of a boat in the hot sun. Gretchen was kind enough to give him one of her two very tough pork chops though there was no gravy, just a slice of apple dyed red. She had ordered a bottle of white wine but he had never thought of white wine as actual alcohol so he opted for a couple of double whiskeys.

"You could say that whiskey is my wine," he said raising his glass and she clicked it with her own.

"Apparently."

"I'll pay for it," he said drawing out a ten-spot.

"Delmore gave me enough to bring you home. He's getting sentimental. We met a number of times and even danced at the American Legion fish fry to a band called Marvin and His Polka Dots."

"It's true if you say so."

"He even asked how women make love to each other and I said, 'Mind your own beeswax,' and then I told him I had given up sex for the rest of my life. He said he gave it up at age seventy because women kept borrowing money from him."

"I can't believe you two being friendly."

"He has a motive. He's eighty-eight years old and he's worried about you and Berry. He's not worried about Red who Cranbrook wrote him about and said was the best young math student they've ever had. Anyway as his nephew you're his only close living relative. I had to tell Delmore that it's unlikely that Berry has any memory of her brother."

"He never admitted I was his nephew."

"Well, you are and we agreed you need a short rope so I'll likely end up as your guardian."

B.D.'s mind whirled and he signaled the waitress for a third whiskey. Most of everything was going over his head because he was not one to think of the future. Up until Berry had entered his life the future was limited to the next day at most. Nearly every day he cooked food when he was hungry and slept when he was tired.

"You were going to tell me why sex is repellent." B.D. could practically smell 6-12 and Muskol in the air though you had to be careful about getting it in your eyes or you couldn't tie a fly on your leader.

"I'm tired of being sunk in mental shit. I can't talk about it now. Besides, you don't look so physically repellent after three glasses of wine." She leaned back, yawned, and stretched revealing her belly button, that sacred nubbin that connected her to a thousand generations before her.

"I'm telling you that if you drink two bottles of wine you'd be on me like flies on a cow's ass." He knew his words weren't quite right but the sight of her belly button was a jolt to his inner and outer beings.

"You can do better than that."

"Like a monarch butterfly on a daisy."

"You're a daisy!" She shrieked with laughter.

"Like an old maid sitting on a warm cucumber in her garden."

She leaned forward smirking and parted her blouse so he could see her left braless titty.

"In high school I was known as Miss Prick Tease," she laughed.

B.D. felt he was bubbling inside as Gretchen walked toward the cash register. Her body mystified him as it was far too slender for his normal taste. She had told him she had taken dance classes for fifteen years to "burn off anger" and that likely accounted for her tight build. On the way back down the hall to their rooms she stumbled and he caught her. She gave him an almost hug at her door and he thought of breaking his plastic key so he could enter through her door but she grabbed it and opened the door for him when he fumbled.

"We could have a nice glass of water for a nightcap," he said through her adjoining door.

"Sorry, kiddo. Right now I'm undressing. The squeaking sound you hear is my butt rubbing against the door."

"You can't do that to me. I won't sleep. I got a hard-on like a toothache."

"Just whack off. Get in practice as a sperm donor. Say your prayers. Think about your mom."

"I don't have a mom."

"I'm sorry. I misspoke."

He lay down on the rug and squinted through the quarter-inch space under the door. He heard her lights turn off. Lucky for him that he had darted next door into a liquor store when they had stopped for gas in Chamberlain and she had gone to the toilet. He sipped at the first of three shooters staring up at the creamy void of the ceiling. He slept on the floor until five AM then rushed to the bed to get fair use of the room cost.

Mum was the word in the morning except when he couldn't work the coffee machine and called out to her.

"Is this a rapist trick?" She rushed in wearing a short robe and while she got the machine going he leaned far over from his position at the end of the bed to get a peek up the back of her robe. His vision reached midway up her thighs so the effort was worth it except that she turned around and caught him.

"You're incorrigible."

"I'm just curious."

B.D. paid for his sins with a long wait for breakfast. Gretchen's eyes were vaguely teary and she drove with concentration buffeted by a blustery wind out of the southwest. She pulled off the interstate in Sioux Falls for a large container of franchise coffee which he declined because he didn't see the point of being that awake.

"Grandpa used to say, 'I'm so hungry I could eat the raw pork around a sow's ass.'"

She glanced at him with horror but stopped at a diner just over the Minnesota line when she turned to take Route 23 diagonally northeast across the state.

"You're not very interested in reality," she said, getting out of the car with a coolish smile.

"Define your terms." This came from his civics class thirty-five years before.

"I'm not being mean. It's just that you're more mammalian than anyone I've met. My father and his friends were fake mammals. For instance I bet you didn't notice that Berry scarcely recognized me."

"Yes I did. Sometimes when I picked her up from the speech therapist in Toronto she didn't instantly recognize me. I could see her mind saying to itself, 'Oh, it's you.'"

"Of course she was your pal more than anything."

"I was a fairly good dad. She always had clean clothes. I cooked her food she liked. We went on walks and fishing. We played games and looked at books though she didn't like words, only pictures. I let her have her garter snake on the table except when we ate at Delmore's. What more could I do?"

"Nothing. That's far more than most kids get. I mean my two cousins raped me over and over when I was ten and they were twelve and thirteen. I told my mother and she said, 'No they didn't.'"

"That's pretty bad reality," B.D. said looking up at the clouds scudding swiftly above them. She was shivering in the forty-degree wind. He tried to put an arm around her but she slipped away entering the diner. To his surprise she laughed at his "country boy special" which he covered with Tabasco and catsup while she settled for a dry English muffin.

* * *

It was never the state, he thought, but the terrain. Once they were out of solid farm country and he saw birch, cedar, pine, and hemlock, his spirits lifted through the top of his head. A sign said that there were ten thousand lakes in Minnesota which he doubted but then he was more interested in streams and rivers. He noted that Gretchen was drowsy by midafternoon when they hit the Wisconsin border and he offered to drive. She reminded him that if a cop stopped them and ran a check on his license he'd end up in jail. The idea that everything with the police was connected by computer distressed him, remembering as he did a time when the world seemed friendlier and more haphazard. Delmore was always carping about Homeland Security but B.D. with his aversion to the news kept himself ignorant. Despite his bluster Delmore was rather timid about authority and kept badgering B.D. for not having a Social Security number. Nowadays, Delmore insisted that even babies are obligated to have Social Security numbers, adding that people in Washington, D.C., knew all of the considerable bad moves B.D. had made in his life to which B.D. had responded, "Why would they give a shit?" Delmore pretended to be an authority on Arabs having known a few in Detroit fifty years before and had told B.D. that the Arabs were pissed off because we had treated them as badly as we do blacks and American Indians. B.D.'s frame of reference was limited to a late-night movie where this sheikh in a huge tent had a harem of thirty women wearing see-through gowns. The women were always dancing and servants brought huge platters of food. B.D. had thought that thirty women was being a bit too ambitious if any were as energetic as Belinda, his big dentist, who had screwed him into the carpet.

Gretchen was suffering from road exhaustion when they entered Wisconsin and began maniacally dithering about her future baby perhaps to keep herself alert. She spoke of day care, the legalities of sperm donorship, and once again the specter of intrauterine pollution. B.D. liked the sound of the word "intrauterine" but didn't care what it meant because he was betting on something confusing. B.D. thought of the outside of a woman's private parts as lovely as a woodland but knew that just inside things got pretty complicated. Way back in biology class the illustrated cross sections of a woman were stupefying whereas a man's pecker was as plain as day.

Near Rice Lake on Wisconsin Route 8 his attention was caught by the core of the legalities.

"You're saying that though I'm the dad of the kid I'm not actually the parent?" She had used the new word "parenting" which seemed slippery.

"Well, yes."

"I'm just a piece of meat that shot off into a gizmo that you squirt into yourself?"

"That's essentially it but I'm choosing you because you're interesting genetically. I'm not picking a white-bread, white-car, white-house American like my dad and his awful friends. Once when I was having a pajama party and they were playing poker his friend named Charley shone a flashlight under the sheets when he thought we were asleep."

"Can't say that I blame him."

"You're disgusting. We were only fourteen."

"They used to say that if a girl is big enough she's old enough."

The car swerved when she swatted at him. She had raised his ire and he was baiting her.

"In other words when I see this baby I'm not supposed to think or say that I'm his dad?"

"It's better that way since we're never going to be married. I also liked the idea that the baby would be one-quarter Chippewa."

"Oh bullshit. I was a fine dad to Berry."

There was silence for many miles and by the time they passed through Ladysmith she became a little jealous of the landscape which had him sitting on the edge of his seat. It was the same latitude as the southern tier of the Upper Peninsula and he was seeing his homeground flora for the first time in nearly six months. At his insistence she stopped the car at a little tourist park near a river outside of Catawba so he could wander around breathing in the pungent smell of cedar and alder along the water and look up at the green buds of birch and aspen. The flowing water made his brain jiggle and he fondled the thin branches of willow and dogwood. At the edge of the woods he lay down on his stomach to smoke a cigarette with a ground-level view. She had followed and stood over him with her arms wrapped across her chest, a defensive posture against the cool spring air and her own out-of-control feelings.

"You seem to think I'm marginalizing you." She stooped down beside him and scratched his head.

"What the fuck else?" he muttered, not quite knowing what "marginalizing" meant except that she was pushing him off to the side. On Grandpa's sofa back home there was an embroidered pillow that said "Love Conquers All." He thought, I'm not so sure. He could tell his huffiness was paying off because he had a clear view up her skirt and he would bet she was doing it on purpose to win him over.

"I'm so sorry. I'm just not explaining it in the best terms."

He buried his face in his hands but not so completely that he couldn't see up past her inner thighs to the delightful muffin captured by white panties.

"Got you." He suddenly reached out and grabbed her ankles.

She pitched over sideways twisting her legs to get loose. He had a quick fine view of her butt before he let go of her ankles. She ran laughing toward the car and he scrambled after her on his hands and knees like a dog barking and howling. She was thinking that her old shameless prick-tease moves had at least changed the mood and he was thinking that playing difficult had paid off.

They reached Ironwood by nightfall still happy though Gretchen was so tired she asked him to pick her up some takeout. Many copper and iron miners had arrived from northern Italy in the mid-nineteenth century and maintained their interest in their own food so the U.P. abounded in Italian restaurants. B.D. walked down the road a scant half mile and ate a large order of lasagna with a whole bottle of acrid red wine and waited for a pizza to take back to Gretchen. She wanted double anchovies and onions and he thought, Strong flavors for a strong woman. He'd drunk the bottle of red at warp speed and treated himself to a double whiskey thinking unpleasantly of the time he came home drunk from an evening with David Four Feet. His grandpa was angry and told him that his mother was a drunk and he didn't want B.D. to die from the same "curse." Grandpa said that his daughter still made his heart ache so that was the most that was ever said about B.D.'s mother. Grandpa had emerged from World War II with a number of bullet holes in his legs and ass but they made out okay on half disability from the government and Grandpa's ability as a part-time cabinetmaker. He couldn't stand up for long but tended a fine vegetable garden on his hands and knees.

When B.D. got back to the motel with the pizza he knocked at Gretchen's door.

"A peek at your beautiful ass for a pizza," he hollered.

"Of course, darling." She opened the door, flipped the back of her nightie up, took the pizza, and slammed the door, leaving him with burning skin.

"I wish to dine alone. Good night, love."

B.D. recalled that there was a smart-ass guy from near Traverse City who used to hang out in the Dunes Saloon in Grand Marais in the summer who had said, "How does a woman's butt crack capture our imaginations? It's only negative space, in essence, a vacuum." This was puzzling and really made you think it over.

They reached Delmore's at noon and were promptly attacked by the pup Teddy whom B.D. hadn't seen since leaving for Toronto. Teddy had grown much larger. B.D. asked about Teddy's mother and Delmore looked into the air while responding as if the mother had ascended.

"She got shot while eating sheep down the road. We saved the hindquarters of the sheep. You owe me a hundred bucks." Delmore was busy giving Gretchen an overfond hug so that she finally pushed him away.

They sat on the porch swing talking and drinking Delmore's poor man's lemonade—too little lemons and too much sugar. It was Sunday and even the landscape was snoozing in premature warmth. The peepers, tiny frogs, were trilling from the swamp down the road in an evident state of spring fever. B.D. had a lump in his throat about life itself and the sight of Delmore sitting in the ragged old easy chair at the end of the porch with the dog in his lap. Gretchen began to fall asleep on the porch swing, then got up and reminded B.D. that he was due at the doctor's at nine in the morning for his checkup.

"Who's paying?" Delmore barked.

"I am, sweetheart. I'm sending him to a vet." She kissed Delmore on the forehead and escaped his attempt to give her a pat.

"She's going to be your stepmother when I pass on," Delmore said as Gretchen drove off down the gravel road with stones tinkling under the fenders. "I'm hoping that you'll fix me some fried chicken and noodles for Sunday dinner?"

B.D. nodded staring at his favorite hill about three miles off to the north. Gretchen wanted him to teach her how to catch a fish and he was busy concocting a fantasy about a riverside seduction. Meanwhile he was going to head for the hill to breathe air where others weren't breathing it. About three-quarters of the way up the hill there was a fine thicket in the middle of which there was a white pine stump to sit on. So much of his life had been solitary that the crowded nature of the past six months had been confusing. He could be confused enough when alone and the addition of the company of others raised the ante exponentially. For instance he didn't really want to teach Gretchen how to catch a fish. Love was love and fishing was fishing, an almost religious obsession that had added grace to his life for more than forty of his nearly fifty years. Sitting in the car with Gretchen from Ironwood to Delmore's a dozen miles from Escanaba had been difficult. By count the highway had crossed eleven streams that he had fished and each stream held a reverie of the experiences on the stream: "Small bear crying at twilight meant get out of there ASAP as the mother would be irritated. Left two trout behind as peace offering." But with Gretchen in the car he would turn away from the bridges, look down at her when she uttered the word "baby." The hugeness of the idea of a baby filled the speeding car and the world around it and the clarity of trout fishing disappeared despite her strange assurances that the baby had "nothing" to do with him. He had long since accepted that she was by far the most hopeless love of his life, for practical purposes as remote as the princess of Spain or a creature from outer space. He was one of those very rare men who, for better or worse, knew exactly who he was.

He reached his thicket in a fast-paced hour wiping the sweat from his face with his shirt and was pleased to find that a female Cooper's hawk still returned to the area, probably recently, and was not disturbed by his familiar presence. Before he could fully relax he checked the contents of his wallet for what was left of Dr. Krider's gift and discovered three hundred and seven dollars, a virtual fortune. If he was careful and avoided too much time in bars he could possibly fish for a month. He would do a little of it locally because Delmore was bitter about his lack of home-cooked meals. He was too far out in the country to be reached by Meals on Wheels and his fridge's freezer compartment was full of Swanson chicken pot pies which were sometimes on sale three for a dollar, and in the pantry there was a long neat line of cans of Dinty Moore beef stew. When B.D. went to the doctor in the morning he would pick up a few things to cook and freeze before he took off on his fishing trip.

Sitting uncomfortably on his stump B.D. lapsed into a state much envied by the ancients. He thought of nothing for an hour and merely absorbed the landscape, the billions of green buds in thousands of acres of trees surrounding him. Here and there were dark patches of conifers amid the pale green hardwoods and far off to the south a thin blue strip of Lake Michigan. He had never thought a second of the word "meditation" and this made it all easier because he was additionally blessed with no sense of self-importance or personality which are preoccupations of upscale people. Within a minute he was an extension of the stump he sat upon. After about an hour he was aroused by the Cooper's hawk flying by a scant ten feet away after which B.D. reached into a hole at the base of the stump for a pint of schnapps he stored there and was delighted by the wintergreen berry taste.

He was the doctor's first patient on Monday morning and the doctor was in a pissy mood because he was a friend of Gretchen's and her choice of a sperm donor was inscrutable to him. He carelessly drew blood from B.D.'s large forearm as if wanting to punish the nitwit.

"Sperm donorship is a serious thing," the doctor said. "It's better if it's anonymous."

"Why?" B.D. knew that he was normally invisible to the doctor and had decided to play dumb in hopes of getting out of the office as soon as possible.

"Obviously there are emotional issues. Have you been sexually active?"

"Now and then whenever it's possible. You can't always get what you want. It's better not to aim too high."

"What's that supposed to mean?" The doctor was clearly irritated.

"If you go to the bar at the alley on women's bowling night you're not likely to score one of the top ten ladies out of thirty so you aim low."

"Have you ever had a sexually transmitted disease?"

"None other than crabs in Chicago thirty years ago."

"Stand up and drop your trousers. I need to check you for herpes and warts."

"No."

"I insist."

"I don't give a fuck if you insist. I'm familiar with my dick and I don't have any warts." B.D. had never been to a doctor in his life except the time when a tree he was cutting down bucked back and shattered his kneecap and then the orthopedic doctor hadn't been curious about his dick.

"I'm afraid I can't recommend you to Gretchen as a sperm donor."

"Fuck you and the train you rode in on."

B.D. left the office whistling a merry tune and headed for the supermarket. Delmore had given him fifty bucks and he figured he could cook up a half dozen dishes from *Dad's Own Cookbook,* put them in the freezer, and still get over to Grand Marais before dark assuming the old Studebaker pickup didn't break down. Delmore had kindly had the windshield replaced the evening before and B.D. had packed his meager camping equipment including a seventy-year-old heavy canvas pup tent from World War II. He had slept outside because the things of Berry's left behind gave him a severe lump in the throat.

Leaving the supermarket he sorted out his own cans of beans and Spam putting them in a wooden potato crate in the pickup bed. Delmore didn't like him driving the old Studebaker except when B.D. used to visit Belinda, the big dentist, the thought of whom agitated his loins. They both got some serious knee burns on her fluffy white carpet. He was supposed to stop by Gretchen's office and tell her how things had gone with the doctor but he was willing to bet top dollar that the doctor had already called Gretchen. The obvious solution was to leave a message on her home phone saying that he could be contacted at eleven-thirty any evening this week at the Dunes Saloon in Grand Marais. Gretchen's office made him dry-mouthed and nervous. It was the rows of file cabinets that put him off along with the many computers. Why keep records on everyone? How could the contents of so many lives be kept in the cabinets and computers? Way back when, a teacher would show them the contents of his "frozen zoo," all the marvelous dead songbirds he had found which he kept in the freezer. His own records began with when he and David Four Feet were caught at age thirteen throwing cherry bombs under squad cars in Escanaba, and went on to include every pissant scrape with the law since then.

He was soothed cooking Delmore's dinners for the week with Delmore sitting there at the kitchen table making uninformed suggestions while flipping through the satellite channels. Delmore talked back to the television. If a character, say in a spy movie, were imperiled Delmore might holler, "Watch out behind your back you fucking nitwit!"

After a couple of hours B.D. was finished making six stews, two each of pork, chicken, and beef, mindful to keep the bites small as Delmore's teeth were sparse among his gums. B.D. slid the Tupperware containers into the freezer, then called Mike in Grand Marais and was pleased to hear the area was currently shy of a constable or deputy though one might be hired in June for the summer when tourists arrived. Tourists were appalled when there were fights at the taverns and someone was needed to unsuccessfully keep the lid on tempers and extreme public drunkenness. B.D. was still legally enjoined from the area due to a past mud bath and the unfairness of the law.

Delmore was asleep in his chair so B.D. tiptoed off for his first actual freedom in six months. At the last minute he remembered to pack a couple of very large construction trash bags in case the weather turned bad so he could crawl into one when the tent began to leak. On the four-hour drive northeast he stopped at two creeks and caught a half dozen brook trout for supper. When he reached

Seney with only twenty-five miles left to go to Grand Marais he relented and stopped to buy a fishing license on the off chance of getting stopped. It wouldn't do to have a game warden calling headquarters for information. He also bought a cold six-pack reminding himself to keep the beer he was drinking out of sight when driving up a hill because there might be a cop coming the other way, an old survival trick of the North.

Feeling rather soothed by the beer B.D. still resisted stopping at either tavern while driving through Grand Marais. It certainly would be stupid to tie one on while it was still daylight. He greeted the lovely harbor and Lake Superior beyond and headed east for a few miles before turning south on a log road for seven miles to a place he loved not because it was the best fishing which it wasn't but because of the gentle, unobtrusive beauty of the place. He was a little surprised about two-thirds of the way in when he felt an unexpected tremor of fear in his stomach. A mile off to the west was the location where years ago he had found a large wild cherry tree blasted by lightning, an object largely held to be magical by all Indians and a few whites. And not fifty yards away in a thicket of sugar plum and dogwood he had discovered a small ancient graveyard of seven graves. When he had told a very old Indian friend about the graveyard the man said, "Don't even tell me where it is. If it's found out college people will come with their evil shovels." Sad to say B.D. had met a graduate student in anthropology from the University of Michigan who had come north to the Upper Peninsula to study possible battle sites of the Chippewa, known to themselves as the Anishinabe, and the Iroquois in the early nineteenth century. It was all in the way Shelley's ample but well-formed butt handled the barstool beneath it. He was smitten, not a rare thing, but this was a powerful smiting indeed. He almost prayed, "Please God, let it be me." Suffused in the mixture of lust and alcohol he had spilled the beans and showed her the graveyard. How could he do such a pathetic and obvious thing? It was easy, though he tried to convince himself later that he had been caught up in a "whirl" whatever that was. He and Shelley became temporary lovers and in the following summer, sure enough, the University of Michigan began their anthropological "dig." By then B.D. was involved with Lone Marten's ill-fated and short-lived project of a "Wild Wild Midwest" tourist attraction. Lone Marten was David Four Feet's brother but also a rotten-to-the-core scam artist and fake Indian activist. Their little Wild, Wild Midwest group attacked the dig one dawn with an improbably large amount of fireworks. Unfortunately the Michigan State Police got wind of the plot and in the ensuing melee Berry's mother Rose had bitten off a cop's thumb. Lone Marten and B.D. escaped and went on the lam with Delmore eventually bailing B.D. out. Rose was the only one to do hard time. B.D. was enjoined from entering Alger County west of Munising, his favorite spot on earth.

But here he was encamped several years later convinced that no one remembered that long ago because he rarely had reason to do so himself. These rehearsals of the past were brutal so he quickly gathered wood and started a fire. The concentration required to cook his trout properly would help abolish the past but then while he was setting up the pup tent and waiting for the fire to get right another behavioral glitch struck him hard. About ten years before in a bar in Sault Ste. Marie he had said something nice to a woman of about thirty who was drinking with her friends and she had responded by saying, "Beat it, creep," and he had poured a big mug of beer down her neck and fled. Unfortunately at the time he was well known around the Soo and the cops quickly found him. Two nights in jail were unpleasant. He and a buddy who ran the job were notorious for illegally diving on old Lake Superior shipwrecks and pillaging what could be removed. An antique brass binnacle could bring a thousand dollars assuming that you didn't get caught but they did get caught with the body of an Indian in full regalia B.D. had found on the lake floor.

B.D. had set up camp and cooked his supper fish hundreds of times and now this simple act soothed him at least temporarily. The beans were in a saucepan off to the side and he scooped some bacon fat into his iron skillet and put it on the coals. He took a handful of watercress and put it on his tin plate which kept the trout from congealing against the metal. He looked up to see the last of the sun's top dropping over the ridge to the west. He saw an evening grosbeak land in a chokecherry and a group of cedar waxwings were doing their twilight limb dance.

He ate quickly and was still hungry wishing he had kept a portion of the pork chops and potato casserole he had cooked for Delmore. Or the chicken and Italian sausage stew. He took a swallow of the peppermint schnapps and made his way down a gulley perhaps fifty yards to the river hidden by alder and sweet-smelling cedar. He flopped down on a grassy patch of bank, a slight groan on his lips, thinking, You may as well fully accept how awful you've been and entertain good thoughts like the glimpse of Gretchen's bare butt just before you handed her the fine-smelling pizza. Finally he was released into the beauty of the river for the last hour before dark. Through the trees on the other side of the river there was still a patch of snow on a north-facing hillside though it was May 5. The river was still high and strong from the snowmelt runoff and he was amazed as ever by how wonderful it sounded, perhaps the best sound in the world this water noise. He heard the drawn-out sound of a whip-poor-will which always made his skin prickle. He hoped to hear a wolf in the five days he intended to camp there as a den was less than a mile away.

The Dunes Saloon was far less idyllic. Taking care of Berry had made him lose his touch at nighttime bars. You had to pace yourself and too many acquaintances from years ago bought him drinks. Three doubles in thirty minutes was too fast and when Gretchen called at eleven-thirty he was less than lucid.

"How could you do this to me?"

"What did I do to you?"

"You were rude to the doctor."

"The dickhead treated me like mixed-blood trash. I've been through this before."

"You were supposed to let him examine your penis for possible herpes warts."

"My penis doesn't own any herpes warts. It's pure as the driven snow."

She hung up on him and he was sorrowful for a full minute but then Big Marcia snuck up behind him and grabbed his wanger. He turned with a smile to see that Big Marcia had gotten even bigger. B.D. thought she had maybe reached two fifty and lost some of her attractiveness. At two hundred she hadn't looked that bad. She wore the T-shirt of the girls' softball team, the Bayside Bitches, and now was perilously drunk and smelling of a cocktail called the Tootsie Roll which was a mixture of orange pop, Kahlúa liqueur, and whatever Dave the bartender might mischievously dump in. Dave was a fan of mayhem. Marcia wanted to go outside and "smooch" and since B.D.'s true love had hung up on him he felt justified in tagging along. However, outside in the yard in the shadow of the tavern she started to waver in his arms and gradually lost consciousness. Her back was sweaty and his hands were losing their grip. She had no belt to hold on to and his hands couldn't get a big enough piece of her capacious ass. He quickly thrust an arm under her crotch and as gently as possible lowered her to the ground. Now he was sweating and there was a twinge in his back. He looked out toward the harbor to the moon above the streetlight and decided to go back to his camp.

B.D. spent a wonderful night sleeping only intermittently in order to keep track of the moon through the open face of the pup tent. He had largely missed the moon in Toronto and since his inner and outer child were pretty much glued together he had been quite disappointed. All that ambient light in Toronto had also made the night sky short on stars. From childhood on he had been an addict of "moon walks" not of the tawdry NASA golf-club-swing type but wandering in field and forest in strong moonlight say from the three-quarter phase onward. Grandpa never minded when his seven-year-old grandson would head out in the dark because there was a fence around eighty acres of pasture, woods, and swamp and the tyke could always follow the fence home.

He fed the coals at the first glimpse of light and made his boiled coffee getting back into the sleeping bag to drink it and to study the fog that had dropped from the heavens. He wiggled like a caterpillar in his bag dropping a half pound of bacon in the iron skillet and opening a can of Mexican refried beans. He searched his mind for the remnants of a dream in which he was a baby sitting on a woman's lap looking up but he could only see the bottom of her chin. Could this be his mother? he wondered. Life was so fantastically inconclusive. The dream was so much more pleasant than the recurrent seminightmare of being painfully thirsty with a wet ass in a crib and looking up at a rough cabin ceiling at boards that varied from narrow to very wide. He'd asked Gretchen about this one and she said it was likely he had been abandoned.

He reserved his grease, pushed the bacon off to the side, and heated the refried beans. This magical combination allowed him to fish eight hours without hunger at which point a thick Spam-and-onion sandwich would fuel another six hours at which point twilight arrived.

Sad to say but in a flat hour he had ripped his cheap Japanese waders on a snag while trying to reach a late lake-run rainbow of a couple of pounds. The fish had snagged the leader on a deadfall across the river and he couldn't jerk the line free. His aim was brook trout but a spring rainbow made a nice chowder fish. When the waders ripped he expelled his air in a whoosh and floundered toward the bank falling forward in the swift waters. Both the air and the water temperature were about forty and he shed the waders and trotted toward camp a half mile away, shuddering with cold but still amused that when he reached the bank the fish had managed to free itself.

He stoked up his campfire to a roar, peeled off his wet clothes, and danced around the fire buck naked to warm up, rather unconcerned because he had dunked himself dozens of times during his fishing life and only irritated at himself because one durable pair of hundred-dollar waders would have lasted through the long chain of cheapies. He generally avoided powwows but danced some Native steps he had learned, laughing at the memory of when he was about ten and told Grandpa that he wanted to be a wild Indian when he grew up and Grandpa had said, "You already are." B.D. frankly didn't see much difference between Indians and the rural poor of the Great North except that the relatively purebloods tended to hang together as if they were members of the same isolated church.

He bank-fished until about noon becoming pissed off because there were so many good riffle corners he couldn't fish without waders. He headed to town to buy another pair of the twenty-five-buck model. At a bridge on the main road he thought he recognized a very old man and stopped to say hello. The old man was trying to fish off the bridge in a hole behind a culvert and it turned out that the man was ninety-two and had been a friend of his grandpa's before he had moved to Muskallonge Lake near Deer Park in the late fifties. The man said he had known B.D. when he was "knee-high to a grasshopper," the kind of thing old men said. He paused a moment looking at B.D. as if questioning whether what he had to say was appropriate.

"I was around that day that your dad came up from downstate all dressed up like an old-timey Indian. His car broke down in Newberry and he stole a pickup. The cops chased him up to Deer Park where he stole Clifford's canoe and went paddling straight out into Lake Superior on a stormy day. They found the canoe miles down toward Crisp Point but never him. I imagine you knew that?"

"Nope," B.D. said, "but thanks for the info." In a lifetime of hearing very slight and flimsy rumors this was the most concrete story yet. He wasn't exactly startled, just a little ruminative and melancholy imagining what it would be like to try to keep a canoe upright in a storm on Lake Superior. His grandpa was his true father. His mother was a whore of sorts but since she was a drunk nothing was probably better having known Berry's mother Rose too well. Who needs someone who could throw a naked kid into a snowbank?

At the hardware store he ran into Big Marcia who was buying some plumbing supplies. "B.D.! It's been years," she said, embracing him. "Maybe we can have a brewski tonight?" He watched out the window as Marcia got into her newish pickup. She always was a hard worker if a little forgetful.

He tossed the new waders into the pickup and walked across the street to call Gretchen thinking that if he fished until dark he might feel up to coming to town tonight. He caught her at lunch on her cell.

"B.D., darling, I'm sorry I hung up on you. I was having issues. Anyway, Thursday and Friday are prime times for conception. I thought I'd take two days off and come over. I'd need directions."

B.D.'s innards began a small spin which actually reminded him there at the phone booth of a big round childhood top where you pumped down on a knob and it began to spin at great speed and make a moaning sound that was supposedly musical. He told Gretchen that he would meet her at noon on Thursday and then walked over to the IGA grocery store to buy a bar of soap. He wished he had a better tent but when he'd checked tents out at a Marquette sporting goods store a good one cost the equivalent of seventy-five six-packs. Gretchen had slept in the pup tent the summer before with Berry when they camped out at Twelve Mile

Beach east of town while B.D. had curled up by the fire in an old green army blanket. The very thought that he'd be in this severely confined space doing whatever with Gretchen caused his heart to jiggle.

He fished hard throughout the afternoon and evening and resisted the urge to go into town for a few drinks. He ate a mediocre pork steak and took a long moonlit walk and the next morning was ready to fish at first light. He headed off toward an area he hadn't seen in a decade past a hilly few hundred acres where the watersheds of three rivers began, the Fox, the Two-Hearted, and the Sucker. He got turned around for a couple of hours near the roots of the Two-Hearted because he had become inattentive in the middle of a pussy trance over Gretchen. It was inevitable that he would see parts of her nude body in the tent and maybe she would hear a bear and throw herself into his arms. Or better yet a big thunderstorm which she was afraid of would cause her to crawl into his sleeping bag. He got a boner while crossing a neck of a swamp which didn't help his sense of direction. Seven years of totally unrequited love and lust and you inevitably build up quite a head of steam. He cooled off and collected his thoughts while sitting on a hardwood knoll eating his squashed Spam-and-raw-onion sandwich. Spam is a decidedly nonsexual meal and he immediately received an insight on just where he was. He walked south about a mile and then traced a small creek that led to the Sucker stopping to catch two fair-sized brookies in a beaver pond. He was thankful to finally hit the Sucker and turned north for a mile until he reached his camp. When you're lost you avoid panic by not quite admitting it but when you finally reach camp you're relieved indeed.

He spruced up his camp and gathered an immense pile of wood because Gretchen liked campfires. He washed some clothes with his bar of Ivory in a river eddy saving his own cleansing until just before he left to pick her up in the morning. They would have to leave her Honda in Grand Marais because the log roads were too rough for its low-slung frame. He made a mental grocery list remembering her fondness for Sapphire gin, expensive but then it might turn the sacred trick.

On a rather timid evening hike to another beaver pond it occurred to him that Gretchen had made a shambles of his fishing trip and that after he had fulfilled his destiny as a sperm donor he'd have to take off on an old-time, full-blast jaunt. It was unthinkable to miss two nights in a row at the tavern but then Gretchen was difficult enough to manage without a hangover. He remembered the Valentines from a distant past where a fat, naked kid with wings would shoot an arrow through a heart which stood for love. The pain was certainly there and its emotional havoc colored everything. For example on his third cast of his fly rod with a No. 12 brown Woolly Bugger fly his backcast was snagged fairly high in an alder bush and it was a fucking chore to untangle it. Just before dark he hooked a fine fish, possibly a rare two-pounder, but the fish wound the leader around a protruding tamarack root and broke off. He howled. He had been visualizing Gretchen on her hands and knees in the tent and he was behind and under her watching the firelight shimmer off her tummy and breasts. If he had been keeping track of his line and fish rather than this the brook trout would have been in his hands. For a millisecond he thought he heard a distant wolf howl, not an infrequent night sound in the area, but it turned out to be the much more comforting coyote. It was a mildly spooky place. A few years back he had fled after hearing two bears fight back in the forest, likely over a female. Even bears are pussy-crazed, he thought, walking swiftly back toward camp so he wouldn't have to wait for moonlight to find his way.

Dawn came bright and clear and he spent a long desultory morning rather aimlessly gathering more wood than they could possibly use. Some puffy clouds moved in from the southwest and he quickly walked to the river to catch a half dozen trout for their dinner. He took off his clothes and soaped himself down in a shallow eddy and when he dunked to rinse himself the water was pecker-shrinking cold. All the tree birds were urging themselves forward into a pastel green mist. He was feeling ever so vaguely religious and remembered a friend from the sixth grade named Skinny who was the Baptist preacher's son. Skinny was always praying aloud for everyone at recess but was indulged because he was by far the fastest boy in class. He would say stuff like, "Who are we that God is mindful of us" which one day B.D. mixed up and said, "Who is God that we are mindful of him," and Skinny was shocked to tears. B.D. had tried to pray when Grandpa was dying but was unsure of the process. Now standing naked by the river he had vague thoughts of how the prayer of love is answered in coupling.

Before noon he was standing on the hillock overlooking the harbor with the gin in a paper sack and studying the weather which was discouraging. It was still warmish with the wind from the southwest but way out there hours and hours away there was a bank of darkness to the northwest above Lake Superior. As a student of weather he knew that it could be the last Alberta clipper until mid-October, wherein the temperature borne by howling winds could drop forty degrees in minutes. Two fishing boats were speeding back into the harbor having noted the oncoming weather.

Gretchen pulled her Honda up beside his pickup, all smiles in blue shorts and carrying a flowery suitcase. There was certainly no point in discussing the weather with her.

"This is the biggest step of my life," she said, cozying up to him on the seat of the pickup.

"It sure is." She likely knew that her blue shorts would prime the pump as it were.

She had brought along his favorite sandwich, liverwurst and onion with hot mustard, and a hummus-and-lettuce for herself. They ate while he drove and had a modest wrangle when he contended that when she became pregnant she should eat lots of meat to make the baby grow in her stomach.

"It will be in the womb, darling."

"I meant the general area," he said, backing away. "I just know that Rose took on the wrong fuel when she was carrying Berry."

"I'm charmed by your concern but I'm thought to be quite smart."

They pulled into the campsite and she floated around in a state of delight while he took her flowery little suitcase out of the pickup bed. He suspected that the contents wouldn't be on the money for the coming weather.

"Let's get the show on the road," she said, kneeling and crawling into the open tent.

"Maybe we should have a little drink first," he said, unscrewing the gin bottle. He felt butterflies and needed liquid courage.

"A small one. We don't want to subvert your motility."

He had no idea what she meant but knelt at the front of the tent and poured two drinks in paper cups. She waved the syringe drawn from her big purse.

"That's a bulb baster like I use for roasting a turkey." He backed into the tent beside her.

"It's not for cooking. It cost seventy bucks."

"Wonderful." He wanted to say, You paid the equivalent of thirty six-packs for that fucking thing, but held back.

"Just take out your penis and get started." She sounded a little floaty like she had taken a tranq.

"I thought this over. I've never whacked off in front of anyone. You're going to have to do it and also show me some skin for inspiration."

"Do you have a glove?" she laughed.

"I don't carry gloves in May."

"Well, anything for the cause. I did this for a boy after the junior prom and he shot all over the place." She opened her blouse and slid down her shorts revealing bikini panties. She grabbed his penis and paused.

"You don't shoot like you did in high school." His voice was quivery as he stared at her body and she began to pump his penis holding the bulb of the syringe near the head. It didn't take long and she caught most of the fluid.

"Turn around and close your eyes."

"Okay." But he didn't. He couldn't help but peek as she slid down her panties and injected the fluid. She caught him looking.

"You cheated, you fucker." She scrambled out of the tent giving him the rear view he so desired. "We'll wait an hour and try again."

He lay there in his depleted postcoital state thinking that this was almost as good as the real thing. Sort of kinky and fun.

They took a slow stroll and then walked down to the river where he gave her a first fishing lesson. She was well coordinated and after a little while could make a modest cast. She checked her watch.

"Let's get down to business." She hadn't noticed that the wind was picking up in the ridge across the river and that the sky was getting fuzzy. She crawled into the tent and stayed with her head and shoulders toward the back. "I need to be near the source."

This time it took longer and the view of her cocked legs and tiny undies so close to his nose beat the hell out of any Hawaiian sunset. He groaned but it certainly wasn't heartbreak.

"You didn't do as well this time," she chided.

"I can only do so much." Without asking permission he took a glug of gin. He was disappointed when she covered herself with her light summer sleeping bag to make the injection.

They napped for nearly two hours waking to the roar of wind and Gretchen had trouble locating herself.

"What the fuck is happening?" she pouted when she heard distant thunder.

"A little storm." He took a wake-up swig of gin and prepared the fire to cook supper before the strongest part of the squall was upon them. She poured herself a drink and looked fearfully at the sky. It didn't take long to cook the brook trout and a can of beans. She wolfed her food as if already pregnant or, more likely, frightened at the rolling thunder in the west. B.D. knew the rehearsal having been caught by such storms a number of times in the Upper Peninsula in spring and fall. It could be real ugly if you were a couple of miles from your car. First came a driving rain and then the wind got colder and it would snow. It could go on for three days in the fall but in the spring it was usually only a matter of hours before it cleared.

They had barely finished their meal when there was a slash of lightning on the ridge across the river and a monstrous crash of thunder. She shrieked, dropped her plate, and burrowed into the tent. B.D. piled an armload of wood on the fire as the first sheets of rain hit.

When he got back in the wind was buffeting the tent and Gretchen was sniveling. He hugged her while listening to the rain pouring heavily onto the tent, knowing where the main leaks would begin. As if on cue he felt water dripping onto his face. Despite the closed flaps there was enough twilight in the tent for him to see the leaks nearest them. He shone the flashlight down the roof line and detected some major problems just as lightning sizzled the air and there was a hollow, raspy crash of thunder.

"I'm supposedly smart so why does this scare the piss out of me?" she said clutching him closer. She craned her neck up. "My feet are getting wet."

"Everybody gets a little scared. Delmore says it's the 'thunder beings.'" He could see in the flashlight glare that they were fucked. The tent was leaking everywhere. Also through the front tent flap he could feel the temperature dropping precipitously. "Just a minute."

B.D. burst out of the tent, trotted to the pickup, and grabbed a big trash bag from his catchall box in the pickup bed. He stooped and shoved the big pile of wood closer to the tent entrance. When he got back in the water was falling everywhere. He shook open the Visqueen bag.

"Get in here. You'll be dry and warm."

Gretchen got out of her wet summer bag and wiggled into the plastic container. Quite suddenly the rain let up but not the cold wind. In the remaining twilight he could see the driving snow through a crack in the tent flap.

"This is already working," she said, curled deep in the trash container.

B.D. leaned out and stirred the remaining fire coals and heaped on a pile of pine branches for quick kindling, then cross-piled bigger sticks of hardwood. He shed his soaked clothes.

"Got room for me?" He had left the other trash bag in the truck hoping for companionship.

"If you behave," she whispered peeking out of the container.

He slid in and grabbed the gin taking a couple of quick gulps. She took a few sips and rubbed his nude chest to warm him.

"We'll be snug as two bugs in a rug," he said.

"Of course, dear, if you say so."

They lay there and then the fire caught and the wind subsided. They were rubbing each other and she parted the flaps to watch the snow falling thickly on the fire. It was dark and the fire's eerie orange light in the falling snow looked lovely to her. Now that the thunder was gone she was feeling better with the help of the gin. She took another slug and passed him the bottle. She slid her hand down feeling the closeness of his erection.

"We could have a third session for insurance. We should stop on an odd number. Three not two."

"Fine by me." For the first time he was being allowed to run his hands closely over her body which was warm and damp.

She abruptly made a decision. She slid down her shorts and panties and turned her back to him, arching out her bottom and thinking wistfully that this was the way all mammals get their babies. He was thinking immediately that this was the grandest moment of his life. He attacked his job with affectionate energy. Afterward they dozed for a while and then he opened the flaps and studied the scene. The world was quiet but the snow was still falling thickly. These storms rarely brought more than half a foot of snow but he couldn't be absolutely sure they wouldn't get stuck there if the snow mounted to a foot.

"We best get the fuck out of here. Sit tight."

He pulled on his wet clothes and boots and walked to the pickup, starting it and wiping the wet snow from the windshield. He would come back the next day and pick up his gear. Despite his wet clothes he was still warm from his exertions. When he turned around she was shining the flashlight on him and half out of the bag.

"Stay inside. The pickup doesn't have heat."

He picked her up in the bag and carried her to the pickup. It took nearly an hour to make their way along the log road to the blacktop that led to town. Off to the east the blackish clouds opened and the moon shone through. She was snoring lightly within her cocoon. He had the absurd feeling of a reverse Christmas in May and remembered the holiday line, "The moon on the breast of the new-fallen snow."

The little village had never looked better and when he knocked on the motel office door he could see the bright lights and the snow-covered cars parked in front of the Dunes Saloon. The new owner of the motel looked at him askance but was pleased to take his cash. Early May was slow in the Great North. He carried her into the room like they were newlyweds. She sleepily got out of the bag and under the covers of the twin beds, getting out of her clothes under the sheets.

"You sleep there," she said, pointing at the other bed.

"It wasn't that bad, was it?" He smiled.

"It was bearable but I'm not intending to do it again. I got this feeling I'm going to be pregnant."

"I did my best. I'm heading down the street for a few drinks."

"Suit yourself, darling."

His heart was light with pleasure as he walked toward the tavern, turning around once to look at his tracks then flopping down in a vacant lot to make a snow angel. It was a fine one and he smelled Gretchen's sweet-smelling sweat on his hands. Somehow the big trash bag had been the perfect place.

He Dog

Part I

Chapter 1

It was late on a cold, windy March night and Brown Dog stood at the open door of the tar-paper shack listening to the dogs howl in chase from the swamp to the south. Above the wind and dogs he could hear the vast slabs of drift ice grinding against each other on Lake Superior a few miles to the north. This storm had come down from the Arctic and across Manitoba gathering force like a hurricane but without warm wind and rain, without a New Orleans to suffer, only Lake Superior and the vast tracts of forest. Trees would fall but not people.

That was the problem. When the storm had hit at twilight a dead oak had fallen across Brown Dog's hastily devised fence impoundment and five dogs had escaped. They began to yip in the distance which meant like it does with coyotes that the dogs were closing in on their prey, likely a deer many of which were yarded up in the deep cedar swamp that offered some protection. The winter had deposited nearly three hundred inches of snow which now had a crust thick enough to support Bruno, the alpha male of the five, a diminutive mean-minded wirehaired fox terrier. Bruno had been abandoned to the dog pound by rich summer people the October before with an ample monetary gift to keep the dog from being euthanized. Bruno would try to bite his owners, often successfully, unless they grated an ample amount of Parmigiano-Reggiano on his breakfast kibble. Nothing could break Bruno's will in this ugly habit until Brown Dog appeared on the scene. B.D. had acquired the dogs by virtue of a snowmobile accident that involved the animal control officer in this small town about thirty miles from Escanaba, the home of his beloved Gretchen and their one-year-old toddler Susi. Gretchen was widely connected through Social Services and wangled the job for B.D. who was connected to nothing practical but thought he should have a job what with being a father though he had no legal connection to the child. Being allowed after a decade of chase to close the deal was certainly one of a brief set of pinnacles in his rather mammalian romantic life.

Frankly, Brown Dog had been stricken by difficulties since the onset of fatherhood. He ever so slightly remembered the story of Job in the Bible but mostly the part where God covered Job's body with boils to test his faith which seemed small potatoes compared to B.D.'s problems. When he picked up the application and employment specs at the county office they were distressingly long. Why did they want to know his long gone mother's maiden name? His only distinct tie to our society was a driver's license. Should he admit his felonies? He doubted it, and there were great spaces in his employment history, which was negligible indeed. When he left the county office building he actually shivered in despair.

The dogs eventually returned shamefaced with bloody muzzles. B.D. stopped at the liquor store not for his own want but to bring a stiff drink for his friend Rollo the former animal control officer, who was still in the hospital from the snowmobile accident. Soon after the first big blizzard in November Rollo had been driving down a county road shoulder at 90 mph and hit a snow covered abandoned vehicle on his Polaris ATV on which he had only made one payment. The state police measured Rollo's trajectory at a hundred and eighty feet which was a record for the accident which was not at all rare. The previous year Rollo had broken a leg at a snowmobile rally on a frozen lake over near Sagola. He had rigged his steering and gas then bet the assembled drunks that he could pee standing on the backseat of his machine while going 50 mph. He succeeded but while taking too many waves and bows his snowmobile collided with a flimsy fishing shanty with someone in it. Rollo managed to jump free at the last moment breaking a leg. The demolished shanty caught fire boiling two pike the angler had in a pail. He was only badly bruised and put the boot to poor Rollo.

In the hospital B.D. had to hand-feed two vodka shooters to Rollo who was hanging there in traction. Rollo was half Blackfeet from near Browning, Montana, and claimed to be the sole child of a wealthy rancher who had been struck dumb by an Indian maiden. To B.D., Rollo was quite the fibber. Rollo had been mostly raised, or so he said, by a dozen English setters in a pen with a platform for baby Rollo so he didn't have to crawl in dog shit. To add credibility to his story Rollo had eaten a bowl of kibble and milk while they were drinking beer in his kitchen just before the big accident. B.D. had wondered why kibble for breakfast when you could have ham and eggs? Rollo had lost his inherited ranch in a succession of three bad marriages in a decade until one spring morning he found himself in his pickup heading east on Route 2, not unique as thousands of riffraff cross the nation back and forth on Route 2 between Coeur d'Alene in Idaho and Sault Ste. Marie in the Upper Peninsula, the northernmost cross-country route. Some are plain addicted to the north despite its absolute inhospitality. Despite being an outrageous fibber Rollo knew his dogs and was famed as a dog man who could correct the most obnoxious problems in hunting dogs and pets most often without saying a word. Rollo had equal success with women which upset B.D. with the mystery of it. Rollo could walk into a tavern on Saturday night and walk out with the best-looking girl or woman within a half hour saying next to nothing. Rollo claimed that he had learned the power of *non-talk* as a child from horses and dogs.

The most critical problem of the animal control job was the employment specs that clearly stated that he must euthanize stray dogs after holding them a week for possible retrieval. B.D. couldn't do it. He had managed in four months to talk people into adopting seven pups and nine strays through superhuman effort but these were hard times. The five he kept out at the shack, sure to grow in number, were absolute rejects. He couldn't kill dogs because they were his spirit animal, or so he had been told at age ten by his closest friend David Four Feet whose uncle was a traditional Midewiwin who lived far back in the woods and had nothing to do with white people. This man had stared long and hard at B.D. and determined the appropriate animal from B.D.'s name, and by asking what creature appeared most in his dreams. B.D had answered "girls and dogs." The man had wailed and sang a song in Anishinabe language and threw a burning log into the lake next to which they were camped.

Now it was May and besides his job, the most insuperable problem in B.D.'s life was Big Cheryl. Her real name was simply Cheryl but she was a strapping woman and an endurance race champion which involved swimming, bicycling, and running for a total of a hundred miles. She and Gretchen had met at a Social Services convention in Duluth the subject of which was "How Can We Best Help Native Peoples?" That was on the marquee out in front of the convention center under which an Indian rebel had spray painted, "Go Home to Yurp." Gretchen loved Cheryl's whimsicality.

In the months since B.D. visited Rollo after his accident, Gretchen and Cheryl had fallen head over heels in love, a homely metaphor if you visualize it. Cheryl was working in Fergus Falls, Minnesota, but quickly found a job in Mackinaw City on the Straits, a three-hour drive to Escanaba which meant for the time being the devout lovers could only be together on weekends.

One weekend the second time they met Cheryl began to call B.D. "dirt bag" and he immediately responded by addressing her as "a cock-knuckling thunder pussy" which he had learned from Rollo. Cheryl promptly threw a five-punch combination which B.D. expertly avoided having been the U.P. champ street fighter in his late teens and early twenties, retiring after a battle in a bar parking lot in Sagola after throwing a hundred hard jabs into the face, stomach, and throat of a huge Finn named Feike Ferkema who had B.D. in a chokehold. The man's head looked like a chunk of chuck roast and his little son was sobbing and yelling, "Kill 'im, Dad." Feike kept charging and trying to get his fatal arms around B.D. who finished him with a gut shot that sent Feike to the gravel puking and flopping. That was B.D.'s last fight mostly because Feike's kid had run in and bit him in the leg and soon after in an Amasa saloon he had seen the boxer Benny Paret die in a televised bout. B.D. never received more than twenty bucks for a bout which translated into ten six-packs, a can of Spam, and a box of Saltines. Why chance killing someone?

"If you can't behave I want you out of my life!" Gretchen said angrily which made little Susi begin to cry. Gretchen was sitting in a lawn chair in her green bikini and began nursing Susi who stopped crying.

"I'm sorry. I'll run it off." Cheryl said with tears in her eyes. She took off at a sprint, leapt Gretchen's picket fence, then headed down the street at an astounding speed. To B.D. Cheryl's body was mysterious. At twenty feet Cheryl looked normal. Close up she looked normal but a lot more so. He figured she was his own size, about six foot and 185 pounds but she was half his age and in impeccable shape. True her butt and other parts were overlarge but they were smooth, solid muscle. B.D. dismissed Cheryl from his relentless sexual fantasizing because he felt a slight tinge of fear over the idea that this powerful woman could kill you while coupling if she so chose. A few weeks before they had all driven down to Charlevoix to see Cheryl compete in a triathlete contest wherein they watched a hundred women swim, bicycle, and run a total of a hundred miles. Two of the contestants even pooped their shorts. Cheryl wept piteously when she only took third because of a bone bruise on her foot. She and Gretchen embraced and wept while B.D. proudly held Susi who stuck a finger in his eye. On the way home Cheryl ate five hamburger deluxes to assuage her hunger. Later when B.D. told his uncle Delmore about the contest Delmore was cynical claiming the race must be "political." B.D. was puzzled but then Gretchen had said that Delmore's slippage indicated a bit of dementia. B.D. was unsure of the word but recalled that there was an Upper Peninsula rock band called Danny and the Dementias one of whose musicians in a drug haze had forgotten he was holding a lit firecracker and lost a thumb.

"Are you paying attention?" Gretchen snapped her fingers to jolt B.D. from his reverie. She was concerned about the chicken he was grilling, two halves for Cheryl, and one half apiece for them. Rollo had spent two years on the lam in Taos, New Mexico, selling fake crystals to religious nuts. He said he wore a turban and sold the rocks which he advertised as being from Kathmandu for a good price. He went out with a waitress in Santa Fe who taught him how to make red chili and he in turn taught B.D. Gretchen sent off for fifty pounds of dried chilies and the die was cast what with the girls demanding genuine Mexican dishes every weekend. They had had Sunday dinner last week in early May at Delmore's and B.D. made tamale pie and had to struggle to get his share. Gretchen had said that when Cheryl was in full training she had to eat five thousand calories. The notion of calories was beyond B.D.'s ken or interest. He had been brooding over the idea that Gretchen was further away from him than ever before. He was now only a cook, handyman, and put-upon uncle despite being an unrecognized parent. Meanwhile at the far end of the table Delmore was questioning Cheryl about the political aspects of her being a triathlete to which she responded with, "You goofy old fuck." For inscrutable reasons they liked each other and after dinner Delmore put in a DVD starring Gene Kelly and Donald O'Connor and managed at eighty-six to get Cheryl to dance saying that back in the forties in Detroit he was known as Delmore the Dancing Wonder. When Delmore played the movie *Singin' in the Rain* B.D. headed outside and into the woods no matter the weather. Delmore was a child again liking the same movies and songs ("I'd Like to Get You on a Slow Boat to China") and books (*Your Income Tax Is Unconstitutional*) over and over.

Gretchen had lined a refrigerator shipping box with aluminum foil for comfort on cool days with wind off the lake and a weak sun. Suntan lotion was an erotic key for B.D. but far less so with baby Susi around, and the equally powerful depressant of having the first actually, bonafide job of his fifty-four years. At that moment, B.D.'s cell phone rang, the call coming from the sheriff's office, his primary obligation as a dogcatcher but Gretchen leapt up from her aluminum foil cave, grabbed the cell phone, and shrieked, "No talking with meat on the grill."

He carried the chickens in the house as Cheryl came bounding up the steps. She looked like she was steaming but it was smoke from the barbecue fire behind her. B.D. moved his plate of chicken and red chili sauce and potato salad to the corner of the kitchen to protect it from Cheryl while he returned the cell call. She was definitely a grabber.

"Chief. You're to answer all calls pronto."

"The Weber tipped over. My baby was in danger."

"That's a personal problem. You're on duty."

"I'll send you photos of her burns. We're at the ER right now."

"Be that as it may the other dog is trapped in the barn. Pick him up. Terminate if necessary."

"Of course. Have a nice day."

"Fuck you, nitwit."

"Let a smile be your umbrella."

B.D. hung up with this salutation from his fourth-grade teacher remembering when his best friend David Four Feet wouldn't smile and the teacher, Mrs. Schmeltzer, grabbed him and with her forefingers in the corners of his mouth stretched out a smile. One of her fingernails cut his lip deeply so he bit down. Mrs. Schmeltzer fell to the floor howling. Two other teachers and the principal rushed in and started beating on David Four Feet despite his bloody face. David kept shrieking "Fuck you *wasichus*," which meant "white people." This was good old golden school days.

B.D. was pondering strategies and eating quickly because Cheryl was eyeing his plate from the table. The sheriff had called about two big dogs who had escaped three days before and wandered over from Arnold to Perkins and had killed and partly eaten a calf. The dogs were in training as guard dogs and owned by a man from downstate Flint who without market research had decided to go into the guard dog business. In a couple of years he had sold only one to a young man who had a meth lab in the woods near L'Anse. Few if any see the need for a guard dog in the relatively crime free Upper Peninsula, especially with a shotgun and a deer rifle in the front closet, and the guard dog business had fallen into neglect.

After being called when the farmer shot one of the dogs, B.D. dragged the calf carcass into the barn and told the farmer to leave the milk stall door open accurately predicting that the other dog, Fred, would return to eat more veal. The farmer hid up in the mow and closed the door beneath him when the dog returned in the pitch dark.

When B.D. arrived at the farm there was a deputy there with a rifle. B.D. was unarmed but told the deputy to put his rifle back in the squad car and that he as the Animal Control Officer was in charge. At first the deputy refused but then B.D. told the man that he might have to relearn to eat without teeth so that the deputy said "Fuck you" and drove off. The farmer said that the dog had been in the barn for at least ten hours and hadn't made a squeak and was likely sleeping off his meal. B.D. went up the side of the barn to the open mow hand over hand with his Ketch-all pole to his side. He usually didn't need it as he was skillful at keeping a dog docile but if the dog was pissed off he'd slap the loop of the Ketch-all pole over its head and tighten the loop which gave him relative control. Oddly his toughest catch had been Bruno the terrier who, though he only weighed twenty pounds, was fast and devious.

Up in the mow B.D. shone his flashlight on the trap door and ladder where you threw down hay. He shone the light down and there was Fred dozing with his forepaws on the calf. B.D. had met Fred several times when he fished the confluence of the main branch and the west branch of the Escanaba River. The first exposure had been a little alarming: the sense of being watched then turning to see Fred's shape emerging from a dark thicket of alders. At first B.D. thought he was a wolf, he certainly had the size, but he was too thickish which meant a wolf-dog hybrid. A generally unsuccessful breeding experiment. You think you have a nice dog and then it suddenly eats your calf or the neighbor's dog. On the river he threw the dog a brook trout and the dog swallowed it whole and then sat down on his haunches next to B.D. who recognized that he had a new friend.

He crawled down the mow ladder and stooped down beside Fred and petted him. Fred flopped his big tail and separated the calf's head from its neck. B.D. attached a leash and led Fred out of the barn. The farmer retreated well back from the barn door and Fred gave an insincere, muffled growl with the calf's head in his mouth.

"Can I shoot it?" The farmer asked eagerly.

"No, I'm obligated by law to painlessly euthanize the creature," B.D. said pompously.

Fred jumped in the open door of B.D.'s pickup and they were off with two worries in mind. Twice while fishing with Fred B.D. had read Fred's collar tag but when he tried to turn on the road to return the dog and Fred growled thunderously at which point B.D. stopped and let him out near a cedar swamp. Taking him home seemed out of the question. Now he dreaded having him join the rest of the mutts at home, especially Bruno. He doubted that the rest of the dogs would pose a problem but the very thought of Bruno made B.D. stop at a country store for a six-pack. It was strictly forbidden for county employees to drink while working and most certainly in a company vehicle but B.D. thought of himself as man enough to say "fuck it." A regular job had worn him thin of spirit and what's more cut his spring brook trout fishing to the quick. The other day the sheriff had told him to wash his vehicle and B.D. had deftly replied that washing his vehicle wasn't in his job description which pissed the sheriff off. He said, "Your days are numbered," and B.D. said, "Go take a look at Rollo. That boy is looking at a lot of hospital time."

At his shack the four dogs in the pen barked happily until Fred got out of the truck with his calf's head, then they stopped barking and lay down with their backs turned. Bruno was inside because he had been napping and always threw a tantrum when awakened from a nap. The only thing that placated little Bruno was a Kentucky Fried Chicken wing of which B.D. kept a box in the propane refrigerator and through the window he could see Bruno standing on the kitchen table.

B.D. had the warrior courage of four beers when he turned the doorknob. Bruno shot out, leapt straight up, and sank his teeth into the calf's head. He hung there in a standoff and then Fred

dropped the heavy calf's head, probably thirty pounds plus, and Bruno yelped when the head landed on him. Fred gave Bruno a look of consolation then lay down beside him. B.D. was waiting for disaster. The dogs touched noses and then Bruno was looking at Fred with a specific fondness as if he had been smoking weed. A goofy smirk to be exact. Had the nastiest animal he had ever met found love, albeit gay?

Chapter 2

It was twilight when B.D. was wakened from his nap by chickadees and song sparrows, that and the bladder pressure of a six-pack. In the dim light he could see Bruno and Fred nestled together on Bruno's sofa that B.D. had bought for ten bucks at a yard sale. It smelled a little peculiar and a bartender at the local saloon had told him that a very fat bachelor farmer had died on the sofa though he had been discovered by his sister in two days. "It adds up," the bartender said. The sister who was known as the loudest voiced woman in the county was selling off everything and getting a little retirement apartment in Pasadena, California.

B.D. occasionally thought about the provenance of furniture because he had never owned any new furniture. In the tenth grade when a very pretty teacher had stepped out of the classroom B.D. had rushed up and kissed her chair seat and all of the boys had cheered and laughed. Unfortunately a minister's daughter loudly told the teacher when she returned and B.D. was sent to the principal who was fresh out of University of Michigan and was totally puzzled by how to handle the problem. He finally said, "Civilized men don't act out their gross desires." "Yes, sir," B.D. said unsure if a comment was expected from him.

He warmed up some venison stew he had made out of a hind-quarter of roadkill after pitching the rest of the carcass to the dogs. Venison was too lean in spring to be good for anything but stews and then you had to add some cubed salt pork to counter the dryness of the wild meat. Gretchen would add a cup of red wine but B.D. was rarely capable of making the twenty miles home from the grocer's with a bottle of wine. There was always a good reason to drink.

As the stew warmed he was trapped once again by thinking. He could have used a beer though he knew that a beer didn't necessarily lead to clear thinking and never in his life had he felt so under the gun. Perhaps the lowest point had been in March when he had had a two-week case of shingles and couldn't see Gretchen in person because shingles would somehow expose little Susi to chicken pox. B.D. wasn't afraid of shingles and he knew it was what he had because he could recall clearly Grandpa once having a case where big red welts grew out of his chest and back and three times he drank most of a quart of whiskey and rolled naked in the snow on a below zero night. Another night he found Grandpa on the floor of his bedroom chewing on the leg of his bedstead. Great Aunt Doris would come over once a day and rub on Chippewa salve and several times had whipped up a poultice made of oatmeal and tea which had a good though temporary effect.

B.D. had been diagnosed at a saloon by an ex-doctor who had been kicked out of the profession for too liberally prescribing narcotics. Gretchen took B.D. to her doctor who said cheerfully, "You're in for a ton of shit, kiddo," but B.D. gutted it out without too many drugs. The drugs made him feel half dead so he tried to walk off the pain a half dozen hours a day. March is the time of frozen snow so that often you were five feet farther up in the world. And he found a hibernating bear's blow hole, the breathing tube shaped up through the snow through which you learn that bears have very bad breath. The breath seemed to come about once a minute in time with the throbbing sores of the shingles. His back was the color of meat spoiling. Then there was a slight movement far beneath him and the soft moan. Yes, it was March and time for the bear to start thinking of waking up if bears could be considered thinking specifically or was it just an upward urge?

The worst evening he actually began to cry a bit pretending he wasn't. He stripped off all of his clothes and ran the hundred yards down to a pool in the creek where he drew his water and jumped in rolling around. Then he flopped around in the snow noting that the dogs hadn't jumped into the creek and Bruno had furiously barked his disapproval. He would have to make cocoa for Bruno who expected a treat for being irritated. The dog was mad as a hatter but then so was he. He walked slowly back to the shack until he couldn't feel his extremities which was the condition he wanted. It was luckily less than zero.

Now he was staring down into his venison stew supper and Fred had gone to the door wanting to pee. This meant he'd have to put the stew bowl on the fridge to keep it safe from Bruno but then Bruno wanted to take a pee with his new friend. It was then that B.D.'s brain lit up remembering that there were a few ounces of schnapps left in the fishing tackle box under his bed. There was one solid four-ounce gulp, the "nectar of the gods" as Grandpa called whiskey. He lightened up but only temporarily because he thought of what Gretchen and Cheryl would be doing at the moment now that they had put baby Susi to bed. B.D. had always been preoccupied with sex and this was a euphemism but he also understood that sexual behavior wasn't susceptible to clear thinking. Maybe the girls were running around the yard in the dark playing kick the can or watching "Dancing with the Stars" or stuck together in bed with Krazy Glue. B.D. hadn't done any reading on the matter.

When he was cured of his shingles in late March B.D. lucked out. Cheryl had to cancel her weekend trip from Sault Ste. Marie to Escanaba to fly home to Bemidji, Minnesota, to see her seventy-year-old father who ran a sawmill. Dad had written a naughty letter to Sarah Palin in Alaska and the law had landed on him with its big boots. First Gretchen and Cheryl were enraged and bitter about losing a love nest weekend when all Dad had written was, "I'd love to go hiking on a glacier with you and see your pooter and butt." This seemed harmless to B.D., Gretchen, and Cheryl. In fact B.D. was given to saying such things at the drop of a hat. Cheryl had retained a lawyer who intended to explain that Dad had been depressed for a decade since his wife had left him for an Amway salesman with whom she now lived in Honolulu. The upper Midwest is saturated with women itching to move to Hawaii. If you don't like pan fishing, ice fishing, snowmobiling, or applying mosquito dope you're out of luck in that area.

It was a bright clear late morning when Gretchen, Susi, and B.D. drove west to Iron Mountain for an outing and early dinner. They would eat at Ventana's where B.D. would have his favorite dinner, a two-pound rare porterhouse, a bowl of spaghetti with red sauce, and a bottle of red vino. Throughout the drive they would stop where the road crossed creeks and rivers so that B.D. could study the massive runoff of the melting snow and the possible effect on trout season. There wasn't even a trace of green in the landscape but then it smelled like spring in the fifty-degree temperature and the sight of the mounds of snow on the north sides of houses, shacks, and log cabins, and the drifts along fence rows, and the glistening drift ice far out on Lake Michigan and the ice piled on shore on the westerly sides of the forested peninsulas out into the lake. Everything looked raw except when you knew what it meant.

Gretchen meant to give B.D. a pep talk but the question was how to approach this creature despite having counseled thousands of Social Services clients. He was uniquely poor and she had long supposed that this was what drew her to him. Having been raised in a very rich white suburb of Detroit her rebellion was to loathe her own class that was notable for lining up at the car wash Saturday mornings. It was a suburb loaded with auto executives who were only mildly embarrassed over losing market share to the Japanese. Even the parking lot of the high school was stuffed with new cars and to her parents' disgust Gretchen would only drive a used Subaru with rusty fenders. Midway through high school she had developed a fascination with the poor and woebegone that continued into college. She had read hundreds of books on the worldwide poor and to the embarrassed dismay of her mediocre teachers she had her facts completely assembled. Naturally, she wanted to be a peasant but was honest enough to recognize playacting.

"How much money do you have in the world?" She broke the ice.

"Check." He flipped her his wallet. He was nervous because she was nursing baby Susi with a protuberant nipple and he speculated whether it was proper to desire a nursing mother. He was relatively inexperienced in self-criticism but then figured if Gretchen was that proud of her rejuvenated tits they deserved his attention.

"Forty-nine bucks and a driver's license."

"Payday's in six days. I'll be fine. Dog food is setting me back quite a bit. Bruno has to have this special kind or he's wildly pissed off. He costs nearly as much to feed as me." B.D. laughed.

"I'm concerned because you've been drag-ass all winter."

"It was the shingles that set me back."

"Nonsense. It was before Christmas that you took a dive."

"Maybe. I was doing well shoveling walks but then Rollo got hurt and I took my first actual job."

Gretchen fell silent thinking it was her fault wangling him the dogcatching job. He did okay shoveling walks in the winter. Work was work and he had no real concept of the menial. He was without self-pity or any sense of being put upon. Grandpa always insisted that if you were good with a shovel you'd never lack food on the table. B.D. was much different than Gretchen's Social

Services clients who tended to think that they had been victims of bad breaks. In truth they actually were but mostly it was sloth and sometimes illness. Gretchen was weekly amazed in her job at how much could go wrong with the human body. Meanwhile on B.D.'s snow-shoveling route there was a daffy old lady who paid for the work with Monopoly money and a piece of bread and butter which B.D. thought was funny. If there was an especially large amount of snow B.D. would also get a small glass of cooking sherry which was much appreciated. He never skipped her walk because she might fall. When Gretchen heard this story she felt deeply hopeless thinking that her friend would always be a corgi in deep snow. Nothing let her off the hook because of her exhaustive knowledge of the despised and rejected. She fell silent because the year before her nutcase uncle, the black sheep of the family, had sent her a poem in an e-mail. Tom pretended he was a cowboy poet in New Mexico but once she passed through she discovered that Tom was a line chef at a wonderful restaurant named Pasqual's in Santa Fe and was obsessed with bird-watching, and on his days off would trailer his horse far into the country and ride around reciting his poems as if he were a troubadour which he thought he was. Gretchen could only remember a single line of the poem but now it struck her hard:

> Birding is time out
> from the heavy lifting of being who we are not.

She thought that was the crux of her sin against B.D. She presumed he needed guidance because guidance was her job. When the chance for substitute dogcatcher came up the lowliest part of her professional training popped up with "gainfully employed" as if it were the ultimate grail. He thought he was doing the right thing as a responsible father but simply wasn't equipped for the job any more than he would be a maître d' of a New York French restaurant. The salary was pathetic and he was expected to answer a cell phone as if it were Mozart. But Mozart didn't call anymore. He had been getting along well with his odd jobs and hunting and fishing and chasing ladies, cooking and looking after his great uncle Delmore who wouldn't last much longer as his only living relative. Gretchen with her access to records had some knowledge of B.D.'s background but not much. His mother died in her twenties and his father a year later drowning in Lake Superior north of Newberry. B.D. had been raised by his grandpa. Early on Gretchen figured B.D. was just another low-rent playful malcontent. She met him at Burger King where he was struggling with his stepdaughter who Gretchen accurately diagnosed as having fetal alcohol syndrome, and in the ensuing years had become part of his small family. Berry and her older brother Red were both off at private schools now and he missed them.

Gretchen became miffed because B.D. got up to go to the toilet and baby Susi grinned and reached out for him which she rarely did for Gretchen. This always pleased B.D. who had said, "We might not be married but we're cut from the same cloth." B.D. came back to the table and his steak and pasta were there. He plowed through the meal with energy and included the leg and thigh of Gretchen's roast chicken. Curiously he was far away transfixed by the odor of pussy willows along the creeks in the woods. They were the first true smell of spring and since childhood the sweet odor had swollen his chest.

"Yup, I took a dive. Two things actually. Or three. First there's Cheryl, and on my job I'm always getting bossed around. And I hardly get to fish. I've been fishing all my life."

"What about my Cheryl?"

"I've been tagging you for years and I'm just beginning to understand. I'm about where I started. That's hard. Of course I had my one fine best night of my life but that's gone."

"I never promised you a thing. I explained to you clearly I don't like men. I like women. It's not my fault. It started early. You know I love you as a friend. I'd do anything for you but I'm not going to sleep with you and it seems that after ten years you could accept this."

"It's always been said that I'm not too good at reality. When I was twelve my dog died and my throat closed up and I couldn't talk for two months. The school made me talk to this expert in psychology." He was embarrassed that his eyes were misting up. So were hers.

He had pulled off the road near the Ford River and the water was so high it seemed unlikely that a trout could live in it. She moved closer and embraced him. He looked down at the baby peeping up at them with a smile.

"I'm sorry you love me," she said.

"I'll live with it," he said.

Chapter 3

As he drove down the log road to his place in the gathering dark he slowed down thinking that he was a trapper who had trapped himself. He infrequently thought about the idea of emotions because he was aware that he had no control of his own impulses. For instance trout season had opened but all the creeks and rivers were too high to fish. When young it pissed him off and still did. Once he was so angry he cut seven cords of wood in one day, collected his money, went on a twenty-four-hour drunk. A woman threw a cup of hot coffee on him in the shower and he yelled but in truth the coffee wasn't much hotter than the shower water. She apologized with one of the best hundred fucks of his life. She was a schoolteacher and later admitted she had thought she was slumming and regretted it adding, "We're all human beings."

Gretchen reminded him of a song he loathed, "You Can't Always Get What You Want." She always made him feel high-minded and he'd come up empty. He couldn't figure out this quality of yearning and thought he never would. He suspected it was what everyone called love, something he couldn't get his head around he supposed because he didn't have a mother he could remember. You start out loving your mother and then you move on. He dimly remembered a human shape in a hot cabin where he was suffocating. The shape poured cool water on him and he could breathe.

Turning a corner between two big pines on the rutted road he was startled to see the lights on. He was sure Big Fatty, who sometimes looked after the cabin and dogs, had driven over on his four-wheeler because there were tracks but then he saw a van parked at the end of the kennel. The three outside dogs were barking and he pitched them a roadkill muskrat he picked up then noticed they already had the forequarters of a deer. It must be Fatty who had had a hard time losing a leg to a falling oak. B.D. had put together a little house a mile down the road for him out of four abandoned fish shanties. There was only room for a bed, stove, and table. Fatty was massively strong and weighed about three hundred. He could easily jerk himself out of bed with one arm using a sling attached to the wall over him. He liked the idea of a four-door shack because he could shoot a deer out of each door though one was nearly blocked by a giant pile of beer cans.

B.D. looked in the door and there was a woman dressed in black sitting at the table eating a sandwich with a pistol beside her plate. He saw a dagger in her purse as well. Bruno was on her lap snarling at him but mostly protecting the sandwich.

"This is my house," he said.

"Then why's the dog threatening you?" She had the pistol aimed at his head.

"He beat up his mother and sent her to the hospital. Big Fred here knows me." Fred was all over him with toothy smiles.

"Are you Brown Dog?"

"Sure enough. You look like Rollo."

"I'm his half-sister. You and I have to drive Rollo to Montana. Momma thinks he'll die here. I'm Long Rita but I go by Rita. You're not too impressive but I can't say I know a man that is."

When she stood Bruno clutched her and wouldn't be put down. She was slender and at least six feet. B.D. figured she had the unfriendliest face on earth.

"This is the first dog that ever liked me." She kissed Bruno, who became a puddle.

"He's Bruno and doesn't like anyone. Consider him a gift. Am I supposed to quit my job?"

"You'll be paid. Mom's got a used-car lot down in Great Falls. She'll get you something to drive home. Be at the hospital at 8:00 AM."

She stood holding Bruno and jumped straight up in the air higher than he had ever seen a girl jump even on the championship Escanaba girls' basketball team. He was in shock as she grabbed her pistol and walked out.

Chapter 4

He sat at the table settling his nerves. He remembered he had misplaced his two-dollar Air Force suitcase but he could pack some clothes in a paper bag. You can always get another paper bag. He kept sniffing the air quizzically because of an alien odor. A horse. Rita smelled like horse. A horse had got him talking again after he quit when his dog died. How it happened is that his favorite brook trout place at the time was a full three miles back in the woods, accessible by multiple turns on overgrown log roads. He was fishing well and looked up and there was a gray horse about thirty feet away and he wondered if he should be frightened. The horse stared at him for ten minutes then walked away. He went back a half dozen times in the next few weeks remembering that a mean-minded local 4-H girl had lost a horse the year before. Maybe someone beat on it with a ball bat? The first person he talked to was Grandpa who was very happy. He asked if a horse could winter over in that area. Grandpa said yes if he had shelter and not up near Marquette where there was too much snow. It would be hard and the horse might not live long but the area had some open fields for forage.

Now B.D. wondered if he should report the horse. One day in a big thunderstorm he followed it down the creek a half mile into an old deer shanty with one side collapsed. The open side was to the south so the horse would have protection from the north and west where the worst winds come from. The thunderstorm was violent so B.D. sat down off to the side of a pile of horse turds and ate his pickled bologna sandwich. He offered half to the horse who sniffed but rejected it. There was nothing quite like the softness of a horse's nose which it would sometimes press against his bare neck He talked a lot to the horse which seemed to like it. Grandpa had pointed out that horses always knew where they were so if the horse wanted to go home he would. Inside of B.D.'s very young head there was turmoil over turning in the horse and lengthening its life or leaving it alone. He left it alone because of his own relentless combative relationship with authority. He still hated and would leave a bar if there was a loud political argument when nitwits thought they were in chains and weren't safe without fully automatic weapons and it might help if you shot the Indians, Blacks, and Mexicans. This was a certain kind of fearful man. A small minority to be sure. One little guy in Rapid River with a big Adam's apple kept yelling, "Live free or die!" It was amazing to him how often he had thought about the horse that lived in the woods.

Fatty came over at seven in the morning with a deer neck soup for breakfast. Fatty was going to take care of the dogs. Lucky for him Bruno was gone so it would be peaceful. Bruno hated Fatty because he had bitten Fatty's artificial leg and hurt his teeth.

The night before he recalled he had a pint of schnapps in the car but after Rita left he was too tired and unnerved to go out and get it. This had never happened before. His memories of Montana were bad. He thought he was in Billings and had been drinking beer for days and had even visited the site of the Battle of Little Bighorn when he got in a tussle in a bar. He was sort of harassing two cowgirls not realizing their cowboy boyfriends were playing pool. After the usual brief argument he got a good punch in on one but the other bushwhacked him with a chair over the head. He wasn't quite that dumb anymore.

On the way to the hospital with his sack of rather ratty clothes his mind naturally drifted to the sexual possibilities of Rita. To be sure she was a bit tall and slender and had not shown herself to be very friendly. His long slump plus the utterly shitty job had put him off the chase plus it was easier to catch someone when the female summer tourists started coming in June. Until then you had to make do with lesser talent. There's nothing like a schoolteacher on vacation to turn loose. There could be hair on the walls in the morning.

He crossed a small river, slammed on the brakes, backed up, and just as the cell phone rang he pitched it out the window into the swiftly moving water with a warm, tingling, happy feeling in his body. He should have called the sheriff first and told him to go fuck himself but that might have caused future problems. He had been crossed with the law enough in his life to know what you wanted was to avoid notice. Wearing a green janitor's suit helped. Then no one noticed you. You had to have a couple of outfits, though, to get laid in. You couldn't check out Women's Bowling Night in a janitor's suit. After a night on the lanes and a few drinks those girls, some a tad large, could get frisky. His favorite was a school classmate who was a stuck-up snot because her family had a little more money. His friend David Four Feet once put both a stink bomb and a whoopee cushion under her seat. It was a big day though he got beat with a leather strap. She married a guy that became the manager of an auto dealership but was a major lardass and B.D. felt that must be where he came in. No way did the guy have ready access to his pecker. She was a kinky Episcopalian and even paid for the motel.

When he reached the hospital they were just finishing loading Rollo. Rita looked taller in the daylight. She stared at him without smiling with a special glance at his paper bag.

"An Indian woman stole my suitcase," B.D. said.

"That's not funny, asshole," she said.

B.D. had noted that more and more women were calling him names especially tall ones. He wondered who between Cheryl and Rita would win a fair fight.

"Did you bring any shooters?" Rollo asked.

"No alcohol on this trip," Rita interrupted.

"You'll make a stop or your life will be miserable, sister."

B.D. noticed she winced slightly. He looked in the big van. There was a hydraulic hoist for a collapsible wheelchair, an electric heater, a mini fridge, a hospital bed where Rollo lay, a bed pan, a big expensive sleeping bed, and fluffy pillows on the floor.

"I suppose I sleep on the floor?" B.D. asked.

"No, in the front seat. I brought you a blanket. The seat goes back a ways."

Off they went with B.D. at the wheel and Rita in the passenger seat with a big notebook with pictures of horses. They were heading south before turning west because Rita said she had a couple of brief horse stops. She said she trained cutting horses but B.D. had no idea what that meant. She also said for him to follow the GPS and he said he didn't know how. She said, "You must be a dumb fucker." More names from tall women. She played Merle Haggard, Captain Beefheart, and Leonard Cohen, the latter always making B.D. teary. He asked her what cutting horses were and she said she'd tell him when they got out of Michigan which spooked her for all the damage it had done to her brother.

It had occurred to B.D. that he had forgotten to say goodbye to Gretchen and asked Rita to dial because Rita's cell phone was a BlackBerry and far too difficult for him to manage.

"Hello darling. I'm headed west."

"You're what?"

"I'm heading west to go into ranching. My love for you will never die. It's farewell for us."

"Be careful."

"That's sad," Rita said.

"She loves another though we had a baby. The other is a woman."

"Oh my God, now it's really sad. You poor man."

B.D. was a bit overcome and his throat clutched.

"B.D. is a pro pussy chaser," Rollo called out, "I need a shooter for my morning Oxycontin."

"In an hour. I'm not stopping until Wisconsin. It's close near Iron Mountain."

Meanwhile, B.D. was feeling good about Rita's sympathy which can be a critical factor in seduction.

"I want my shooter," Rollo yelled. "When Rita was fourteen she was selling her ass in Great Falls."

"That's smarter than pissing off a snowmobile seat."

"Please. I won't tell what you did with the Choteau basketball team."

She pointed out a combination gas station liquor store of which there are hundreds in Wisconsin. They were having a sale and he managed to get twenty for the twenty bucks she gave him slipping three in his coat pocket. Back in the van he gave two and an Oxycontin to Rollo who could now drink on his own with a quivery hand. Rita was still deep in her horse folio. He handed her the paper bag which she put at her feet. He was a little confused about what he was doing in Wisconsin never having agreed to the trip in the first place. He was on a command performance for his friend Rollo, exact destination unknown. On further thought this didn't seem to matter as he had been slowly sinking in small increments. You had to "get out of Dodge" as everyone says. The predominant problem was the need for affection and the mere presence of a female in the front of the van was causing a specific heat beneath his belt. A wobble in his driving caused her to announce it was time for her to take a six-hour shift. He pulled over and walked into the woods for a pee and a shooter followed by a stick of gum to mask the shooter. Rita ran past at an alarming pace evidently to loosen up. B.D. questioned the expanding tribe of rude-mouthed amazons. Cheryl threw dozens of punches and Rita pointed a gun!

Rita made some fine roast beef sandwiches saying that they had raised the beef. Rollo had lost the best ranch but "momma'" had earned another smaller one with a modest amount of cattle and her horse operation. She added that when they reached home Rollo wouldn't be allowed anything but a '53 Ford pickup and he would be locked in at night. Because of the Oxycontin Rollo responded with dog and meadowlark noises.

B.D. napped for an hour and had a marvelous liberating dream. He had been Gretchen's love slave and now she let him go after screwing him again in the pup tent in the snow. He was riding the horse in the woods with his fly rod and stopping to fish here and there. The forest and creeks were radiant. He had the clear vision of when he and his friend David Four Feet snuck up on a little lake where 4-H girls were skinny-dipping. There was a great big one and David said, "I want that one."

Rita nudged him awake to see the Mississippi near La Crosse and he wondered how the hell he'd fish this vast water. He had a hard-on which was pushing against the limits of his lightweight trousers. She gestured at it and said, "Don't point that at me or I'll cut your throat."

"That's not a kind way to say good morning."

They were going up the steep hill into Minnesota on the other side of the river when B.D. pointed out a gray horse. "That looks like the horse I used to hang out with."

"I didn't know you rode."

"I don't. I just hung out walking and talking with her during five months of trout season. We were a couple miles back in the woods. She led me to her shack which was a partly collapsed three-sided deer shack. I thought of living there with her but I was only ten and Grandpa wouldn't allow it. I heard that fall that this girl who owned the horse had a mean brother that beat it with a ball bat so it ran away."

"If you shoot the guy I'll give you five grand," she howled.

"That was forty years ago and I'm not into killing. One day we came around a sharp bend and there was a medium-sized black bear and she chased it across a field about a mile wide hauling ass. I liked it when she put her soft nose against my neck. A horse's nose is a wonderful thing and they smell best of any animal."

Of course B.D. was trying to find common ground, her good side if there was one. He had never made love to a full-blood, just mixed-bloods like himself or whatever he was. His Uncle Delmore wouldn't tell him and might not before he died. Likely Gretchen would cook Delmore Sunday dinner.

"You're not a bad sort but I gave up men twenty-five years ago when I was fourteen. It's no secret since Rollo blabbed. I ran off from Browning to Great Falls. I fucked for a living because no one would hire a tall, skinny Indian girl my age. I was into volume for food, booze, and drugs. Most were quickies in alleys with teenagers or college-age boys. Some were older men in motels, and there was a low-rent doctor whose office I'd sneak into through the back door after hours. He made the best money offer, twenty bucks, but he was too kinky. Finally I spent the night with a mixed-breed rodeo rider and liked him. He knew a neighbor rancher in a valley to the south who needed someone to look after thirty expensive quarter horses. I was good with horses very young and got the job and lived in a pretty nice bunkhouse. I could never deal with men. I believe I would kill if I was around one more than a day.

"How?" B.D. was appalled and didn't know what to say. Sex diminished with the idea of death. He also remembered the violent stories of women and how he asked Gretchen. She said that our mythologies have a soft stranglehold on us but manage to change slightly every day. The same for both women and men.

"My pistol or my knife. Or this perfect crime I've devised. I own a real rank stallion that hates men and would likely kill them if he got a chance. I call him Bowie after the knife. I get the guy drunk and drag him and tip him over the fence into Bowie's pen. Presto!"

They stopped wearily at a rest stop near Council Bluffs. Rita had changed to a more southern route because of bad weather in the Dakotas. Many have felt the brunt of a late April, early May snowstorm. South of the Dakotas she buried her nose in her driving but her head bobbed after a dozen hours on the road. B.D. yearned for a six-pack. It also occurred to him that it was only twenty-four hours after Rita had shown up at his shack and now here he was on a high hill off the freeway looking at a real big-ass river, the Missouri, in the distance. It felt a whole lot better to get out of town no matter that his life was out of control. The simple fact was he needed to be out of control and it had never occurred to him not to go.

"Rollo, you miserable cocksucker!" Rita was lowering Rollo out of the van on a hydraulic lift and a little bag of pills had fallen off his lap. He had somehow mooched extras at the hospital. She had worried about him talking so little when he was normally voluble.

"You stupid fuck. You're killing yourself." She slapped him but pulled her punch and the slap was light. She was washing him with bottled water and then drained his pee bag onto the ground. Now Rollo was crying and she leaned over to hug him.

Meanwhile B.D. stood there and noted that tall, slender Rita had a bit more flesh on her butt than he had perceived before. His weenie tickled itself even though he was convinced that the odds of his ever mounting this heifer were poor indeed. He kept thinking of her ominous dagger and a knife fight he had seen in Chicago thirty years before that made him nauseous.

"Wheel him around for fresh air. I need to run," Rita said, taking off at a speed that exceeded Cheryl's back home. B.D. quickly swallowed one of his vodka shooters though he would have preferred a cold beer. Rita said that they were turning north to Sioux City since the bad weather had passed. They were going across the top of Nebraska because she had to look at two horses she had sold, one in Valentine and one in Chadron.

Now he grabbed the handles of Rollo's wheelchair and trotted around the rest stop with Rita frequently whizzing by at warp speed. He enjoyed the job and wondered if there were any openings to push attractive women around. The drawback was that they would have to be pretty crippled up to need a man to push their chair. He had a fine time for a month or so with a waitress with a short leg so a lot was possible.

Rollo had begun to detox and requested a vodka shooter. B.D. couldn't see why not, opened one and slipped it to him not seeing Rita coming up behind.

"You miserable cocksucker. I saw that. I'm docking your pay," she yelled while passing.

B.D. wasn't concerned as he had had a lifetime of having his pay reduced. One thing people liked to do is cut your pay.

Back in the car Rollo croaked that he had dreamed that he should go back to raising and training hunting dogs. He could partition the barn or chicken coop for kennels and B.D. could build a five-acre fenced running area.

"No fucking way," Rita said. "No fucking dog near my young horses. You can set up near the calving shed a mile down the road."

Rollo dozed off under the powers of the vodka shooter. B.D. didn't like building fence but a job was a job. Rita was driving but a little slow. On the southern outskirts of Sioux Falls it was sleeting and she gave up. It was ten in the evening and they had had no dinner. "I don't want to sleep in this fucking van. We'll try to get a room with two double beds." She stopped at a truck stop with a diner, a motel, and fuel pumps. He watched Rita trot into the office then dozed until she came out of the diner with a big sack. In their room which had the heavy dense smell of smoking and a bit of manure from truckers hauling cattle Rita unpacked the large bag including a six-pack which lightened B.D.'s heart. Come to think of it he had noted that his heart had been lifting by the hour with the growing distance from his job.

"I figure we'll need a beer to eat this shit," Rita said.

"I don't get why there's so much celery in the chili," B.D. said, draining his first beer in one long swallow.

Part II

Chapter 5

He awoke with a screech. His foot had strayed out of the sleeping bag he had grabbed from the van and now Bruno's teeth were attached to his big toe not altogether playfully. Rita stood at the opening of the decrepit calving shed.

"Why are you here?"

"Where should I be?" he said, looking at dried cow plots and old straw from ground level.

"Next door in the cabin." She actually laughed now standing near his sleeping bag.

To B.D. she had become even more of a giant and he felt sad that you couldn't look up the legs of Levis. After two more days of driving, she had dropped him off in the dark without a flashlight and he evidently took a wrong turn. They had been quarreling about sex and alcohol in some manner beyond memory and she had shoved him out the door into a place without water or his toothbrush. Before sleep he had concocted an image of himself, somewhat lugubrious, as a black slave, then dropped it for a captured Indian. The problem had started in Valentine, Nebraska, when he used his emergency twenty-dollar bill to buy fifteen shooters and Rita's twenty dollars to buy ham and cheese sandwiches with very little ham and cheese. When he had been a Bible student in Chicago a local grocery store gave you a half pound ham and cheese for fifty cents but that was thirty years ago. At his request he had bought Rollo a sweet roll that was at least a foot wide. B.D. did not ask what was becoming of the world because he was poignantly conscious that everywhere the chiselers were in control.

Meanwhile, the fifteen shooters would not make the rest of the trip better.

"Where did Bruno come from?" B.D. asked struggling to get his pants on in the sleeping bag over the painful morning hard-on ever more firm with the presence of Rita.

"Your lesbo girlfriend shipped him by flight. She thought I lost him. Now I owe her four hundred bucks for this fucking nitwit dog's transportation."

Bruno crawled into the sleeping bag perhaps to check on the wounded toe. It occurred to B.D. that he rather liked waking and not knowing where he was. It could mean a new life or at least the old life with new clothes. There was the old lesson of not leaving a foot straying outside a sleeping bag which could leave the foot swollen with mosquito and blackfly bites or nips from a beloved dog. He looked up and noted Rita was sweating. He had thought of her in the night when he lay cushioned on a bed of manure listening to coyotes and nighthawks. He struggled out of the sack turning away from her to capture his dick with a zipper remembering her sensitivity to the organ.

"What are you sweating for at this hour?" he asked examining the blood on his toe.

"I worked a few horses then ran. I have to drive my body or I might fall back into booze and drugs, you know, the old ways where I'd be dead by now. Meanwhile we got to get something on your toe. Bruno's been chewing horse turds."

He followed her out the wide opening of the calving shed into a new world of mountains to the west and the wide Missouri to the east and nearby in a grove of young cottonwoods surrounding the trim little cabin he should have slept in but hadn't noticed in the dark.

When they entered Bruno shot in growling in case there were enemies. He grabbed a trapped mouse in the kitchenette shaking it manically. Rita tapped his ass with a book and Bruno rolled over in supplication which he had never done for B.D.

"This is the most obnoxious fucking dog God ever made." She took iodine and cotton from the toilet cupboard gesturing him to sit down and stick out his bloody toe. She poured on the iodine and daubed the toe with cotton.

"I deserve a drink," he said, wincing.

"When I was looking for you I was directed to your Gretchen in the Social Services office. She said while drawing me a map that you were partial to fishing, drinking, and fucking. That won't be going on around here." She glanced here and there checking the cabin. "The owner and top hand would stay here when they were dropping a couple hundred calves. It's round-the-clock work to make sure there were no problems. Sometimes they have to pull one."

B.D. had seen this as a teen when he worked on a farm up near Arnold. He and the farmer pulled and pulled but the calf was dead. He had never seen anything so dead until later when he found Grandpa facedown on the kitchen floor. B.D. sat down on the floor beside him reflecting that Grandpa was eighty-three but it was hard to figure out what this number actually meant. B.D. was nineteen at the time, possibly the age when a young man is furthest from wisdom.

"You're drifting, asshole." Rita took his arm and led him to the door. "You'll live here for the time being. Mom got ahold of an old Chevy pickup that won't go more than 45 mph. Rollo must be kept from speed."

"I was thinking of dead calves and my dead Grandpa who raised me." B.D.'s thoughts stopped in their tracks at the sight of three very large rattlesnake skins mounted on the wall near the door. "What the fuck do we have here?" he said loudly.

"Local residents. Sometimes they live under the floorboards here. You'll hear them when it warms up." He touched a skin and shivered before following her to her pickup.

Rita drove unnecessarily fast to the ranch house or so he thought. He was struggling with a memory about rattlesnakes. He must have been about seven and having problems learning to read. He would sit with Grandpa on the sofa and they would go slowly through *Life* magazines with Grandpa reading the choice parts and then helping B.D. repeat the portion. There had been a big flood down south and a pretty girl, or so he remembered, had swam to a tiny island in the flood waters. Unfortunately on the island there were dozens of rattlers that bit her to death. It was the saddest tale imaginable and in his young heart he swore vengeance against these vipers and forty-plus years later he was to have an opportunity. Rollo had told him that at county school when they found a rattler in the yard they bet they could jump over it high enough not to get struck. A fat kid tried and failed and got bit. An ambulance came from Great Falls. Rollo said the kid's legs swelled up and split and he was never the same.

Rita pulled in the drive of a fair-sized stone house with a yard full of flower beds. Out back were sheds and corrals and a long, low horse barn.

Rollo was in his wheelchair in the yard shooting at blackbirds with a shotgun. Bruno would scoot around giving a coup de grâce by biting and tearing at the birds and then several barn cats would retrieve them and run off and hide them at warp speed.

"Mom doesn't like blackbirds shitting on the sidewalk and porch."

"I've never seen Indians living so high on the hog." B.D. said. He observed that Rollo was a pretty good shot.

"Mom was good at marriage and her used-car lot in Great Falls. She could sell shit as Shinola especially to Indians. They like those big old Pontiac sedans or fast Crown Victorias they could die in drunk. She bought twenty down in Denver and tripled her money."

Mom turned out to be tall and broad-shouldered though not so tall as her daughter but even more ominous. She had had a ramp built up to the porch and B.D. wheeled Rollo in for breakfast which was eggs, potatoes, and pork chops apparently cooked up by a white girl who stood in the corner. B.D. couldn't recall ever using a cloth napkin. Mom didn't eat but stared at him sizing him up. She wore a trim blue business pantsuit.

"Five bucks an hour. Rollo needs a dog kennel. A big one."

"That's below legal minimum. I never work for less than ten."

"You're getting room and board."

"I'd live in a snake den before I work for five." This was definitely not true.

"Seven and a half and a bonus of two hundred when you finish plus a vehicle to get home in."

"Nine or I leave now by thumb."

"Okay but no messing with the help."

B.D. nodded in assent. He had already stolen a few glances at the girl in the corner who was now blushing. She was a bit small and slender. He idly wondered why when people met him the low-wage lightbulb lit up in their heads. A teacher once told him that he wasn't "presidential material."

Chapter 6

It took B.D. nearly four hours to shovel the dried cow shit out of the calving shed into the bed of the '73 Chevy pickup, a virtual mountain of manure. The day had warmed and B.D. was dense with sweat. He enjoyed the freedom of the exertion. He began to be homesick early on the job but he was thinking clearly enough to see that the homesickness was fucked-up like a soup sandwich. Between Gretchen and the dogcatching job he had been stomped into roadkill. He had teared up at the mere idea of euthanizing. To B.D. it was as if dogs were a different species of human who deserved a good retirement. One of his mongrels called Old Bob would emerge from the doghouse shortly after dawn madly wagging his tail and walk the big perimeters apparently in a state of ecstasy because of the world around him.

At about noon Mom and Rollo arrived from a trip to the doctor's in Great Falls. Rollo was pouty and yelled, "The fuckers are cutting off my drugs." Mom swatted him, "No 'F' word in front of Mom." Rollo demonstrated his new walker slowly but surely. They were both impressed at B.D.'s job on the calving shed and Mom told him to dump the load near her garden. She then handed him a huge ham and Swiss out of the van. A sandwich and a compliment made him warm inside. Rita drove down with some lemonade when a six-pack would have been better.

Late in the afternoon Rollo directed him down to the river while sipping from a pint of bourbon and rigging fly-rod tackle.

"I got a boat but that's for a long day. Without pills I'm afraid I'll become an alcoholic."

"You always were. So what?"

"Maybe so. We got to draw up kennel plans. You don't want to stay here forever. Mom and Rita are real bossy. They're going to work your ass off."

"I'm hoping to save up five hundred bucks for retirement, go home, and fish until fall."

"That's quite a retirement plan. You might want to throw away your fake Social Security card. Mom said they can get you for that. You don't want her worrying about you or she'll take over your life. That's why I headed east after the second divorce. You should also send the cell phone back to the sheriff or he'll get on your ass when you get home."

"I threw it in a body of water. I don't recall where right now. My head is buzzing." It occurred to Brown Dog that telling everyone about the fake Social Security card might not have been a good idea.

They were parked on a two-track near the Missouri which was high from snowmelt runoff. B.D. wondered how trout could survive in such a vast river but Rollo had showed him photos of huge brown trout in an outdoor magazine. He was disturbed because he had noted that a small photo between the pages, a memento, had ripped in half and was blurred. It was of their East Side gang that had a hideout near the coal docks in Escanaba.

There were five of them so tough that in the fifth grade even seventh graders avoided them. David Four Feet had been killed in prison, Eddy Murat was doing life without parole for shooting someone in a bar fight in Detroit, and the Lambert brothers took off for California and weren't heard from again. Bobby Lupa tried to be a boxer, failed, and died from drugs in Grand Rapids. He, B.D., was just getting along, Grandpa's term for doing okay but nothing special. He was known far and wide for doing a good day's work if you could find him. He usually lived in deer-hunting shacks in trade for doing repairs outside the two-week season. Once he lived in a tent for the two-week deer season in an especially cold November but it was profitable. He had three stray dogs with him and they threw off a lot of heat. He shot four bucks and sold two for a hundred bucks apiece to unsuccessful hunters. A game warden stopped by but didn't notice the other two butchered in the tree above him. So he was getting along though one afternoon in her kitchen recently Gretchen had said that he was having a "midlife crisis." He didn't hear her explanation very well because he was attentive to what he was cooking, a pork shoulder with pinto beans and red chili sauce. You had to cook it slow and then the pork shoulder would get so tender it would fall apart. To B.D. the pork shoulder was the best cut of meat partly because it was the cheapest. Meanwhile Gretchen's lengthy explanation was lost in the kitchen air. Grandpa used to say you could walk or fish yourself out of a slump. Until he was seventy and then arthritis in his hip got too bad he could walk all day and then work in his garden and make dinner in the evening.

Now in the Missouri B.D. jumped out of the pickup and rigged the fly rod quickly because black storm clouds were approaching from the south and he wanted to get in a few casts before the rain hit. He cast a small female muddler five times and on the fifth a large brown trout rolled the fly and took it then shot out into the main current. B.D. put on too much pressure and the line broke.

"The fucking leader was too light," he said, turning to Rollo who stood off to the side in his walker.

"If the leader's not light on this river they won't take the fly. Look at how clear it is. You just can't horse a big fish like that, asshole. I've been fishing this river since I was three years old. I was once swept away in the current for a mile before my dad caught up to me. I was wearing a life preserver. I saw a lot of big trout, some the size of an all-night log in the U.P. when you need a good fire." Rollo had to add a fib to anything he said.

Then the rain suddenly hit and Rollo hobbled to the pickup while B.D. stood there as if he was a mallard. B.D. had come to the conclusion that he wouldn't have lost the fish, by far the biggest brown trout of his life, if he hadn't been thinking too much. What's with this five-hundred-dollar retirement fund? He wasn't one to think about money and had spent a life living day to day and now suddenly the figure five hundred loomed. It occurred to him that maybe as he aged just past fitty his brain had changed a bit. That didn't seem possible but it could be true. In Gretchen's terms this might be the *midlife.* Grandpa had inherited the small farm and after he died B.D. sold it and pissed away the money quickly. He didn't really sell it for money but so as not to live with memories. Now he wouldn't mind owning a place way back in the woods near a creek rather than moving from cabin to cabin. This was also a new idea.

Rollo began beeping the weak horn of the pickup. B.D. was soaked but unconcerned. After they had cut and split fifteen cords of wood in the fall Grandpa would say, "Now we can den up." He had canned everything possible from the garden though by spring they would mostly be eating macaroni cooked in a jar of canned tomatoes and illegal venison and rabbits. They basically lived on a one-quarter disability check from the army, $160 a month at the time. Grandpa had been shot through the thigh by a small caliber rifle at Monte Cassino in Italy. All in all he thought it was a fair trade especially since he discovered garlic in Italy. He and B.D. were certainly the only garlic eaters in the area except for a few Italian families that arrived in the late 1800s from the Piedmont to work in the mines.

"I think I remember where I hid some whiskey in your cabin a few years ago," Rollo said triumphantly. "Mom was drying me out and I had to get cagey. Mom was good at drying men out. She was quite a looker years ago."

"She still looks good." B.D. did not avoid older women. "Eureka," he said, drawing four shooters from deep in his wet coat pocket. He was going to save them for himself but Rollo was a friend and critical to his five-hundred-dollar retirement plan. There it is again, he thought.

The world was blurred and beautiful through the rain that lashed against the windshield. It occurred to him that he was liable to fish all summer, five hundred dollars or not, because he had always fished all summer. It wasn't an intention, just something he had always done since he was a child. At Grandpa's he had always done his chores fast. That was where he learned to work hard and fast. All so he could go fishing. After all if he ran short of food he could cook for Gretchen or Uncle Delmore. He had been avoiding Uncle Delmore because he was always loudly playing with his ham radio or had the TV on loud and was talking back to it with his crackpot theories. Delmore wanted B.D. to live with him mostly for his cooking but also because at eighty-seven he was getting fearful at night. When B.D. wasn't cooking for him he only ate Dinty Moore beef stew. Period.

"I got my eye on a whole litter of English setters," Rollo said dreamily. "I always wanted to train a litter. They're five weeks old down in Helena right now. I'll have to get you out here to hunt. Just imagine hunting with seven dogs at once."

Brown Dog had raised his tremulous spirits by imagining what it was going to be like to teach little Susi how to fish, pick berries and morel mushrooms, and avoid poison ivy. He would have to write Gretchen a letter though he had only written a few in his life.

Chapter 7

Before dinner Rita figured out a list of what they would need to fence five acres and a seven-compartment kennel. She also advised acquiring a sizable child's plastic swimming pool for the coming heat of the summer. It's a peculiarity to the United States above forty-five degrees latitude that the temperature can vary from forty below zero to one hundred above. Few properly understand that Montana is classified as high desert and wouldn't exist as is without an immense amount of irrigation for crops. The water comes from the buildup of snow in the mountains that begins to melt in May.

Rita was dressed to go to a meeting after dinner about the fatal equine virus that threatened the horses of the west. The horses had all been quarantined against travel and all events canceled. You would have thought that the horses were Rita's children, but in fact for all practical purposes they were.

B.D. and Rollo sat beside her at a desk while she added up the figures. B.D.'s attention wavered with her scent which he finally determined was Camay soap. He couldn't help but be aroused but she looked at him with dismay rather than anger. His single spare shirt after the rain soaking was Hawaiian with a tear in the collar that he had bought in a thrift store for its dancing hula girls. He was amazed at the sketch and page of figures where she figured out the yards of fencing and poles they would need plus the kennel material that would be constructed in the calving shed.

"I'm getting Roy a Pro-Fence to help you. I am also borrowing a power auger for the holes. Roy's deaf but he'll work your ass off."

"We'll head for Great Falls tomorrow for the material," Rollo said as if he were a pro.

"No you won't. I'm ordering by phone. Mom said you were grounded. You'd just get drunk at the tiki bar and go to the strip club. Maybe I'll take you in when you're all done."

"At the tiki bar you just sit there drinking whiskey and eating free popcorn and watching girls in the motel pool through the glass partition," Rollo said lamely.

"Sounds good to me," B.D. said, a bit amazed at Rita's competency. She had whipped Bruno into shape in no time announcing she was going to make a cow dog out of him. He had made friends and was hanging out with her vicious stallion when he wasn't hunting pack rats. He was obviously pissed that Mom didn't allows dogs in the house but when he scratched at the door, she yelled at him so loud he ran for it.

B.D. walked home to his cabin in hopes of tamping down a couple of pounds of spaghetti which had made him a tad homesick for the U.P. He readily admitted that it was better than his own and quickly corrected the tinge of homesickness by recalling the mud bath he had escaped. Throughout his adult life a closely held tenet had been that a regular job was the worst of all worlds. One of Grandpa's friends had been a school janitor for thirty-nine years and had only lived five months into retirement. It had been a huge community funeral but B.D., though a mere nine at the time, had figured that Freddy likely didn't know.

B.D. had borrowed paper and a ballpoint to write a letter to Gretchen. He hurried along wanting to reach the cabin before dark, because without a flashlight he figured he was susceptible to rattlers though Rita said that the evening was fifty degrees and they wouldn't be active.

He arranged his paper and pen just so on the kitchen table and then made the mistake of turning on the radio, a mistake for an inexperienced writer. There was a dismally sad song by Merle Haggard that blew away his thoughts which anyway were ill formed. He recognized the enemy and turned the radio off thinking that if writing was so hard it might not be natural. Way back when, a probation officer had told him to write down his thoughts and it had been brutally difficult. One had been, "If a girl gives you a six-digit phone number that means she doesn't want to hear from you." That didn't seem especially smart as time passed. He went to the fridge thinking that a beer might get him started remembering only as he opened it that he didn't have one. But then my God there was a six-pack with a note from Rita, "You get two a day, buster." A beer did it. "Dearheart, I am building a dog operation for Rollo. He's buying seven pups. I should be home in two weeks. I nearly caught a big brown trout but it broke off. Kiss Susi for me. I miss you. Love, B.D."

He was fairly proud of his work but more than a little exhausted. He put his head down on his arms on the table for a rest as he had done all too often at school. He'd sneak out the back window when he was sure Grandpa was asleep to create a little mayhem with his toughie gang. At school he'd hope for a few minutes of sleep before the teacher shook him awake.

It seemed very long in dreamtime with choruses of singing mice and rattlers in the manner of early Disney movies and a troubling fish that was neither brown or brook trout but part of both. There was a hand lightly on his shoulder and he wrenched himself away from the table with a shout nearly knocking over Rita who stood there with a large full sack.

"Calm down. I got you some clothes at Walmart. You look homeless."

"You got your knife?" B.D. was confused.

"Of course but my pistol is in the car. I'm edgy when I travel. At home I'm nice. Plus it looks like my horses are safe from equine virus." She helped herself to a beer from B.D.'s ration and shook the clothes out on the table.

"I usually favor used clothes. They're broken in." He was still edgy to be alone with Rita and her knife and told her so. "A beer might help." Now she was sitting on his bed and his compass suddenly tilted toward hope. She patted the comforter beside her.

"Let me tuck you in in the best way possible."

And she did. He had the feeling that her legs went around him twice. When she left in about an hour she told him not to expect it to happen again but then they were always saying that. It was rarely true except for his beloved Gretchen who only wanted a baby. For the first time it occurred to him that she might want another child. Hope again.

Chapter 8

B.D. awoke feeling manly, certainly a set of dubious emotions. He was listening to the dawn flurry of birds which didn't offer the dense music of the warblers in the U.P. where the dense arboreal home was so vast. Bird music along with the scent of Rita was a kind way to awaken. Was her soap Dove or Camay? Rita, suspecting his abilities, had set up the coffee machine for him so that all he had to do was press *on*. For decades he had simply boiled his coffee dropping in a fresh eggshell toward the end to clarify it.

He stepped outside in his skivvies and there was a young man Rollo called "Roy the Deaf Boy" sitting on the cottonwood stump. B.D. waved but Roy shyly looked away. B.D. went back in and checked the refrigerator where there was sausage and also eggs and he had a half-pound patty. Many had told him that too many eggs were unhealthy. He never replied because Grandpa had always cracked him a half dozen for breakfast. He also liked to slather his eggs with hot homemade horseradish but there was none to be had. Three cinnamon rolls helped though the sausage was undercooked. He didn't care because he felt as pleasant and dumb as any well-fucked man. He barely had time for a cigarette when Rita arrived with a tractor and auger followed by a big truck from the Great Falls Fencing Company. Rita had said that a dog fence didn't need the solidity of a cow or horse fence though the corners still had to be thickish wood poles to bear up under the two-way strain.

Later B.D. figured it was one of the hardest stretches of work he had ever done. It was a matter of keeping up with Roy who at about 180 pounds was the strongest man B.D. had ever met, and also the fastest. They worked from six in the morning until three in the afternoon, when Rita said Roy had to be back at the home ranch to work until dark. Roy ate his lunchtime sandwich standing up while B.D. sprawled in the grass trying to stay awake. He had the added strain of Rita's nightly visits which he thought of as too much of a good thing given his daily work. Such arduous work frees one from mental problems as it does any beast of burden. Occasionally Gretchen, essentially a lost love from the time they had met, passed gently through his mind but he didn't have the energy to think of rude Cheryl and her manly triceps.

The disappointment came the fourth day on the job. Each day he would rest from 3 to 4 PM, and then he and Rollo would go fishing until dinner, generally at 7 PM. They would drive up the lane of a friendly neighboring rancher and then B.D. would help Rollo and his walker across a shallow channel in their mud boots, knee high for the ubiquitous mud of corrals, then easily reach the far side of the grassy island and the river. B.D. had fine brown trout fishing on a bristly blackfly called the wooly bugger. Fishermen have a tendency to have a fidelity to their home ground where they habitually fished but B.D. doubted there was any place on earth where the brown trout fishing was as good as here. He even caught a hot acrobatic rainbow of three pounds that jumped pretty high five times. Half of the fish he caught would be trophies back in Michigan.

The fourth afternoon the shit hit the fan as it were, from unexpected quarters. B.D. had pretty much ignored anything Rollo had said about the snowmelt coming from the mountains. The weather had turned warmish the last two days, so much so that Rita had brought him one of those sports drinks with his lunch. It didn't taste very good but it was full of potassium and other trace minerals to counter profuse sweating that occurred when he tried to keep up with Roy the Deaf Boy on the fencing job. B.D. had wondered if Roy was taking meth but that seemed unlikely.

So they got to the Missouri that fourth day and it was baby-shit brown. B.D. stood there with his rigged fly rod shivering with horror.

"It's the Dearborn," Rollo said.

"What the fuck are you saying?" When Rollo said "Dearborn" B.D. immediately thought of the place near Detroit where Henry Ford worked on developing the Ford car. It was confusing.

"It got warm and the Dearborn River is upstream. It comes out of the high country and the snowmelt started. It picks up mud in the low country. It will clear up in a week or so."

B.D. felt tears coming. If he couldn't fish he wanted to get the fuck out of there and go home. Of course the rivers and creeks in the U.P. ran high when the snow melted, sometimes nearly three hundred inches near Grand Marais but everything cleared pretty fast. He had the homey image of cooking a brook trout lunch for Gretchen, old Delmore, but then Cheryl intruded on his fantasy hogging the fried potatoes. In the fatal present Rita was spooking him. She had to have all the lights out. One night she had a crying jag because she had had an abortion at fourteen and she thought she couldn't get pregnant and now at thirty she wanted a baby. B.D.'s cock had wilted and she said, "What's wrong?" and he had said "life."

"Got 'im," Rollo yelled near the pickup. He was on his knees in the grass and grabbed a large, writhing snake that wrapped its thick length around his arm. He patted it to calm it down and noticed that B.D. had jumped up on the hood of the pickup.

"You fucking moron!" B.D. yelled. "That's a rattler!"

"It's not a rattler, it's a bull snake. It just looks and acts like one. It actually kills rattlers by squeezing them to death. You should feel its strength." Rollo offered his snake wrapped arm to B.D. who slid off the far side of the pickup hood.

"You must get over your fear, son." Rollo said in the manner of a preacher. "I had a bull snake as a pet when I was a kid. I took it to school in my lunch bucket in the third grade. When I let it loose it emptied the room. Snakes get pissed at everyone except if they know their owner."

Chapter 9

On the seventh day they rested. It was a very warm morning and all that was left to do was to assemble the kennels themselves to be assembled in the opening of the calving shed. B.D. couldn't figure out the directions and all the parts didn't quite fit. Rita stepped in with her quick wit.

"You got it backward, asshole," she said daintily.

"Thanks." B.D. was all played out. He was thinking about Roy the Deaf Boy not getting paid. All of his hard labor was in trade for Rita breaking three horses for Roy's boss. Rita told him that Roy was forbidden by the authorities to be around girls and he said, "In the movies all ranching people are normal."

"Fuck you. Tell me what's normal." She was throwing around heavy pieces of the kennels and her strength was that of a man he thought. He had watched her briefly breaking a horse but quickly withdrew because the horse's violence made him fearful for Rita. Watching Rita sort the kennel pieces was enervating and he drifted off to sleep thinking of ranchers and movies. Roy the sexual predator was awkward. In his difficult winter it made it much worse that

Delmore had returned to his old fascination with the *Planet of the Apes* series of movies after they started remaking them, which drove B.D. quite mad. Delmore at age eighty-seven accepted the movies as gospel. The apes were at work somewhere and needed shooting. Meanwhile we were wasting our time in Afghanistan. Delmore had known Arabs in Detroit and said you couldn't change them because they had been Arabs for tens of thousands of years just like Indians.

Rita had the kennels assembled by noon while B.D. slept in the shade of the calving shed. He had worked twelve hours the day before with Roy, finishing the fence, and had had a big dinner, but then Rita tracked him to the cabin and had a fit. It was near the anniversary of the death of her father in a car wreck seventeen years before, the event that caused her to run off to Great Falls at fourteen. Her mom had slipped into a depression and was no help. B.D. felt an anguished empathy and struggled to stay awake. They made love in the evening light but he was so fatigued he could barely see.

She nudged him with a toe to the neck which didn't work and then screamed "*Brown Dog*," and he sprung to his feet in a state of shock.

"That was for fun," she said.

"Lucky you didn't have a pail of water."

They all had a lunch of hot chili with the beans on the side which B.D. felt could have used a few beers. Mom was going pretty hard on Rollo. She was letting them go to Great Falls to pick up a plastic swimming pool for the pups which would be fetched from Helena the next day. It was to be a no-drinking trip according to her. The seriousness of her words were lessened by the fact that Bruno had climbed the ladder she had been using to wash windows and was barking furiously.

"Bruno likes Mexican food," B.D. said and Rita took out a small portion. Once while cooking he had dropped a jalapeño which Bruno ate and spit out too late. Bruno tried to bite his leg but B.D. had pretty much cured that biting behavior by grabbing him by the scruff of the neck and running a little cold water on his head which the dog found humiliating.

On the way to Great Falls B.D. felt a bit of ice in his stomach. He felt Montana was too large for him. He didn't want to see thirty miles in so many directions. You could see farther than the distance between Seney and Grand Marais. It also bothered him that he had lost his fake Social Security card within a few days of receiving it via Gretchen's address. He had hesitated to put it in his superthin wallet which contained his only identification on earth, his driver's license. He was gun-shy about wallets because as a child snoop he had poked in Grandpa's and found a miniature photo of a pretty young woman who wasn't Grandma as there was a framed photo of her in the parlor. She had died of breast cancer in her thirties just after her daughter's death. That meant the photo in the wallet must be his mother. The shock meant that he never again wanted to touch a wallet. There was a chance that Bruno had eaten the Social Security card that he thought he had left on the table. Maybe there had been a speck of gravy on it from the venison stew. Some dogs will eat a head of lettuce if you put a teaspoon of venison gravy on it. Once Bruno had eaten the contents of the sugar bowl and was off the wall, literally, for an hour then slept the rest of the day.

B.D. drove at 50 mph, all the pickup could manage, so that cars and trucks whizzed by him, some beeping because his slowness was a menace. Meanwhile Rollo was irritating him with attacks on his mother's obsession with AA. It seemed peculiar since booze had given Rollo several near-death experiences not to speak of the loss of two fine properties through divorce while Mom's sobriety had done well by her. Rita had said her mom had drowned her grief for a year after her husband's death in the auto accident. Then one warm summer night her mother had fallen down out in the yard and awoke at dawn with a rattlesnake coiled on her stomach. The rattlesnake told her to quit drinking so she joined AA and was able to retrieve Rita from the ranch west of Great Falls where she was taking care of a herd of horses.

B.D. had real trouble dealing with Costco. He had never been in a box store because the need had never arisen. The rack of goods seemed to go up a thousand feet and gave him vertigo. He began to sweat profusely. What if there was an earthquake? Rollo was off looking for the plastic swimming pool and B.D. was somewhat consoled by the great array of meat and wine.

Back in the parking lot Rollo thought that it might be time for a beer though it was against the rules. Because of his fearful Costco experience B.D. agreed. He wished, though, that he had hung around to look at more of the ladies that worked there. Rita's melancholy was wearing him out though it was better than her knife, pistol, and murderous stallion. At the stop light he glanced off at some mountains to the east and thought they looked pretty unfriendly compared to the woods back home. He probably should walk up one while he was here but then Rollo told him that a female grizzly had slapped the whole face off an elk hunter up in the mountains which put a stop to the idea.

They went into the tiki bar which was part of a big motel. B.D. was mightily impressed because the whole place was decorated like the South Seas and the drinkers at the tables were enjoying baskets of free popcorn. Behind the liquor bottles there was a big window that looked into the subsurface of the pool. A couple of real big girls swam by but didn't excite much interest among the drinkers. The bartender gave Rollo a real unfriendly look.

"Rollo, you know you're banned for life."

"That was ten years ago," Rollo said humbly, emphasizing his walker as he approached the bar.

"Ten years isn't life. Get outta here or I'll call the cops." The bartender reached for the phone.

"I'm showing the sights to a very important visitor from Iceland," Rollo persisted.

"Are you bullshitting as usual?" The bartender paused because tourism was important. He had never met anyone from Iceland.

"Good to meet you," B.D. said in Chippewa. The bartender poured him a shot and a beer ignoring the plaintive Rollo.

"You fucking prick," Rollo yelled, throwing a full basket of popcorn at the startled bartender. Rollo made his way to the door as the bartender came at him. B.D. drank his shot and beer and a second and grabbed the bartender's elbow in a painful vise grip.

"He's a cripple," B.D. said.

In the parking lot Rollo admitted that he had driven past one day and had seen one of his ex-wives and her boyfriend enter the bar. He dove into the pool and mooned her in front of a full bar. The cops caught him south of town.

They stopped at a convenience store for a twelve-pack and then Rollo directed B.D. north of town to see a spring that he said poured out a *million* gallons a day which B.D. doubted. They didn't have a cooler and agreed to drink the beer fast so it would be pleasantly chilled. The spring turned out to be huge and there was also a waterfall that B.D. considered frightening. Rollo said that one of the Lewis and Clark boats went off the falls and a nearby woman said, "That's not true." Rollo ignored her because he was trying to keep up with two teenage girls in shorts on the narrow walkway across the spring. His legs, still weak from the accident, slipped but when he fell he managed to grab the walkway. He sprawled with his feet trailing in the water.

"You can't keep up with young girls," B.D. said, hauling Rollo to his feet and stooping to grab the walker before the current swept it way.

"All of this water comes from the Belt Mountains to the east. Science has proved that it takes fifty years for the water to reach this location." Rollo was trying to retrieve his dignity. Meanwhile the teenage girls were giggling at the end of the walkway quite aware, as usual, of the fuss they had caused.

B.D. and Rollo retreated to a picnic table for a rest period. A twelve-pack drunk at judicious speed isn't too much for a couple of grown men but drunk at top speed it holds a punch. Rollo was immediately asleep with his face in his arms. B.D. tried it but immediately was looking down through a crack at an ant wandering in a confused circle on the top of one of his shoes. What chance did this ant have for a good life he wondered. He had watched them on the sandy banks of creeks and they seemed to work from dawn to dusk. He remembered from school that ants work entirely for their queen and so do bees which didn't seem to be a good deal. Of course when he took the dogcatching position it was to impress Gretchen who had helped him get the job. He wondered what she was wearing now. She changed her clothes every day, sometimes more than once while tavern girls tended to hang with the same outfit. And over the past thirty years he had noted that women's undies had gotten smaller and smaller. Was there a hidden meaning to this? Sometimes subservience to this immediate consciousness bothered him. He suspected ordinary homesickness but that didn't quite cover it. You had to try to be honest with yourself and he knew that if the Missouri had stayed clear he could have stayed in Montana indefinitely. But the Missouri hadn't stayed clear so he was high and dry. Nothing was holding him here except picking up the setter puppies the next day and his troubled fondness for Rita. He turned and discovered his problem. It was a chokecherry tree about thirty feet behind him and about to bloom. He walked over and stuck his head within the branches inhaling deeply. It was now May 19, and almost always in the U.P. the chokecherries bloomed in the last weekend in May up near Grand Marais and earlier down near Escanaba. He always picked two creeks and a river to camp near while fishing brook trout in location near blooming chokecherries. Their odor was a wonderful narcotic to him. There was also the odor of dogwood and sugarplums mixed in. He thought he better get moving or he was bound to miss the chokecherries which was unthinkable.

Driving back through Great Falls Rollo insisted on stopping for a pint of whiskey and some Motrin for his beer headache. He took a half dozen Motrin in his hand and took a long swig of whiskey. B.D. limited himself to a short snort because he was still in a chokecherry panic. On the way south on the main drag Rollo spotted a strip club and demanded that they stop for a "pussy fix" for their morale. They put the plastic swimming pool in the pickup cab to protect it from thievery. The Saturday afternoon crowd was thin and they had barely gotten out when a mammoth bouncer near the door glared at them.

"Rollo, you know you're banned here."

"That was years ago," Rollo said plaintively. "I need a lap dance from Minnie Mouse for my health."

"She took off for Denver and besides you ain't coming in here."

"Just for ten minutes. My friend here is a visiting guest from Iceland and I'm showing him around. He's bound to spread the word of your club in Reykjavik." Rollo tried to push past the bouncer who put his huge hands around Rollo's neck, lifted him off the ground, and started to shake him.

"He's a cripple," B.D. bellowed to put the bouncer off guard. He strained to remember his once famous seven-punch combination from thirty years before then delivered two stiff jabs to the bouncer's nose to affect his vision, a strong jab to his Adam's apple to choke him, two mighty punches to his lower gut to make him feel ill, and a left and a right cross to the head to knock him out. It worked. The bouncer fell like a tub of shit. A small crowd had gathered and an older business type took out his cell and said he was calling the cops. B.D. hurriedly carried Rollo to the pickup. He drove farther east and north through areas of residences and small business until he parked between two Dumpsters behind a Mexican restaurant. Rollo had fallen back to sleep so B.D. went inside for three very good beef enchiladas and a beer.

Back in the truck he noticed that Rollo had drunk all but an inch of the pint so he finished it for energy. He drove east about ten miles through farm and ranch country and then headed south. It would take longer this way but if indeed the cops were looking they'd likely check the interstate. Up in Michigan the cops weren't much interested in strip club bouncers and he hoped it was the same in Montana.

It took more than an hour to reach the ranch because he had gone too far south following a wonderful looking creek but the land was posted. When he reached the ranch he carried Rollo into the house in the twilight knowing Rita would be pissed. In fact she was in tears when B.D. put Rollo on the sofa.

"You assholes are enablers," she sobbed.

"What's that?"

"People who encourage each other to get drunk."

"I'm not drunk. You ought to send your brother to Hazelden for six weeks." He was bullshitting because he didn't know anything about Hazelden except that it was a place in Minnesota where rich people dried out.

"Maybe. And maybe the pups will help. He's a pure dog person like his dad."

"I'm hoping for the car and money so I can leave," he gave her a hug on the way out feeling a tinge of desire.

Chapter 10

In the cabin B.D. ran cold water on the swollen knuckles of his right hand. He felt badly about the fight though the bouncer clearly had it coming. He noticed a letter on the table. It was from Gretchen so he was immediately dry-mouthed and quivery. He could have used a beer.

Dear B.D.,

I'm lonely for you and wish you'd come back. I had a falling out with Cheryl. She arrived very late from the Soo for the weekend. I smelled Cheryl's skin and something was wrong. I accused her and she broke down and admitted she had wrestled naked with her sixteen-year-old protégé athlete. By the way this is against the law. I said we're through. I can't stand unfaithfulness. I need you. So does Susi.

Love, Gretchen

B.D. felt somewhat paralyzed. This was way too much to happen in one day, or even a week. There was a knock on the door and he dreaded the arrival of Rita. It turned out she had just gotten her monthly but was bringing him a half chicken and two beers for a late dinner. He was upset but not too upset to eat. In the movies when there was an argument they would abandon the dinner table which was stupid. He showed Rita the letter. She meditated a few minutes.

"It's just like men and women. I had this girlfriend once and we slept together a few times. It certainly didn't hurt me and was even fun. You should bargain for once a month but from what you said she's a hard case. But it's just bodies."

"She's got these high standards so she doesn't have friends," B.D. agreed. "When I had shingles I figured that we're only meat."

"Hardly anything turns out well. I mean I like you but you would fuck up my horse business."

Bright and very early the next morning B.D., Rita, and Rollo headed for Helena to get the pups. Rollo slept in a large fleece dog bed with sides about a foot high. The kennel turned out to be clean and well run. Rollo and the owner had an interminable bird-dog conversation until Rita interrupted and completed the transaction by writing a check. B.D. was close by and saw that the price was thirty-five hundred dollars which meant it was five hundred dollars a pup which was beyond his comprehension. The pups are worth a lot more than me, he thought.

It's hard on any infant creature to get weaned and the pups cried a lot. Where was Mother? Calves bawling are the worst. Rita brought along a pile of dog toys and then Rollo crawled back into the dog bed with them and petted them to sleep, one across his neck. At the cabin B.D. had filled the plastic pool early so that the hot sun had warmed the water. First only the boldest pup jumped in the water and then they all hopped in except the runt, a female, who began to cry. B.D. picked her up and rubbed her tummy. Our inborn leftist sympathies are always quite taken by the runt. Now that B.D. was leaving and Rollo was moving to the cabin Rollo said that he intended to let the runt sleep with him.

In the afternoon B.D. and Mom drove to Great Falls to take a look at the car lot. There was a big sign in front that said "CHEAP." There must have been a hundred cars that though spit polished were definitely older models. She specialized in the poor and Indian customers and was respected in the business community for filling this gap. B.D. couldn't resist a gray 1979 Subaru because it had a built-in winch and skid plate, ideal for the back roads of the U.P. As he had gotten older becoming stuck in the snow had become more unpleasant. They sat in the Subaru and she took B.D.'s pay envelope out of her purse and handed it to him.

"Count it," she said.

"What's the point? I helped you bring your son back and there was seven days of fencing. We never agreed on the pay. So I have to take what I get."

"Count it. You'll never get ahead if you don't count."

"I'm never going to get ahead." He counted it and there were ten one-hundred-dollar bills, his ambition for retirement. He asked for change for the hundred which she gave him and he put the rest in a sock. "Grandpa said you know you have your money when you can feel it in your sock."

They went in her office and she made out a bill of sale and gave him a temporary license. He was impressed by her big desk. He had the impulse to take off for home from there.

"We're just trying to keep Rollo alive," she said.

"Good luck on that. He just needs something he likes to do. Raising dogs might work." He was more uncomfortable with this big question. "I got a lot I like to do. You know, walk and fish. I'm lucky I'm not as crazed for booze and pills as he is. I'm heading out now."

"Don't you need your luggage?" she asked, forgetting the paper bag he arrived with.

"I only got the Walmart stuff Rita bought and a jacket I paid two bucks for at a yard sale. I don't like to say goodbye. The only thing I'm missing is stretching out in the pool with the pups but I've swum a lot with dogs."

He had chosen Route 2 for its simplicity rather than its scenic quality. He caught it north of Great Falls in Havre and it took him all the way to Escanaba and Gretchen. The car shimmied at 48 mph and 60 mph so he settled for 55 mph, a slow but reliable speed rather than the 90 mph a few of his friends had died at after leaving a tavern. It was a fine trip visually as the pastels of mid-to-late May are more interesting than the dense greenery of full summer. He stopped at a yard sale near Glasgow to pick up a jacket and blanket for sleeping in the car. He certainly didn't want to use any of his retirement money on motels. Besides the backseat went flat and would be a fine bed. It was hard to believe he had only been gone about two weeks but he felt a lot better than when he left. He owed the sheriff a cell phone but maybe he could buy one used.

In Williston, Montana, he stopped to get some dinner and two young women pulled in at the same time in a new Volvo station wagon with a bicycle rack in the back. They were in shorts and expensive sporting wear. They had very nice legs if a little muscular. He waited in the Subaru until they went in and chose their seating. He wanted to get a seat near them for the leg view. He ended up right across from them and could hear their chat which included:

"You can't be healthy without a clean colon."

"Tell me about it! Mine was a mess when I still ate meat."

This made them a tad less attractive but he enjoyed them whining about the food. "Only iceberg lettuce!"

His only complaint was the lack of a pillowcase when he slept a few hours. There was also the question of how you knew your colon was clean. All the way across North Dakota people were worried about the oncoming floods so that he was not sure he was safe until he was well into Minnesota and felt more at home. Gretchen always listened to NPR stations but then he wasn't quite the concerned citizen she was. He preferred the mournful banality of country music though he couldn't handle more than an hour at a time since most of the songs were complaints, bad form in his code. His intentions were to stop and see Gretchen for a day or two for brook trout and chokecherries. He'd take along the three dogs at his cabin for warmth and friendship.

PART III

Chapter 11

He arrived at dawn, about 5:30 AM, after driving all night. He knew she would be up giving Susi her first nursing. She unlocked the door in tears and hugged him with Susi between them. She looked pale and had lost weight. She gestured and he sat down on the easy chair and she sat on his lap in her nightie and began nursing Susi who immediately stopped being cranky and burbled something as if she recognized him after his absence.

"I suffered horribly," Gretchen said, shifting her butt on his lap and glaring at him comically. "Why are you ruining a family moment by getting a hard-on?"

"It's not my fault. It does it by itself."

"Women have control over themselves."

"Not always. I've been abused."

"Fuck you." She gave a sassy wiggle to her butt which put him up in the farther reaches of heaven. She suddenly became morose. "That bitch Cheryl betrayed me."

"I'm sorry." This was all he could think of to say.

"You hated her."

"She was mean to me."

Susi was finished nursing and Gretchen got up nestling her in the corner of the sofa. B.D. thought, "That's that," getting a startling view when she bent over with Susi but then she sat back on his lap crying with her face in his neck. He held her by the waist moving her nightie slightly so a breast would emerge. It seemed like a cement mixer motor started in his head.

"I might want to get pregnant in September," she snuffled.

"We should practice before then."

"You've got to be kidding." She swiveled and poked his penis hard with a forefinger beneath his trousers. "I saw the boy next door's penis. It turned right. It was ugly as a dog's."

"You're talking about something that gave you a beautiful daughter."

"You put it in too far."

"You should have said something. Women have different depths."

"Make me some Mexican chicken."

"Now?" He was trying to remember something Rita had advised, about being more difficult so he wouldn't get walked on.

"Yes. I'm starved for it. I tried to make it but I burned it so I gave it to the dogs next door along with some water because it was spicy."

"I'll make it if you kiss me for thirty seconds like you would the prettiest girl in the world."

She paused as if trying to get her bearings. She was looking at life again after having emerged from a total cave of a couple of weeks. B.D. had been startled to see that the house was a mess which it had never been in the decade plus that he had known her. Now she was looking at him with a cockeyed smile and he wasn't sure if she would begin slapping him or pull a hidden dagger like Rita.

"At long last, Laura." She collapsed against him kissing him with an open mouth and grinding her body against him straddling a leg with a convincing sob, both breasts free of her nightie and tears falling profusely in her amazing insincerity.

He was poleaxed having fallen into a ladylike swoon, his limbs paralyzed, the Lord Byron of trashy ladies had helplessly risen to a new place of romance and was ill suited for it.

"Make chicken, Bozo," she said jumping up. Susi's eyes were now open and Gretchen picked her up. "Time for your Cheerios, carrots, and peas."

B.D. was waiting to be able to move. Nothing seemed possible except his heart that still fluttered. He would make a double batch of chicken and drop some off to Delmore on his way to Grand Marais for the chokecherries and brook trout. He was in retirement.

Luckily she had bought two chickens so he began cooking at 6 AM in his gathering fatigue. The chili sauce was an ass kicker which he knew Delmore would complain about. He was nodding as he ate this unorthodox breakfast which immediately soothed Gretchen and made her happy.

"I'm thinking of buying a house on forty acres outside of town about ten miles. There's a creek. I'll build you a cabin on the creek in the far corner of the property. You can take your bulbous girlfriends there."

"What's bulbous?" He was sweating from the hot sauce and wished he had a beer.

"A woman shaped like an enormous tulip bulb."

He fell asleep telling her about his retirement fund. She guided him to the sofa and when he awoke before noon she had cleaned the house. She brought him a cup of coffee and he sat up regretting that she had changed out of her nightie into jeans and a T-shirt.

Susi sat in the high chair pounding the tray with her tiny fists. He was pleased she was grinning at him.

"Maybe I'll adopt in September." She had returned to her melancholy. "Which means I don't need you."

He realized at that moment that he could have taken advantage of her weakened condition when he had arrived but above all else Grandpa said one had to be a gentleman with the female of the species and eventually a suitable one would fall into his arms. He was aware that most of his conquests were tawdry and alcohol related, and alcohol was merely a fluid that allowed sexual impulse to surface in reality. The summer before a small glass of wine had turned an off-duty camp counselor into a banshee in the darkened Marina Park in Marquette. She had pulled him to the ground evidently not all that far from a dog turd which could be overlooked. Gretchen was far too wary for him to try slipping vodka into the fruit juice that she drank frequently. Back in high school it was a surefire aid to seduction as long as the girl didn't puke from too much alcohol. Vomiting tends to squelch the sexual urge for both partners. Nevertheless it was grand to have her sitting on his lap and the challenge of kissing him as though he was a pretty girl was one of his smarter moves in years.

"Why can't you treat me like Laura more often?" Susi was on his lap and dragging a finger through the hot sauce on his plate, then licking it off. She didn't seem to mind the spiciness but bounced on his lap grinning and shrieking.

"Sorry but you don't look like Laura. We seduced each other as freshmen at Michigan State."

"Where," he asked irrelevantly.

"What do you mean *where*."

"I need to locate events to picture them."

"On the banks of the Red Cedar River on a warm September evening. We took off our miniskirts to avoid grass stains. I admit it was like an explosion. She went straight but then so many of us could have gone both ways usually with disastrous results."

"You could try it. It's old-fashioned but it's historical."

"I could also jump off a cliff but I know better. We had a taste didn't we? It wasn't as bad as I thought it would be but nothing like my kind of love. I mean I cherish you as maybe my best friend ever but our sexuality is in another category. You can't talk yourself into pleasure."

"I can."

He was thinking of the surprise that Long Rita kept in store. She could also be a little rough, a wild creature, in fact. B.D. felt melancholy descending from wherever it came from, clearly a bad place. From the distance of Montana things had looked so good what with a comparatively sizable grubstake for lots of time fishing. Now he was sitting, a dead-ass, while Gretchen bathed Susi in the bathroom off the kitchen. Susi was cooing and madly splashing her mother. B.D. glanced snoopily at the papers on the desk which included the mysterious bill of sale for a Toyota pickup of recent vintage and also a Swede newspaper ad for something called a country *estate*, fifty acres bisected by a creek, and a fine house at the edge of a clearing, all for three hundred thousand, to him an unimaginable number, merely a social phenomena wherein money from a prosperous family is passed on to a daughter, the only heir, who had proved her worthiness by producing an heir with a man who looked to them like a handyman, someone always slightly dirty who fixed the furnace or the garage door. The parents were aware of Gretchen's sexual inclinations early on and when they had met B.D. in Escanaba a few months back, they felt that someone is better than nothing.

B.D. in contrast thought the senior couple looked peculiar in their Lincoln Town Car, useless on logging roads, in their well-tailored clothes you wouldn't want to pick blackberries or blueberries in and were doubtless changed everyday for no good reason. The father was a pronounced stiff who plainly disliked the idea that B.D. had screwed his daughter despite the wonderful result, an ebullient granddaughter. As a peace offering the father had purchased B.D. a beautiful Orvis fly rod with B.D.'s name engraved on the helve.

The parents were radiant at a nice restaurant when B.D. gave Susi a bottle while Gretchen had dessert. When he burped Susi and she spit on his shirt the mother-in-law dabbed it off with a wet napkin. It was certainly an illusory family dinner à la Norman Rockwell. On the way out a very fat man stumbled and B.D. caught him. The man yelled, "I can't believe you caught me! No one can catch me!" and his wife shrieked, "You should hire him, Roscoe!" B.D. bowed, taking one more glance at a pert waitress standing in the door. He recalled that she was last year's local homecoming queen and her dad was the obnoxious logger, an unlikely father for a lovely daughter B.D. would like to see spread on a table with good sauces.

When they drove out in the country that afternoon B.D. was as dumbfounded by the sprawling size of the house as he had been at the three-hundred-thousand-dollar figure he had seen on Gretchen's desk. Why would Gretchen want such a big house for her and little Susi? He didn't know that people nowadays buy big houses merely because they can. Her grandma had been rich through no fault of her own and when Gretchen and Susi had flown south for a visit the ailing grandma had been thrilled, holding the baby in the way one only sees in families, with a kind of glow.

Gretchen showed him the remote location of *his* cabin but he was curiously repelled by the split-rail fence surrounding the clearing that kept nothing out or in. He recalled a drawing in a high school history book of Abe Lincoln splitting rails. He himself had split rails for rich summer people but it was unpleasant work. He finally didn't want this lovely woman to build him a cabin. He told her he could build the cabin for half the estimate she had received and she said okay with a melancholy tinge. It's a mixed

blessing to give a present and not very far in the back of his mind he knew that people who were kind to you often wished to control you or change your life in unpleasant ways. A loose male is not a good thing in the culture. Everyone knows that. He was still smarting from his work as a dogcatcher. Oddly, Long Rita was the perfect owner for the obnoxious Bruno. His friend Fatty the dog sitter wanted the other two dogs but not big Fred, the wolf dog, who scared him. Fatty had shot two deer in his absence to feed the dogs his patented venison stew. The deer wouldn't be good for human consumption until July when the cedar swamp flavor from their winter yarding grounds would be out of their flesh. Cedar swamps with their close-knit trees offered creatures the most protection from the winter's unremitting blizzards. In high cold winds a cedar can be relatively quiet with the gaunt deer chewing on the bitter branches. Once B.D. had entered a swamp with a chain saw and cut ten acres of aspen, their favorite food, for a starving herd. The deer closely approached him among the fallen trees and began feeding, their hunger outweighing their fear of man. A game warden visited one day but thoroughly approved of his struggle against deer starvation and besides it was Delmore's back forty.

Delmore was nearly hysterical when they arrived. He had just heard on the radio that there was to be a new *Planet of the Apes* sequel and the idea was nearly unbearable. Delmore took these movies as God's truth, considering the apes to be *spirit animals* though siding with humans. B.D. could tolerate almost any movie once, but loathed these from overexposure. One of Delmore's heroes was Charlton Heston and Delmore had yelled warnings when the apes stole Charlton's clothing when the great man was swimming beneath the waterfall. Charlton was from West Branch, really St. Helen, Michigan, and there were Chippewa in the area and Delmore believed it was likely that some of his own fine blood was in the veins of the great leader. Delmore thought Charlton had been a little excitable about gun possession. Delmore's own old hunting weapons were in hiding and he doubted if any government nitwit could ever find them.

B.D. heated up the Mexican chicken while Delmore dandled little Susi on his knee. He considered Susi to be B.D.'s finest hour and said so repeatedly including that comment that Susi looked like her grandma which gave a chill to B.D.'s tummy. He only knew enough of his parents to understand that their behavior was questionable and that they had been involved in the rise of Red Power in the sixties. B.D. had never had the heart to rummage though Grandpa's trunks after he died in hopes of finding old photos of his mother. And here he was at Uncle Delmore's with no truly positive proof that Delmore was an uncle or truly a relative. Delmore referred to all relatives as gold diggers which didn't help much as his cousins were skins at Lac du Flambeau down in Wisconsin. This was all of minimal interest to B.D. who was mostly interested in "getting by" and if you never had parents they are mostly an abstraction. When he heard the rumor that his father had victored over three state cops at a Munising dance hall it fell short of heroic as he had done well in that area himself.

Meanwhile Gretchen was disappointed over B.D.'s lack of enthusiasm over the gift cabin. She recalled that in college no one actually believed in any reality surrounding the notion of the noble savage but people largely envied people who lived a simple life, not that they couldn't do so themselves. It is actually easy when people aren't fond of clutter. You strip the life down to the bare boards underneath, the barest elements of shelter and food. Once a month Grandpa would scrub the wood floors of their small house on the edge of the forest. B.D. figured if he actually built the cabin it would be all wood and not drywall to paint. But right now holding Susi on Delmore's porch swing he meditated on Gretchen's stranglehold on his being. She was on her hands and knees weeding Delmore's small garden which consisted mostly of cabbage, cucumber, and rutabaga. Delmore insisted that supermarket rutabaga were always "spoilt" compared to one pulled fresh from the ground in September. B.D. put up with Delmore because so far as he knew Delmore was his only relative and B.D. was doomed to take him to *The Planet of the Apes* sequel. It would be a struggle to keep Delmore quiet during the movie. Delmore felt obligated to shout all sorts of warnings and instructions. "Cornelius, goddammit, listen to me!" he would howl.

After supper B.D. packed up his shabby camping equipment wanting to set up before dark and maybe do a little fishing. Everything, mostly his love for Gretchen, had been interrupting his official retirement plans. When Gretchen questioned his plans and the minimal amount, he said, "It's the most I've ever had." It was safely in the sock he wore. Now she was going to trap him in the cabin, the only advantage being that he could peek in her bedroom windows. Even that lacked the old fire now that he was convinced that their love was doomed. She had hit him over the head dozens of times with her predilections though he could never quite believe they were fatal. It had been a decade of heartsickness but then his life before Gretchen had scarcely been ideal. When Berry had run amok in McDonald's, Gretchen had been able to calm her down. Now she was helping him pack the car and when she bent over in her short flowery summer dress the usual strong tremor was there and he recalled a song he disliked that the girls in high school used to sing, "I'll take romance." He kissed Susi goodbye and she jerked painfully on his lower lip. He laughed so she laughed too. This was obviously the greatest thing he had ever had a part in. All in all, he thought, nearly everything was impossible but then along came things as marvelous as creeks and Susi. He had to include the puppy Grandpa once got him from the dog pound that he named Warren after a third-grade teacher who got the kids packets of Audubon cards so that they could tell one bird from another. He loved them dearly but promptly got them wet and ruined and then sobbed when he told the teacher after school. He got a new packet mostly because the teacher was also a brook trout fisherman. B.D. directed him to some good places, not the sacred best which are always saved for oneself, but good ones and Mr. Warren was thankful. The best was actually a deep spring in a marsh that B.D. used sparingly. If anything it was his church.

Back to Gretchen's fanny emerging from the back of the Subaru trying to neaten up the mess of B.D.'s gear.

"I'm camping at the site of Susi's conception," he said.

"That's sweet," she responded, receiving his gratuitously tight hug with grace.

"You and Susi could jump in the car."

"No, thanks. I got work tomorrow."

She let her lips touch his, doubting that anyone would love her like this goofy man. He was clearly the virtual opposite of anything the culture thought was acceptable.

He made the Dunes Saloon in Grand Marais by 8 AM after picking up Fred at the cabin. Fatty had the other two dogs but B.D. didn't want Fred to be lonely just because he was huge and ugly and half wolf. Delighted with his freedom B.D. had a couple of double whiskeys and beer chasers and flirted with the barmaid with whom he had had a beach wrestling match a few years back. She was cool and didn't seem to remember him, saying she had been recently married to the love of her life, a big young man who glowered at him from the end of the bar. B.D. tipped her a twenty as a wedding present, feeling lonely, and headed out for Barfield Lakes. He quickly set up camp in the location where he had fathered Susi. Big Fred quickly ran off and about a mile away he began howling like his wolf relatives. B.D. was undisturbed and inhaled deeply the odor of chokecherry tree flowers that surrounded him. The brightly flowered surroundings lightened up the gathering dark and he had a quick half an hour of fishing, then gathered enough firewood for the night. Fred returned with a fawn in his jowls, upsetting but there was nothing to be done about it except to swallow the cruelty with the beauty. He boned and fried two small brook trout and had a trout sandwich with beer. He put Fred in the car so he wouldn't get his ass killed by the wolves who had begun howling in the west with Fred growling from the car. He poured a cup of coffee from his thermos wanting to stay awake for a while and think things over which was generally not what he was best at. There was an unpleasant memory spark of Gretchen's desk and a sketched architect's rendering of the cabin to be built. He had pushed it from memory because it reminded him of a children's story that Grandpa used to read that included a silly little house made of gingerbread. He couldn't live in such a cabin. Grandpa felt obligated to read these stories with gusto while B.D. preferred tales from outdoor magazines of heroic men catching giant fish throughout the world or getting attacked by giant animals. He didn't want to hear about little girls getting lost which oddly frightened him what with having been lost himself. If only the cabin did not smack of a huge dollhouse. He would have to talk to Gretchen and put on the brakes. He preferred it to be built of logs and have a simple front porch, one large room and a sleeping loft, a small kitchen, a toilet inside or out, plank flooring, and sizable windows for keeping an eye on nature.

After a couple of health giving glugs of schnapps he slept well though occasionally Fred howled from the car perhaps to warn visiting curious wolves or coyotes. In general B.D. didn't care for huge dogs as often they were bullies which he also loathed in humans. Grandpa taught him to box so he didn't have to put up with bullies. In both dogs and men it was ugly.

The dawn walk among the chokecherries and sugarplums was all that he had hoped for. He had been upset in the saloon that a front was coming through but only the smallest signs were visible in the northwest. Meanwhile he was walking in waist-high ferns wet from dew and basking in a world of profusely flowering trees thinking it must be natural to be overwhelmed by flowers as he had been since childhood. Late in the afternoon when he drove to town for a drink he would check the forest bordering the sand dunes where there were valleys matted with white trillium. Fred happily walked with him and B.D. was able to call him back when a gamey scent was picked up. Fred growled wildly at a pile of bear shit. B.D. sat down on a white pine stump shaped like an easy chair that he had used for years. On waking he split his ham and cheese sandwich with Fred telling him to chew thirty-two times as B.D. had learned in school. He noted that the front was mounting with a rolling black rim of clouds to the far west. He headed for the car and tent not wanting to be caught out without a jacket. He could see the car in the distance when he heard the roar of the storm and by the time he got to the car he was in a blizzard of flowers with lightning ripping the sky like canvas tearing. Fred was frightened but then what did he know about thunder? B.D. had never had the right time to be in a virtual blizzard of chokecherry flowers and it was an astounding version of January. The high winds and moist air made the odor even more poignant. In the car with the shuddering Fred he saw the wind collapse his pup tent and figured that he might squander a little of his retirement money on a motel rather than have an uncomfortable wet night in a tent.

Sitting there in the aura of Fred's bad breath he studied how the first rain pasted the blossoms against the car windows and was thankful that he was in the right place at the right time which was similar to good fishing or getting laid. An irksome detail arose about the gingerbread design of the cabin. At community potlucks he hated gingerbread. Once he thought he was eating chocolate cake and spit a gob of gingerbread on the floor. What was this strange shit but then he never had a mother who made gingerbread cake and cookies around Christmas. On Christmas morning he'd open a present or two and then he and Grandpa would go ice fishing or rabbit hunting. He was proud at potlucks when everyone headed for Grandpa's "dish to pass" which would be a twelve-pound brisket in a roast pan cooked at low heat for a dozen hours and tender as a baby's butt. When young Grandpa cooked at a logging camp he could flip flapjacks high in the air and would make fine sausage out of a whole hog he butchered and would smoke a couple of hams and slabs of bacon with wild crabapple wood in his smokehouse.

There was a stillness for a while after the first brunt of the storm passed and B.D. and Fred strolled around on a thin blanket of sweetly odorous flower petals. B.D. rolled in them in a small culvert where the flowers were thicker. Fred jumped on him for fun and B.D. developed a lump in his throat that Gretchen wasn't there for this beauty. What a beautiful situation to father a child. By the time he treated himself to a few shots of schnapps and hung his tent and sleeping bag on the bushes he felt a bit lunar as if he were blessed after all.

His serenity didn't last long when he drove to the saloon for food when it opened midmorning. He had tried fishing locally but wasted a lot of time bathing both himself and Fred and spraying down the car with Lysol. Fred had rolled in some desiccated carcasses and B.D. had taken a divorcée to the motel even though they didn't like each other having been caught red-handed years before by her husband. The husband had broken B.D.'s windshield with a ball bat, nothing serious but the expense, about fifty six-packs B.D. figured. She wasn't worth it back then and still wasn't. She jabbered endlessly about an extension course she was taking from a professor in Marquette on how to open herself to her own creativity. B.D. had no idea what this meant but noted that she had hogged her way through most of the remaining schnapps. He was unsure of the word *creativity* though it was being used a lot in recent years. It likely had nothing to do with his life. The woman made him miss Long Rita very much. She had been a gymnast and could walk on her hands in the nude which curiously wasn't as sexy as you would think. She also wept and hooted at orgasm. He abandoned her at the motel to get back to the saloon for last call for a much needed double whiskey and when he got back she was infuriated. She dressed and left, a specific relief. He meant to ask Gretchen about this creativity thing. It certainly made people pissed off.

He was back fishing near his campsite and caught a nice fat brook trout about a foot long which he kept to cook for Gretchen who loved to eat them, including the crispy fried tails. He didn't mind being generous with her though she seemed to regard him as a lump of coal. On the way home he detoured to the shack and there near the front door stood Fatty next to a Sky Kennel. He pointed to the woods with a hand holding a sixteen-ounce can of beer. As B.D. let Fred out of the car Bruno shot out of a thicket and jumped way up on Fred's back like a horse. Fred began barking and then the dogs huge and small rolled in the ferns yelping with pleasure. Fatty handed B.D. the note that had arrived with the Sky Kennel. "Your mutt tried to hamstring a new foal. I loved him but you can have him." Also a note from Rollo, "Your dog Bruno wouldn't stop beating up the setter puppies then he bit my hand badly when I punished him. Sorry." Bruno and Fred came out of a tall patch of ferns with Bruno still riding Fred, holding on with his teeth in the back of Fred's neck.

He loaded the dogs and headed for Gretchen's presuming that Bruno would be gentle with Susi. On the way to town Bruno saw some cows and threw himself against the closed window as if he intended to send them into meat chunks. B.D. was often a bit mystified by animals. Several years back in a blueberry marsh loaded with ripe berries he watched from a presumably safe distance as two male black bears argued over a female who continued eating berries through the noisy fuss. The males charged each other howling and growling. B.D.'s ass was tight with fear but the bears ignored him and also neglected to injure each other. Finally the smallest male wandered away from the sex argument but when the dominant male approached the female she angrily chased him off snapping at his ass then went back to her blueberry feast. She clearly wasn't ready for affection.

It was a sunny overwarm late May day when he reached Gretchen's driveway. She was sunning herself in her blue bikini and Susi was in her Johnny Jump Up on the porch. B.D. remembered Grandpa had been shocked when he saw a girl in a bikini in *Life* magazine. Before B.D. could stop him Bruno jumped out the open window and ran to Susi squealing, writhing and licking her bare foot at which she laughed. Bruno didn't forget their earlier meeting. Here was a human, albeit miniature, that he could like. He rolled over kicking his feet to show off. When Fred approached he snarled viciously. This was his toy alone. Gretchen hugged and kissed B.D. on the lips when he handed her the brook trout but pushed him away when he trembled.

"The sheriff was here," she said. "I told him you'd be here pretty soon."

"Why the fuck tell him?"

"Why piss him off by making him look for you like a desperado? He wants his cell phone back. Not unreasonable."

"I gave it to an Indian girl and she threw it in a slow moving river."

"That won't work. Were you having a romance?"

"You might say that. You saw her. Rollo's sister."

"You did pretty well by yourself." She looked cool and mean. "Maybe I underestimated you."

"You certainly do," B.D. said a bit smugly and she thumbed her nose at him. Susi had fallen asleep with Bruno tickling her toes with his tongue while Fred watched with curiosity. He weighed one thirty at least and Bruno twenty-five at most, so it was a Mutt and Jeff combination.

The sheriff swerved up in his glossy squad car, and swiveled and trundled his heavy way out the door. Bruno was immediately on the attack but B.D. intercepted him which made him furious.

"I think the rich people might want that dog back, God knows why. Also hand over the cell phone."

"The dog is owned by my daughter," B.D. said. "An Indian girl threw your phone in a Minnesota river." He had momentarily forgotten what had actually happened to it.

"I'd extradite her if I wanted. You owe for it."

"Bobby, I'll pay for it, I don't need trouble," Gretchen said. The sheriff admired her bikini. They had worked in the same county building and he loved it when she called him Bobby though she regarded him as an obnoxious toad. He deeply mistrusted B.D. and guessed that he had no idea where he left the phone which was true.

As the sheriff was leaving B.D. remembered that the publicly owned cell phone was at the bottom of a stinking creek along with a naughty magazine of Rollo's he had also thrown in on their way west. B.D. had been ashamed that Bruno had bullied Rollo's setter puppies. Both dogs and men can be ready-made assholes. He had been tempted to let Bruno bite the sheriff. It would have been fun and utterly worthwhile. Now he was dancing around to amuse Susi while Gretchen was doing calisthenics. She had changed into a sweatsuit after the sheriff's eyeful. Girls sent Rollo nude photos of themselves on his cell phone and that seemed an extraordinary technical advancement. Grandpa wouldn't have believed it. His long-term girlfriend had been the secretary to the high school superintendent who whenever she visited their house would greet him with "clean your room Mr. Piggy." One weekend night B.D. came home late and was sure he heard them making love and it amazed him that people that age still did it. She made little screeching noises like an owl.

B.D. was at the kitchen table assembling ingredients for the locally famous tamale pie, which was not really Mexican but more of a border recipe that had crept its way north, partly because there's a lot of melted cheddar on top of the Mexican ingredients to which people often add a generous dollop of sour cream, both ingredients much loved by Americans to their peril. Beans not dairy products allow Mexicans to work fourteen-hour days.

The architect's rendering of the cabin was next to him on the table, a culinary crime because when you are cooking that should be the sole item in your attention. A quarrel loomed. Gretchen, sitting across from him, didn't seem to notice.

"You look pissed, darling. And you've been so pleasant lately." She swore as Susi in her highchair lifted up and poured out her pureed pear.

"I'm feeling like I ate several pounds of gingerbread." He waved at the drawing.

"So go to the architect's office and tell him what you want changed."

"I've lived in and remodeled dozens of cabins all without gingerbread. This looks like a sissy cabin."

"Don't be a sexist. I'll call him and tell him to do what you want."

"I wouldn't feel right."

"For Christ's sake it's over. I don't give a shit. I want it to be what you want. I just thought that Susi would eventually like the cute gingerbread."

"No daughter of mine could like it."

"You fucking nitwit." Gretchen couldn't stomp in her barefeet but left the room.

It wasn't unlike the average marital quarrel where one gets their way but won't leave it alone.

He wasn't experienced at much but he believed cabins and shacks were his specialty. One of his life's mainstays.

Gretchen had called ahead to the architect believing that something might go amiss and it did. He recognized the man, a snotty kid from the ninth grade whose parents had sent him off to school in Connecticut before he could be permanently damaged by the U.P. which in truth didn't guarantee future success. The kid had been a prick and the man maintained the average. B.D. had been condescended to so often that he usually didn't mind it anymore but this time he had the upper hand and was adamant about the filigree, the more decorative aspects of the design. He even made a sketch at which the man snorted and sucked his upper lip.

"It's certainly plain," he said.

"Yes, it is," B.D. said and walked out wanting to tip the desk over on the asshole.

Walking home he saw Cheryl's car a full block away, a red compact which was fine if you like getting stuck in the winter. At that moment he felt he needed a toilet. It was an astounding jolt. She nodded and he nodded back as he approached the front yard.

"I might need a character witness, darling."

"I wouldn't be too good over in the Soo. I had some scrapes over there."

"Just kidding, handsome. Maybe I'll go to Brazil."

When Gretchen had told B.D. about Cheryl's crime he was frankly amazed that girls of that persuasion must limit themselves to those over eighteen. He had noted that the Park Service had spent a fortune on signs saying "Stay on Trails" or some such. Everyone bullying everyone else or snooping into their business.

B.D. gave up Gretchen's spare bedroom to Cheryl and spent a restive night on the sofa in the middle of which he heard Cheryl sneak into the kitchen and sneak the tamale pie leftovers cheating him of his intended breakfast. He stepped out of the house at first light, about 5 AM to go fishing. He saw Cheryl looking out her bedroom window and waved goodbye. She flipped him the bird. There would never be peace between them what with her thinking he might be a competitor for the princess. He stopped at a gas station and ate half of one of those premade sandwiches, ham and cheese, thinking the egg salad might be fatally infected. The tamale pie would have been good but mighty Cheryl had scraped the bowl clean. Her internal engine evidently needed a lot of fuel. At times she belched loudly, a backfire in the exhaust system. He had no religion but was irked that she would give him the finger on Sunday morning. The girls had requested green chili chicken enchiladas for dinner, which was annoying as he would have to quit fishing by afternoon to cook.

He parked on the road near a culvert that passed the water from Gretchen's property. There was quite a bit of volume so he guessed there must be a feeder creek between the road and Gretchen's house. One of the surpassing pleasures of his life was exploring the courses of creeks both for finding new fishing holes and for the mysterious nature of free-flowing water, the way it chose its path, and its purling sound. The previous owner had left "No Trespassing" signs and he hoped that meant this creek wouldn't be fished out though he ignored such signs himself. After about a hundred yards of difficult walking through a cedar swamp he came upon a spring feeder creek from the west, pure cold water. He would look into it at some point but not on this shortened fishing day. There was a fine deep hole which the two streams joined and he sat on the bank studying it while the water totally quieted from his wading. There were a group of mayflies swirling in the air across the small pond by the joining of the two creeks and some smaller fish raising to them and then in cooperation to every angler's dream the dorsal fin of a much larger trout arrived from under the bank. B.D. had used up his artificial mayflies in Montana and took a chance on one female muddler that resembled a heavy moth and expertly tied it on the line and flipped it over in the path of the moving dorsal. The fish gulped the muddler and when B.D. set the hook the fish shot off toward the emergent spring creek. B.D. guessed that in size it would be in his top ten so he had no choice but to plunge into the pool over this waist, scrambling to the other side and crawling up the creek after the trout. The greenery formed a close tunnel so he abandoned the rod and played the fish gently by holding the line by hand and crawling along. In a half dozen minutes of struggle the fish didn't seem to be weakening but then the line caught on a large dead branch. He feared that the line would break but he held on. He slid his hand under the fish and flipped it up on a sand spit.

Assuming that Cheryl was still there he released the beautiful fish because he did not think she was worthy of it but then grabbed it again because it was bleeding from the gills which meant it would die. He would cut it in half and give her the slender ass end.

Only Susi smiled when he entered the front yard. The adult girls were sunning themselves and evidently having a serious love talk.

"Look what the rats drug in," Cheryl said to the wet, bedraggled B.D. who held up the fish.

"Be nice darling. That's a whopper, love."

"Don't call him love," Cheryl hissed.

"Calm down. I bought a chicken to make you green chili enchiladas."

B.D. nodded and went inside to work on his favorite dish. He fine chopped some garlic and a half dozen jalapeños and serranos.

Cheryl came in for a glass of water and began to needle him.

"Whoever told you that you could cook?"

"You don't have any trouble overeating. The food won't be so good in prison."

"You miserable fuck!" she screeched just as Gretchen walked in the door. Cheryl grabbed the saucer of minced hot chilis and threw them in B.D.'s face including his eyes. He rubbed his face in panic then splashed his eyes with water groaning, "Fuck me."

Gretchen cupped running water against B.D.'s eyes, then said coldly, "Go away, both of you."

Cheryl tore off and B.D. sat in his car until he could see clearly, and then drove to the liquor store and bought a pint of schnapps and a six-pack with his precious retirement money. Gretchen guessed his moves and called but he said no to coming back and finishing dinner. His feelings were deeply hurt and he felt that getting drunk was the only answer. He'd fish a week before coming up for air. Meanwhile he hoped that Fatty had moved back to his own place with the remaining dogs. He had forgotten Fred but Gretchen could be trusted with the noble dog.

On the way to the shack he drank three of the beers and half the pint of schnapps which was a fair start. The shack was amazingly clean and tidy which meant Fatty's sister Rhonda had been there. She was sweet on B.D. but he was past the age when he was eager to mate a plus-three-hundred pounder. He felt a little saddened by this as if he had vitally narrowed his versatility. Just before he left Gretchen came out the door and picked up Susi and Cheryl shouted out her car window, "Fuck you rich bitch," which B.D. recognized was not a wise thing to call someone who spent her life aiding the poor. He had had a lifetime of lame lover's quarrels and was remarkably inept at them preferring to cut and run. He was melancholy indeed about Gretchen's unjust anger feeling it was he who was the insulted and injured with the only pleasure being that Bruno had nipped Cheryl in the heel on the way out of the house. She had turned around to kick him but Bruno was far too deft and gave her an extra nip in the knee. Huge passive Fred would turn away in embarrassment when Bruno was violent.

B.D. rigged his tackle in the car and had a final swig of schnapps before setting off down the creek toward Gretchen's house. His eyes still stung but profuse tears were helping. He avoided stepping on a large bear turd and thought of the hunger after six months of hibernation. Years back a bear had eaten an Indian who had passed out. Some years bears became fat in May from winter-kill deer after a severe winter. Right now it was damp and still and the mosquitoes were thick but the weather said it was due to be windy by noon which would drive them away. When it became consistently warmer it would be the turn of the deerflies to drive him crazy. Once when being tormented by deerflies he cut across a field flushing many dragonflies in the deeper grass and the dragonflies killed the deerflies pushing them off in the air like a war game. It was a delightful discovery especially for someone who never noticed the balance of nature that schoolbooks make much of.

When he reached the secret pool where he had caught the fine trout the day before he sat on a white pine stump and merely watched the water for any sign of disturbances due to a fish underneath. There were no mayflies today and no feeding trout except for a small school of minnows near the outpouring of the spring deep in the woods. Of the hundreds of places he fished this had immediately become one of the most beautiful despite any gingerbread intentions. There was a specific flare of anger in his chest when he heard an unfamiliar vehicle making its way up the two-track to Gretchen's house despite having spent a lifetime trespassing himself almost always with impunity. Brook trout are most often in creeks sunning through low swampy areas and are not much patrolled. Right now however he laid his fishing tackle down having decided to sneak up on the criminals and kick some ass. Luckily the car took another turnoff.

It was a fairly long stalk with lots of mosquito bites from crawling on the forest floor. He edged his head cautiously out of the two-track and saw Gretchen's car near the house. She was sitting on a porch chair with a notebook on her lap sunning her legs in an old pale blue frock he revered that she wore for housework. The blue set off her brown eyes just so. He did his best imitation of a basso growl and she shrieked and ran into the house. He was inordinately pleased. A new career in frightening people.

He walked up on the porch and she stuck her head out the door and yelled, "Asshole, you scared me."

He sat down on an actual leather sofa and she plunked down beside him waving her tablet.

"Your eyes look awful. That's quite the girlfriend I have."

He couldn't respond. He was still angry.

"It's almost Memorial Day. If we want a spring cabin next year we better get started."

"I don't want a baby unless I'm the legal father on paper. What am I to Susi? Or what will I be?"

"She'll know."

"I want to be a legal father."

"My dad's attorney thought we should do it this way. Lawyers are always thinking about money."

"I don't give a shit about lawyers. I grew up not knowing who my parents were. It makes you feel bad."

"I'm sorry, darling. This one will be proper. I can also have you adopt Susi. We'll pretend we're married."

"Will that make it legal?" Tears were falling profusely which had the residual effect of making his jalapeño eyes feel better.

"Of course," she said unconvincingly.

They embraced and she dabbed at his eyes with a tissue. In the ten years she had known him she had never seen him shed tears. It was curiously upsetting and she tried to imagine growing up without actual parents but couldn't do so. She recalled his profound attachment to his adopted daughter Berry and how long it took him to recover from losing her. A note would come from Rapid City every month or so, often with a photo of Berry on horseback and he would be quite overcome by the messages. "Berry is already the best rider in our 4-H club. Horses love her," or "Berry loves garlic and the family is trying to get used to it. They don't eat it out here." He did not seem to have a wide or deep emotional life but he was thrilled to the core when he taught Berry numbers with garlic cloves when the school had failed to teach her anything standard. But then no one but he and Delmore could make Berry remotely cooperative except for running around the woods on Delmore's eighty acres.

Gretchen walked into her spacious bedroom and sat on the edge of the bed stiffly confessing that Cheryl had opened a letter for him from Long Rita. She took the opened letter from her purse and handed it to him. He wasn't angry because he was stuck back on the issue of not having any regular parents, just old Grandpa. He glanced at the note seeing a passage where she said she missed his body which embarrassed him and Gretchen admitted it made her jealous. "How could it?" he asked. "I've always been yours for the taking." She flopped back on the bed with the blue dress halfway up her thighs and for the first time ever he didn't feel stimulated. It was startling. The spring light was eerie and misty with many musical warblers through the screened window.

"You don't want another baby?"

"I'm confused. My mind is jumping around. I might have found my father's body way back when I was diving for salvage. He was an Indian radical. I saw a photo of my mother in Grandpa's secret things after he died. It was in a metal box. She was his daughter or Delmore's daughter I was never sure. So there it is." He was feeling that very mortal sense of the loss of love. A hollow chest and pain in the temples and looking at her a sense of the fragility of mere beauty.

"You don't love me anymore?" she said blankly.

"I don't know if I should. You're like absent parents. It's painful. Once I found a perfect hidden cabin and then I never found it again. I wondered if it was a cabin I stayed in with my mother with the memory of extreme thirst. The furniture was small and so were the windows. It was hot." He frequently returned to this cabin in his dreams. Could the dream woman be his mother from fifty years ago?

She hated the feeling that he was drifting away. It was painful. "What do you want from me except sex?"

"I want to be a family with Susi and whoever else comes along."

She was startled. Her sexual predilections passed through her mind and she couldn't summon up what mattered anymore except Susi and, somewhat, this man.

"You build your own cabin. You can make money, then we'll have a pretend marriage but a real family. I'll hope I don't fall in love again. Does this work? You can have me now and then. We could have a big family or not. I don't want us to lose each other because I've been mean." She got some more wet cotton to dab his eyes. She stared at him trying to figure out this newish mood.

He was trying to figure it out too. He was totally unaccustomed to his feelings plummeting to the bottom of their reservoir toward the hidden places we all keep, but also where we protect and try to hide from ourselves and others. Now he felt thoroughly numb as if it were a photo of her next to him rather than her body and a breast wagging next to his chin. Could he remember his mother's breast? He asked her. Maybe in your memory storage, she lied. He tongued a nipple and she wiggled then placed it between his lips. Normally this would have made him feel explosive but he was still remote.

"Playing hard to get?" She teased and unbuckled his belt which worked because it was so unlike her. He sighed a long sigh as she pulled his pants down. "Do you want a boy?"

"It doesn't matter. Just a child." He thought that for a man who loved the natural world Berry had been more than enough what with fooling the bird-watchers in Toronto with her uncanny chirping. He missed Toronto a bit partly because of the food and in part because of the nice people who seemed to know what they were doing. Why did they watch birds more in Toronto than around here where there were so many?

Before she left to pick up Susi from the babysitter they walked out a hundred yards to the cabin site half encircled by a grove of hardwoods and firs that would give nice wind protection. They wrangled a bit but then agreed on a north-facing front which was unorthodox but had the only clear view of Gretchen's house which he wanted. Gretchen had gotten rid of the architect and had found a set of plans from the Vermont border. The plans must have spread because he had seen such an old-time cabin over near Ontonagon on Lake Superior. He would start tomorrow working ten-to-twelve-hour days then fish for three straight through. He had done this before and it worked fine. Fishing places popped up haphazardly from dozens of years of wandering in the U.P. Right now he was thinking of the Grand Marais area and taking a short canoe called a Sportspal and paddling through five sections of land, five miles, through a particularly dense area, on a deep creek. Other anglers were unable to penetrate this area without physical suffering but he was conversant enough with the area to take hidden channels. Years ago he had seen a photo of a record brook trout of six pounds taken by a trapper who shot under the fish with a thirty-thirty stunning it, a questionable manner of angling.

B.D. stood in Gretchen's shower wondering at the femininity of the bathroom. He was standing in a warm hard rain with a big lump of melancholy in his chest. His was not a life of thought and he had felt his innards were strangling when he said, "I want a family." He certainly was inexperienced sinking that deep into his own soul if that was where it was. How could a thought cause that much emotion? The dream image could slip in at any time. The woman in a hot cabin giving the baby, him, a nippled bottle of cold water that he guzzled, then washing his sticky face. Later in school an irate principal said, "You're as wild as your father," and then, "It's the twentieth century, the warpath is over."

At that moment an animal lunged through the shower curtain at his dangling pecker. It was Bruno. He swatted him away and Bruno floundered nipping his ankles. B.D. hadn't realized she had brought him out but then there was no possible babysitter for Bruno. Meanwhile big Fred was standing on his hind legs outside the bathroom window watching the violence with bright eyes. He dried off with one of Gretchen's huge expensive towels, snapping at Bruno in the air with it and careful not to get bushwhacked in the ankles. Outside he set up his transit and staked the corner borders of the cabin. He would do two rows of cement blocks and then a plate to make it easy if the cabin ever had to be moved. He was pretty fast at building forms, lowly work. He would pour cement tomorrow and have his list of supplies trucked in. He would leave time for a snack this afternoon because Gretchen had said she was making chicken curry which he didn't like. She merely bought a supermarket roasted chicken, chopped it up, and mixed in a little curry powder and chicken stock. She had no real interest in cooking only eating and he could see a long trail into the future of doing the cooking. If you got good at anything you were in demand. Delmore had left word that he wanted a slow-cooked chuck roast on Sunday in two days. Gretchen had called to say they were married and Delmore had asked, "What are you, stupid?" Luckily, Delmore didn't mention that B.D. might still be married to Rose.

Fatty came chugging up in an ancient war surplus Jeep saying the sheriff needed to talk to B.D. immediately. B.D. felt a tremor of fear but it proved worthwhile. The sheriff was willing to drop charges over the stolen cell phone if B.D. would take care of a "vicious Lab" at a public beach at a local lake. The current substitute dogcatcher was a "chickenshit." B.D. said okay never having heard of a vicious Labrador retriever.

When he reached the beach he immediately perceived that the dog was only trying to bully bathers to throw a stick in the water for him to retrieve. There were two squad cars with flashing lights and cops with drawn pistols. B.D. borrowed a nearby rowboat and rowed down the lake where the dog had cowed a little girl into throwing the stick for him. She was plainly getting tired of the snarling dog. B.D. rowed nearby and whistled. No Lab could turn down a boat ride. The dog came at a dead run and jumped into the boat with the stick in its mouth, then lay down for a quick snooze. B.D. could think of nothing else to do so he rowed out in the middle of the lake and dozed himself. The dog had one eye open and was growling lightly, staring at him as a possible enemy. After about an hour a motor boat headed toward them from shore. The boat pulled near and an elderly couple began yelling, "Wolfie," the woman in a high screeching voice. The dog ignored them, looking the other way. Evidently they had failed him by not throwing the stick often enough. When Wolfie was immovable the man offered B.D. twenty bucks to dock in the distance which translated into five six-packs. B.D. rowed in but Wolfie wouldn't get out of the boat. The old couple knelt and begged him as he chewed his beloved stick to pieces. Finally B.D. stepped out of the boat, took the man's twenty dollars, and walked to his car saying that he had to catch a plane. Bruno wasn't the only dog asshole, Wolfie was the master of that family.

On the drive to Gretchen's he stopped at a bar for two doubles and a cheeseburger to make up for the curry lacuna. He felt airy from the pleasure of rowing a boat and the mystery of dog behavior; all a guy wanted was someone to throw a stick. And the extreme pleasure of owning your first cabin. He had often regretted selling Grandpa's little farm but what did he know then? And only a bit more now. It had been a yearlong booze and pussy run and then he woke up broke. Now at age fifty the love of a woman and your own cabin sounded dandy and best of all, a family. A wife and two children whom Gretchen said would take care of him in old age. He had always been able to take care of himself but not necessarily well. Over the years he had remodeled dozens of deer cabins in exchange for staying there off-season. The trouble was waking in a cabin in January when the interior temperature was only ten degrees and it was a couple of hours before it was warm enough to hold a hammer. Also the appetite developed was enormous. He'd put a pork shoulder with lots of fat in the oven on waking and work on it all day, then start eating the minute it was done. You often had to begin the day by shoveling the heavy snow off the roof, scarcely a dream life but quite solitary and independent. He once shot a mostly albino deer but was too superstitious to eat it. Because of the message from David Four Feet's relative by the lake he was superstitious about the spirituality of dogs except possibly Bruno. Maybe Bruno was sent to haunt him because he, B.D., had acted like Bruno in school. On the last of the drive to Gretchen's B.D. felt wary of the cabin wondering if it could be compared to his ill-advised job as a dogcatcher to prove his worth after Susi was born. No, all his life he had wanted his own cabin in the forest. The only fear is that she would fall in love with another woman but then it was his cabin, and also his kids, and it was certainly better than her falling in love with another man.

Gretchen was planning a picnic at the new house tomorrow or Sunday. They would put the chuck roast in Delmore's oven and take him along. She also insisted that he show Susi, at one, how to catch a fish, plainly impossible, but no point in arguing about it. He had a difficult night on the sofa from the abominable curry plus he ate an entire four-dollar bottle of chutney which she warned him about. She had told him that Delmore had a surprise for him about which he lacked optimism.

In the morning he hated pouring an entire half bottle of good red wine in with the chuck roast but that's what the recipe called for. Once he'd been unable to see the point of good wine, but Gretchen had had an influence. He saved a goodly swig for himself like a Frenchman would. At Delmore's he slid the chuck in the oven before he noticed something covered with a pillowcase on the sofa. Delmore made a little inappropriate speech about Brown Dog's mother traveling all the way to Frazer, Montana. A lot of Chips lived there, having migrated after the whites strongly invaded the U.P. in the nineteenth century. She had fallen in love with a Lakota, the enemies of the Anishinabe, a member of the famed He Dog family (He Dog was Crazy Horse's best friend). Delmore claimed the match was a "bad mix" and the young man as a Lakota was warlike and contentious. It was thought that he drowned in Lake Superior in a canoe while being pursued by the police up north of Newberry. He had assaulted a number of police officers. B.D. had once found the body of an Indian in the lake but it was never proven it was his father.

Delmore took the hands of Gretchen and B.D. "Since you are married I'm giving you the wedding painting of B.D.'s parents." The painting was amateurish but still powerful. It answered some questions and opened up more. A very big Indian in traditional dress and a lovely girl with long sweeping black hair. B.D. had had no idea his father was a Lakota but had heard rumors that he was a Montana Chip. He felt his chest would burst. Why did they have to die so young?

"It's for your cabin," Gretchen said, noting that B.D. was overcome. They all drove over to Gretchen's. Susi liked to hold Delmore's hand when she walked which gave him an elaborate sense of self-importance. Bruno kept a sharp eye on him.

When they got to Gretchen's B.D. led Delmore and Susi down to the forest pool formed by the creek and tossed out a humble worm with his fishing rod to show Susi how to catch a fish. He hooked a small brook trout immediately. Unfortunately Bruno saw it as a threat when B.D. swung the fish toward the laughing Susi. Bruno leapt through the air and ripped the small fish from the hook, ground it in his teeth, and swallowed, spitting out most of it in dismay as he did with the snakes he tried to eat. B.D. jumped in the pond to rescue Bruno who had never shown signs of having figured out how

to swim. B.D. rescued the head of the brook trout for Susi who put it in the pocket of her playsuit for Gretchen to hopefully find in a few days. It was a local joke to slide a fish under someone's car seat in the summer. Quite a find for the owner.

They nibbled on some wretched hors d'oeuvres Gretchen had bought at a deli except for one pan of oriental chicken livers she had made herself which were good. She had hung the painting of his parents temporarily in the living room. One lifelong puzzle resolved. What his parents looked like. His father was obviously a hard-ass as rumored. Delmore said he had a book about the He Dog family but B.D. felt intimidated about reading it. He was aware of the Lakota dying violently in the old days. That was over now though peace was rarely grand. The living room was a tableau of everyone watching shyly as B.D. stared at the painting. There was the worry that if he came from the famous He Dog family who helped defeat Custer he might try to do something famous. He knew it was always a grave danger to raise your head up above others. People who get their names and picture in the paper are always fucked and always get picked on. The rule was to run to the forest at the sign of any ambition. He once saw four men fishing together which is three too many.

That night when he dreamed he didn't have that semi-empty place. His mother had long black hair and maybe dad was outside cutting wood for the oncoming autumn or fishing for dinner. He felt cool water in his throat. They were looking after him.

The next day at Delmore's for the chuck roast Delmore whispered to him at the stove, "I didn't mean to knock you off your feet."

"No, it was good. Everyone wants to know where they came from."

"It wasn't pretty. Your dad was a hard man. Imagine a Lakota leading us Chips. He wouldn't take any shit from the county or state about any of our rights. It was only a matter of time before they cornered him. He's buried in Lake Superior which is big enough for him."

That evening they ate the splendid chuck roast and Delmore hogged as much of the gravy as possible despite Gretchen warning him about his health. "Between health and gravy I'll take gravy. I'm seventy-seven."

"I thought you were eighty-three," she said.

"Who gives a shit? What's important is who is taking me to the new *Planet of the Apes* next week."

"I will," Gretchen said with humility. "Those apes are sexy."

"So is Bruno," Delmore said with a guffaw.

Susi was being obnoxious eating her mashed potatoes with her hands and refusing to stop so B.D. took her out for a stroll. Susi rode on his shoulders and sang nonsense songs while she tapped on his head in rhythm. Bruno was on the lead and ran a small raccoon up a birch tree which put him in a frenzy.

"Bruno, that raccoon could kick your ass in a minute."

Bruno seemed to understand and left the challenge behind. They walked out to the entry in the bright early summer evening only three weeks from the solstice which meant this far north it wouldn't get really dark until ten, a great time to fish but it was lovely carrying his daughter on his shoulder to the music of tree frogs and birds near sleep, the odor from ferns and wild flowers and the musical sound of a whip-poor-will which as a child he was convinced was a ghost.

He slid out of bed just before dawn seeing Gretchen's bare butt and wondering if fishing were worth it if he could make love. He touched her butt and she swatted his hand away as if it were a mosquito; the answer. Susi was standing up in bed in her Peter Rabbit pajama suit so he waved and she waved back. He had left his clothes and tackle near the front door and made a speedy exit after noting Bruno on the kitchen counter with the remains of a pound of butter. About a hundred yards down the two-track toward the creek pool he heard the muted call of "Daddy" behind him. It was Susi with her watchdog Bruno beside her. "Shit," he thought then decided to make do. As luck would have it a big snowshoe rabbit ran across the road and Bruno gave chase yelping. At the pool he hooked a fish pronto and handed Susi the rod. She looked up not knowing how to work the reel. She dropped the rod, grabbed the line, and dragged the fish by the line up into the grass and ferns. He unhooked the fish and she clasped it to her chest giving the head a kiss, a proper beginner's attitude he thought. Off in a clearing he could see Bruno and Fred playing tug-of-war with the snowshoe rabbit. Fred of course was winning, twirling Bruno in circles but Bruno wouldn't let go. Susi stared and said, "Peter Rabbit." Gretchen met them halfway, concerned about the empty crib. Susi handed her the fish which she properly accepted as if it were crown jewels. B.D. was touched, his mind so clear he needed a drink.